PHOTO: JONQUIL MACKEY

Karen Viggers is a writer, veterinarian, mother and wife. She was born in Melbourne and grew up in the Dandenong Ranges riding horses and writing stories. After finishing her veterinary degree Karen developed an interest in Australian native wildlife and has worked with many different species, including kangaroos. She loves landscapes—especially wild places in the mountains and on the coast—and she loves to escape with her family whenever she can.

Karen lives in Canberra with her husband and two children. She is the author of two other published novels: *The Lightkeeper's Wife* (2011) and *The Stranding* (2008). You can find out more about Karen and her books at www.karenviggers.com.

D1528294

Also by Karen Viggers

The Stranding
The Lightkeeper's Wife

For Chris

The GRASS CASTLE

KAREN VIGGERS

Thankyou for having us
at wonderful Eden Rd wines

Karen Viggers

ALLEN&UNWIN
SYDNEY · MELBOURNE · AUCKLAND · LONDON

First published in 2014

This edition first published in 2015

Allen & Unwin
83 Alexander Street
Crows Nest NSW 2065
Australia
Phone: (61 2) 8425 0100
Email: info@allenandunwin.com
Web: www.allenandunwin.com

Cataloguing-in-Publication details are available
from the National Library of Australia
www.trove.nla.gov.au

ISBN 978 1 76011 300 1

Internal design by Lisa White
Set in 13/17 pt Adobe Garamond Pro by Bookhouse, Sydney
Printed in Australia by McPherson's Printing Group

10 9 8 7 6 5 4 3 2 1

For my parents
Jim and Diana Viggers

Here, everything moves,
Mists, weather and people move
confusedly over the mountains
only the monoliths stay
peeling their onion-skin faces back
a thumb's width in a century.

—*Where the Body Lay*
MARK O'CONNOR

That the clouds should change so swiftly,
you and I so slowly,
and the mountains least of all.

—*Skiers*
MARK O'CONNOR

From
The Olive Tree: Collected Poems
MARK O'CONNOR

PART I

PART 1

1

Night spreads its thick blanket over the valley. There is no moon, no light. Abby is alone in the car park, staring into darkness. She sees a wink of tail-lights somewhere along the road: two red fireflies flickering briefly in the bush. She hears the distant rumble of a car engine going too fast, now slowing for a corner. Then it is quiet. The national park is all around her—she can feel it. The soft hoot of a boobook owl somewhere in the distance. The muffled coughs of kangaroos. Higher up, against the sky, invisible granite crags hunch their stony shoulders. They are watching, always watching.

At the back of the four-wheel drive, she turns on a light and loads the last of her gear: her backpack, the esky. The journalist is gone and she's not sure what to think; whether she should think at all. Probably not, none of it means anything. He's a reporter and he was doing his job. That is the extent of it. She must take this afternoon for what it was and surf on, skimming surfaces, landing lightly. It's the easiest way.

She's been in the valley since morning, following her kangaroos through their monotonous herbivore day. Early, she tracked her radio-collared animals and watched them bounce among their colleagues before settling to graze. Kangaroos don't do much, it seems. They sleep, graze, recline, hassle each other. But their movements are points on a map which tell her what their lives are made from: how the range of each animal overlaps, and how this changes when the grass grows . . . or doesn't grow, as in this drought. Her work doesn't sound like much, but it forms the shape of her career. She's a researcher in training—paid almost nothing to wander among kangaroos, taking measurements that might help explain an ecosystem.

The lack of money doesn't matter, or so she tells herself. Hopefully she will be paid more once she's established her career. What matters is that she is doing something she cares about, something meaningful, and that she is making a contribution to saving this beautiful, complicated world. Equally important is that she is outdoors, not cooped up in some dreary office bathed in fluorescent light and surrounded by people staring like zombies at computer screens . . . although she does her share of screen-staring too, when she's entering data or tussling with the strange and slippery discipline of writing up her research.

Working here returns her to her childhood. It reminds her of horse-riding through the bush with her mother, when often a kangaroo would appear suddenly on the track, startling the horses. Abby was always impressed by the kangaroo's power as it surged away. She loves the way kangaroos move, the elegant efficiency of it. Where else on this planet can you see animals bound so gracefully with a muscular tail for counterbalance? She likes to watch how they interact, the liaisons that form in the mob: bands of mothers with young at foot. Did her own mother tend to her with such vigilance? Surely she must have felt her mother's attentive hands stroking her hair. But she can't remember. Ten years since her mother died and she still misses her. There's a wall in her mind she can't look behind, places she can't go for fear of memories.

She switches off the light and slams the back door of the vehicle, pauses and listens to the quiet of the night, the rustle of air moving in the grass. Usually she goes straight home after work, but today the journalist came for the interview, so she stayed late. They talked, and now he is gone, driving back to town in his fancy sports car. The park is empty: just her, the kangaroos, and the wind.

She clambers into the vehicle, starts the engine and puts it in gear. She's comfortable behind the wheel. Working here day and night, her body knows the road. She can drive almost without thinking.

She comes to the corner where perhaps she saw the journalist's tail-lights blinking several minutes ago, and she brakes reflexively—it's a sharper curve than you might think. The four-wheel drive slows smoothly, swings the turn, wheels gripping. Then she sees lights ahead and her heart lurches. It must be him, the journalist. And something must have happened. She knows already what it is.

The WRX is angled across the road, headlights flaring. She pulls up on the roadside and drags on the handbrake. The journalist is standing in front of his car looking down, and he's folding his hands over and over. She slides out, her boots crunching on tarmac as she walks around the car.

A kangaroo is splayed on the road: its body crumpled, head erect, nostrils wide, ears quivering. The hind legs are skewed, dark clots of blood on its furry coat, a black pool expanding around it like oil. Abby sees the exaggerated lift and fall of the kangaroo's chest, hears the laboured suck of its breathing. She sees the soft pale underside of the animal's exposed belly, notices the pouch. 'Can you turn off your headlights?' she says quietly.

The bush hisses and sighs and the journalist looks at her, not understanding.

'Your lights,' she says. 'They're too close and bright. She's frightened.'

He jerks with delayed comprehension then strides to his car and reaches inside. The road falls to sudden darkness and Abby swallows the beat of panic in her chest. She knows how this must end.

'Perhaps you could leave your parkers on,' she suggests.

There's a faint click and the dim glow of parking lights softens the curtain of night. Cameron, the journalist, is staring at her, eyes and hair wild. He expects something of her—something she knows she can't deliver.

'You think it's a girl?' he asks, voice gravelly.

Not a girl, she says to herself. A female. Aloud she states: 'She has a pouch.'

'I hope I haven't killed her baby,' he says.

Pouch-young, she wants to say. It's called a pouch-young. Even now, with this before her, she can't suppress her inner scientist. She gazes up and finds a faint sliver of moon edging above the ridge. Then she looks at Cameron, still watching her, his face pinched.

'Will she be all right?' he asks.

The loaded question. She had known it would come as surely as she'd known what had happened when she saw his headlights on the road. Placing a hand on the bonnet of his car, she tucks her emotions inside. She'll have to explain it to him as kindly as possible.

———•———

Cameron had come to her via her PhD supervisor, Quentin Dexter—an ecologist with an international reputation for scientific excellence. Quentin had handballed Cameron's phone call on to Abby so she could do a soft-touch kangaroo story. Thanks, she'd thought at the time. *Soft-touch* wasn't a term she would use to describe her research. She'd tried to worm out of it; she'd never had direct contact with the media before and she was afraid she would say the wrong thing. But Quentin insisted this was part of being a scientist. He said she should get used to it if she wanted an academic career.

Cameron suggested they meet in Abby's office or at a café on campus to go through a few questions. Then he would hunt down some kangaroo shots from the wildlife archives and write his article for the Wednesday environmental supplement . . . if they could just fix a time? But Abby knew the university wasn't right. It had pretty spreading grounds, carefully cultivated and manicured. But it was a bit like a museum—especially when the students were on holidays and the grounds were empty—and it seemed unlikely anything of consequence could happen there. Even the cockatoos, screeching regularly overhead, seemed to be laughing.

No, if they had to do this interview, Cameron should come to her valley where she could explain her work more clearly and he could get a feel for the place. In the morning she'd be busy, and later in the day the kangaroos would retreat to the wooded slopes. So late afternoon would be best. The kangaroos would be grazing, and the journalist could see them doing their thing.

She waited for him in the car park, but he was late, and she passed time tidying her gear, brushing grass seeds from the back of the work vehicle, checking her notebooks, watching the weather. By the time he arrived, she had almost given up. When his blue WRX came rushing too fast across the tarmac, she knew she wasn't going to like him. He was tardy, flashy and impatient. He would want to finish the job and get back to his office. She watched him unfold from his sports car, rising to ridiculous heights above her. Let him try to patronise her and the interview would be over before it began. He reached into his car to tug out a black leather shoulder bag, before turning to meet her.

'I'm Abby Hunter,' she said, extending her hand.

'Cameron Barlow.'

'You're late,' she said.

He smiled without hint of apology. 'Yes, I know. It's genetic. Hope you had something to do.'

'My work truck has never been cleaner.'

He was undeniably attractive, with tousled black hair that needed a cut, and he wore a hint of arrogance—something in the tilt of his head, or maybe it was the way his lips twitched as he looked down at her. His beige trousers and light suede coat were office-smart beside her work uniform of jeans, thermals and saggy woollen jumper. She felt small beside him, and he peered around the valley with an undisguised assessing stare that annoyed her. What did he see here, she wondered. Not the beauty of it, that was certain. Even she, with her upbringing in the Victorian mountains, had taken some time to warm to the different grandeur of this place, to love its tawny colours, the scabby peaks, the harsh blue skies—absent today.

'Dry, isn't it?' he said, offhand. 'Pity we couldn't have arranged some green grass.'

'It's a drought,' she said.

'Green would have been good for the photos, but no matter.' He shrugged and peered about. 'Where are the kangaroos?'

'You didn't see any?' She couldn't conceal her surprise. From the park gates the road ran alongside open meadows where grass grew in frost hollows even in the driest of seasons. Kangaroos were always there, grazing or sleeping. He must have passed dozens without noticing.

'I was concentrating on the road,' he said, smiling blandly. 'I don't get to navigate such lovely twists and curves very often.' He glanced at his shiny blue car. 'The beast took control, I'm afraid.'

The beast—he said it in such a tender way she wondered if he was referring to himself or to his sports car. Perhaps he hadn't even noticed the trees and the valley—it seemed all he'd appreciated was the road. 'You'll see plenty of kangaroos,' she said, pointing up the valley. 'But we'll have to walk. There's not much to see in the car park.'

His eyes and nose crinkled and he looked down at his shoes—nice leather lace-ups with polished toes.

'It's okay,' she said. 'It's too dry for mud. And there's a track. We'll wander along and find some kangaroos for you.'

'Good,' he said. 'I want to see them move.'

She felt reluctance in him as she led him from the car park along the old four-wheel drive track that ran among tussock grass and the dug-out furrows of a rabbit warren, recently ripped. Perhaps he seriously didn't want to be here and she'd made a mistake inviting him. It was obvious he didn't get out of his office too often, at least not to places where his hair might get ruffled and his shoes dirty. For a moment she was tempted to lead him the long way, skirting round the edge of the valley and up the steeper, rougher hills, so she could see him puff and struggle in those inappropriate shoes. But, glancing more carefully at his physique, she noted he looked fit—no soft city belly or double chins. Maybe he was worried about the time; he kept glancing at his watch. She hadn't any idea of his other commitments, and perhaps it was a bit much to force him to come all the way out here simply to feel the atmosphere . . . her purist values running amok. She grappled with a flash of guilt, but was over it almost immediately. He'd manage. And the fresh air would be good for him.

As they walked up the valley, the interview looming, she felt a clutch of shyness, and was suddenly tongue-tied. What should she say to impress a journalist? What would he want to know? She waited nervously while he paused to stoop over his shoulder bag. When he straightened he had a small digital recording unit in his hand.

He nodded at her encouragingly and smiled. 'Mind if I point this at you while we talk?'

Her shyness ratcheted up a level. 'I'm not sure,' she said. 'My voice sounds horrible in recordings.'

'Don't worry.' He flashed a reassuring grin. 'It's purely for reference in case I forget things. And I find it easier than paper and pen. Plus, I like to see where I'm putting my feet.' He grimaced at the terrain as if she was dragging him across a glacier.

'Next time, wear your hiking boots,' she said. And he raised his eyebrows at her.

They wandered up the valley beneath the scattered bellies of wind-shuffled clouds. As they walked he began to prod her with light conversation, slipping in questions along with self-deprecating jokes. She discovered he knew a few things about kangaroos—not much, but enough to lift him above the average level of ignorance. He was good at getting her to talk, an attentive listener, and soon her shyness faded and she found herself sprouting information, facts she thought he'd find interesting, threads unfurling spontaneously as he unknotted her with his genuine interest.

She told him about droughts, and how kangaroos were adapted for breeding. A female could have two young at the same time, she said, a young in the pouch and a fertilised embryo waiting in the uterus. When the pouch was vacated, the embryo would develop to become the next pouch-young. It was an ingenious survival mechanism. In hard times, a starving mother could ditch her young, saving energy and increasing her chances of making it through the drought. When conditions improved, she didn't need to find a mate because she was already pregnant; the previously fertilised embryo would grow into new young, ready to take advantage of the fresh grass. When a suitable male came along, the mother could mate again, and soon another embryo would be waiting.

'It's lucky humans can't do that,' Cameron said. 'Imagine the number of unplanned babies and custody battles.'

Abby smiled. 'Humans aren't so different,' she said. 'We have our alpha males, and devious usurpers mating on the sly.'

He arched an eyebrow at her. 'Don't you call that cuck-olding? Having an affair?'

'Same thing, minus the ceremony and the wedding rings.'

'. . . as well as the divorce and legal wrangles,' he added. 'Thank Christ for that.'

The valley narrowed as they walked and soon they were traversing Abby's favourite section, dotted with straggly clumps of dwarf eucalypts with trunks streaked olive-brown and gangly branches dripping bark. Beyond the grassy flats, the taller forest reached up-slope to bony ridges and great domes of grey rock. They passed a pile of boulders and the burnt remains of an old hut, then they were among the kangaroos, grey-brown lumps that merged with the landscape.

Cameron didn't see them at first, which made Abby smile—city people often brought their urban blindness with them when they visited the valley. He'd walked to within fifty metres of a large mob before he finally noticed them. By then the kangaroos were upright, alert and watching. The big males were sitting on bunched haunches, ogling warily, while mothers with flighty young were already moving away, ears swivelling.

'Will you look at that?' Cameron's voice rang in the quiet, and the big old bucks spun and bounded off. In moments the valley had cleared, distant crashes marking the passage of some of the mob as they disappeared uphill into the trees. 'What did I do?' he asked, turning off his recorder.

'They don't know you,' Abby said.

'How can you study them if they bolt like that?'

'They habituate. They don't take much notice when it's just me.'

He looked down at her. 'Maybe it's my aftershave,' he said, sniffing at his collar.

'That's possible.'

'Don't you like it?' A smile hovered about his lips.

'I think I'm with the kangaroos,' she said. 'It's a bit sweet.'

He switched the recorder on again, and they followed the stragglers up the valley, pausing every now and then to look at a few kangaroos half-hidden among the trees. They came across one of Abby's radio-collared animals and she described how the government vet had come to help her fit the collars, armed with his dart rifle and sedatives. It had taken five mornings to capture sixteen animals, an even mix of males and females.

There was a lull in conversation when Abby thought the interview might almost be finished, then Cameron looked at her and his lips tweaked. 'What do you think about kangaroo culling?' he asked.

Abby hesitated a moment before answering. Quentin had warned her about this. He'd said it was likely to come up. 'I don't want this to be an article on culling,' she said slowly.

Cameron grinned knowingly. 'It won't be.'

'So I can speak off the record?'

'If that's the way you want it.'

'Yes please.' Quentin had said she should request this if the discussion wandered onto controversial ground—if this was to be a soft-touch kangaroo story, they didn't need to address emotive issues like culling. Abby noticed Cameron regarding her with heightened interest, but he'd turned off his recorder so she felt a little more comfortable.

'I gather this is a touchy subject for you,' he said.

'Not really. But it's a sensitive topic, isn't it? It upsets people.'

'So what's the solution? Surely it can't be that hard to sort out.'

Abby almost smiled. Quentin had coached her on this too. He'd said journalists always wanted simple answers to complex problems. As a country girl, she used to think managing kangaroos ought to be straightforward, but now she's studied ecology for a few years, she knows it isn't. 'It's complicated,' she said. 'Kangaroos are efficient breeders, and we humans have opened up grazing land and removed predators, so there's nothing to control them anymore. There can be so many of them they damage the environment, and that affects other species.'

'So we have to shoot them? Is that what you're saying?'

Abby paused again. She didn't like shooting. She hated guns. But in the absence of a suitable alternative what else was there? 'There isn't any other way yet,' she said. 'There are labs working on kangaroo contraception, but that's years off. Shooting has its problems too. It's a practical short-term solution, but it's never-ending. Once you start, you have to keep doing it because the kangaroos keep breeding.'

Cameron laughed. 'The confused biologist!'

'Not confused,' she said, 'but definitely challenged.'

In a grove of twisted snow gums, Cameron paused to yank one of the springy branches, pulling off a sprig of leathery leaves which he attempted to tuck behind her ear. She ducked away, laughing, embarrassed, then jerked to a halt as a large old-man kangaroo appeared from nowhere, rearing on its hind legs, and jolting towards them in short sharp hops, snorting loudly.

'Move!' she yelled, thrusting hard against Cameron and shoving him backwards.

He caught her urgency and leapt back while she reversed slowly, hands raised, palms open. As she put cautious distance between them, the buck subsided to a wary crouch, still watching them. He was a big lone male with sharp hooked claws and forearm muscles like a gym junkie. Abby's heart battered and a hot adrenalin sweat tingled on her skin. She faced the kangaroo till he lowered his head to snatch a mouthful of grass, strong jaws grinding.

'What was that about?' Cameron asked, shakiness deepening his voice.

'We got too close,' Abby said. 'They don't like anyone inside their personal space.'

'Tell me about it.' Cameron was flushed and stepping lightly now, surprisingly agile despite his height.

Abby relaxed a little. 'You look ready to run.'

'You bet,' he said.

Looking up, Abby noticed that clouds had snuffed the sun and late afternoon light was leaning creamy and soft across the valley. A freshening wind was rolling among the trees and ravens cawed overhead, flapping up-valley. The old-man kangaroo was distant and harmless now, uninterested in them, a bulky grey hummock only half-visible among the trees. But he had altered the mood of the day.

Cameron glanced at his watch. 'Perhaps we should head back,' he said.

By the time they stepped onto the tarmac in the car park, Cameron's recorder was buttoned away and an awkward distance had reasserted itself between them. They were strangers again. They'd met for a purpose which had now been achieved and the interview was over. Abby watched as he slung his shoulder bag onto the front seat of the WRX then politely reached out his hand.

'Thank you,' he said. 'That was great. I wasn't too keen on coming. But it was good.'

She shook his hand, feeling something like sunshine in his grip, and suddenly she didn't want to let go. 'Look,' she said, diving on submerged courage. 'You don't have to leave immediately unless you're in a hurry. There's an old hut further down the valley that you might like to look at. It's historic, an old slab building.'

Cameron seemed to hesitate and Abby's brave moment faded.

'I suppose you need to write this up,' she said, assuming his silence meant no. 'I noticed you looking at your watch.'

Cameron laughed. 'The watch is a habit. Part of being a slave to time. The life of a journalist. But actually I'm not in a rush to get back. I've already done my columns for tomorrow, and I'm going to write your interview as a feature, so no pressing deadlines. I wouldn't mind seeing the hut . . . might give me some ammunition for another story.'

'It'll be nice to get out of this wind,' Abby said. 'But it's a bit of a walk. Do you have a warmer coat?'

Cameron shook his head.

'I have a blanket you could toss round your shoulders,' Abby suggested.

'That'll be fine.'

She opened the back of her work truck to fetch the blanket then she turned to Cameron as another idea occurred to her. 'Are you hungry?' she asked. 'I was planning on staying back tonight to check my radio-collared kangaroos, so I brought along a roast chicken and a few bread rolls for supper. I'm happy to share.'

Cameron smiled. 'Sounds great. And I have a bottle of wine in the car. Left over from dinner last night with some workmates. Do you have anything we can drink from?'

'A couple of thermos lids,' Abby said. 'They're not quite wine glasses . . .'

'But they'll do,' Cameron said.

Abby shoved everything in a backpack, gave Cameron the blanket, and they set off, weaving their way among the wind-whipped tussock grass.

2

The old slab hut, huddled on the valley floor, was Abby's hideaway where she often took shelter in bad weather. It was a wonderful old building, oozing history, and laden with fragments of the forgotten lives and faded voices of the families who had settled the region.

Usually she closed herself behind the latched wooden door and listened to the hollow moan of air scooping around the walls. The outside world seemed to dissolve and she became a presence among ghosts. Sometimes, as she sat cross-legged on the battered wooden floor, she thought she could almost hear snatches of conversation swirling in the stone fireplace and mumbling under the eaves. Beneath the peeling wallpaper that lined the hut were sheets of yellowed newsprint from another era. She pictured shadow-people snuggling against the colder wetter weather of those times. She thought of snow in winter. The smell of burning wood, sodden timber, woollen clothes drying on nails. The snort of a horse in the yards.

On calmer days, she sat outside on the grass, boiling water to make tea, and she imagined men in dirty trousers working the land, felling and ringbarking trees. There wouldn't have been fences, and cattle would have roamed the valley and slopes, crashing through undergrowth, stripping bark from trees with their muscular tongues. She liked to think of the settlers, and she wished she knew more of their history, how they had changed the land, inadvertently paving the way for the mobs of kangaroos she was now studying.

But today she was distracted by Cameron's presence. She was excited to have another human being sharing her valley, someone who seemed interested in her and her kangaroos. On the rattly boards of the veranda she dug into her backpack, pulling out the roast chicken, the crispy bread rolls and Cameron's bottle of wine.

He watched her lay out the food on plastic plates. 'Do you do this often?' he laughed. 'Seems I'm in the wrong job.'

She gave him a withering look and ferreted the thermos cups from her pack, plonking them unceremoniously on the deck. 'Only the best for this scientist,' she said. Then she held up the wine. 'It has a cork,' she said, dismayed. 'And I don't have a corkscrew. I thought corks went out with the ark.'

'I have one.' Cameron jingled his car keys at her, displaying a sheathed silver corkscrew. 'Sign of a true wino,' he said. 'Always prepared.' He detached the corkscrew and handed it to her.

She made a mess of the cork, embarrassing herself, until Cameron reached over with a casual arm and took the bottle from her. With fingers long and fine as a pianist's, he eased out the broken cork remnants and poured generous portions of wine into the thermos lids, passing one to her. 'It's a pity to drink out of plastic, but hey,' he bumped his cup against hers, 'who am I to complain?'

She drank, flushed with a strange jittery sense of anticipation, while the mountains watched on.

They sat on the porch, looking across the valley towards the shadowy ridge. 'Peaceful here, isn't it?' he said. 'I didn't know all this was so close to the city.'

Abby loved the emptiness, the ravens cruising overhead. 'Hardly anyone comes here,' she said, 'just a few bushwalkers; sometimes some rock climbers up on the ridge. Mostly I have the place to myself.'

'You don't get lonely?'

'No. I have things to do. Work's busy. It's not all about picnics and wine.'

There was a short silence during which they both sipped from their cups and reached for food; then, just as Abby was beginning to feel awkward, Cameron broke the quiet. 'Is your family from round here?' he asked.

This shift in topic wasn't quite what Abby desired, but she had to go with it. 'They're in Victoria. Mansfield.'

'Hey, I love Mansfield,' he said, smiling enthusiastically. 'We used to ski Mount Buller in my teens. Was it a good place to grow up?'

'It's a typical country town,' she said. 'It has a nice feel to it, and it is beautiful country: the mountains and the bush, the rivers. But it's a small place—people living in each other's pockets.'

He laughed: a musical tone that floated under the eaves. 'Isn't that what you call community?'

She thought of her father living on the farm with his pushy, possessive new wife. 'Being nosey is the same wherever you are. And it's not my definition of community.'

'Canberra then?' His eyebrows lifted slightly. 'Is that your idea of community?'

She couldn't suppress a grin. 'Maybe if you're a politician or a journalist.'

He smiled. 'Why did you come here?' he asked. 'Why not Sydney or Melbourne?'

'I was offered a scholarship here.'

'Not too far from home for you?'

'I'm twenty-three,' she said. 'Old enough to fly the coop. And home's not what it used to be. Mum died when I was thirteen. Dad has a new wife.'

'Tough losing your mum,' Cameron said.

'Yes,' she said, and shivered. 'How about you?'

She was hoping he wouldn't notice her discomfort when it came to talking about herself. He picked up a bread roll and started gnawing on it, and she was relieved when he took hold of the conversation and carried on.

'I'm from Melbourne,' he said between mouthfuls. 'Inner-suburban city boy. Man of neon lights, cappuccinos and nightclubs.' He stopped chewing to scoff at himself. 'Private-school educated, of course.'

'I went to Mansfield High,' she said. 'No other options.'

He took a morsel of chicken and popped it in his mouth. 'My parents are wealthy, so it's all about options. Theirs, not mine. A government school would have been fine for me, but my parents wouldn't have it. They wanted to stamp the renegade leftie out of me. So it was Melbourne Grammar then Melbourne University. They're barristers, both of them. They wanted me to tread the same track they did. Journalism is all I ever wanted to do. But they slotted me into law. It didn't last, of course. I hated it. I was going to drop out of uni altogether, and they couldn't cope with a bum for a son, so they agreed on a compromise, a shift into literature. It was terribly humiliating for them—a son with a classic career-less Arts degree, but at least it was at the right univerity, and they supposed it might lead to something. Soon as I finished, I took the first cadetship I could sign up for. The *Herald Sun*. Not exactly my political line, but it was runs on the board. You need those before you can get ahead. I was born a journalist. I just had to make my parents believe it.'

'And they believe it now?'

He tore another bread roll into pieces which he arranged in a circle on his plate. 'I don't have much to do with them. I'm a disappointment. When I go to Melbourne I mostly stay with friends. It's easier that way. My parents are busy. I take them out to dinner or the opera. Then I've done my duty and I can do my own thing. I catch up with my journo mates, and we drink and tell stories and talk politics. It's fun. Journalism suits me—despite what my family thinks.' He laughed derisively. 'I can tell you this much: my family isn't normal.'

Abby held his gaze. 'There's no such thing as a normal family,' she said quietly.

'Hell no,' he agreed. 'But I bet mine's less normal than yours.'

She said nothing. He couldn't compete on abnormal, but she let it go.

He reached for the bottle again. 'What about the rest of your family?'

'I have a brother, Matt.'

'What does he do?'

'He skis, works on a vineyard and shoots kangaroos with his mates.'

Cameron chuckled. 'Your brother shoots kangaroos and you study them. Ironic, isn't it?'

'Life's ironic,' she said.

They finished the wine, and chatted into the darkness, talking about politics, music, films and books. Cameron was easy company, talkative without being overbearing, up-to-date on everything. Abby supposed this was part of his job, to be able to talk to people, to make them feel comfortable.

As the chill night air sank from the ridges, she became aware of the inadequacy of his clothing, and when she saw him shiver, despite the blanket, she knew it was time to call it a day.

They made their way back to the cars by the light of her head torch. In the car park he lingered, watching her toss things into the back of her four-wheel drive. She thought perhaps he wanted to say something, that maybe the valley had worked its way under his skin like a splinter of wood picked up from the veranda of the old hut. It was possible he liked it here, that he might ask to see her again. For a moment she felt a flutter of excitement. What if he reached out and touched her? But he held his distance then thanked her and said goodbye. She masked her disappointment as he slotted into his car and took off down the road.

And now he is standing over the kangaroo he hit driving too fast in his sports car. 'Will it be all right?' he asks hopefully.

KAREN VIGGERS

Abby is thrown by the expectation in his voice. He wants the kangaroo to be fixed so it can hop away into the night, but she can't protect him from the truth. 'No,' she says slowly.

His stare is disbelief. 'Why not?'

'Legs are broken.'

'Broken legs can mend.'

'Not the hind legs of a kangaroo. A joey in the pouch perhaps. But not an adult.'

'I don't understand,' he says. 'We should call a vet.'

She shakes her head. 'Nobody will come. Not at this time of night. They'll tell you to shoot her.'

'So what will you do?'

He hands over responsibility just like that, and now it is *her* problem. She steadies herself before speaking, draws a ragged breath. 'The most humane thing is to put her down.'

His eyes widen and his body tightens, then he turns and strides to the WRX, reaches in and pulls out a packet of cigarettes. She watches him flick one out of the box. He puts it in his mouth and lights it with a lighter that has materialised from his pocket. The tip flares red in the night. She didn't know he was a smoker—he hasn't smoked all afternoon.

'Emergency supply,' he grunts. 'It's only moments like these I need them.'

He sucks on the cigarette, his face illuminated in the faint orange glow, deep lines etched around his mouth. He is bent in on himself. He glances blankly at her then swings away and walks down the road into darkness.

She waits by the kangaroo, watching its agonised breathing and the slick of blood on the tarmac. The animal has lowered its head, its life-preserving flight response dulled by pain. The

24

bright eyes are glazed, eyelids drooping. With a shudder, it lays its cheek on the road. Anxiety knots tighter in Abby's throat. She feels for the poor animal; in its agony it is almost human, she sees the suffering in its eyes.

'Do you have a gun?' Cameron has come silently back and is standing in the shadows beside his car, leaning against the roof, his face gaunt, eyes haggard.

'No.'

'Then how are you going to do it? We'll have to find a farmer.'

'There aren't any farms for miles.'

'What do you suggest then?'

She breathes deeply and tries to look strong. 'I'll have to do it.'

'How?' His voice is blunt and tight. He wants this thing over, she can feel it. He wants her to deal with it so he can disappear down the road.

'There are two possibilities,' she says, knowing he isn't going to like either of them. Neither does she, but she can't bear the animal's distress. 'I have an axe in the car. I can strike her on the back of the head.' Not really. She can't do it—her stomach contracts at the thought.

'What's the other option?' He is staring at her, his face taut with a new expression: separation and distance.

'I can drive over her head and crush her skull.' She says it flat and quiet, trying not to grimace, her gut twisting.

He regards her coolly. 'You biologists are hard people.'

She wraps her arms across her chest like protective wings, folding her sadness inside, toughening against him. 'We can't stand here watching her. It's cruel.'

They look down at the kangaroo. Cameron is pulling away. Soon he will climb into his car and drive off, leaving her with the kangaroo and the night.

He glances at her, eyes cold. 'What will you do?'

She swallows. 'I'll use the car. I can't do it with the axe.'

He turns from her, withdrawing. 'I don't think I can watch. Do you mind if I go?'

She watches bleakly as he climbs into his car and rolls down the window. For the first time tonight, she feels lonely. But perhaps it's better this way; he won't have to see her crying.

He peers out at her. 'What if I hit another one?' he asks.

'You won't,' she says, but he isn't reassured. 'Okay then,' she suggests. 'Drive a few hundred metres down the road and wait for me.' Not only does she have to kill the kangaroo, she also has to guide him home. It's almost more than she can manage.

He starts his car, the engine throbbing throatily, and snaps on the lights. The kangaroo claws at the tarmac, trying to drag itself away.

'Turn your lights off,' Abby yells, but he doesn't hear. He's backing away, taking care to dodge her work vehicle. She watches him disappear down the road and is relieved he has gone.

Shaking with apprehension, she clambers into the four-wheel drive and lines it up near the kangaroo's head. Several times she has to pull on the brake and check the positioning with her torch, and by the time she has it right, the kangaroo is blowing bubbles of blood from its nostrils and she is already weeping. Behind the steering wheel, she clenches her teeth and prepares to finish it. The vehicle judders as she revs forward, then she jerks on the brake. Hesitantly she climbs out to look.

The animal is dead. Its body is twisted, the head mashed, but mercifully the breathing has stopped and all is dreadfully still. Abby is taken by a horrible adrenalin sweat and she thinks she might be sick. Weakly she leans against the car. She can't give in to it: there is more to be done.

She shifts the vehicle away then approaches the poor dead body to check inside the pouch, slipping her hand inside the warm moist fold of skin. She hadn't expected to find anything so she's surprised to discover a small young wriggling there. Her gut clenches as she directs her torch into the pouch—is she going to have to dispatch a joey as well?

Peering into the musky shadows of the pouch, she sees that the joey is covered by a fine layer of grey fur and that it has whiskers and its eyes are open, its mouth firmly wrapped around a long, pink teat. The reality of her next step overwhelms her. She will have to kill it. A quick blow to the head will suffice.

Sobs threaten, but she locks them inside. Grasping the kangaroo by the forelegs she drags it off the road, the crushed head dangling. She can't bring herself to touch the hind legs, doesn't want to feel the grinding sensation of bone against bone. The skull bumps against her knee, the warmth of fresh blood. Fighting tears, she pulls the limp heavy body into the bush.

When the kangaroo is concealed behind some shrubs, she lifts the head and gently straightens it. The skull is shattered, an eye protruding. She wishes she hadn't seen it, thinks she might vomit, bile rising in her throat, an involuntary choking sensation. The eyes are glassy, staring into emptiness. This animal, still warm, was alive only five minutes ago. Now it has departed, its body a shell; such a fine line between life and death. Abby knows about that.

She works to compose herself, listening to her own breathing as it rasps into the night. The kangaroo's legs remain skewed, and there's something not dignified or respectful about leaving them that way. Despite her reticence to touch the broken bones, she forces herself to bend and gingerly, tenderly, untwist one leg then the other. Then she squats to stroke the kangaroo's shoulder before turning away. The stickiness of blood is on her hands, the smell of death in her lungs, the taste of it in her mouth.

At the back of the four-wheel drive she rummages agitatedly for a drink bottle and flushes water over her trembling hands. It seems she will never be clean. Then finally the gush of tears comes and she sobs against the back of the car.

When the first wave of reaction passes, she digs around in her backpack and pulls out an old grey windcheater, ties off the arms. Then she goes back to the kangaroo. Reaching inside the damp cavity, she scoops the young out while it struggles and hisses and barks, jabbing with all the pointy angles of its gangly joints. She tugs the determined little mouth free of the teat and folds the joey into the windcheater. Then she walks to the car.

Within the jumper, the little body squirms wildly—Abby can feel the desperate thrust of limbs. She stills the joey's panic with the crook of her arm, hugging it close. She can't kill it, even though she knows she should. Instead she tucks the pouch under her clothing against the warmth of her belly and the joey seems to quieten. She will keep it safe for tonight. Tomorrow she will hand it on to a wildlife carer. That's the best she can do.

3

Abby lives in a small bungalow in the inner north of Canberra. The rent is cheap, she doesn't have to share with anyone, and this suits her perfectly. Her bungalow is at the back of a large old renovated house in a quiet wide street lined by oak trees. She likes the trees—especially in autumn when the brown leaves refuse to be shed and they rattle in the wind like castanets.

Five minutes away there is a scrubby hill where she often goes walking. The locals call it a mountain, but what would they know? Her home in Mansfield is overlooked by *real* mountains. The mountains here don't even qualify as foothills . . . but perhaps imagination thrives when you don't have anything to compare with.

The large old Canberra house and Abby's rooms are embedded in a rambling garden which, in spring, sports a profusion of flowers in all the primary and secondary colours. When the owners are absent, it is Abby's job to splash some water around when it is needed. The rest of the maintenance is left to the gardener who comes once a fortnight.

The owners leave Abby alone, which is exactly what she wants. They are married but childless. Their dog is their child—a pampered, well-groomed, over-washed golden retriever called Maxine that bounds joyfully through the garden beds crushing plants and flowers, heedless of their discouraging cries. Abby tries not to smile when she sees the damage Maxine inflicts. She likes the dog's happy attitude—a canine could easily become suppressed and neurotic beneath the anxious eye of the wife, but fortunately Maxine is immune. When the owners are away, which is often, they take her to the home of a sympathetic relative. Abby suspects those visits are good for the dog. She is happier when she comes home because she has been treated like a dog.

Sometimes Abby takes Maxine walking, and Maxine smiles all the way, eternally delighted at escaping the yard and the house. Abby has discovered that a dog is a ticket to conversation. People remark on Maxine's beautiful floaty combed coat and her soft brown eyes that speak of love and pleasure and hope that a human hand might reach to touch her silky head. She is easy company, and the interactions her presence initiates are suitably brief and superficial—no time for people to ask questions, which is good because Abby likes to keep to herself. It's harder at university where, if you make friends, you are expected to confide all the details of your life—which is not something Abby does with anyone.

Her bungalow is small and untidy. The largest room is the combined kitchen–living area which has floor-to-ceiling windows looking out on the garden. Even this room is small, but it is adequate for one. There is also a bedroom, a bathroom and a tiny laundry. In the living room, piles of books and newspapers have taken possession of the coffee table. Unwashed dishes live on the kitchen sink. Dirty washing is flung in the corner of the bedroom, and her mess of shoes is a mound by the door. This is how she lives.

Disorder is normal for Abby. She grew up that way and it feels comfortable, no energy wasted on obsessive tidiness. That's how it was with her mother, who was focused on more ethereal things or, at other times, on nothing at all. She was either loving or absent, thrilling or withdrawn, rarely anywhere in between. Abby learned to capitalise on the good times, to absorb affection when it was given, and not to take it personally when the tap was turned off.

Her father hadn't the headspace to clean things up. He was frenetically busy with work, the vegie garden, the horses, the chook pen, kids' homework, the cooking, his wife's wanderings. Consequently, Abby has learned to be self-sufficient. She's a lone wolf, doesn't rely on anyone to hold her together like other girls do. She has friends at university, and she's slept with a few boys over the years, but she hasn't let herself get emotionally entangled. Anyway, her fieldwork isn't conducive to boyfriends and in-your-pocket friendships, and night work is a real killer for partying.

She has the potential to become a social isolate, she sometimes thinks, a real hermit, except the university has thrust her into a large open-plan office along with all the other PhD students, so it's impossible to hide. Luckily she managed to score a desk tucked away in the corner where she can hunker down and keep herself small, work on invisibility and getting things done. She has her career to think about; she's more than two years into her studies and time is closing in. She has to set herself up for her next job by writing some good scientific papers, otherwise the path is difficult. It's a tough gig being a female scientist, but it's what she's always wanted to do. She can't think of a better way to make her mark, to *do* something rather than *be* someone—she's not interested in fame.

It's hard to be a reliable friend with all this on her plate, and mostly she's out in the field alone anyway, which is what she prefers. Nobody wants to come to the valley with her—or they think they do, and then one visit is enough. They get bored hanging around while she does her work: counting kangaroos, measuring pasture and radio-tracking. It amazes her they can't find anything to do. There are walking tracks and the historical hut and trails for mountain biking, but all her friends can do is gripe that there is no mobile phone coverage and mope as if their arms have been cut off. No phone, no life—Abby is glad she's not as dependent on constant electronic connection as the rest of them.

It's the day after the interview with Cameron, and Abby is sitting on the doorstep of her bungalow playing guitar. She's had a torrid twenty-four hours, and she's feeling traumatised, tired, disappointed and sad. No wonder, after all she's had to deal with: the accident, killing the injured kangaroo, confronting her emotions, and then caring for the orphaned joey. Last night after she'd finished with the kangaroo, Cameron followed her from the national park to the edge of town then he'd taken off, accelerating past her in his WRX and disappearing down the road. It would have been nice if he'd called to see how she was faring. But she hasn't heard from him, and a heavy feeling congeals in her belly every time she thinks of him.

It had been close to ten o'clock when she arrived home; too late to call for assistance with the joey, so she'd fed the little creature some warm sugary water using an old syringe she keeps in her cutlery drawer. It wasn't an easy task with such a wriggly head and tiny mouth, but she'd managed to get a bit of liquid in, hopefully without drowning the joey's lungs. Then she'd filled her hot water bottle and set it in a box alongside the joey tucked up in her jumper.

She'd spent a restless night, worrying whether the joey was warm enough. Several times she'd clambered from bed to check and refill the water bottle. This morning, she'd found a wildlife group on the internet, and she'd called the number then delivered the joey to a farm near Queanbeyan. The lady seemed pleased to take the joey. The way she handled it with gentle expert hands was reassuring, and Abby was happy that at least one thing had turned out well.

Cameron is another issue. She can't muster the courage to phone him. And isn't it his responsibility to call her after all she did for him last night?

She bends over her guitar and immerses herself in the music.

The weather is cool but clear, not a cloud, the light intense, the sky blue. Early autumn is often like this in Canberra. The temperature doesn't look promising on the news report, but the weather is crystalline. Soon the cold starts will come, followed by still, translucent days. The garden is finishing its late flowering and the frosts will short-circuit the blooms. In the back corner, the vegie garden is starting to go to seed.

Abby strums the guitar and hums to herself; it's like meditation, the peace it brings to her. She likes the feel of the instrument in her hands: the hard lines of the strings beneath her fingers, the vibration of the body against her chest.

When she plays, it seems the music moves right through her, connecting her to larger things. Her mother Grace used to play the guitar. She had a beautiful voice which floated like a kestrel on the wind. It was her gift, and when she sang the house filled with glorious sound. Like angels, Abby used to think, when she was young enough to believe in such things.

Abby loved to listen to her, and even now she plays the songs her mother used to play, mournful lyrical pieces that suit the melancholic tone of the guitar. Songs by James Taylor, Jim Croce, John Denver. Abby knows these singers are long out of fashion, but these are the songs she grew up with.

She remembers the time after her mother's death only in patches. Her mind has blotted things out, and perhaps parts of it are safer forgotten. But there are things she can't erase, like the quietness that came on the skirts of her mother's departure, time losing its shape and definition, hours when Abby lay alone in her room watching patterns of light moving like liquid across the walls. She recalls someone taking her to the window one night to look at the stars so she could find her mother. *She's up there*, they told her. *She'll be watching for you, waiting for you.* It seemed like rubbish even then, silly sweet fairytales when she was already well beyond star-people and the concept of heaven.

Then there was the time of humming, a period of vivid clarity and bright light in which all things presented in sharp and wonderful detail. Abby was transfixed by a persistent and monotonous sound that permeated everything: her chest, her feet, the air. At the funeral, it fused with the hymns that echoed in the church, floating up near the lofty ceiling. Then she was outside in warm daylight with the arm of a buxom woman around her shoulders, and her collar was wet with tears she didn't know she was shedding. *Poor darling*, the woman said. *You must stop that dreadful noise.* But when she shut the humming off, the silence was overwhelming, and she was lost in it, lonely, shapeless without her mother.

After that came visceral sobs and the onslaught of unwanted hugs as women from all across town marked her as a target for sympathy. Abby was defenceless and numb, small and easy, so they captured her in their grip. Her face was crushed into the bosoms of everyone else's mums trying to fill the hole her own mother had left.

Her memories of the angry time are more defined and full of shouting, the sound of plates breaking. Yes, she threw things. People accepted her behaviour and she played on their pity. She had a good excuse to be horrible: a girl without a mother was like a yacht without a mast. Back then Abby didn't realise the consequences of it—the isolation that awaited her, the unexplained mysteries of puberty. Her brother Matt had their dad, Steve, to guide him through adolescence—although Steve was as useless then as he is now. Lost without Grace.

The day Abby attained womanhood was one of her worst. Blood leaked through her clothes at school, leaving a murky stain which everyone sniggered at. The teacher was sympathetic—Abby saw it in his eyes. But he was a man, and the facts of life were not his duty to impart. He sent her to sick bay, where a female teacher said *Poor you* and handed her a sanitary pad and gave her permission to go home to change her clothes.

It was a long walk. Abby could feel stickiness between her legs, the pad, bulky and uncomfortable. The knot inside her wasn't embarrassment; it was fear. She needed someone to talk to. She walked the lonely stretch of road alone and looked to the purple mountains for answers, finding none, of course. At home she put on a clean dress and threw the tainted one in a bucket in the laundry for her father to find later (he washed it without a word). Then she sat on the couch feeling surreal as a cloud, detached and floaty, as if none of this was really happening.

Eventually she thought to ring Gran, who came over immediately with everything Abby needed, including compassion and explanations. Gran gave the kindly, loving help and guidance she'd always given, the help that Abby's mother could have provided if she was still alive . . . or perhaps it would have ended up Gran's job anyway, as it had so often before when Grace wasn't up to mothering.

But Gran died only a few months later, and Abby was left to suffer the mood swings and uncertainty of puberty alone. Her father ducked away from it—what he didn't acknowledge couldn't touch him. By seventeen, when her hormones had levelled, she was already planning her future. By then she knew what she wanted. She was young to be so certain, but she'd learned how to take care of herself. She had to get out, make her own life in science, which was her passion, and outdoors, which was where she needed to be. Matt had moved into a ramshackle house on a friend's property. He took a job at a local vineyard—anything to be independent. There was nothing to hold Abby at home. She finished school, applied for university, shifted to Melbourne, worked a night job in a bar. It wasn't nirvana, but she had to set herself on her path, away from the past.

Now, sitting on the step of her bungalow, she hears her phone ringing inside on the coffee table, and she unhooks the guitar from around her neck and sets it gently aside. The flyscreen door bangs as she swings it wide and rushes to find the phone among the jumble of books on the table. The battery is low—after this, she will have to recharge it.

'Hello?' She flicks to speaker-phone and goes back outside to retrieve her guitar.

'Hey, Abby, it's me.' Her brother's rough voice scrapes down the line. He rarely rings.

'What's up?' she asks.

'Dad's not good. Had a fight with Brenda. Anniversary of Mum's death.'

The anniversary. Abby is surprised she has forgotten it. 'What happened?' she asks, suppressing a surge of guilt.

'He got drunk. Pissed off his head. Walked round the streets shouting Mum's name. Singing to her. Brenda had to rescue him. Serves her right. But she made him sleep in the chook shed.'

The chook shed may not sound like much to anyone else, but to her family it has special significance. Abby's trampoline-heart knocks hard as old visions rise and she works to squash them down. 'He didn't have to stay there. He's a man, isn't he?'

'Not when it comes to Brenda.'

Abby pauses. She knows what she needs to do. Matt wants her to fix things like she always does. She rolls in when there's a need and finds solutions. That's how she manages. She sees a problem, gauges its shape, sizes it up, resolves it then moves on. No looking back. 'Do you want me to come down?'

'Be a good idea. Soon as you can.'

'My car's not running well. I'll have to catch the bus. Can you pick me up?'

'Just let me know the time.'

4

The bus trip down the Hume Highway the next day is quicker than it used to be—at least that's what the driver claims in conversation with the passenger seated just behind him. All the new bypasses have cut the transit time, which is good for passengers and drivers alike.

Three rows back, Abby eavesdrops without wanting to. The bald-headed driver, in his dark blue shorts, pale blue shirt and long white socks, seems hungry for chat. Abby supposes it must be dull driving the same stretch of road over and over, pulling into the same roadside stops, day after day. The driver must be hungry for food too, she notes. He has an impressive stomach presumably won from countless deep-fried meals and fizzy drinks. The rubbish bin, located down the front, already holds two empty Coke cans and one of Red Bull. Abby reserves those sorts of drinks for exam time, but highway driving must be tedious.

She feels sleepy as she sits slumped in her seat watching the farms flicker by. The bus is not full, so she doesn't have to share her seat. At the bus station in Canberra she used her daypack as a deterrent to would-be trip companions who eyed her seat with interest. She doesn't fancy conversation with strangers at the best of times, and today she has other things to think about . . . like that horrible incident with the kangaroo, and Cameron's failure to ring—she's still smarting about that. Honestly though, she'd be better off contemplating how to deal with her father. He can be evasive and he won't discuss anything if he doesn't want to. He finds smokescreens to hide behind—generally women or alcohol. And Abby ought to know.

When Grace died he became a beacon for assistance, and women came flocking to him like white cockatoos settling on a gum tree. Abby had watched them claim the house, stacking the freezer with pre-cooked meals and taking liberties in the kitchen, filling the kettle to make their own cups of tea. They took other liberties too, planting themselves at the table to immerse in long conversations with her father. Mostly they oozed sympathy and condolences, but sometimes they came drenched in other things, like perfume and verbal diarrhoea and flirtatiousness—even Abby could see it.

Whenever an invasive matriarch arrived, Matt vacated the house, rifle in hand, to blow the crap out of some poor defenceless rabbit in the bush. Abby hated it too. But her father seemed to like the endless talk-fests and female attention.

His first betrayal had been the worst. Abby had come home from school to strange noises disrupting the familiar quiet of the house: rhythmic thudding, a woman's voice. At thirteen, Abby was naïve, but not stupid. She tossed her school bag to the floor with a deliberate clatter, pausing to enjoy the subsequent strained silence and then the rustling that came from her father's room. She knew he was trying to make himself presentable so he could explain with some pathetic mash of excuses. She didn't wait, banging the door behind her as she raced across the paddock towards the trees. She was almost to the fence when her father's voice came on the wind. Glancing back she saw him, standing half-dressed and barefoot in the grass by the house, his unbuttoned shirt flapping against his chest. Self-righteously angry, she turned away, barely breaking stride as she dived through the fence, ripping her T-shirt on the barbs before continuing up-slope. On the ridge she stopped. Around her, the bush whipped and sighed, and the tree crowns seemed lashed by a windswept fury that matched her own.

It was almost dark when she crept downhill again, sliding on the scented bark of peppermints. Her father stood in the paddock, swaying like a drunken scarecrow and calling her name. From where she remained hidden in the gloomy shadows, Abby watched him taking regular gulps from a bottle. When he finally staggered back to the house, she slipped from the bush and followed him home.

After that, there had been many dalliances, and sometimes it seemed to Abby the whole lonely-hearts brigade of the town had worked their way through the front door of the house and into her father's bedroom. Neither she nor Matt became accustomed to it or was able to forgive him, but over the years they learned that it was unreasonable to expect him to remain true to their mother. Available women were few in a country town, but he found them. Or they found him. This was something Abby and Matt had to live with.

When the bus arrives in the main street of Mansfield it is already dark. Abby sees Matt waiting for her beneath a streetlight outside the post office, hands in pockets. He's wearing his usual uniform: checked flannelette shirt, stained jeans, toe-worn boots and a worried frown. He has none of the smooth style of Cameron, Abby thinks, and then she feels guilty for comparing them. It's hardly fair to line her brother up against a private-school educated city boy.

Hooking her daypack over her shoulder, she alights from the bus and goes to hug him. He's awkward with her, stiffly resistant to her affectionate embrace. This is not unusual, but a small part of her had hoped he might have melted a little and become more amenable to a sisterly hug. Naturally, he hasn't changed.

It's been a while since she's seen him, but he's still thin and rangy. His blue eyes shift when she locks him in her gaze, and he scuffs his boots on the pavement while the driver unloads her suitcase. She smiles to herself. He's never been one for eye contact. Who knows how his girlfriends get near him.

'Good trip?' he asks, not looking at her.

'No, it was boring.'

He nods his agreement. 'I hate highway driving.'

She cocks an eyebrow at him. 'Is that why you never come to visit? I've often wondered . . .'

He grabs her case and grins sideways at her as he leads the way to his old bomb Nissan. 'You know why I don't come,' he says, tossing her case in the back. 'I hate cities. Hate fake dudes.'

'There's none of them here, of course,' she says, leaning on sarcasm.

His grin widens. 'No. Here we only have good wholesome country people with charity in their hearts.'

They clamber into his car and Abby kicks aside takeaway containers to find a home for her feet. She dusts the dirty seat with the back of her hand. 'Nice car for royalty,' she says.

He grins again. 'No room for airs and graces here.'

They drive out of town, the headlights cutting haloes in the dark. The car rackets over the bridge, inky water gliding beneath.

'How's Dad?' Abby asks.

Matt firms his hands on the wheel and shrugs. 'Sucking it up to Brenda, I reckon.'

'Is he back in the house?'

'In the spare room.'

'I can't believe she banished him to the chook shed. Maybe he deserved it.'

Matt tenses. 'Brenda's a bitch. Worst thing she could have done.'

'She holds him together,' Abby says. 'I suppose we should thank her for that.'

Matt's brow furrows into an angry black line. 'Thank her for nothing. He shouldn't let her wear the pants.'

They could both remember when nobody wore the pants and it was all about harmony and survival, keeping their mother afloat. 'Maybe she was the best on offer,' Abby suggests. 'I mean, after Mum.'

Matt's mouth is hard and straight. 'Brenda just spread her legs the furthest.'

They swing into the farm driveway and jolt up the rutted drive. 'How long since they had the grader in?' Abby asks.

'Who knows.' Matt's face shines green in the dashboard light. 'I try not to come here. Only emergencies, like now.'

'You coming inside?'

He shakes his head. 'I'll leave it to you.'

'Thanks. Such a kind brother.'

He chuckles, pulling up in front of the house.

The movement of the car trips the sensors and the outside lights flare suddenly, flooding the house, the yard and the turning circle. Even in the dark, the sight of home tugs at Abby. There's something reassuring about returning to the place of your roots—a sweet twist of nostalgia tangled with good memories. Your mind blanks out the bad. And it's just as well.

She lingers for a moment in the car with Matt, psyching herself up to face Brenda. The familiarity of the house steadies her. It snuggles in its hillside nest, somehow solid and unchanging. The oaks reach their leafy arms over the roof as if in a protective embrace, and around the house, the garden rambles and leaps in its usual chaos. Brenda has tried to alter the rustic look of the place, but even her gargantuan efforts can't contain the garden. The veranda remains cluttered with chairs and gumboots, brooms and rakes, just as it was in Abby's childhood. Brenda has managed to subdue the mess inside the house, but out here, Abby's father remains in charge. The past continues to hover, and this is reassuring.

Abby opens the car door. 'Thanks for the lift,' she says to Matt.

He nods. 'When are you heading back?'

'Hopefully tomorrow or the next day. I'll see how things go. I have an open ticket.'

'Give me a call. I'll take you to the bus.'

She gets out, hoicks her case from the back seat.

'Good luck,' he says. 'Hope Brenda doesn't cut your throat.' He chuckles. 'Reckon she'd like to.'

Abby slams the car door, and Matt takes off, spinning his car too fast around the turning circle and deliberately spitting up gravel to leave his signature on the driveway. The headlights roll crazily off the walls of the machinery shed. Then he's gone, a set of lights bobbing down the driveway.

The front door of the house opens, spilling light.

'That you out there, Abby?' Brenda's thready voice echoes.

Abby turns towards the house. 'Yeah, it's me.'

'Well, don't just stand out there in the cold. Come on in and have a cuppa.'

Abby steps from the floodlit driveway into the entrance hall of the farmhouse and leaves her luggage by the door before following Brenda into the kitchen. She has never enjoyed Brenda's company and tonight is no exception. The two of them don't even pretend at niceties. Step-mothers, Abby tells herself, haven't changed since Cinderella's time.

Brenda is a short, rounded woman with a glowing ruddy face and small eyes which glare out at Abby from puffy cheeks criss-crossed by fine broken blood vessels. She's fat from eating too many of the cakes and desserts she bakes for Steve—at least that's her excuse. In the kitchen, she folds her arms across her generous bosom and sets her stout legs wide, proclaiming ownership of the house. 'Did you hear what your father's been up to?' she barks.

'Matt gave me a brief summary,' Abby says.

'Sounds like Matt.' Brenda juts her chin. 'Brief.'

Abby allows herself a smile. 'He's not a man of many words.'

'Shame I can't say the same for your father,' Brenda huffs, filling the kettle. 'There's at least one word I'd like to delete from his vocabulary, and that's your mother's name. He doesn't mention it for months then gets drunk and sings it all over town.'

'You shouldn't let him go out on the anniversary,' Abby says. 'That date just brings everything up again.'

'Don't I know it! Though God knows why he'd want to sing about her. She wasn't much of a wife or mother, from what I hear.'

'Don't talk about things you don't know,' Abby says stiffly, suppressing a flash of anger and refusing to give Brenda the satisfaction of a response. They've been through this before and it gets them nowhere. 'Where's Dad?' she asks.

Brenda sets the kettle on the stove and nods towards the hallway. 'He's licking his wounds in the spare room. Not allowed out till he's made a full apology.'

Abby ignores this last part. 'Think I'll go and see him.'

Brenda raises supercilious eyebrows. 'You don't want a cuppa first?'

Abby shakes her head. 'Maybe later.' Maybe *never* with you, she thinks. How has her father fallen so low?

She wanders down the hall to Matt's old bedroom. Her father is lying on the bed, hands behind his head, staring at the ceiling, just as her mother used to in times of illness. Brenda's cooking has thickened his waistline and he's no longer as thin and wiry as he used to be. 'Hey,' she says, shutting the door and sitting on the edge of the bed.

He looks at her without smiling and she notices the silver hair multiplying at his temples, invading the thick crop of black that springs from his scalp. The frown lines between his eyes are deeper than she remembers. 'Where did you come from?' he mumbles.

'Came to dig you out of trouble.'

He winces. 'Got an excavator?'

'It's hard to organise one at this time of night.'

'No doubt she's told you what happened.'

'You're supposed to serenade people when they're *alive*,' Abby says. 'How much did you have to drink?'

He shrugs. 'Lost count.'

'Great.'

He frowns. 'Don't judge me. The drinking only started when your mother died.'

'So it's her fault now, is it? The way you've ended up?'

He glares at her.

'How are you going to make it up with Brenda?'

He scowls. 'Can't bring myself to do it.'

'She's hurting. You've humiliated her.'

'Don't tell me,' he says. 'I don't want to hear it.'

Abby can't believe she's sticking up for that woman. But she knows how hopeless her father is when he's on his own. He gets lonely, doesn't eat properly, drinks too much, doesn't shower often enough. The sad fact is he needs someone to look after him.

'Did you hear where she made me sleep?' her father says.

'What do you mean *made* you? Or were you too drunk to get yourself out of there?'

He closes his eyes. 'Too drunk.'

Abby shakes her head, disgusted. 'No wonder she's pissed off.'

'But the chook shed,' he says, with emphasis.

Abby sympathises, but she can just imagine how he must have been the other night, too drunk to walk. She wonders how Brenda got him home, tries to picture her swinging him into the car, pushing him in with her knee. She thinks of them stumbling down to the chook shed: Brenda strengthened by rage, dragging her father along. Abby can see where Brenda's cruelty might come from—who wants to live in a small town with a drunkard?

'I'm not always like this,' her father mumbles, eyes still closed. 'Just once a year. I miss your mother. Don't you?'

'Yes,' Abby says. 'I miss her. But she's not coming back and this doesn't fix anything. And when you're ready we'll practise an apology. I'm not going anywhere till we've got this sorted.'

He opens one eye and peers at her. 'How about I come and live with you?'

She gives him a sharp-edged grin. 'Not an option. I live in a shoe box. There simply isn't room.'

'You're right,' he says with a self-deprecating smile. 'It wouldn't work. You don't cook well enough. And how would I survive without my desserts?'

Abby pokes the soft layer of fat over his ribs. 'A diet might be good for you.'

He chuckles and Abby is pleased to see his sense of humour re-emerging. 'I'm with Garfield on this one,' he says. 'Now that Brenda has converted me to sweets, the word diet has become die with a t.'

5

Abby spends the night in her childhood bedroom . . . although it's not really hers anymore, Brenda has stamped herself all over the place. That was the hardest thing to accept: Brenda's efforts to rub out all evidence of Grace's existence. Matt won't come here anymore; he doesn't like Brenda and refuses to pretend. Abby doesn't like her much either, but she accepts that Brenda is something they have to endure.

Before Brenda, Abby lost count of the women who passed through her father's life. She had moved to Melbourne to study science, so she wasn't around when Brenda began to feature. Matt told her all about it though. He couldn't believe he was meant to take Brenda seriously. Abby tried to counsel him from afar, which wasn't easy, given his aversion to chatting on the phone.

Then Brenda moved in to the farmhouse and took over. Next she tried to bulldoze the rest of the family. She had offspring of her own who Abby and Matt were expected to like. Abby recognised that her father had no choice. Brenda's grown children were in the farmhouse all the time so he had to accept them. But Matt was furious. He resented that Steve saw more of Brenda's family than he did of his own.

Gatherings were planned, and Abby was expected to come from the city to attend. It annoyed her that she and Matt were supposed to join in and play happy families. They were supposed to stand by and watch Brenda's kids bagging Steve out. It was humiliating. Brenda and her family laughed at him, denigrated him, made him look small. Abby tried to switch off, and Matt fumed, barely containing a violent eruption, while Steve watched on with a glass of beer in his hand and a detached, bemused smile on his face. Abby concluded that although Brenda's family was a twisted nasty lot, her father had grown tired of living on his own. It seemed he was prepared to stomach put-downs and derogatory digs as a trade-off for leaving loneliness behind.

Then they were married. Matt refused to go to the wedding and Abby couldn't blame him. She went only to remind Brenda that Steve had a life and family before her. It was a strangely tragic day: watching her father relinquish his independence and his past for a compromised future.

But despite Brenda's efforts, there's obviously a corner of her father's soul that hasn't been subdued—he shows it every year on the anniversary of Grace's death—and this brings Abby a significant degree of smug satisfaction. Brenda has done her utmost to delete Abby's mother—she's bought new furniture, new drapes, new carpet, had the kitchen renovated—but Grace is still with them. There's no escape. While Brenda is living with Steve, Abby's mother will always be present. This is Abby's consolation.

Abby's family has lived in this staid brick farmhouse for twenty-five years. They moved here after Matt was born—at least that's what Gran said. Before that they were living in the flat suburbs of Melbourne where Abby's father worked as an accountant and her mother taught at the local primary school.

Abby still remembers the day Gran presented a tray of scones with jam and cream for afternoon tea and sat down to explain how Abby's family was different. Abby was eight and already aware that her home life wasn't like everyone else's. Until then she'd simply accepted it, but Gran said there were things she should know.

Apparently Abby's parents were 'normal' until Matt arrived. Then Grace became depressed like many other first-time mums. Medications prescribed by the doctor didn't seem to work. Grace tried to care for Matt, but simply couldn't do it. Gran offered to help, but the family house in Melbourne was small and Abby's father hadn't seemed receptive, so Gran had given what support she could from her home in Mansfield—listening to Abby's dad's concerns over the phone. It hadn't been easy for Gran to stay away while her daughter's life fell apart, yet she had to allow them their independence, at least initially.

As the weeks passed, Steve had become increasingly desperate, living in a filthy house full of flies and dirty nappies and stale milk and food left on the kitchen table. Gran heard about it all. She said Steve had feared for Matt's safety while he was away during the day. But what could he do? He had to work to bring in money and pay the mortgage. Gran was afraid for Matt too. She was worried Grace might forget the baby when she drifted away—let him drown in the bath. From what Steve had described, Grace was completely disconnected from the baby, unmoved by him.

Steve was exhausted. Gran knew he was trying to do everything each night after work, racing from one disaster to the next: cleaning, washing clothes and dishes, heating bottles, settling Matt, shopping, cooking. He was losing patience with Grace, and with the crying baby, and the mess.

That's when Gran went to the city to take control. She'd found Grace sitting blankly on the couch looking at Matt as if he was a doll, a red, angry toy that screamed. And it seemed that Grace didn't care. Time and again, Gran would find her in the bedroom staring out the window or vaguely flicking at the bedspread with her fingertips. It was a sad and stressful time, Gran said, but it was far better when she was there to watch out for the baby.

In the end they all moved to Mansfield. Steve took a job with a local accountant and they lived in Gran's house for a couple of months until Steve bought the farm. Gran understood it was a decision he made for himself; Grace was too vague and misty to contribute to running the family, let alone choose a home. The farm was Steve's solace, a base from which to manage the rest of his life. Gran knew he needed it.

Then things looked up. A new anti-depressant drug seemed to move Grace out of the clouds. Gran said it was wonderful to see her become a person again. She started singing and playing the guitar, and she cared for Matt with revived interest. She didn't work—that would be too much for a fragile mind—but she began riding horses, something she had enjoyed as a child. Gran had been happy to see Steve start a vegie patch. It was a good sign. Then he built a chook shed, bought a tractor and cows.

Grace secretly weaned herself off the drugs and fell pregnant. Both Gran and Steve were concerned, but Grace seemed to remain even. Abby was born.

At first everything was fine. Grace had managed to breast-feed little Abby, the house was messy, but not dirty, and Gran minded Matt three days a week so Grace had time to rest. But Grace nose-dived and it took longer to recover than the last time. At least Gran was close and knew she could help.

It was tough for eight-year-old Abby to hear all these things about her mother, and at the time she'd been more focused on eating scones with cream than listening to Gran. But the stories stayed with her, and she'd been proud Gran considered her old enough to listen and understand. After that Abby had become more aware of her mother's cycles. She'd noticed how her mother would lift slowly from depression and re-engage with life and people and music, until she began to wind up, becoming faster, busier, more hectic. Grace was entertaining and funny, and Abby would laugh and feed off her mother's energy. She would watch her mother whirling around the house, singing, or pouring out great chunks of Shakespearean plays in character. In the space of a day her mother could be Cassius, Lady Macbeth, Portia and Puck. The couch in the lounge room was her mother's stage, where she would stand with an actor's erect posture and distant gaze, unloose her wavy auburn hair and let the words flow. Abby remembers being an enraptured audience.

As a child, she loved her mother's weird and potent energy, her creative impulsivity: dances in the rain, Christmas laden with cakes and presents, singing in the kitchen, pots banging.

She remembers cooking frenzies of butterfly patty-cakes, carrot and walnut muffins, sponges with enormous whorls of cream, fruitcakes doused in brandy. The kitchen was always cluttered with used bowls, cracked eggshells, stray mounds of flour. When Grace was energised, it was feast or famine. The cake tins would be crammed with treats and the fridge would be stuffed with food (both fresh and rotting—Grace never knew what she'd stashed in there). Or, when Grace shifted focus, the cupboards and pantry would be empty. After-school snacks became snow peas from the vegie patch.

Often when Abby came home from school, she would walk down the drive to the sound of music. Her mother would be sitting on the doorstep, playing guitar, singing to the chooks pecking on the lawn. Once, Abby found her perched on the roof, guitar slung around her neck, picking out a tune.

What are you doing up there? Abby called to her.

Why sit on the step when you can be up here? her mother said. You should come up and see.

Abby had tossed her schoolbag aside and scaled the ladder. Young children navigating gutters and steeply gabled roof-lines—Abby knew it wasn't sensible. But her mother made no move to help. Abby was on her own up there, stepping breathlessly across the tiles while her mother smiled and watched. She sang again while Abby sat with her, and in those moments Abby felt she understood. She saw how her mother's craziness gave her enlightenment. Her mother was right. The view was different up there. The beauty of the landscape was heightened by the headiness of elevation.

Other times Abby would be sitting at the kitchen table doing her homework and she would hear the drumming of hooves. Out on the flats, her mother would be galloping her horse, helmet-free, her lithe shape fused to the horse's back. When she was surfing a wave of exhilaration, she was reckless, without a sense of self-preservation. Her horse seemed to respond to her effervescence and revert to its wild, flighty self, leaning into the joy of a frenzied gallop with matching verve.

Abby and Matt learned to ride too. Their mother would lead them up into the foothills of the mountains where she loved to fly her horse along the tracks and trails. They would follow her on their ponies, pulling up when she careered ahead on some manic dash. They feared for her safety and their own. When she was gone, they could still hear the thud of her horse bolting up the hill. They would follow at a more sedate pace. Often she would be waiting on a high ridge, looking out over the forest that rolled down into valleys then climbed to the nearest peaks. When she turned to look at them, her eyes would be shining, while her horse blew and heaved from the effort of the uphill pull.

The journey home was even more frightening. Grace would gather her reins without warning and charge downhill. It was much more difficult to restrain the ponies on the homeward run, but Matt always stayed back to help Abby control her pony, grasping Abby's reins and checking the pony himself.

Occasionally the ponies took off before the children could contain them. Abby would dig her fingers into her pony's mane, hook her fingers beneath the pommel and cling on while the pony scrambled headlong down the hill. She would be too terrified to breathe. If the pony stumbled she knew they would roll into the scrub. The pony could break a leg, could fall on her.

Their mother would meet them at the gate and the ponies would reef and chafe while she swung it open, knowing this was the last homeward push. Once the gate was secured, Grace would turn her horse and gallop off with the ponies trailing madly behind her, Abby imagining legs twisting in rabbit holes. Grace would be oblivious. Abby still remembers the musical sound of her mother's laughter on the wind, the way Grace would fold herself over her mount's wither and seem to become a part of the horse, her hair streaming like the horse's tail as they hammered back to the house.

Grace climbed trees too. She loved to press up high where the branches thinned and the wind spun through the leaves. Occasionally she scaled one of the oaks near the house, but she preferred the pines down the paddock. She would drag Abby and Matt down there and coax them to climb with her, leaving them behind once they started to cower at the dizziness of height. Ensconced safely on the lower sturdier limbs, they would watch as she worked her way higher while the wind whined in the pine needles.

Those times were full of a bright happiness, colourful and vibrant. It seemed to Abby that her mother touched on the very essence of life. She showed them the thrill of freedom, of living without kowtowing to risk. But things would always change. Abby would notice her mother's speech accelerating, her thoughts cluttering, and she would look on with dread as her mother became confused, rushing so fast from one task to the next that she finished nothing. Chaos would overtake the thin veneer of order in the house. Then it was a case of keeping her mother safe until she broke.

When the crash came, Grace would be back in bed, staring at the ceiling. The horse would stand in the paddock under the tree, swishing its tail with boredom. The house would be quiet: no singing, no music, no Shakespeare. And Gran would come again with her old brown suitcase and her gentle smile to tend to them all in her patient methodical way.

These were the hard times for Abby, and they would last for weeks. Her mother would emerge only when everyone was sleeping. Abby would hear her wandering as if lost through the house and sometimes outside. That's when her dad would emerge and quietly intervene, gently retrieving Grace from the doorstep, folding her against his chest and guiding her back to the bedroom.

Several times, Abby remembers staying with Gran while her father took her mother to Melbourne to see specialists, psychologists, psychiatrists. They tried different drugs, new therapies, natural products, acupuncture. Sometimes the medications seemed to lift the blanket of depression for a while and Grace would normalise—whatever that meant. But she hated the side effects. She said the drugs dulled her and she forgot who she was. She was vaguely acceptable as a human being, but she felt like a zombie, a ghost, bland and absent.

Abby also preferred the roller coaster of her mother's emotions to seeing her drugged out. Eventually Grace stopped taking the drugs, and they all learned to endure the ride. Life wasn't easy, and home was never normal as other people knew it, but love is love, and family is family, and they found ways to work around Grace's illness, learned tolerance.

The only good thing was having Gran move in to help. Even though Abby knew her father didn't enjoy having Gran in his space, Abby loved having her grandmother to stay. Gran was someone Abby could talk to, someone to hug, a listening ear. Abby loved the sense of order when Gran was in charge. Clothes were washed, folded, and put away. Dishes cleaned and put in drawers. Food appeared in the fridge. There were kisses goodnight, long talks about issues at school, knitting lessons, jigsaw puzzles on the dining room table, a fresh fire set in the fireplace each morning, hot scones after school.

For Abby, Gran was the light when her mother was in darkness. It was a double whammy when Gran passed away so soon after Grace's death. And for a long time Abby wasn't sure who she missed most. Fact is, you expect your grandparents to die while you're young, but your parents should last till you don't need them anymore. At least, that's how Abby used to see it. It seemed she just didn't have enough time with her mum, felt like she hardly knew her. Even now, it still didn't seem fair.

6

When Abby wakes, milky light is weaving its way through the swaying shadows of oak leaves to fall softly across the bedroom floor. She forgot to pull the curtains last night and now she is glad of it, allows herself to drift in and out of consciousness like a snowflake wafting on the wind. She figures there's no rush to impose herself on Brenda and her father this morning. Hopefully the very fact of her presence will remind them that reconciliation must somehow be achieved. And it's pleasant to wallow in bed, reminds her of the unhurried nature of childhood, when unplanned days stretched lazily in front of her, waiting to be filled.

She emerges from bed slowly and wanders into the kitchen where Steve is sitting at the table, hunched over a cup of coffee. Brenda stalks and parades beside the bench, rattling dishes and cutlery. Resolution must be nigh, Abby figures, although punishment and retribution are obviously still incomplete. Brenda has a point to make, and Steve's contrition, however absolute, will be insufficient until she has had her fill of huffing and posturing.

Abby slides into a seat, smiles at her father, and winks. At this stage of recovery the only asset Steve requires is endurance. He must stomach Brenda's moaning and accusations without retaliation, and soon all will be back to normal.

Brenda is a whirlwind of hurt and anger. She inflicts upon Steve the smart of humiliation she has had to bear due to his drunken performance: an eye for an eye. Steve is like a reprimanded child, and Abby would like to protect him, to stand up to her step-mother. She can think of many scathing things to say, insults that would put Brenda back in her box, such as: 'you old bitch, you're only in this for the farm', or 'did you know they crucified the last person who was as perfect as you?' But she knows this would serve only to prolong Brenda's attack. It's best to observe in silence and let the storm pass.

After breakfast, while she is showering, Abby thinks perhaps she hears the sound of shouting, maybe Brenda's shrill voice above the hiss of water. But it seems unlikely; her father is generally non-confrontational, and after a decent night's sleep he seemed genuinely remorseful this morning. Abby rushes her rinse-off anyway, and as she dries herself she is certain she hears Brenda in full cry, like a scalded rooster calling in the dawn. Abby dresses in a flurry and tiptoes to the kitchen, pausing outside the door to listen.

'That's not an apology,' Brenda is shouting. 'But it's exactly the sort of rubbish I'd expect from you, you pathetic man. What were you doing, singing to a dead woman! How am I supposed to live with that? Oh, I don't want to hear your grubby explanations. Ten years that woman's been dead and I still have to live with her. Then your daughter shows up to make sure you say sorry because you haven't the strength to do it yourself. What did she offer you? A lollipop for good behaviour? I don't know why I put up with this.'

Abby lingers in the hallway, afraid of butting in on Brenda's outburst, and sure she's not supposed to witness it. She hears the low defensive rumble of her father's responses as he attempts to fend off Brenda's wrath, but she can't make out his words.

'Don't give me that utter garbage,' Brenda yells. 'And don't cower away from me. Anyone would think I'd been guilty of beating you, which is so damned tempting when you flinch like that.'

There is a moment's silence, during which Abby can only imagine the fury in Brenda's small pale eyes and the anger feeding along the tight line of her lips. Then there is a thud, followed by a gasp, a clatter and a groan. Abby opens the door to see her father bent over with a hand pressed to his forehead and a spurt of red, like tomato sauce, spreading through his fingers. There is Brenda near the kitchen sink with her mouth rounded into a shocked O, her hand flying wildly to her face as if to shield herself from the scene. On the floor at Steve's feet, a ceramic saucer that Brenda has thrown at him, broken into several pieces, rocks on the remnants of its curves before settling into guilty stillness. Steve looks up at Brenda, disbelief etched into his craggy features, fingers covering his forehead. He says nothing, but his expression says it all. Brenda has gone too far.

Abby steps centre-stage into a drama which has frozen mid-scene. Brenda seems paralysed, as if she can't quite believe what she has done. Abby grasps a blue-checked tea towel from the back of a chair and goes to her father, loops an arm around him and guides him to a chair. He sits slowly, like an old man, and gently she levers his fingers away from his brow and dabs at the oozing gash that weeps blood like water seeping from a cracked hose. She finds herself uttering cooing sounds like a mother comforting a child, reassuring verbal music that takes its origins from the beginning of time. Her father recoils in pain, winces as she wicks the blood away.

'I'll have to take him to the hospital,' she says to Brenda, who still hasn't spoken, and who stands limp and somehow deflated by the kitchen sink, sagging now, all her anger departed.

'I didn't mean to hurt him,' Brenda says, a notch above a whisper.

Abby turns a searing gaze on her. 'I hope this is over now,' she says. 'You both need to move on.'

In the ute on the way to the hospital, Steve holds a fistful of cotton wool to his head, which Brenda fearfully offered to him as Abby ushered him out the door.

'Sometimes I wonder what you see in her,' Abby says, hands firm on the steering wheel.

Steve says nothing, sits curled into himself in the passenger seat.

'You can't tell me you love her,' Abby continues. 'And if you do, it's a strange kind of love.'

He grunts something she can't hear and she asks him to repeat it.

'All love is strange,' he says. 'That's nothing new.'

Abby considers this for a moment and supposes it is true. Her father's love for her mother was no ordinary love, and he didn't walk out on that roller coaster relationship. Perhaps this is his strength, the skill to wait things out, to cut through where nobody else would persist. 'So you wouldn't consider leaving?' she asks, just to put it out there.

He shakes his head. 'Can't live on my own, and she's bearable most of the time. It's just me. I bring out the worst in her.'

'What would happen if you did leave?' Abby asks. 'Would you have to sell the farm? Hand it over to her?'

Steve shakes his head again. 'Nah. I had the brains to organise a prenuptial agreement. The farm is yours and Matt's. Brenda can own me, but she can't take that from you. The farm is a gift from your mother and me. The only thing we've got to give.'

He says it in the present tense, as if Grace still lives on the farm, alive in the wind that blows through the leaves of the oaks and the pines down the driveway, sweeping down from the mountains where her soul might still exist within the symphony of landscape and sky. *A prenuptial agreement*; Abby hadn't expected such foresight from her father.

At the hospital, they wait two hours even though there's no-one else in the waiting room. Abby wonders if perhaps the doctor has a special date and won't appear until a breakfast of eggs Florentine and strawberry crêpes has been eaten and digested. She kills time staring at the TV mounted in the corner of the room, volume turned down. There's nothing worth watching anyway—just electric shadows moving meaninglessly, dulling impatience.

The doctor, when she appears blank-faced with a clipboard, is only marginally apologetic, mutters something about a cardiac patient and waiting for blood results, which Abby reads as being caught up with a cup of tea and Scotch Finger biscuits. She directs Steve to an orange plastic chair in a small room with bright lights, and pulls away the fibres of cotton wool which have stuck to his congealed scab.

'You didn't have any Steri-strips?' she asks, as if this should have been sorted without medical assistance.

'If I'd had any, I would have used them,' Abby says.

The doctor flashes her a look and dabs at the wound with an alcohol swab, making Steve grimace. 'Suppose I'd better stitch it.'

'That'd be good,' Abby says.

The doctor pulls from a cupboard a plastic bag of instruments, a brown bottle, a syringe and needle, and a stainless steel kidney dish which she fills with some sort of pink liquid. She absently draws up some other liquid in the syringe, then sets it on the bench and turns her attention to cleaning the wound more thoroughly. 'How'd you cut yourself?' she asks.

'Flying saucer,' Steve grunts, and the doctor frowns with annoyance, thinking he is joking. Steve refrains from elaborating.

The doctor slides the needle in under the edge of his wound and he flinches. 'Hey, steady on.'

'It's local anaesthetic,' she says. 'Stings at first, then you won't feel a thing.'

The doctor's smile is as tight as a cat's arsehole, Abby thinks.

'You new here?' Steve asks.

'Been here a few months,' the doctor says, biting her lower lip as she slips the needle in again and injects more local anaesthetic. 'I have to complete a country stint before I can get a city rotation.'

'Enjoying it?'

'It's okay.'

The doctor opens her kit, then she washes her hands in a cursory manner, as if sterility is only a marginal matter with rural beasts like Steve. She draws out a length of white thread for stitching and does a quick job of pulling Steve's forehead together. He frowns and winks involuntarily every now and then, as she probes into areas not quite numbed by anaesthetic.

'Am I better looking now?' he asks, as she secures the last stitch. Abby is impressed by her father's joviality with this seemingly disinterested young woman who manages only a half-smile at his game joke.

'Depends on your perspective,' she says.

'Starting from a low base, eh?' Steve adds with a grin.

On the way home, sitting beside a scrawny Frankenstein's monster with a patched forehead, Abby asks if he and Brenda will be okay now.

Steve smiles wanly. 'We're even,' he says, 'at least for another year, till your mother's anniversary comes up again.'

'Or until you step out of line.'

'I guess that's possible.'

Steve's grin reminds Abby of Matt. It's good to know a measure of spunk still runs beneath his skin.

The next morning Abby calls Matt and asks him to pick her up. He's amazed she's still alive, and he comes willingly to save her from the house of monsters. She waits for him outside, sitting on her suitcase in the middle of the turning circle, her goodbyes said and accepted. Her father has retreated to the vegie garden, a lonely figure leaning against his shovel like a scarecrow on a stick, small and stooped, older. But what can Abby do? She can't change his life, can't alter the fact of Brenda—it's his choice, not hers. Consumed by guilt, Brenda has immersed herself in the fine art of constructing a caramel slice in the kitchen—Steve's favourite. From here, the path to peace may still take a few days. There's no point in Abby hanging around; at least they've declared a truce.

Abby likes the stillness and emptiness of the yard, the large quiet of the shed where the battery for the electric fence ticks with monotonous regularity and the orange Kubota tractor stands in oily sleep, and the hay bales sit neatly stacked, waiting for winter. She can hear the soft clucking of the chooks turning over this morning's scraps in their pen, the wispy voice of the wind sounding in the pines, the distant rattle of Matt's Nissan coming down the driveway.

Now that yesterday's tension is subsiding, and she is relaxing into peace, she's aware she could almost live here on the farm if it wasn't for Brenda. The air carries the thick rural scent of her childhood, rich with good things, and coloured with memories of her mother. But it's the same each time she comes back now—if she stays too long, the cloudiness returns, and she begins to think of her mother's death. Today, however, the sun is warm on her skin, and here is Matt, swinging open the car door for her. He's wearing that perpetual frown, so quirky and quizzical it's almost funny.

'Get in before Brenda appears,' he says from the driver's seat.

'What, you're not going to lift my bag for me?'

'You're strong,' he says. 'And I have to prepare for a fast getaway.'

'Afraid Brenda might inflict dessert on you?'

'Afraid she might invite me to dinner.'

Abby deposits her bag in the back then settles herself beside Matt. He clunks the old car into gear and performs his usual wheel-spinning exit specifically to irritate Brenda.

'You must have worked your magic pretty quick,' he says as they bounce down the driveway. 'Thought Dad would be held hostage for days.'

'They're on the mend. All I had to do was show my face and Dad sank down on his knees in apology.'

'Bullshit!' Matt laughs and the pleasant spread of his face renders him close to handsome. 'Did you threaten him?'

'No. He threatened me. Said he'd come and live with me in Canberra.'

Matt flings her a glance of horror. 'Christ. That was good motivation for you.'

'Yep. I thought it was all done and dusted before I got out of bed yesterday. Thought they'd kissed and made up. Then she threw a saucer at him and cut his head open and I had to take him to hospital to get stitched up. He's uglier than ever now.'

'It's like a bloody soapie.' Matt's lips kink with amusement. 'Still, I suppose it's easier for him to apologise and be done with it.'

'Easier for me too,' Abby says, 'both of them eating humble pie. I need to get back to Canberra. I have work to do.'

❖

In town, they find a café near the bus stop and sit at a small round table by the window. Abby shouts a coffee for each of them, a pie for Matt, a croissant for herself. Matt slumps in his chair, shoulders rounded, his hands cupped around his coffee mug; it's obvious he doesn't socialise very often. He stirs two lumps of sugar into his cappuccino, focusing on the swirling patterns his spoon makes in the froth. She notices his nails are rough and dirty, could use a trim. His face is shuttered and lonely. She wonders if there's a way to reach him. More hope, she thinks, than trying to undo her father's self-imposed messes.

'I'm sorry I can't stay longer,' she says. 'It would have been good to go for a hike or something. A bit of soul-time in the mountains. But I suppose you have to work.'

His brow crinkles as he raises his eyes to look at her, his skin brown as a walnut—the product of his outdoor life. Then he's distracted by something in the street and his glance shoots out the window. Abby follows his gaze, but nothing's happening out there—just a few cars driving by. 'I'm out of work at the moment,' he says, avoiding eye contact. 'It's quiet at the vineyard. Vintage is done. Nothing much on now till pruning. They put me off for a while.'

Abby is worried by this. Matt has never been good when he's under-occupied. Too much time to think isn't constructive for anyone—it's too easy to tie yourself in irrational knots. 'How are you managing?' she asks.

'I have a few savings,' he says, bum-shuffling on his seat. 'I'll get by. I don't mind having a bit of time off so I can get some other things done.'

'Like what?' she asks.

'I dunno. Might service my car. The engine's a bit off. Could use a tune-up.'

'Will you get another job?'

Matt's eyes speak of hurt and injury, and Abby suspects she is a burr digging under his skin. But who else will push Matt out of his unemployment hole? She tries to lighten the atmosphere. 'Looks like I should have brought my pack down after all,' she says. 'We could have gone for a bushwalk.'

Matt stares out the window again, silent, and Abby waits. His face has changed. She sips her coffee, allows time for him to work up to whatever it is he wants to say.

'I've been thinking about Mum a bit lately,' he says, still fixed out the window.

'Me too,' Abby says. 'I think about her all the time.'

He shakes his head. 'Not like that. I think about what life was like for her. The way she saw things. I think I might be similar. More than I thought. Maybe I'm a chip off the old block.'

Looking at him, Abby sees for the first time the dark smudges under his eyes, the jitteriness in his fingers around the coffee cup. 'What do you mean?' she asks quietly.

He hesitates, flashes an agonised glance at her then flicks his eyes away. 'I get down sometimes. Can't seem to lift myself out.'

A knot of worry hitches in her throat. 'But you're all right, aren't you?'

'Yeah, I suppose so.'

'Isn't it better when you're working?' she asks.

'Yeah, I'll look for something. Keeps me busy, I suppose.'

'Maybe you should see someone,' she suggests tentatively.

He frowns. 'Like who?'

'I don't know. Maybe a psychologist. Talk things through.'

He tightens, and shakes his head. 'Hell no. I'm not going to some shrink. None of that helped Mum anyway.'

'How do you know?' Abby asks. 'We were too young to understand.'

Matt straightens and his face hardens. 'I was sixteen when she died. I understood.' Then his eyes soften and sadden, like butter melting, as if Abby has tugged on some deep inner string and unravelled him.

'Will you talk to *me* then?' she asks. 'Not that I'd be much use, but at least I can be on the end of the phone. Would that be any help?'

He's evasive, takes a long sip from his cup, places it down with slow deliberation, avoids answering; then, 'Maybe.'

'If you're having unsettling feelings you should talk about it,' Abby says.

'Best I keep that stuff to myself.' His face shutters, and the opening is gone.

'If you don't tell me, how can I help?' she insists. 'You're all I've got apart from Dad—and he's more than half owned by Brenda.'

Matt smiles briefly.

'Tell me the signs,' Abby says, 'so I have some idea.'

He meets her eyes. 'You wouldn't be able to tell. I can hide it. You wouldn't ever know.'

He drains his coffee and she senses the topic is closed. She should press him for some sort of commitment, some reassurance he'll contact her if things get bad.

Then the bus pulls up in the street. She has to go. The turnaround is quick. If she's not on board within two minutes, the bus will leave.

'Call me,' she says as she gathers her bags. 'And I'll call you. Don't be a stranger.'

On the bus she can't stop thinking about him so she rings him on her mobile.

'Hey, it's me,' she says.

KAREN VIGGERS

'You again.' He sounds amused. 'Didn't I just put you on a bus?'

'Yes, but I'm worried about you. I want you to call me every day. It doesn't have to take long. Just a quick *Hello I'm fine.*'

'Nah,' he says. 'Too much trouble.'

'I need to know you're okay.'

'I'm fine at the moment.'

'But what about when you're not?'

'It doesn't happen very often.'

'I want to be there for you when it does.'

There's a momentary silence on the other end of the phone.

'Look,' she presses, 'how about I ring you? All you have to do is say you're okay, then I'll leave you alone.'

'You don't need to call. I don't want you trying to be my mother,' he says, grumpy.

'We don't have a mother, so I have to be,' she points out.

'I don't need a mum,' he grunts. 'I can look after myself.'

But Abby knows this isn't true. Everyone needs a mum. The sad thing is that those who've got one often don't appreciate it.

PART II

7

A wattlebird is drinking from a Coke can in the car park. Daphne sees it as she comes out of the doctor's surgery. The world has changed since she went inside. Half an hour, that's all, and suddenly everything is different. Colours are fresher, more vibrant. There is beauty in the way the wind moves in the trees. Clouds seem miraculous, the sky so blue. She feels the texture of the air, smells food cooking somewhere over at the shops: takeaway fish and chips, hamburgers. And here, right in front of her, a wattlebird is sipping Coca Cola.

She watches the bird at its work: dipping its narrow beak into the can then lifting its head so the liquid trickles down its throat. That is how birds drink. They are not designed to sip out of Coke cans, and yet this bird is managing it. How ridiculous. But it is also marvellous. Daphne has never seen a bird do this before.

During the appointment, the doctor said many things, and now Daphne is full of words. Some are familiar, some are not. She went for a check-up and came out with all this jargon floating in her head. Does she really need to know?

The doctor had started by asking questions and ticking them off his list. Daphne answered dutifully, but she disliked the doctor's cool impersonal manner, the way he stared right through her as if she wasn't really there, querying symptoms without truly wanting to know. He is Pam's doctor after all, and Daphne supposes she shouldn't expect much of such a fresh-faced youngster.

Her favourite doctor retired a few years ago. That's what happens when you are old: your compatriots age too. They give up their jobs because they have their own health issues. Good doctors retire to armchairs and become files in other doctors' surgeries. Then you have to see someone else—someone young with attitude and arrogance. They think they know everything, and they have no patience. They are bored, and they talk through you, and they spend half the time glancing sidelong at their iPhone on the desk, wanting you out of there so they can check their messages. That is what this doctor of Pam's is like.

Then Daphne must have given a wrong answer. The doctor's drooping posture disappeared and suddenly an attentive young man sat up in his place. 'What did you say?'

Daphne had shifted uncomfortably in the hard vinyl chair. She gave the answer again, and the doctor's clean young brow twisted in thought. He checked her over again, peppered her with a barrage of other questions, then he started tapping words into his computer, his fingers flying over the keys. It seems all young things know how to touch-type these days.

Now, outside the surgery, Daphne looks down at the envelope the doctor has given her—a referral. On the front he has written an address and phone number in blue pen, the letters pressed deep and dark into the paper with a scrawly, heavy hand. Daphne wonders what she should do with it. Tell Pam and ring for an appointment? She looks back at the wattlebird as it continues to dip and sip from the Coke can. The world is going crazy, including the birds.

She thinks of her home in the valley, wishes she was there right now, back in the mountains where she lived for so many years. Pam is taking her there this afternoon. They are leaving soon, after this appointment which is now finished. It's a good thing. It will give her time to consider.

She thinks of her husband, Doug. How the land shaped him. How he loved it. Part of his bones, he said. And it is true . . . or at least she assumes it to be. Who knows where he rests. He is up there somewhere, that much is certain, and definitely dead—there's no question of that, even though he was never found.

She feels the weight of the envelope in her hand. Does she want to go through all these tests? Probes stuck onto her? Into her? The possibility of surgery? Absolutely not. She'd rather let things happen as they will. Her mind is good, and she's still healthy—at least she was until today. But she's eighty-six and she can't live forever. If heaven exists, Doug will be waiting for her.

She thinks of her daughter Pam, a thoughtful girl—or rather not a girl, but an ageing woman now too: a grandmother. She thinks of her granddaughter, Sandy, whose three children make Daphne a great-grandmother. She never thought she would have all this, thought she'd be dead long before, like Doug. Perhaps she should have gone when he did. It might have been easier. Is she in the way? A burden? She's certainly not much use to anyone anymore.

She examines the referral again. Maybe she should ignore it. Perhaps she should let things run their course, live fully and well until nature takes her.

She walks across the car park, past the wattlebird, which is still drinking. She crosses the road to the supermarket where Pam is picking up a few things for lunch out in the valley. On the footpath near the sliding doors she hovers. She'll wait outside. Pam shouldn't be long.

Just outside the supermarket there is a bin. Daphne looks at the envelope, looks at the bin. Then she walks over and drops the envelope in.

———

They drive out to the valley in Pam's car, winding through the suburbs. There is no convincing short cut, and they must pass through many traffic lights: stop, start, stop, start. Pam complains about waiting due to the lack of synchronisation, but Daphne is sure synchronisation is an urban myth. Life is dictated by road sensors and luck. While Pam fusses and frets, Daphne is patient, accepting. This is something she has learned with age.

Beyond the housing estates at the southern edge of the city they drive past grey paddocks dotted with bored cattle and dirty brown sheep. This is the colour of the drought. Daphne is sure it was wetter when she lived out here. They had dry times of course, but she can't recall anything like this. She doesn't know whether she believes in global warming or not, but perhaps she is looking at it now.

The drive lulls her, the way the road curls through hills and over dips, threading away from the city. It's spacious out here, rugged and harsh and spare, country that breeds tough people: people hard on the exterior, but with soft buttery hearts and a strong attachment to the land. None of them ever wanted to leave, but what say had they, in the end, when the government bought back the land? A signature on a piece of paper and your rights are removed. And what do you do when everyone is gone? You can't stay on like a lone grasshopper in the snow. You have to transfer your lives elsewhere. But it's not the same to live among concrete and street trees and air-conditioning. Yes, you soften with luxury, but it's not what you want.

She always feels good when they drive through the gates and into the national park, car tyres juddering over the cattle grid. Once a month, Pam brings her on this pilgrimage. It's a nice thing Pam does for her. Better than a café or an art gallery.

Pam drives as far as she can, wending slowly through the park. On one side of the road, the bush grows down to the verge, all glossy and fragrant, the sharp tang of eucalypts and mint bush. On the other side, the valley spreads. It is wide at the park entry, visible only in patches between the trees. As the valley progresses, it narrows, pulling its long arms in and tucking them beneath its waist. There were fewer trees when Daphne lived here. These days the bush is creeping back down-slope from the forest. It is taking over again, reclaiming the margins that were so hard fought for by her family.

Pam pulls up at the locked gate above the old homestead. It would be useful to have keys for the gate so they could drive down the long track to the building, but Pam is reluctant to ask at the parks office, and Daphne is still too miffed about losing her family property to beg for access to land that should rightfully be hers. They get out of the car and Pam retrieves the folding chair from the back seat. As they walk through the wooden chicane and slowly down the track, reclining kangaroos heft onto their feet and bounce away. Watching them, Daphne stumbles on the uneven ground, scattering piles of dried dung. Every time she comes here, it is the same. She can't believe the number of kangaroos. There are always joeys in pouches, always young ones at foot, following their mothers.

When finally they are down by the old slab homestead, quite some distance from the car, Pam sets up the folding chair in the lee out of the wind, then she pats Daphne on the shoulder and walks back up the track. She likes to give Daphne her space, and Daphne appreciates it—she's freer to let her thoughts wander when she's on her own. While she has her fill of valley-time, Pam will sit in the car up at the road and read, maybe even take a nap.

Daphne settles in her chair and looks around. She is always disappointed at first. What she sees initially is the decay: the crumbling yards, the collapsing sheds, the fallen chimney further up the hill where the brick house once stood. And the weeds! The overgrazing, thanks to all those kangaroos! Who says farmers don't take care of the land? When she lived here, the place looked better than this.

But soon she begins to look wider and deeper, and memory distorts her vision. She starts to see what she wants to see, rather than what is actually here. She sees the slab homestead as it used to be, with its kitchen block out the back, smoke threading from the chimney, the fire always lit. She sees the horses in the yards, the black cattle scattered across the valley like crumbs of burnt toast. She sees Doug riding his horse, the dogs following. She sees her father, further back in her memory, hustling a mob of cattle, her mother on the veranda hanging washing, the sheets flapping.

Her family were settlers here, but they weren't the first white men. The first were cattlemen. They rode with a black man who showed them the way through the mountains en route to markets. The settlers—her father's people—weren't far behind. They built wattle-and-daub huts, then stronger and more permanent homesteads, sheds and yards. They brought long lines of cattle that grazed their way up the valley. Then families came, women and children. They subdued the land, cleared and ringbarked trees, making way for better pasture. They planted fruit trees, pine trees, vegetable gardens.

Daphne's father grew up here. He married her mother, had a son and a daughter, other babies that didn't survive. He broke horses, ran cattle, chased brumbies. He lived and died on the property—the land made him, and he was the land. Then it was Daphne's turn. She and Doug had a family, worked hard . . . But of course, life isn't that simple. There are many stories, and every story contains birth, secrets, death or loss.

She thinks of Doug: a quiet, proud man, honest and hard-working, patient and kind. It killed him when the land was taken. The government bought it back, claiming they had reason to do so. They had authority and there was nothing Daphne and Doug could do. The government took Doug's life, though they'd never see it that way.

She wonders what Doug would think of the doctor's referral letter, and it takes only a moment to decide he would agree with her. She did the best thing. The bin is the right place for the envelope.

She stands up and walks down to the yards, leans against the old silver rails streaked with lichens. Across the valley the wind is playing in the grass, making waves in the tussocks, the only tucker the kangaroos won't eat. She feels the afternoon breeze freshening, a touch of cold on its breath.

Then she feels something else. A strange flash in her head, and a distant pinging sound. A whirring and swishing. A brief impression of the rails tilting.

8

Daphne has been having a misty dream. The landscape is a blanket of fog from which domes of granite loom and fade. She is in a different time. Black people drift among the hills and shimmy through the trees. Veils of smoke sit over the valley. There are fires out there: slow smoky cooking fires with glowing embers. Dark-skinned women squat by the coals, grinding yams. They use round white stones to crush the bulky roots, pressing them into tongue-shaped grooves worn into flat rock slabs by generations of women before them.

The sound of stone clunking against stone echoes from the crags. Someone is working on a weapon, chipping sharp edges into a sliver of rock. Maybe a spearhead to drop a kangaroo. Birds, kangaroos, black people, these are the only things that move, apart from the wind. The valley changes slowly, time wearing the rocks away. People come and go, their bones bleaching in crevices between boulders on the high tops.

Then Daphne sees a young woman looking down at her. The woman has blue eyes, fair skin, a chaos of unruly reddish-brown hair. Daphne feels a strange slow spinning. She remembers falling, doesn't know how long she's been out: minutes or seconds.

The young woman's face is puckered with concern. Daphne has seen her in the valley before, but from a distance. She's just a girl in Daphne's estimation, maybe in her early twenties. They have passed each other several times near the homestead, maintaining polite separation, acknowledging each other with miniscule nods. They have never spoken. Daphne comes here to remember and she knows other people have their reasons for being here too.

Now she accepts the hand that is offered in assistance, and sits up, wavering a moment before the girl reaches down to circle her waist with an arm and helps her to stand. The girl is saying something Daphne can't hear because there's a thumping in her head, like a water hammer juddering through pipes in the walls of an old house. She leans against the girl and they walk slowly to the homestead where Daphne sits down on the boards of the veranda and slumps against one of the uprights. She watches vacantly as the girl drags a backpack onto the veranda and empties the contents: a jumper, notepads and pencils, a raincoat, a lunch box, a range of other paraphernalia. Then the girl sets out a mug and pours something into it from a silver thermos.

'Here.' She places the mug into Daphne's hands and helps raise it to her lips. 'It's hot chocolate.'

Daphne feels something warm and rich trickle into her mouth. She almost gags before she swallows.

'Drink up,' the girl says. 'It's good for you.'

Daphne is vague and fluttery. She sips the warm liquid, clears her throat, tries to speak. Her voice comes out rough, like sandpaper. 'Thank you.'

The girl nods and sits beside her, takes her hand. 'You're cold.' She lays her jumper around Daphne's shoulders. 'Are you here on your own?'

Daphne shakes her head but can't elaborate; she needs more time to rest and re-gather. The girl seems happy to sit, and together they gaze across the valley. The light is clear and strong. A currawong flaps over.

'I should introduce myself,' the girl says. 'I'm Abby.'

She has a pretty face, Daphne thinks, as she tells the girl her name. But when you are craggy as the hills, all youth seems beautiful.

'Are you feeling better?' Abby asks.

'A little,' Daphne manages. It's hard to talk.

'I'm glad you're okay,' Abby smiles. 'What would I have done if you weren't? My first aid is out of date. I'm no good at CPR.'

Daphne taps her chest. 'I'm fine,' she says. 'My heart's still beating.' Her head is beating too, she notes. It's not supposed to—that's why the doctor wrote out the referral that is now festering in the bin at the shops beneath layers of soggy hot chips and dripping drink cans.

The girl smiles. 'What do they say? While you're breathing you're having a good day.' She points over the rise. 'I was coming down the valley when I saw you fall. Nobody came to help, so I ran to see if you were okay. I didn't know I could move so fast. Did you say someone is here with you?'

'My daughter is in the car up at the road,' Daphne says.

The girl stands up. 'I'll go and fetch her.'

Daphne raises a hand to stop her. 'Not yet, dear. She'll come eventually.' She shifts her gaze across the dry vista of the valley, and Abby sits down beside her again.

'You come here often, don't you?' Abby says. 'It's a special place. I love it.'

'I grew up here,' Daphne says. 'My family were settlers.'

Abby gazes up among the eaves. 'Really? You lived in this old hut? It seems they've preserved it fairly well.'

'There used to be a kitchen out the back,' Daphne says, strengthening a little. 'That's gone now, just the old stone chimney left. And there were other buildings. Some were taken down. Others have crumbled away.'

'This hut's my best friend in bad weather,' Abby says. 'Not that we've had much rain this year. I'm tired of the drought.'

'The land looks poorly, doesn't it?' Daphne agrees. 'It's sad to see it so run-down. All these kangaroos.' She thinks of the past, and its place in the present, and how much things have changed. Then she thinks again of the doctor's appointment and the referral letter and the rubbish bin at the shops. Suddenly she feels tired. 'I'm sorry,' she says, 'I don't feel well.'

Abby jumps up immediately. 'I'll go and get your daughter. I have a key to the gate so she can drive down.'

Daphne sits back weakly while Abby disappears round the side of the homestead. Soon Pam's car noses around the corner and parks on the grass. Pam leaps out and gushes over her anxiously. 'What happened? How did you fall? Are you all right?'

At the sight of her daughter, Daphne feels suddenly feeble and teary. 'I'm tired. I need to go home for a rest.'

Pam helps her to stand up, then Abby returns, smiling. She has a long loose stride like a brolga about to take flight.

She and Pam assist Daphne to the car. They hoist her into the passenger seat where she sags, drained. 'Don't forget the chair,' she says.

Pam goes to get it.

Through the window, Daphne reaches for Abby's hand and grasps it. 'Thank you for helping me, dear. If I was in better nick I'd stay longer.'

The girl rubs Daphne's hand with small pale fingers. 'I'm glad you're all right.'

Daphne lets go of Abby's hand reluctantly. 'I'd like to see you again,' she says. 'We could make morning tea for you. To thank you.'

Abby's blue eyes hover on Daphne's face for a moment as if she's considering something. Then she pulls a mobile phone from her pocket. 'Tell me the number and I'll call when I have time,' she promises. She punches in the numbers as Daphne announces them.

Then Pam is back. She tosses the folding chair in the back seat of the car and they drive slowly up the track to the gate. They wait for Abby, who swings the gate wide then closes it behind them and pushes the padlock shut. She leans against a post and waves.

As they pull away Daphne twists in her seat to look back, and what she sees is an outline of Abby's pale face framed by a crop of wild hair.

9

The big brick Queanbeyan house where Daphne lives with Pam and Pam's husband Ray is double storey and a tad ostentatious for Daphne's taste, but Ray has worked hard for his money—there's good business to be had from selling curtains—so Daphne supposes he's allowed a status symbol or two. Ray ought to be retired by now, but he's addicted to his job. He doesn't do as much as he used to, so Pam doesn't mind. She says work keeps him out of trouble. These days he mostly manages things from home—or interferes, according to Pam. He has enough staff to run the business, but he can't quite let it go.

Daphne was independent till a few years ago. She had a small house in old Queanbeyan that she and Doug bought when they moved down from the mountains. She liked having her own space, living among the possessions she'd accumulated over a lifetime. But her arthritis worsened, and now it's so bad she needs help to dress, and she can't lift pots and pans anymore so she can't cook. She wasn't eating well, started to lose weight, and it was clear she wasn't managing on her own.

When it had come time to downsize, she had considered moving into a retirement village with a hospice attached to it, but she was afraid she'd rot or die of loneliness. Who do you talk to in places like that? Someone told her it was good socially, that you make friends with similar interests. Daphne couldn't face talking aches and pains all day. She couldn't imagine herself in a museum with other old artefacts. It was denial, she supposes. Plus, she was worried nobody would come to visit her. Young people have such busy lives—where would they find time to come to a retirement village or hospice? Those places are for people without family, or for those with illness and dementia. She's fortunate she doesn't fit either of those categories. She still has all her faculties—although Pam says sometimes she's not so sure.

Moving in with Pam and Ray seemed like a good solution. Daphne was hesitant about imposing on them, but she has her own bathroom, and her bedroom is away from the main activity area of the house, so she can retreat if she senses a need for it. She even persuaded them to construct a vegie patch for her. It was her only request. Pam joked about keeping her working and saving money on vegetables, but a vegie garden has always been important to Daphne, and she was relieved when Pam and Ray agreed to humour her.

One weekend, not long after Daphne had moved in, Ray donned a worn shirt and his thirty-year-old, paint-spattered work boots, and built raised garden beds at the back of the yard. That was five years ago, and to his credit, he still periodically collects bags of manure from a friend's farm and digs it into the soil. Daphne appreciates his thoughtfulness.

She's always had a vegie garden, can't remember a time when she didn't. On the farm, it was a source of fresh produce, especially in days long past when they didn't drive to town very often, and salt beef and flour and tinned vegetables kept them going through the lean periods. There were no fridges back then so there was no way to keep fresh meat cool. In winter, they used to hang a side of beef from a shady tree and carve slabs of meat from it each day, keeping it trussed up to stop the wild dogs from attacking it, and the currawongs and ravens—always out for a taste of meat. But the warmer months were the season of salt meat and rabbit, and vegies . . . whatever was left after the kangaroos, possums and rabbits had been through.

Daphne had a vegie garden at her old Queanbeyan home too. It was the first thing she and Doug did when they moved into town. Those were hard times, and looking back, she can see that the garden kept her busy during the difficult transition to city existence. Even as her soul withered and curled up and dried out, somehow it helped to watch green things growing. There was a kind of therapy in standing there with a hose, spraying water onto the dark soil.

In her garden at Pam's, she plants things that grow without effort. She should put in only a plant or two, but when the seedlings come in punnets it seems cruel not to give each one a chance, so she plants too much, harvests too much and hands out her produce to everyone she knows. In summer, Pam's window sills are crammed with lines of ripening tomatoes, and the fridge is full of zucchinis, silverbeet and basil. In autumn and winter, she prods cloves of garlic into the soil, and broad beans for nitrogen. Pam refuses to eat the broad beans, so Daphne puts them in plastic bags and takes them to the bowls club, leaves them on the table in the kitchen for whoever wants them. There are plenty of old-timers down there who, like her, appreciate fresh food, lovingly grown and generously given.

Working with the soil also brings Doug back to her. She remembers watching him dig over their vegie patch in the valley, his muscles flexing and popping like potatoes. He was a strong man, his body wiry, tough as an ox. On a warm day, he'd sometimes shed his shirt and she would watch from the kitchen, shirking her tasks to enjoy the view of him down there—all man, with his beard floating around like a cloud. When he came in later in the day, she liked the smell of sweat and soil on him, earthiness clinging to his skin. She would kiss him hungrily, knowing sex might follow in the dark, once the chores were done and the babies were in bed. But that was a long time ago.

Living with Pam is mostly a good thing. Daphne gets on well with her daughter and fits herself into the lives of others as best she can. Sometimes it's a bit much when the great-grandchildren invade. Daphne's granddaughter, Sandy (Pam's daughter), has three children. The eldest two, Jamie and Ellen, are at school, but Ben is only four, so he's still at home. Often he stays with Pam while his mother is at work. Sandy has a part-time job as a dental nurse, and, as if that's not enough, she also has commitments with the local wildlife group. There are many meetings and gatherings, so Pam looks after the children then too.

Through the wildlife group, Sandy cultivates her interest in caring for orphaned kangaroo joeys. Neither Daphne nor Pam can see the point of it when there are so many kangaroos around . . . you only have to go out to the valley to see them.

Kangaroos everywhere. But Pam says they have to humour Sandy. It's Sandy's passion, and Pam says they have to respect that even if they don't agree with it. Daphne sees it as a kind of madness. The world is changing, and people have lost their sense of balance and order. They prioritise strange things: animals equal to people. It's craziness. Modern generations haven't experienced hardship—they need a good Depression or a war to normalise them. Not that she'd wish such suffering on anyone . . . while it imparts an understanding of reality, it also damages people: her father, for instance. But sometimes it seems to Daphne that everyone around her has lost their mind and she is the only rational one.

Today she is sitting at home with Pam, glad of a quiet day. Since her episode at the valley a few days ago, she's been quite exhausted, and even though she hasn't done much, she's eternally weary. Pam has been fussing and worrying over her, but Daphne insists she's all right. It's just as well Pam doesn't know about the discarded referral.

The phone rings and Pam goes to answer it. Daphne has been hoping Abby might call, but she hasn't yet, and perhaps she won't. What use would a young woman have for spending time with an old lady? As usual, it is Sandy on the phone. She has a sick joey and needs someone to look after her youngest child Ben while she takes care of it. She wants Pam to go out to the farm because she doesn't want to stress the joey by putting it in the car. Daphne feels too tired to travel, but Ray has gone into the shop today and Pam doesn't like to leave Daphne alone, so she will have to go too.

They have lunch and get organised then Pam helps Daphne into the car.

The property is a twenty-minute trip along a twisty road that passes through open woodland and dusty farms. Daphne would like to drive out here herself sometimes, but she doesn't have a car anymore, thanks to an old woman who backed into her in the main street two years ago. Daphne hadn't been ready to give up driving, but after her car was written off it was hard to justify buying a new one. She discussed it with Pam and Ray, and they encouraged her to accept what life had served up. It was time for her to retire from driving anyway, they said. And Pam could take her wherever she needed to go. Still, it was a relinquishment of independence. Daphne would have liked to make the decision herself. To have it made for her by some other silly old woman's mistake was unfair.

When they arrive at Sandy's property, the house is in disarray, which is not out of the ordinary as Sandy is often too busy to attend to details like tidiness. Today, however, it's worse than usual, because Sandy has been distracted by the sick joey. Daphne notices that the breakfast dishes haven't been done, the cereal boxes are still on the kitchen table, and half-finished cups of cold coffee lurk on the bench.

Sandy is sitting on the couch with the sick joey in her lap, and her face is puffy and blotched from crying. Pam goes immediately to hug her, and fresh tears loosen down Sandy's cheeks. She has two joeys at the moment—Daphne knows all about it because Sandy and the children are at Pam's so often it's impossible not to know. The younger joey, Milly, is still pouch-dependent. This one in her lap, Zeek, is being prepared for release. He's been living down at the holding pens for a few months now, learning to be a kangaroo before being let out into the wild. Yesterday he was fine, Sandy says. But this morning she found him in a mess of faeces.

Now she has him tucked up inside a large home-made pouch—a bag made from one of her husband Clive's old windcheaters. Only the joey's head is visible, and Daphne can see he is limp and lethargic. It doesn't look good. The kindest thing would be to put the poor thing down, but Sandy is not one to give up without trying. She subscribes to the belief that where there's life there's hope, something Daphne has never understood. Daphne hates to see an animal suffering.

The youngest child, Ben, is sitting in front of a DVD. It's a Harry Potter movie, and Daphne sees Pam bristle when she notices. Pam believes four-year-old Ben is too young for these films, but Sandy shrugs and says how hard it is with two older children. Young ones get broken in early. It frustrates Pam that Sandy uses the video as a babysitter. Parents these days are all about keeping children quiet and out of the way rather than interacting with them. It's easier, Daphne supposes, and at least, living on a farm, the children are often outside, so they know how to entertain themselves too.

At Sandy's suggestion Pam delivers a banana and fruit juice to Ben, then a lengthy discussion of the joey's symptoms ensues. 'It's a bad case of diarrhoea,' Sandy concludes. 'I've treated him for absolutely everything.'

Pam's lips seal into a straight line. She understands the joey is dying, but she's not sure how to handle her daughter on this one—Daphne can see it. Pam puts the kettle on for a restorative cup of tea. Perhaps after that Sandy will come to her senses.

Sandy lays the pouch aside and fetches a large syringe of sterile fluid which she injects under Zeek's skin. She says she got it from the vet the other day for emergencies like this. 'He's dehydrated,' she says, as she caps the needle. 'I can't get him to drink.'

The joey doesn't move—a bad sign. Daphne hopes Sandy will take heed, but Sandy follows up with a bottle of warmed joey-milk, trying to encourage Zeek to drink. He feeds listlessly and Sandy weeps when the teat slips from his mouth.

'What should I do?' she says, looking to Daphne and Pam for answers.

'Maybe you need to let him rest,' Pam, offers gently. 'Perhaps there's nothing more you can do.'

Sandy sits down heavily. She knows Pam is right. They all know it. They can't help little Zeek. He's heading slowly out of here; the life is seeping out of him. Later Sandy will start on the *if-onlys*—it could go on for hours. Pam pours tea while Sandy sits miserably on the couch, Zeek in her lap. The pouch is almost flat—there's nothing of him. Daphne sees the bag lifting slightly with each breath. Sandy gives in to tears again.

'A year of snuggling with this little fellow,' she says. 'A year of watching him grow. His first hops. Watching him emerge from the pouch and dive back in. His little head peeking out. His little whiskers. I've done everything for him. I've fed him, toileted him, moisturised his skin, cleaned his pouches. And now this! He doesn't deserve it. *I* don't deserve it.'

Pam strokes Sandy's hair then takes the pouch and hangs it from a doorknob in the laundry beside the other joey. 'You go and have a shower,' she says when she comes back. 'You'll feel better.'

Daphne watches her granddaughter trail sadly from the room. She can't fathom why Sandy rears joeys; it's a form of self-torture—too much death and grief. Sandy does have her successes, but joeys seem to be fickle creatures. When a new one comes into care it's touch-and-go for a while. This one is particularly tragic for poor Sandy. Losing him after so much time and effort seems unfair, but that's the way it goes with wild things.

'I wish she'd give these joeys up,' Pam says, echoing Daphne's thoughts.

'She already has three children to care for,' Daphne points out.

'Yes, but I suppose the joeys are her hobby,' Pam says, 'the one thing she does for herself that doesn't involve the kids. She does it because she likes it.'

When Daphne was growing up on the property she tried raising a few joeys that her father brought home after shooting kangaroos for dog-meat. Most of them died, despite plenty of good rich cow's milk to drink. Sandy has told her this is exactly why they died—because they shouldn't have been drinking cow's milk. She says they can't handle the lactose, but Daphne doesn't believe it; everything grows well on cow's milk.

One of Daphne's joeys survived to adulthood. Big Joe, a large muscular male. He would hang around the homestead hoping for treats. Eventually he took off looking for females, but he came back every now and then for some bread or a handful of oats. He died when a pack of dogs brought him down. Dogs were a problem in the mountains back then. Daphne's father, and then Doug after him, shot every dog they saw, both dingoes and wild dogs, which were mostly farm dogs that had taken to the bush. Dogs and eagles played havoc with the lambs. That's why Doug got rid of the sheep.

Plus it was too cold for them up in the High Country; they never did well.

Daphne accepts a cup of tea from Pam and sits in an armchair by the window, looking out at the property. It's a sad place, she thinks, not a patch on the valley in the mountains. Here the paddocks are steep and dry, the garden is scraggly, there's no stock to help control the weeds, and rocks keep floating to the surface. Daphne has never been quite sure why Sandy and Clive decided to buy a farm; for urban people it seemed a strange thing to do. Sandy had such big dreams for the place. She and Clive wanted to do some replanting and restore it as habitat for wildlife—but it's a mess in this drought. Part-time farming simply doesn't work. Sandy is too busy with children and joeys, and Clive doesn't have time to be a farmer. He knows nothing about it and he's not handy like Doug, who knew how to fix things like chainsaws and mowers and tractors. These are skills you must have if you own a farm because tools and machines are always breaking down.

Daphne supposes Sandy grew up hearing about life on the land. Daphne and Pam often reminisce, even now, about their time on the family property, and Sandy has visited the mountain country many times. It would have been her inheritance if the park wasn't gazetted. She has heard all the stories, and she knows how Daphne loved the place, still does. Perhaps Sandy needed to build her own grass castle. Daphne can't blame her for that—it's in her blood.

She leans back in the armchair and listens to the drone of the TV in the background. Soon she is sleepy in the sun.

10

By the time Sandy brings the older two children home from school, the joey is dead. Daphne stays out of the way in the armchair while Sandy carefully shares the news with the children over afternoon tea. The kitchen fills with wailing and tears: Jamie and Ellen are bereft. Ben doesn't really understand, but he joins in for effect; if there's drama going down he obviously wants to be part of it.

After milk and anzac biscuits, Sandy wraps Zeek's limp little body in an old pillowcase while Ellen drips tears onto the soft fuzz of his coat. 'Mummy, he smells funny,' she says. Daphne knows that strange pungent smell of death, slightly sour.

Jamie insists on carrying the joey down the paddock to the pit. He's trying to be a little man, attempting to take responsibility to help his mother. Daphne decides to accompany them—she's sat too long in the armchair and needs some fresh air. As she leans against the doorjamb to slide her feet into a pair of Sandy's old gumboots, she sees Jamie standing silently outside on the lawn, the angular bag containing the joey hugged tightly to his chest. Ellen waits beside him, clutching her favourite doll. Then Sandy comes out with Ben grafted to her hip. He refuses to let go, probably sensing his mother's sadness and frightened by it. Pam comes too. She fetches a long stick from the woodheap and hands it to Daphne for support.

They make a bizarre and tragic procession, Daphne thinks as she plods along behind them: Jamie fighting to be brave, Ellen sobbing, and Ben mute and grave, his face pressed to Sandy's shoulder. Looking out across the paddock, Daphne sees several kangaroos grazing in the long shadows of late afternoon. Why save orphaned joeys in a drought? she wonders. Perhaps their mothers have tossed them from the pouch to survive the big dry themselves. Either that or they've been hit along the roadside. She's sure there weren't so many kangaroos when she was young. They shot the few that hung around the homestead and broke into the vegie patch. Kangaroo was poor man's mutton—tucker for the dogs. The only good kangaroo was a dead one.

As they trudge towards the pit, Sandy quietly tells Pam about the last animal that was buried there: a road-kill swamp wallaby hit along the lane. Apparently her husband Clive had trouble digging the hard dry soil, and Sandy is worried she might not be able to cover Zeek's body properly.

Daphne hears Jamie emit a small strangled sob. He stumbles on a rock and accidentally drops the joey, which flops to the ground with a thud, head lolling out of the pillowslip. Jamie crouches beside the joey's body and folds into tears. 'I didn't mean to drop him,' he wails. 'The bag was heavy, and you were talking about burying him, and then my arms gave up.'

That's when everything goes pear-shaped. Sandy tries to set Ben down so she can reassure Jamie, but Ben clings to her, crying hysterically, and won't let go. Ellen is crying too. She stands there with her doll hanging from her hand and her face streaked with tears. Pam attempts to intervene, without success.

Daphne leans against her stick and watches, shaking her head. The noise is enough to wake the dead. Then Sandy succumbs to grief and starts sobbing too—it's all too much. While the three children pile on top of Sandy, howling, Pam quietly picks Zeek up and slips him back in his pillowcase. 'I'll put him in the pit,' she says. 'We won't try to bury him. Clive can do that later. And how about we all go back up to the house and have some ice-cream?' She smiles and winks at Daphne, and they both know this will be an effective, if temporary, cure. Ice-cream is a good salve for misery.

Back in the kitchen, the children hoe into the ice-cream while Pam cooks dinner so Sandy can have some time off. Ensconced in her armchair, Daphne watches Pam peeling and chopping vegies and putting them into pots: potatoes for a hearty mash, corn, carrots and zucchini. There's not much she can do to help—if she went into the kitchen, she'd be in the way.

Ellen appears from the laundry and comes to sit with her. She's carrying the pouch with the other joey in it—the smaller, younger one that has been left hanging from a doorknob most of the day. She places the pouch on Daphne's lap, and Daphne can feel the joey squirming inside the bag. She doesn't want it, tells Ellen to take it away.

'But I want you to feed Milly,' Ellen says, her face serious. 'Mum's too upset.'

What can Daphne do when her great-granddaughter asks with such gravity? She looks down at the bundle in her lap. The joey is still now. She places a tentative hand on top to make sure the bag doesn't roll off.

Ellen fetches a bottle from the fridge and warms it in the microwave—such an advanced task for a seven year old. She brings the bottle back, dribbles a few drops on her wrist to check the temperature, just like a mother. 'I think it's okay,' the girl says. 'What do you think, Great Gran?'

Daphne offers her wrinkled wrist and Ellen shakes a spattering of milk onto her blotched skin. 'Yes, I think that will do,' she says.

Now the joey starts to wriggle and a small furry head pops from the pouch, nose bobbing, ears swivelling. 'Here,' Ellen shoves the bottle into Daphne's hand.

Daphne doesn't want to feed the joey, hasn't the slightest maternal urge for the creature. 'Can't you do it?' she asks. Ellen shakes her head. 'Mum lets me warm the bottles, but she doesn't let me do the feeding.'

Daphne twists the bottle in her hand and regards Ellen. Then she considers the joey—the shifting, poking legs in the bag. It must be hungry, but Daphne is awkward and unsure.

'Mum says it's easy,' Ellen reassures, watching hopefully, 'like feeding a baby.'

Daphne looks at the joey—its little furry wizened face, the tiny whiskered snuffly snout. How can this be just like a baby? She tries to poke the teat into the joey's mouth, but the teat is long and it kinks against the joey's lips. She tries again and this time the joey grabs it eagerly and starts to suck.

'There, I told you it was easy.' Ellen smiles triumphantly.

Daphne watches the joey feeding: the gentle nodding head, the soft snicking sound of suckling and swallowing, the look of dreamy bliss in the little animal's dark eyes. Ellen looks on like a doting mother. She has a small smile on her tired little face, a glow in her brown eyes not dissimilar to the joey's.

Daphne realises with a moment of great warmth and appreciation that she has just received help and advice from a seven-year-old child.

She sits there feeding the joey with Ellen sitting by her side, while the household carries on around them.

11

Abby's car is the most unpredictable thing in her life—an old silvery-blue Laser hatchback with worn seats, and cracks in the dashboard like the bottom of a dried-out farm dam. It has character, she supposes—not like new cars which have pompous faces and all look the same. Her father bought it for her when she left home to study in Melbourne. Owning a car meant she didn't have to remain captive in the suburbs on the weekend. She could come home and escape the city, catch up with Matt, dose up on soul-time in the hills, maybe go for a ski or a hike.

She loves her old car but these days it has become a liability. It has done too many miles, traipsing between Mansfield and Melbourne, and more recently between Mansfield and Canberra. But it hasn't been running well and the sad fact is Abby has no money for a service. It's just as well she uses a university vehicle for field work, the Laser just wouldn't manage.

Today she is driving to Queanbeyan to see Daphne, the old lady she helped in the valley a couple of weeks ago. She's been thinking of Daphne often and wondering what the land was like when Daphne lived there. She'd like to know how many kangaroos were around back then and how the numbers have changed—how farming, and then the lack of it, has altered things. It might be useful information for her PhD.

Her student life has been hectic lately; round-the-clock radio-tracking means she's been out in the valley most of the time. Sometimes she camps there and snatches a few hours of sleep before she has to get up and complete her dawn recordings. She's been phoning her brother Matt most days too, even though he's gruff and short with her. *Yeah, I'm fine. Yep, still looking for work. See ya.* He might not be up for a chat, but at least he knows she's looking out for him.

The Laser stalls a few times at roundabouts on the way to Queanbeyan—and Canberra has plenty of roundabouts—but Abby isn't too concerned. This has been happening for a while, and the car restarts every time, so she hasn't been worried. Perhaps she should ring her father and ask for some money to have the car serviced—hopefully she'll remember tonight.

In the backstreets of Queanbeyan she finds the house where Daphne lives: a large imposing red-brick place with a double garage, curtained windows and a wooden front door with frosted windows etched with palm trees. The street is quiet, no cars driving by, no people out gardening, no-one on the footpath, not even any barking dogs to break the silence. Abby tramps onto the front porch and rings the bell.

Daphne's daughter Pam meets her at the door, a tall thin woman, with silver and black hair pulled back tightly in a bun. Her face is pale and severe, but the smile that lights her eyes is grateful and welcoming. She holds the door open and invites Abby in. 'Thank you so much for coming. We really appreciate it. Mum's excited about seeing you.'

Abby can't help looking around as she steps inside. The entrance hall is spacious and airy with cream-coloured floor tiles that must be a nightmare to keep clean. There's an antique hall stand hung with sunhats and a red umbrella. No piles of shoes and boots. No dirty footprints. No mess. It even smells clean—order instead of decay.

She follows Pam through into a tidy renovated kitchen which is large and light and white, as neat as a display home and a little soulless, Abby thinks. Adjoining the kitchen is a carpeted living area with beige leather armchairs, a glass-topped coffee table and a massive TV. Daphne is sitting by the window doing a crossword puzzle, and a small thin boy is crouched on the floor working on some sort of Lego construction. The boy looks up, and Abby wonders if perhaps Daphne is going deaf as she doesn't seem to have heard them come in.

'Hello,' the boy says. 'Who are you?'

'I'm Abby.'

'What are you here for?'

'She's here to visit Great Gran,' Pam tells him.

The boy's face shows surprise. Obviously Daphne doesn't receive many visitors. He bends back to his Lego, which is plainly more interesting than Abby.

'That's my grandson, Ben,' Pam explains. Then more loudly, 'Mum, Abby is here.'

Daphne peers up from her puzzle and a smile spreads across her face. 'Abby, dear. How lovely to see you.'

The light in Daphne's eyes infuses Abby with a cosy flush—it's nice to be so warmly welcomed. She sits and takes the old lady's withered hand, presses it between her fingers, notices the paper-like fragility of Daphne's skin and cold bony joints. Seeing Daphne reminds her of her own Gran—that same sense of steadiness and lack of rush. It makes Abby feel secure, happy, comfortable. 'It's good to see you too,' she says. 'Hopefully you're feeling better than the last time I saw you.'

'Much better.'

Daphne has pale-blue watery eyes—Abby hadn't noticed this out at the valley—and soft pink lips that quiver as she looks at Abby. Her gaze is thoughtful and inquisitive, not at all judgemental. 'I'm not sure I thanked you properly for your help when I fell,' Daphne says, closing her other hand over Abby's. 'I was a bit dazed at the time.'

'You did thank me. And it was no trouble. I'm glad you're okay. No more tumbles?'

'No. I've been fine.'

Abby thinks perhaps she sees a hint of concealment in the old lady's eyes—maybe there has been another unreported fall and Daphne doesn't want to mention it. 'Have you been out to the valley since?' she asks. 'I've been looking for you.'

Daphne shakes her head, thin white hair shifting slightly. 'We only go once a month, although I'd like to be there more often. But it's a hassle for Pam. She spends so much time looking after the little ones.'

'I work out there,' Abby says. 'So maybe I could take you sometime. I wouldn't mind.' And it's true, she wouldn't.

'Really?' Daphne glances at her daughter for approval. 'That would be good, wouldn't it Pam? I could sit in the car. I wouldn't even have to get out.'

Pam is at the kitchen bench setting slices of cake on a plate. 'That'd be a first,' she says smiling. 'Mum loves to be out in the wind, even though it's no good for her.'

'I think we can work something out,' Abby says. 'I'll just have to find a suitable day. One that suits both of us.'

Pam brings over a tray with a teapot, cups and saucers, a jug of milk and a tub of sugar, all in matching crockery: white with delicate pink roses and gold trimming. Everything is so perfect Abby feels as if she might accidentally step out of line and somehow mess things up. The cup rattles in its saucer as she takes it from Pam with anxious hands. It'd be just her thing to spill the tea and stain the carpet. For a moment she is a small girl again, in trouble for dropping a pot of red paint at school.

'What do you do out in the valley?' Pam asks as she offers a piece of chocolate cake.

'I'm studying kangaroos,' Abby says. She takes a slice of cake and tries to balance it on a plate as well as juggle her cup and saucer. 'I'm looking at their numbers and movements and how they change with the seasons,' she adds.

Daphne chuckles. 'Give them grass and they breed,' she says, clutching a spoon with her chunky arthritis-thickened fingers.

'Yes, they are good at that,' Abby agrees. 'But they're interesting creatures. I like studying them. If we can understand them better maybe we can find better ways to manage them.'

Daphne grunts and Abby wonders if perhaps the old lady has a different opinion, but is holding back. It's kind of her to restrain herself, but Abby is used to hearing what people think about kangaroos. Most people don't hesitate to express what's on their minds. Some want to shoot them, others want to save them. Abby suspects Daphne is probably in the *shooting* camp, given her rural background.

Pam smiles gently. 'My mother has a very old-fashioned attitude towards kangaroos.'

Daphne's lips compress for a moment before she speaks. 'In my day, kangaroos were pests, dear. Only good for dog food. My father managed them with a gun. These days I suppose we try to do things differently.'

Abby nods. 'Guns are still the most practical way, but it's good to be looking at other options.'

'In this house we have agreed to disagree on this topic,' Pam says. 'My daughter is a wildlife carer. She looks after orphaned joeys. Sometimes I take care of the joeys too.'

With a twinge, Abby remembers Cameron the journalist and his collision with the kangaroo out in the valley. It's been nearly a month and she still hasn't heard from him. As far as she knows, the article hasn't appeared in the paper yet. Perhaps he's decided not to go ahead with it, which would be a shame. If nothing comes of it, then that poor kangaroo will have died in vain. The whole thing will have been a waste of time. 'I was with someone who hit a kangaroo recently,' she says. 'He was a city guy. Didn't have much idea how to drive on country roads at night.'

'They never do.' Daphne nods sagely.

'It's pretty bad in the park,' Abby says. 'So many kangaroos. I rescued a joey from the pouch and handed it on—maybe to someone from your wildlife group.'

'Possibly,' Pam says. 'My daughter only has one joey at the moment. She lost one recently. They're not easy to care for.' She glances at Daphne. 'Mum's not so sure about hand-raising joeys. She worries that there are too many kangaroos.'

Abby definitely agrees with the 'too many' assessment. She's seen how little grass there is in this drought. 'Were there many kangaroos in the valley when you lived there?' she asks Daphne.

'There were hardly any,' Daphne says. 'We used to shoot a few, but there are so many more these days. They're everywhere.'

'Maybe your people unwittingly created better pastures for them,' Abby suggests, considering.

'Maybe,' Daphne agrees. 'We certainly opened that country up. Cleared plenty of trees. That's what makes those valleys so good for grazing.'

'The kangaroos sure like it there now,' Abby says.

'Yes, but it's a pity about the weeds. We never had so many weeds when I lived there. Now the place is covered with them. A good herd of cattle would clean it up.' Daphne's lips press firm. 'I'm glad my husband isn't around to see it.'

'The drought doesn't help,' Abby points out.

'It's all those kangaroos,' Daphne insists. 'We've had drought before, but I've never seen it so overgrazed. My family goes back a long way in that district—back to the mid-1800s—and we always looked after the land. It was in our care for generations.'

'Living there must have been tough,' Abby says, 'especially in winter.'

'Yes, it was damnably cold.' Daphne leans forward to tell her story. 'Some years the freeze was so deep the stock couldn't find food, and kangaroos sat under the trees and froze to death. We had chilblains on our fingers and toes. Icy wind driving through the cracks in the homestead. The water freezing over. I was born in the old homestead, you know. It didn't go quite to plan, mind you, because I came early

107

and my mother wasn't ready. She intended to go into town for the birth, but she didn't make it. The river was in flood and couldn't be crossed, so she had to give birth at home. No doctor. No midwife. Just the help of one of the other women on the property. Plenty of babies died at birth back then, so it was lucky I came out all right, eh? Just as well I was strong.'

'Good bloodlines,' Abby says.

Daphne shakes her head. 'We weren't blue-bloods, that's for sure. We were mountain people. The rich ones lived down on the plains in the big ritzy homesteads. We were bush people. Horse people. But we did all right. We lived within our means, and when the Depression came we expanded our holdings. Those that had spent their money had troubles and had to sell off their land. It wasn't an easy life, but we loved it. I would have liked to stay till I died.' She falls quiet, her eyes fixed somewhere in the past.

'Not very practical though, Mum,' Pam says, 'even if it could have been done. And it's been a while now since you moved to the city.'

Daphne dabs at sudden tears. 'Yes, a lot of time has gone by since then. Many births and deaths. I'm not sure what it all means anymore.'

'What are you talking about, Mum?' Pam says quietly.

'I'm a burden.' Daphne's voice wobbles. 'I should be gone like Doug. Dead and buried.'

Pam smiles kindly. She stands up and puts an arm around Daphne's shoulders. 'Mum, we love having you here. The kids love having a great-grandmother. How lucky are they?'

Daphne sniffles and blows her nose on a handkerchief that she tugs from the sleeve of her blouse. She waves Pam away, saying, 'Don't fuss.'

Embarrassed, Abby squats on the floor with the boy and asks to see his Lego, giving Daphne and Pam time to sort themselves. Ben is focused on his task—he's been amazingly quiet for a small boy. 'What are you making?' she asks.

'A spaceship,' he says without looking up. 'It's from *Star Wars*. See, here are the guns.' He points out several features and Abby makes appropriate grunts of approval. Then he swings the construction and aims for her head, making shooting noises. 'Peeow, peeow.'

Pam moves quickly and grasps his elbow, pulling him up. 'We don't shoot people,' she says, frowning. 'Come and have some morning tea, Ben.' She guides him to the kitchen bench and directs him onto a stool where he sits obligingly, banging his feet against the legs.

Abby smiles at the grandmotherly discipline. Her Gran was the boss of the house too, given that Abby's mother wasn't much of a correctional officer. She moves to join Daphne again while the boy scoffs a piece of Pam's fine cake and prattles about *didn't mean to* and *that's what guns are for* and *sorry Grandma*. But as Abby starts to sit, Daphne pushes up onto her feet and slowly unfolds the stoop in her back.

'Come with me,' the old lady says. 'I have something to show you.'

12

It was only the other day that Daphne had retrieved the boxes from the garage. It had been a quiet afternoon: Ray was working in his office and Pam had taken Ben out shopping, so Daphne had the place almost to herself. Usually she likes it when the house is peaceful, and sometimes she naps in her chair. But that day she'd been restless and didn't know what to do—she'd already been through the newspaper and done the crossword. It was then she'd thought of the boxes in the shed: boxes of memorabilia that had been sitting under a dustcover since she'd moved in with Pam and Ray.

This is what she wants to show Abby now: the contents of one of those boxes.

She leads Abby down the hallway and into her room, which is tidy and minimalist, the pink bedspread tucked without a wrinkle, all her clothes folded away in the drawers, her books stacked neatly on the bedside table beneath the white lamp, not an object out of place—because she knew she might bring Abby here today and she didn't want to make a poor impression.

She is strangely and girlishly nervous as she unhooks the lid of the first box, and as she peers inside, she feels an unexpected shiver of nostalgia and regret. It surprises her—she hadn't anticipated such a revival of youthful emotions today. Perhaps it is the presence of Abby that has done it—the girl has such an interested look on her face.

Daphne pulls out a folded length of coarse black hair, cut from the tail of the old mare when she died, and she hands it to Abby who takes it carefully. The wiry hair is crimped in a crazy zigzag, not free and floaty in the way it used to hang from the mare, but altered now into the imposed creases of many years' storage.

'Horses were my childhood out in the valley,' Daphne says, her voice scraping a little, like sandpaper over glass. 'We used them for everything: work, pleasure, mustering, hauling, brumby-running, racing, transport.' She ticks her list off, hoping she hasn't forgotten anything. 'The yards were my second home. Whenever I could escape my chores, I'd be down there, watching the men working the stock. I used to climb the fence and sit on the rails while the animals milled below like a pack of swarming beetles.'

Abby is running her hand along the length of tail hair, stretching the kinks and releasing them again.

'I was only four when I learned to ride,' Daphne goes on. 'That hair is from my horse's tail—Bessie, my old black mare.'

She remembers how her father had lifted her in his strong wiry arms browned by the sun, and swung her up into the saddle, how tall she felt, how large the world seemed, how important she was sitting on top of a horse. Bessie was ancient, slow and safe, happy to shuffle along at a walk, and Daphne had devoured the freedom. On a horse she was a different person, older and more responsible.

Learning to ride was her very first rite of passage, and soon she was allowed to roam the valley on Bessie's back. When her jobs were done, her mother would saddle up the horse and help Daphne to mount. Then Daphne would kick the old mare into action (her legs barely reached below the saddle-flaps), and Bessie would plod away from the homestead. It was the opening of a whole new world. Daphne would visit the men out working as they fixed fences, dug up rabbit warrens, grubbed out saplings and stumps. She wasn't much use, sitting there watching them, but they didn't seem to mind her company. And they told her stories, showed her things.

'My favourite worker on the farm was Johnny Button,' she says, 'the Aborigine who came to work with us sometimes.'

Abby lays the horse hair over her arm and looks at Daphne with bright attentive eyes. It seems the mention of Johnny has pricked her interest.

'My father used to call him in after the muster to find our missing cattle,' Daphne continues. 'He had a way with animals, and somehow he knew where to find them. He would go out alone and there they would be, hidden in pockets of bush, waiting to be gathered like butterflies in a net. But he never stayed very long. He would work with us for a while and then he would be gone, up into the High Country somewhere. I'm afraid my father didn't like him very much. He was happy to use Johnny's bush skills, but he wasn't comfortable when Johnny was around. I didn't understand about racism when I was young. I liked Johnny because he knew the bush differently from the others. He knew secrets about food and animals and he didn't mind sharing his knowledge with me.'

She remembers how she used to seek him out on her old black horse.

Hey girlie, he would say, smiling at her, his white teeth gleaming in his shiny face. *What you doing in these parts?* She would tell him she'd come to see him, to learn things. He would show her echidna-diggings around the dirt castles built by termites, and he would point out nesting-hollows in trees where black cockatoos laid their eggs. While she sat on Bessie's back, watching, he would shimmy up the tree and steal eggs that were shiny white like pearls. Once, he'd lit a small campfire and cooked the eggs, shelled one and given it to her. She'd closed her mouth around the firm white flesh, savouring it, while Johnny grinned up at her. *Special, eh?* he said. *Better than chicken eggs.*

One time she had found him digging up yams at the edge of the forest. *Lots of things to eat in the bush*, he'd said. *Yams are good. You throw him on the campfire and cook him up. Then eat him. Or you grind him up and make flour. Make patties. They're good, but not so good as moth patties. Those are the best. Come from big fat moths up in the mountains. Full of nice sweet fat.*

She remembers Johnny's smile as he told her things, his dark lips spreading over his teeth. She liked his friendly face, the way he spoke to her like she was important, as if she knew something. He had a bushy smell about him, a tangy aroma of smoke mixed with eucalypt and a tinge of sweat. It was his own particular scent: strong, but not offensive. His way of moving was unique too. Limbs long and loose, he had a fluid gait over uneven ground. His eyes were black marbles and his nose was wide, lips dark-brown and full. Daphne liked his manner of speaking. When he was explaining something he cocked his head to the side like a sheepdog and stood on one leg, the other foot crooked against his knee. She respected him, and he always had time for her.

Daphne gently takes the horse hair from Abby and places it back in the box. 'As I grew up, I longed for a horse with more energy than Bessie,' she says. 'But my father wouldn't let me move on. My mother said I had to be patient. There was a reason he was being cautious, you see. It was because of what happened to my brother. A terrible accident. My father didn't want anything like that happening again.

'My brother died before I was born. He was thrown from a brumby that had been brought down from the hills. My father thought it was tamed, but it hurled itself against the rails in the yards one day and crushed my brother into one of the posts. My father never forgave himself for it.'

She reaches into the box again and picks up a neatly folded child's jumper, her son Gordon's favourite when he was six. She had knitted it from coarse homespun wool that Doug had clipped from the sheep. Gordon had loved it, despite its scratchiness. It was warm and grey, the colour of the rocks on the ridge. And it was a rarity—Doug had got rid of the sheep soon after.

Daphne rubs the wool with her fingers, feeling its rough texture, and her eyes become misty. The never-ending well of tears for Gordon still hasn't run dry. She swallows and lays the jumper on the bed. Today she's too fragile to enter the shady corner of her mind where Gordon lives. It's not something she can share with Abby.

She peers in the box to see what's left and pulls out a stirrup iron, rusty and corroded, which she hands to Abby. 'This came from my husband's saddle,' she says. 'His name was Doug, and he was a fine horseman.' That's all she can say for now: Doug is another story she can't contemplate today. She lost him to the mountains too.

Abby takes the stirrup and inspects it, then she gives it back to Daphne.

Daphne sets it aside on the bed.

Now only two items remain in the bottom of the box: a coiled stockwhip and a stone. Daphne reaches in and touches the stone, runs a fingertip around its sharp edges. Without removing it from the box, she wraps her hand around its ovoid shape and measures its weight in her palm. She remembers a warm summer's day. Riding down the valley in the shimmering heat. Having lunch in the shade of a rock shelter. Finding the stone. Taking it home. Her father's irrational anger when she showed it to him. So many stories and secrets. So many things she can't possibly know. When her father died he took his secrets with him. She picks up the stone and slips it into her pocket without showing it to Abby.

Then she lifts out the old stockwhip. The handle has small cracks in it and the lash is stiff and dry, bent permanently now into twists and loops. She turns the whip over, admiring the handiwork, the neat close criss-crossing pattern. 'My father used to make his own whips,' she tells Abby. 'I used to watch him plaiting the thin strips of hide around the core. At night, he would sit by the fire, huddled beneath the yellow light of the hurricane lamp. His big rough hands were so deft with the fine strands of leather.'

115

He knew how to wield his stockwhips with skill, and he used them liberally—on cattle and men alike. Daphne pictures him now, down at the yards, breaking a young brumby. The horse is tied by a thick hemp rope to a large solid post in the middle of the yard. Daphne, young and skinny, nut-brown from the sun, sits on the top rail to watch as her father carefully passes a scarf across the horse's eyes with slow and gentle hands, and blindfolds it. By nature, her father is strident and impatient, fearsome and quick. But something softens in him when he's with a horse, and he changes, becomes patient, calm and alert. It seems to Daphne he understands horses better than people, that he speaks the language of their shivery skin and inherent flightiness.

On light feet he moves cautiously around the horse, his body relaxed and soft. The brumby strains on the end of the rope, muscles bunched, then it twists into a desperate fight, hooves flailing. Her father steps aside and waits quietly. When the horse is done struggling, its sides heaving and dark with sweat, head dropped low, the rope still taut, her father moves close again and restores contact with his palm on the horse's hot skin. He lifts a hessian sack and touches it to the horse's shoulder, slides it gently up and down. The horse tenses and raises its head, nostrils flared. It feels the rope on its head, holds itself tight and quivery, braced for flight. Slowly Daphne's father shifts closer, rubbing the sack along the horse's neck. The horse breathes loudly, lifts its nose, sniffs the air, tugs at the rope. Then it releases a juddering breath that vibrates through its nostrils and shudders along its flanks.

Daphne knows the unpredictable strength of a wild horse and she's afraid for her father. It's frightening to watch, but it is also beautiful. Her father is an artist of sorts: lithe, and in tune with the horse.

Other workers leave their tasks and gather to watch. Johnny Button is there too, the best horseman in the district. He hooks his long dark arms over the railing and flashes a white smile at Daphne, gives her a nod.

At first Daphne's father doesn't notice his audience. He is focused on the horse, feeling its mood, shifting carefully with its nervous movements. As the horse circles the post, sidling away from him, he follows its evasive shimmy. Then he sees the gathered crowd, and for a fraction of a second he loses concentration, but it is already enough. The young horse swings and Daphne's father is caught out. Leaping out of the way, he ejects a shout of alarm, and the horse lurches wildly. It leans back and yanks at the post, then hurls itself impossibly in the air and tumbles. One of its legs hitches over the rope and hooks around the post. The horse twists and struggles, thrashes like a demon. There is a loud crack like a fired bullet and the horse lies suddenly still, breathing raggedly. Its leg and body are skewed, its head still tied to the post.

Daphne's father stands in the swirling dust and stares down at the horse, his face blank. It's clear the leg is broken, and the horse's stillness reflects its agony. He looks up at the crowd, hell burning in his eyes, then he strides to the fence and vaults over it, landing lightly and continuing past them all and on up to the homestead. They hear the thud of his boots on the veranda, the door banging open, silence as he passes inside.

He comes out with the gun. His face is dark and terrible as he charges down the hill. He opens the gate and re-enters the yard, eyes grim, his mouth is set straight and hard. He loads a bullet and cocks the gun, lines it up with the horse's head, fires. The horse slumps. Breathing heavily he puts the gun down, and with his knife he cuts the rope to release the horse's head. Then he looks up at his audience, his face livid and his eyes snapping. Snatching his stockwhip from the fence, he storms through the gate towards them, cracking the air with the whip. Everyone splits except Johnny, who holds his ground and meets Daphne's father's glare. They all know the horse is dead because Daphne's father made a mistake. He is shamed, but he's the boss and he hates to lose face. He needs to blame someone, and Johnny will do. All the men know the boss doesn't like him.

Johnny stands poised and defiant, and for a moment Daphne thinks her father will hit him. But Johnny stares her father down, black nostrils flared like the horse, dark challenge in his eyes. Then, in his own time, Johnny turns and walks away. Sitting on the rails, Daphne is the only one who sees the stockwhip twitching in her father's hand. She knows her father wants to lay into Johnny with the whip. He's itching to do it.

Now, breathless and a little weary with the strain of recollection, Daphne turns to Abby, sees the gentle smile on the girl's face.

'Where were you?' Abby asks. 'You've been gone for a while, haven't you? I've been standing here waiting for you to come back.'

Daphne waves away the last shreds of disorientation. 'Sorry,' she says, embarrassed. 'It happens sometimes. I get lost in memory.' She tucks the stockwhip back in the box and Abby folds in the top and interweaves the flaps before setting the box on the floor. 'Would you like another cup of tea?' Daphne asks.

Abby smiles and Daphne thinks perhaps she detects a twinge of sadness in the girl's eyes. 'Unfortunately I need to get on the road,' Abby says. 'I have some work to do. But we'll catch up again soon. I'll let you know when I can take you out to the valley.'

Daphne pats her arm gratefully. 'That would be lovely, dear. I'd really like that.'

***

After Abby leaves, Daphne drifts back to her room and lifts the other box from the floor. It is light, comparatively weightless, easy for her to tote to the bed. She opens it. Inside sits a cloud of pink fabric, a dress in pale-rose hues, almost coral. Reverently, she inserts a hand among the concertinaed folds, slides her fingers over the satiny surface, notices water stains, the cloying aroma of mothballs.

The texture of the material arrests her. She is young again, lifting the dress out of its box for the first time. The fabric whispers softly as she shakes the dress out. If her shoulders were still good, she would gather the dress and shuffle it over her head, feel its silkiness against her skin. The dress is a remnant of her dreams: life, seemingly gone wrong, but actually coming right.

She didn't show the dress to Abby because she wasn't sure how she would explain the wisdom that the dress contains, inherent in its antiquated folds. The girl would have to have the vision of an older woman to understand.

Everything in its own time, she thinks.

Carefully she slides the dress back into the box and closes the lid. When she lifts her hand to explore a patch of dampness on her cheek, she realises she is crying.

13

Abby is sitting at a bar waiting to meet Cameron the journalist. It's been more than a month now since he came out to the valley and she'd almost given up on him. Then he called yesterday and suggested she read his kangaroo article before it goes to print, explaining it had been delayed by other deadlines.

Abby has been busy in the field radio-tracking her marked animals, day and night. It's tiring, but she doesn't mind. She likes night work: the clear dark skies sprayed with stars, the cold clean air. Sometimes when her tracking is done, she lies spread-eagled on the grass, wishing she knew the names of the constellations. She has a book somewhere which is supposed to enlighten her, but she can't work it out. Instead she focuses on the layers of stars, the near and the far, scattered dot-points of winking silver.

Some days she has pre-dawn starts, odd hours. It's hard to get up and her body is overtaken by a bone-deep weariness.

But it's part of her job, and somehow she drags herself out each day and gets going. People think field research is romantic, like a holiday. They don't realise how hard it is to have a regular life. She doesn't go out much and her social life is non-existent. Being here in this bar is an aberration. Luckily, her night work is almost finished for a while—so she can afford to cut herself a little bit of slack and socialise.

She has a beer while she's waiting. When Cameron rang she told him she'd be happy to look at his article and suggested he email it to her, but he said he'd rather meet for a drink after work. Now he's late. She left some important data analysis to be here—sitting around is a waste of her time.

She drinks another beer. The bar is dimly lit. It has heavy wooden tables and dark wooden benches—not very comfortable; Abby hopes she won't have to sit for too much longer. She doesn't usually drink by herself, but what else do you do when you're waiting in a bar? There aren't many people here, just a few old blokes checking her out between watching horse races on the TV. With their TAB stubs and half-empty beers in front of them, they look bored. Abby hopes Cameron shows up before one of them musters the courage to try to chat her up.

Eventually he arrives, entering the bar bold and fast, slightly flustered, his dark features flushed with the effort of hurrying. It's been so long since Abby saw him that she has forgotten his poise, the directness of his gaze. His eyes connect with hers and he smiles, flexing his blocky jaw as he approaches. He's wearing jeans and a white shirt, a black jacket, nicely fitted. Abby feels rather too casual in her garb of cargo pants and a top she made herself from fragments of clothes she bought from St Vinnies.

'Sorry I'm late.' Cameron reaches to shake her hand.

She gives him a reserved smile, shakes his hand briefly then circles her fingers around her beer. He places a couple of printed A4 pages on the table then goes to the bar for a beer. She picks up the sheets and reads them. The article is reasonably well written, but idealised, as if working with kangaroos is a picnic. Perhaps she gave the wrong impression with the roast chicken and bread rolls. She'll speak to him about that.

'What do you think?' Cameron is standing over her, sipping the froth from his beer. 'Satisfactory?'

'Yes, it's fine.' She points out a few corrections, some over-simplified details that don't make sense. It's a pretty good overview, she concedes. He pencils in her suggestions with neat heavy script. Everything about him is considered and orderly—the discipline and privilege of his private-school education shine through. He doesn't realise how he wears his class.

'What have you been up to?' he asks, slipping his pencil into a pocket inside his jacket.

'Fieldwork,' she says. 'What about you?'

He takes a gulp of beer. 'There's a lot of climate change stuff going down at the moment—hence the delay with the story about you. Unfortunately politics takes precedence. All the posturing about climate policy has been front page. Have you been keeping up with it?'

Abby hasn't looked at a paper in weeks. Saying she can't afford to buy the paper sounds pathetic but it's close to the truth. 'I haven't had time to read the papers,' she says. 'I've been busy doing night work.'

He laughs, his eyes bright with amusement. 'What? Partying at the uni bar?'

She feels unjustly accused. 'No. I've been radio-tracking my animals out at the valley.'

'You go out there on your own at night?' His brow crumples. Is he actually concerned?

'Yes. Why not?'

'Are you sure it's safe? Anyone could go out there.'

'But they don't. It's only me. And I don't mind. I'm used to it.'

'Doesn't the university insist people work in pairs?'

'They'd prefer it, but it's impractical. Who's going to come and hang around each night while I traipse up and down hills with a pair of earphones and an antenna? I don't need anyone with me. I drive, I get out of the car, I climb to a high point and take a reading, then I drive some more. It's more efficient on my own.'

'We journalists tend to travel in packs,' he says. 'I guess that's why I find it hard to relate. Wherever I go, others are there—although, these days I do most of my research from my office. It's amazing what you can do from your desk with the internet.'

'Field scientists still go out in the field,' Abby says. 'That's what we do. If you want a desk job you take up a different area of science. Like lab work or computer modelling. But I get edgy if I sit for too long.'

He grins. 'Like now?'

She gives him a smile. 'I think I'm managing okay.'

They talk over several beers. Cameron loosens with the drink, divulging information about his work. He tells stories about interviews he's had with politicians, confidential stuff that Abby suspects ought to remain behind closed doors. He shares knowledge about who is sleeping with who among the world of journalists and MPs—there are some surprise liaisons, well-concealed. If this was the USA, these details would be all over the paper. In Australia, he says, there's a sense of discretion about such things. Public and personal lives remain separate to some extent . . . unless someone decides to write a declare-all memoir and deliberately forgets to include the important bits. Then it's different. Under those circumstances journalists feel justified in making sure necessary details aren't missed.

Abby wonders if Cameron is trying to impress her. It's fascinating hearing about his life—the world of scoops, opinions and intrigue, so different from her existence of facts and figures. You could sum the two of them up as subjectivity versus objectivity. But he has a good grip on a wide range of issues, and it seems he's keen to chat, so she nods and drinks and tries to appear intelligent—unaware if she's succeeding.

Eventually the alcohol catches up with her; several beers and no food and suddenly the room is tilting. She goes to the bathroom, all staggery, and leans against the wall in the cubicle while the world does a slow spin. When she returns to the table, Cameron offers to drive her home. He seems relatively sober, so she's glad to accept, beyond embarrassment.

The cold air hits as they step outside. It's dark now; in the dim light of the bar, Abby hadn't noticed daylight escaping. Cameron guides her to his car, which is angle-parked a short way down the street. He opens the door for her and she slumps into the passenger seat, misjudging the low height of the sports car.

He is quiet as he follows her directions, driving fast around corners. She says little, afraid she might be sick. Then they are out the front of the big old house, and she is swinging open the heavy car door, trying, unsuccessfully, to leap out. He comes round, grabs her hand, and hauls her out. Then

KAREN VIGGERS

he walks with her down the pathway alongside the house to the bungalow round the back. She feels his arm around her waist and is glad of his support; her knees are saggy.

At the door, she fumbles the key from her daypack then pushes the door open and switches on a light. Her mess sprawls around them. She sees Cameron silently taking it in. He guides her to the couch, where she flops ungraciously. Then he goes to the kitchen, finds a glass on the bench among the clutter of dirty dishes, rinses it and brings it back full of water. She takes a sip.

'Are you all right?' he asks.

She nods yes.

He is standing looking down at her where she sits in a clumsy coil on the couch. She glances up at him, but his thoughts are unreadable. He bends and kisses her, his lips pressing briefly against hers.

Then he is gone.

14

He phones the next day while Abby is in her office entering data. It's boring work and she's pleased to be interrupted. She has had a slow morning, weighed down by an unaccustomed hangover.

'How are you?' he asks.

'I'm still standing,' she says. 'But I've been better.'

'Are you up to dinner? I'm going out with a few workmates tonight. I thought you might like to come.'

She feels a flutter of excitement. 'I'll come,' she says. 'But don't expect intellectual conversation. My brain's still hurting from last night.'

'The best cure for a hangover is another beer,' he says, and she can hear the smile in his voice.

'I'll stick to mineral water,' she quips. Prudish but appropriate.

He offers to pick her up, but she says she'd prefer to make her own way there. If she drives it will be extra motivation not to drink—she doesn't want to lose it among a group of journalists she doesn't know.

But when it's time to go, she can't find her car keys. She has already flustered too long over what to wear, annoyed at herself for being so vain, and now her keys have gone missing. They could be anywhere among the chaos of her bungalow. The bed is strewn with discarded clothes and hangers. The floor is covered too. And there is also the mess of books and magazines. She shuffles through it all without success.

In the end, she decides she will have to go by bicycle. The spare key to the bungalow is hidden under a brick in the garden, so she can let herself back in when she gets home. She'll have to find her car keys tomorrow.

She leaves without her helmet so she won't mess up her hair, wheels the bike out into the street. Then she is on and flying, spinning the pedals, the cold wind freezing on her cheeks.

At the Kingston shops, she dismounts from her bicycle and wheels it along the footpath, looking for the right address. She hopes they haven't chosen an expensive restaurant, but judging by the austere look of the place, the few tables and the subdued lighting, she figures it's beyond her usual budget. She locks her bike to a signpost in the street.

She's sweaty and breathless from the ride—so much for her ridiculous vanity. Her jeans are uncomfortably tight, her shirt and cardigan are skewed, and her hair is wildly wind-blown. She tries to pat down her curls, wishing she'd thought to shove some product in her daypack. She snorts at herself. A daypack in a classy restaurant like this! Her image is shouting *student* and she hasn't even walked through the door.

They are sitting at a table in the back corner. Abby follows the waiter's nod and sees Cameron waving, a bashful smile on his face. She pauses nervously to compose herself then walks slowly across the room. Cameron pulls out the seat beside him. He reaches for her arm and drags her down. Abby sees empty wine bottles on the table. Cameron and his mates are obviously well ahead of her.

She looks around the ring of faces: four men (including Cameron) and two women. Cameron introduces her, and she shakes hands and smiles. Michael, Jason, Imogen, Greta and Andy: no way will she remember them all. Michael leans back and calls to the waiter for an extra glass. It appears quickly and he fills it to the brim with white wine and pushes it towards her, sloshing wine onto the tablecloth.

'Drink up,' he says. 'You've got some work to catch us.'

She glances around shyly, hoping she won't have to initiate conversation. But she needn't be concerned. Almost without pause they dive back into the discussion they must have suspended on her arrival: the latest political wrangle on Capital Hill. Abby is quickly aware she is with people who know politics, and all its shenanigans. She sits back and listens. There's not much she can add to a discussion of this nature.

It's an interesting evening. Cameron and his journalist friends talk and drink big—Abby can't believe the amount of wine they go through. Periodically, two or three of them go outside for a smoke. Cameron doesn't join them. Abby remembers his emergency cigarette in the valley after he hit the kangaroo, and she wonders if he is abstaining simply to impress her. He is certainly having a good time, joining the discussions and arguments with buoyant enthusiasm. Some of the conversations are heated. They escalate gradually. Cameron and his friends posture and gesticulate, and the volume of their talk increases. They lean forward, huff and snarl. Then they laugh. Abby can barely keep up with it.

Throughout the dinner, Cameron reaches for her hand under the table. He holds it and presses it. Sometimes he puts an arm around her shoulder, removing it when he needs to make an animated point. He's so different among his peers—so much more combative and competitive. It's fascinating to see this other side of him, but it makes her feel inadequate. He and his friends are so intelligent and informed. They discuss issues she knows little about: the conflict in Israel, US foreign policy, the modernisation and development of China and what this means for the rest of the world.

Abby feels her country upbringing. She feels parochial and small, comparatively uneducated. She thinks of her childhood in Mansfield: going bush with her father and Matt, camping, riding horses in the hills, skiing back-country, swimming in the river in summer. What does she know of the world? Most of these journalists have travelled widely. Europe, the US, Asia. They include travel anecdotes among their stories. In comparison, her experience is limited: Mansfield High and Monash University. She hasn't had the money to travel, or the time. Cameron's friends are older than her, and far more worldly.

She's relieved when the topic shifts to rural unemployment and the death of country towns. At least she can weigh in on this: closure of facilities in country communities, lack of funding for infrastructure, the negative selection pressure for unambitious people, the impact of highway diversions on rural businesses, salinity, the problems of the Murray–Darling Basin. It feels good to participate at last, to have something worthwhile to say.

Mostly she wings it by drinking. She wasn't going to do alcohol tonight, but there wasn't much choice when Michael thrust that first glass of wine at her. Plus the wine gives her confidence. She can never belong in a group of people like this, but the drink helps her to merge, to be less of a grinning idiot.

When the bill is passed around at the end of the evening, Abby feels anxious. She's not sure she can cover her share—all that fancy food and the multiple bottles of wine. She's relieved Cameron insists on paying. He doesn't even let her see the bill, sweeping it beyond her reach then putting his card on the pile.

Afterwards, they leave together, stepping out into the cold Canberra night. Abby is sobered by the chill air. Cameron has her hand grasped firmly in his as he offers to walk her to her car. She points to her bicycle and he laughs: a hearty chuckle that warms the night. Then he leads her to his car.

'You're not riding,' he says. 'I won't allow it.'

He unlocks the WRX and hands her in. Abby's not sure how drunk he is, whether he should be driving—with the amount of wine he consumed, he ought to be smashed, but he seems to be holding it well. He goes to the driver's side and slides in beside her, closes the door, starts the car, turns on the heater. Then he pauses and looks at her. He seems restrained somehow, as if he's holding himself tucked in tight.

'I think I've probably had too much to drink to take you all the way to your place,' he says. 'But my flat isn't far from here. Would you consider staying the night? There's a spare room.'

A knot of tension weaves itself in Abby's throat, but what can she do? She agrees reluctantly. A taxi fare from here would be too expensive.

Cameron's face is inscrutable as he puts the car in gear and pulls out into the street. He drives slowly, as if doubtful of his own judgement. His apartment block is along the foreshore, overlooking Lake Burley Griffin. He uses a keycard to open the gate to the underground parking. Abby sits silently in the passenger seat as he parks the car, then they get out into the echoing concrete space.

'This way.' He guides her to the lift, not touching her.

They stand in the lift as it glides up to the third floor. The corridor is softened by pale grey carpet. He walks ahead of her to a heavy white door and unlocks it, swings it open for her, flicks on some lights. Then he motions her inside, entering quietly behind her while she moves forward, drawn to the windows and the hint of winking lights on the inky lake.

The apartment is airy, ceiling to floor windows. Outside is a spot-lit balcony with leafy green plants. The living area is large; dark brown leather couches are scattered with green cushions. On the high white walls are Aboriginal dot paintings, some in earthy ochres, others in bright acrylics, cascades of coloured spots depicting abstract landscapes. With her hands behind her back like Prince Charles, Abby peruses them, exploring the shifts in colour and shape and depth. Cameron is standing away from her, hands in pockets, his face bland and closed as if he is suppressing something in himself. She puts a hand on the back of a couch, her heart skittering and her breathing fast. He glances at her then he looks away.

'The paintings are good,' she says.

He inspects his collection thoughtfully. 'I like Indigenous work,' he says. 'They're clever the way they see the landscape. You'd think they'd seen it from the air, but most of them just know how it is. The shape of the land. And it has such deep meaning for them. I like that. And the patterns. The way the colours sweep across the canvas, clashing then merging. It's like a journey through time and space.'

The paintings must have been expensive, Abby thinks. And this apartment makes her humbly aware of her own student squalor. She wishes Cameron hadn't seen her bungalow last night—her world of disastrous disorder. She wonders how he manages to afford all this—perhaps his rich parents have invested. But he is much older than her, thirty at least. He's had time to establish.

'How long have you been working as a journalist?' she asks.

'Started my cadetship when I was twenty-two,' he says, his gaze still fixed on the artwork. 'After the *Herald Sun* I worked in Alice Springs for a while. That's when I bought most of these paintings. I got to know a few of the local blackfellas and I bought some of their art. I probably didn't pay as much as I should have. I still feel guilty about that.' He looks at her. 'I've been in Canberra close to four years now, climbing the journalistic ladder. It's a good time to be a science and environment writer—plenty of stories. You have to make mileage where you can.'

Abby sees his jaw tighten. Her breathing escalates and she can't look away. 'The spare room,' she says weakly.

'This way.'

She follows him down a short corridor.

'The bathroom,' he says, pointing. 'And this is my bedroom.'

She peers in reluctantly. It's another spacious room, lamp-lit, with a large bed covered by a tasteful dark brown doona and several cushions.

'The spare room is down the end here. The sheets are fresh.' He shows her to another neat, elegantly decorated room, and suddenly she can't help laughing.

'What did you think when you saw my place yesterday?' she says. 'I'm surprised you managed to keep a straight face.'

'I didn't,' he smiles, sharing her mirth. 'You were just too drunk to notice.'

She wonders what he sees in her—a broke student, still studying, with limited experience of the world. What's he looking for?

He moves close and she feels the bigness of him. A strong hand reaches and sweeps her hair from her shoulder then he leans forward and gently, so tenderly, kisses her neck. She lets him bend her against him, his arms wrapping smoothly around her back, his lips on her neck, her face, and then her mouth. He is leisurely and unrushed. It feels good, but she hadn't planned on this—perhaps they are diving in too deep too quick. A little bit of restraint might be better. She likes to have time to think.

'Maybe I should go,' she says, pulling half-heartedly away.

'You don't have to,' he says quietly. 'We can sit and talk for a while. We can just hold hands.'

She stands there, her heart juddering, her hands lightly resting in his, and she reads the words in his eyes. He wants her, that's clear. Wants her badly, mystifying though that is. And she wants him too. Wants to feel his hands beneath her clothes; her skin is singing for him.

He closes his arms around her again, and kisses her till her knees soften. Then he slips the cardigan from her shoulders, his fingers unbutton her shirt. His lips and hands are warm and she's suddenly happy to give in to it, craves it in fact: the feel of his hard body against hers.

He pulls her against him and leads her to his lamp-lit bedroom.

In the morning, Abby wakes in the light cast through the large uncurtained window. Beside her, Cameron is slackly asleep, the weight of his arm threaded around her. They are naked: a tousled fawn sheet screwed up between them, the doona half-pulled across their waists. She feels the heat of his skin against hers, the hairiness of his thigh alongside her own, the flush of his breath on her shoulder.

It was good sex. Cameron is a man well in tune with his body, and he focused on giving her utterly satisfying orgasms. But the after-effects of the wine hang heavy in her head. Despite the ecstatic release, she is anxious. Doubt surfaces. Without meaning to, she has succumbed to an entanglement of sorts. It's against all her personal rules. What is she doing?

She moves slightly, wondering if she can disengage from Cameron without waking him, but his arm tightens instinctively around her; there will be no easy escape. He shuffles close, eyes still shut, his lips tracing the line of her shoulder and collar bone. Then his lids sweep open and those dark eyes connect with hers. She feels other parts of him awakening and she knows they are destined for more lust before she can extract herself and go home. She gives in and allows her skin to meld with his. It's a sensual kind of poetry, despite her blurry alcohol-laden head.

Afterwards, cosy and sated, she lies back, closes her eyes and lets him pull her up against him. He curls himself around her, heavy and hot, her buttocks pressed to his groin, his lips tasting her shoulder. Dragging the doona up, he wraps her in the cocoon of his heat, and she has never felt more keenly possessed. It amazes her she can feel so physically comfortable with someone she barely knows. The easy intimacy frightens her—it's possible this man might worm his way under her skin, and how would she deal with that? She's going to hurt him: that much is certain. How can she navigate her way out of this?

Gently he strokes the length of her with a warm hand, and she feels feline beneath his touch. She rolls away and lays her head on his arm so she can look at him. 'I have to go to work this morning,' she says, her voice breaking the quiet of the room.

'Take the morning off,' he says. 'I put in a couple of late nights at work earlier this week, so I don't need to go in till lunchtime. Reckon I can keep you entertained.' His smile is calmly confident and his hands are very certain on her skin.

'A student's work is never done,' she says lightly. She sits up and pushes her hair back, and he reaches and tangles his fingers in it.

'Shower first?' he suggests.

She sniffs her skin. It smells of him and sweat and love-making. 'Might be a good idea.'

'I'll show you the bathroom, but don't bank on getting out of there quickly.'

She frowns at him. 'I do have to get to work, you know.'

He kisses her stomach then swings out of bed. 'An hour won't make any difference.'

15

Cameron calmly inserts himself into her life, and Abby finds herself caught up in him despite her hesitation. Sex is the first and last of everything—it's both erotic and exciting, and it's never been like this before with other men. At night she lies awake in his bed, studying his sleeping face, and when his eyes open, he reaches for her, kisses her. Daytime, in the office, she's unable to concentrate, stares vacantly at the computer while spreadsheets of data blur irrelevantly in front of her eyes. In the field, she wanders up the valley singing. The sky seems wide open: blue smiling down on her. Even the breath of the wind seems sensual. The kangaroos observe her from a distance, lifting their heads to chew on swatches of grass.

She's so schoolgirl-silly and so alarmingly besotted, she can't even contemplate food. She toys with lunch, knowing she ought to eat, but she's tingling with something greater and more insistent, something that consumes her and lifts her and floats her up with the clouds. Out at dinner together, they order plates of food and ignore them. Within the space of a couple of weeks, she becomes a captive by stealth. It's only human, she supposes, to enjoy the warmth of Cameron's body, the intimacy of his arm flung casually across her in bed. He's a passionate lover; expressive and experimental. She likes his way of leading, of gently taking charge and directing her. He's attentive and tender, and it astounds her how quickly she becomes accustomed to him, almost falling in love with him.

Each night they first dispense with lust, then a meal is vaguely possible. After that they have long conversations that wind their way into the small hours of morning, punctuated by repeated love-making. Cameron is an intellectual challenge and sometimes he unnerves her—controversy is his realm and his tactics defy social rules. He oftens assumes an adversarial position simply to test his persuasive skills, and his arguments are so convincing she never knows quite where he stands on an issue or what his true feelings are.

He likes to extend himself by expanding his general knowledge, which is the polar opposite of Abby's life trajectory. Her studies demand she learn more and more about less and less, and, as a scientist, her training insists she never make claims beyond the limits of her information, qualifying her statements with terms like *may* and *might* and *probably*. Cameron, however, thrives on thrashing out a topic as assertively as possible using whatever compelling language he can muster. Lacking authority on a subject is irrelevant. The skill is in the art of argument.

Climate change politics is his pet issue, but it leads them into uncertain territory. Abby's concern is that neither of the two main parties will tackle the problem seriously, and she's annoyed that the media skews the argument. Cameron refuses to accept his profession's responsibility in this. Each time they discuss it, he takes a predictably journalistic stance. To his mind, it's important for journalists to portray both sides of an argument—he calls it balance. But Abby insists there is no balance if journalists give equal air-time to a few dissenting voices purely to present another side. These dissenting views are in contrast to an overwhelming wealth of established evidence, so to give them credence represents bias, she argues, not good reporting.

Cameron smiles and accuses scientists of failing to communicate their findings adequately while Abby asserts this is not their role. Scientists are trained to do science, she says. Providing information to the public is the job of journalists, but their approach is flawed. Political leaders are being confused by reporters who fuel controversy where there is none.

On it goes. Cameron sticks to his line on the need to maintain balance, and Abby strives not to succumb to depression over his views. She reminds him that around the world glaciers are retreating and ice caps are melting. The science is there to prove it, she says, so why do the sceptics refuse to believe it? Further, she points out, there is this stupid argument that climate change is not due to human activity. How can it not be? she asks. She lists for him all the ongoing damage being inflicted on the earth by humanity: expanding cities, burgeoning human populations, booming industry, carbon being pumped into the atmosphere to generate power and run millions of motor vehicles, tree-clearing, water being poured onto land to grow food to feed more and more mouths. How can so many humans *not* be changing things? she asks. The buildings, the pollution, the destruction of natural systems.

Cameron finds her views amusing. He argues that humans have always managed to solve problems. Technology and development are the only way forward, he says. Otherwise they would be back in caves, grunting instead of talking. Then it is sex again, of course. Whenever an impasse is reached, a romantic gambol is the solution. Grunting, instead of talking. They are not so far evolved from cavemen after all.

Mostly she stays over at Cameron's place, but sometimes he comes to hers. She sees the humour in his eyes as he peruses her mess. It's a minor humiliation when he washes her dishes and puts them away, or stacks her magazines and books into piles while she's in the shower. One time, she hears the vacuum cleaner humming in tune with her hairdryer as she dries her hair. He attempts to disguise his small efforts to tidy her life, but hopefully he will soon work out it's a losing battle. In between times she makes a feeble attempt to clean up, then she can't find anything, which makes her grumpy. He laughs at her frustration, grabs her into his arms, and makes love to her with such passionate abandon she is almost able to chuckle at herself.

It feels strange sharing her space with him, having him in her house. He's so big and his limbs are so long he makes her bungalow even smaller. Often he sits on the doorstep talking to the dog. He says that as a boy he'd always wanted a dog, but his mother is wedded to cats. His mother insists cats are easier, but Cameron thinks dogs are more interactive. Cats, he says, interact only on their own terms, whereas dogs give real love. Abby laughs and says he's been duped. Dog-love is entwined with food. But he shrugs and expresses his interest in pack behaviour. He, of course, would have to be an alpha male. What would that make her? she wonders. Alpha female?

He fondles the velvety ears of the landlords' golden retriever as he speaks, and the dog regards him with doughy, adoring eyes. As he tugs the dog's ears in long soft strokes, Abby thinks of his fingers on her skin.

One morning over breakfast, he notices her guitar standing in the corner and asks her to play. She's dismissive, embarrassed, says she doesn't play like that—on demand. She plays when she feels the need. When the urge comes over her, she picks it up and plays, that's how it is. She plays for herself, not for an audience.

He lifts the guitar, sits on the couch and nestles the instrument in his lap. It's too small for him—or rather he's too big, and it looks wrong, like an oversized ukulele. Tentatively he plucks a few chords, fumbles out a rusty 'Smoke On the Water', his fingers clumsy and vague on the strings—he probably learned it as a teenager like many pubescent boys. His brow is creased with concentration and he looks bear-like, hunched over the guitar. But his clunky musical rendition stirs something in her, and she takes the guitar from him, pushes him sideways on the couch with her hip. He shuffles to make room for her. Automatically she thumbs the strings, listening, tuning, her head cocked sideways while she completes the task. Then, unselfconsciously she begins to play. The music comes out of her—'Talkin' 'bout a Revolution' by Tracy Chapman—and the words flow soft and clear. As always, when she feels the music like this, the lyrics fit the way she feels. The stir to change moves through her like a whisper. Her need to run. She's telling him indirectly that she can't commit, not sure if he'll hear.

She feels him close to her as she plays, feels warmth and a strange unexpected happiness. She is connected to him, her hip against his. The music ties her to him and to happiness and to her mother's weird, energetic, on-again-off-again love.

Cameron's face is luminous when she finishes playing and looks up at him. His eyes are adoration mixed with respect. It frightens her. She feels a rabbit kicking in her chest.

'Something else?' he suggests.

She focuses back on her instrument, feels safe again as she picks out a note, the firm line of the string pressing reassuringly into her fingers, grounding her, giving her something solid to hook on to. She waits for the song to rise in her, something lighter, fun. Ben Lee, 'Catch My Disease'—it tumbles into her, rolls out. Cameron's foot taps in time with hers, with the beat, the rhythm of the lyrics. Why is she playing this song? Is she admitting she's in love with him? That she's fallen for him, even though she's afraid?

When she's done, she stands and places the guitar back in its corner. She chances a look at him, sees the lust in his eyes. He scoops her up, ferries her through to the bedroom, lays her on the bed, tugs her clothes off and takes her body. Desire crunches through her. All good.

After sex, they lie loose in each other's arms, legs tangled, the musky smell of their love-making lingering in the air, the sheets, on their skin. His lips press against her shoulder and his hand scrapes an untamed hank of hair from her cheek. He pulls back a little, leans his elbow on the pillow and cups his chin in his hand while he looks at her.

'You transform when you play,' he says. 'You're like a different person. Where do you go?'

She dodges his gaze and glances up to the corner of the room where a delicate daddy-long-legs huddles beneath the cornice. 'My mother used to play,' she says. 'Playing reminds me of her.'

He is quiet. 'She died when you were young, didn't she?'

'I was thirteen.'

'Girls need their mums.' A sigh huffs out of him as he lies back and stares at the ceiling. 'Not so much for guys. I've never been close to my mum. She was always closer to my sister. A girl thing, I suppose. Mum was busy with her career so we had a nanny. We saw more of her than our parents, so she became our mum in a way. I was bereft when she left. When we were at high school Mum figured we didn't need her anymore and gave her the sack. That was it. I still remember the tears in my nanny's eyes as she picked up her bag and walked out the door. So much for attachment.' His head shifts on the pillow so he can look at her, eyes sad.

'What about your father?' Abby asks.

'My dad?' Cameron snorts. 'He's a hard and arrogant man—I can say that now. He had high expectations, a clear vision of what he wanted me to be. But I wasn't that person. I tried, God knows, I tried.' He sighs again, his body heavy with it. 'Eventually I had to give in to my real self. I was an angry teenager. Sometimes I wonder if I chose different views intentionally to separate myself from him. It seemed every thought I had was contrary to what he wanted me to believe. But I grew into my skin, or maybe my skin grew around me, I don't know which. And I gained confidence. I was happy when I became a journalist. I was good with words, enjoyed lacing them together, putting down all the ideas I knew my father would hate. Do you call that retribution? Pay back? In the end I became my arguments. But I grew beyond that eventually. Luckily my sister fulfilled my parents' hopes and expectations and became a high-flying solicitor, so that let me off the hook in a way.' He glances at her. 'What about your family?' he says. 'Seems you don't much like to talk about them.'

'These days, there's only Dad and Matt and me,' Abby says. 'My dad's an accountant and a farmer. An odd mix. And I've told you about my brother. He works on a vineyard and skis. We grew up outdoors with the bush for a backyard. No fences—or none that held us in anyway. We had it a bit different from you. Few expectations. Not many rules. Now there's Brenda too, Dad's wife. She's not my favourite person, but she holds Dad together.'

'They still live on the land?'

She feels the gentle enquiry in Cameron's question. He wants her to keep talking, wants to know the person who lives inside her skin. She can give him snippets, but not too much, or who knows where it will lead. 'Still on the farm,' she says. 'But they've become rather parochial these days—they've lived in the country too long. All they talk about is stuff that doesn't matter outside Mansfield. Pot-holes in the road, lack of opportunities for teenagers, weeds and erosion, road signs having the crap shot out of them, the lack of doctors at the hospital. When I go down there, I'm expected to sit and listen. It's painful, but I do it. I nod at all the right spots. They don't want to hear what I've been up to. They just want to talk about themselves, Dad as much as Brenda.'

'What about your brother?' Cameron asks. 'Are you close to him?'

'Matt's a good guy,' she says. 'But he's no talker.'

'Same as you,' Cameron says with a hooded smile.

She bumps him on the chest with a fist. 'I talk,' she says. 'What do you think I'm doing now?'

'I don't know,' he says. 'But it feels like you're keeping me at arm's length. I'd like you to let me in sometime. I'm keen to share.'

'Give it time,' she says, getting up and heading for the bathroom. Time to run, she thinks.

16

Daphne is in the four-wheel drive with Abby on the way to the national park. It's an overcast day and grey clouds muscle against the horizon. It has been like this for a week: the skies threatening rain, but delivering nothing. Abby says she has given up hope of a decent autumn, and Daphne agrees. The land is brown and hungry, and the cool wind suggests winter is coming.

It's been a few weeks since Abby visited Queanbeyan, and Daphne has been worried that she frightened the girl off with her trip down memory lane, spilling the contents of her boxes and blurting parts of her story like that. Then Abby rang and invited her out to the valley, said she'd found a suitable day. Daphne has been spinning with anticipation ever since, counting off the days. Perhaps Abby didn't mind her reminiscences after all.

But when Abby collects Daphne from the Queanbeyan house, she seems distant somehow and hesitant, as if she's changed her mind about taking Daphne with her. For a while she is silent, and Daphne feels uncomfortable. Then Abby looks sideways at her and mumbles 'I've met someone.' And finally Daphne understands. She almost laughs, relieved that the girl feels sufficiently relaxed to share her news. She also notices that Abby has a pretty radiance about her, a coy self-awareness that comes with physical loving. Daphne remembers feeling that way with Doug early on. It had been a surprise to her that sexual charms lurked beneath his veneer of gruff hairy reserve. She hadn't expected it of him—the shock of tenderness and intimacy and the ability to arouse the woman in her.

On their wedding night, she had anticipated pain and fear and awkwardness, and there had been some of that, yes. But from the beginning Doug had been attentive to her needs, focused on her pleasure. He wasn't the rough bushman he appeared; there was sensitive magic in his work-toughened fingers. He leaned over her that first night, in the muted glow of candlelight, thoughtfully lit for psychological warmth, and unravelled her slowly with careful gentle delight shining in his eyes, as if he was unwrapping the most exquisite present. And she supposed perhaps she was a gift to him. Doug was not a young man when Daphne married him. He was in his early thirties, a hard worker, on the cusp of bachelorhood.

Theirs had been a restrained and cautious courtship on the tail of her father's death. Doug had been almost painfully respectful of her grief, and she'd been in no hurry, striving to recover from the loss of her father. She was emotionally fragile, and had he rushed her, pressed her, made demands of her, it is likely her bruised heart would have ruptured and she'd have run into a different life. As it was, Doug's patience was so profound she was well recovered when he bashfully offered his first gestures of affection—a deliciously restrained and gentle caress of her cheek with the back of his hand, his eyes brimming with the power of his feelings. By then he was sure she wouldn't reject him. He had visited at the farm often, accepted invitations to dinner, selflessly assisted with many jobs too difficult for Daphne and her mother after her father's passing. He had humbly made himself available and displayed his interest subtly, through service, allowing Daphne to come to him in her own time.

It was a beautiful form of romance—Daphne sees that now. Back then, it took some time for her to appreciate it. Initially, she had resented his presence. But his was such a gentle and furtive way of slipping beneath her skin. From her thanks and gratitude grew the first stirrings of affection, and from there came awareness of the bright light in his eyes when he looked at her, followed, eventually, by the desire for his approval and his touch. It was a masterful breaking in, like her father's skilful handling of a young horse.

'Well that's lovely for you,' she says to Abby, hiding these recollections of Doug which must surely be glowing in her eyes. 'Do you mind if I ask what he does for a living?'

'He's a journalist,' Abby says. 'Very smart.'

Daphne smiles. 'I'm sure you'll run rings around him.'

'I doubt it. He's streets ahead on general knowledge.'

'That's his job, isn't it? To know a little about many things. Or at least to appear as if he does.'

Abby looks glum. 'He pulls it off well.'

'So long as he's nice,' Daphne says. 'That matters more.'

'Yes, I suppose he's nice.'

'That's good then, isn't it?' Daphne sees the nervous jitter in the girl's hands as she grips the steering wheel.

'He's very keen,' Abby says, suddenly miserable.

Love's supposed to make you happy, Daphne thinks. But she knows the fear that can roil in your belly when infatuation first strikes, the tussle between lust and decency, the terror that this might be the forever you've been looking for, and for which you are suddenly and completely unprepared. She learned this herself with Doug when she was a girl becoming a woman. 'So long as he's good to you,' she says gently.

'Yes, he's good to me.' Abby looks away, one of her fingers twisting a hank of hair into a curl.

Daphne wants to tell the girl that love will work itself out in time, but she's not sure how much she should impose her opinions, so she says nothing.

'I'm sorry to burden you with this,' Abby says. 'Being with you reminds me of my Gran. I feel like I can tell you things.'

'I'm glad you're talking to me,' Daphne says.

'Have you ever felt like this?' Abby's lips tremble as she combs her fingers through her hair.

'Like what, dear? I'm no mind-reader. You'll have to tell me.'

'I really like him,' Abby says. 'But I don't want him too close. I want to stay safe.'

Daphne understands. She sees the anxiety in Abby's face and she wishes she could convey that everything will be all right, that Abby's terror will pass and that something softer and gentler will take its place, something longer lasting that will survive highs and lows and troubles, and metamorphose into real love. 'Nothing's safe, is it?' she says finally. 'Not even walking down the street to the shops. Anything could happen. And some of it might be good.'

'You think so?'

'Don't you?'

The quiet smile that spreads on Abby's lips tells Daphne she has hit the spot.

They drive into the park at last, through the forest and then across undulating flats to the car park at the end of the road. Abby cuts the engine and they sit for a moment in the new silence while soft fists of wind buffet the windows and gusts of swirling air sift through the trees—tall cypresses and pines, a pair of oaks, all out of place in this valley of grass and gum trees.

'This is where the tracking station used to be.' Daphne waves towards the concrete slabs beyond the parking area. 'There were several buildings and an enormous dish. When the space race was over they were taken down. It's hard to believe they were here, isn't it?'

Abby gazes out on the empty area where the buildings once stood. 'I knew about the space program being here, but I find it hard to imagine. If it wasn't for the concrete and all these introduced trees there'd be nothing here. No evidence. Was your family still living here then?'

'The government started buying up land in the early sixties just before the space program took off,' Daphne says. 'We had to let go of this country so we moved further south onto one of the other runs. There were no choices for landholders back then. If the government wanted your property you had to give it up.'

Abby's face puckers thoughtfully, as if she's trying to put herself back in that era. 'The space race must have been exciting. Man on the moon and all that. Don't you think it was amazing? Considering how basic technology was back then?'

Daphne has mixed feelings about that time. 'Some people were quite taken with it,' she says. 'And I suppose there was a definite atmosphere round the place. Lots of new faces. Security gates. Enormous trucks. The satellite dishes. We were quite overrun, like an invasion. Up till then this place was ignored, even though it's only an hour from Canberra. Then suddenly we were the centre of everything. But I can't deny how proud and excited we were when they announced our dish was going to be involved in the moon landing. Everyone went to the local school to watch because none of us had a TV.' She laughs. 'Funny, isn't it! The dish could see the moon but there was no TV reception in the mountains.'

She remembers all the cars and trucks lined up outside the little schoolhouse. 'We had to crowd into a single room,' she says. 'All squashed in like sardines, trying to see the screen. It was a terrible blurry picture by today's standards, but there he was, Neil Armstrong, stepping onto the surface of the moon.'

Daphne is surprised by the warm glow that accompanies her recollections. Generally she feels only the conflicting emotions of that period—the anger and resentment that their world had been taken over by foreigners and out-of-towners who had never shown any prior interest in the place. But she sees now that her memories are also embedded in an aura of nostalgia. She had forgotten the good bits. Yes, land was taken over and families were forced to move away, but there had also been local pride, a certain status that had come with being involved in the moonwalk. Afterwards, they thought they could go back to living as they had before. The dishes and buildings were dismantled. All the workers and officials disappeared. But the space program marked the beginning of the end.

'We didn't realise what would happen when it was over,' she says. 'We thought we'd be left alone again. But once the government had their hooks in, they began to take over the region. There was talk of a national park. If a property came up for sale, the government resumed the lease. Farmers who'd lived here for generations were pushed out. And there was worse to come. They didn't just move people off the land, they rubbed them out. Once the park was declared, most of the buildings were knocked down. People's homes, farm infrastructure—if they weren't old enough to be historic, down they came. People were trying to make new lives in places they didn't want to be—in towns and cities—and when they came back to look at what used to be theirs, everything was gone. Perfectly good homes demolished. It was a slap in the face. People were already upset at leaving their properties. Then the way the government scrubbed everything—well, it bred a lot of anger and resentment.'

Daphne remembers her neighbour crying on her shoulder. The hurt of it! There was no consolation to be had. It was an appalling way to treat people. The government thought money and resettlement was enough, but they didn't understand people's bond with the land. They didn't care. All these years and Daphne still feels the despair.

'Doug and I stayed as long as we could,' she says. 'But by the early seventies almost everyone was gone. Families that my family had known for generations—they all left. A whole community, gone. The government kept telling us that sooner or later we'd have to go too. Not in so many words, mind you, but the message was clear. People gave in to it. Some were getting old and they thought they should take what they could and get out. Saw the writing on the wall. Then time was up for

Doug and me too. We were the only ones left—empty land all around us. There was so much pressure to leave, and in the end, we had to give in. It was bullying. We had no rights.'

Daphne remembers packing up. They sold their tractors and machinery, equipment accumulated over decades, the animals. The horses were advertised in the paper and they went quickly: Doug's favourite grey gelding, the brood-mares, Daphne's staid bay mare. The cattle went to market—the cows and heifers, the old Angus bull. It broke Doug's heart to truck them out. He couldn't face going to see them off. It was the last time the yards were used. Not long after that, they were pulled down—almost as soon as Daphne and Doug stepped off the place.

They sold most of Doug's tools at a garage sale—all he kept was a basic kit, his favourites, set on doing some woodwork and repairs in his new garage at the Queanbeyan home. He hated leaving his old farm shed. It was a solid dark wooden structure with big posts cut from mountain-gum logs, and rough-cut beams and slabs for walls. His shed had been his cave—a quiet retreat, sheltered from the wind, with a dirt floor beaten hard from decades of use, and a heavy wooden bench he'd made himself years ago. He'd made furniture in that shed, mended things, pulled apart engines and put them back together again. He'd fixed and serviced pumps, cars, trucks, chainsaws, mowers. He'd worked there in the company of his dogs, always heelers, which he preferred with the cattle. He liked kelpies too, but they were lighter-framed and softer, better for sheep; they tended to get knocked about by the larger, more aggressive stock.

At last they had to leave. On that final day, they walked up the valley together, said their silent goodbyes to the mountains and the trees. They could come back and visit, but they knew it would never be the same. Daphne wandered through the homestead one last time—it would soon become a ranger's residence—then she went in search of Doug. She found him in the shed, crumpled on the floor, weeping harsh wretched sobs that no man should ever have to cry. It broke him, the wrench of leaving the place—just as it had broken the others who'd departed before them, torn from their land. Doug had wanted to stay till he died. He would never be a city man, would never adjust to the crush of the suburbs.

Daphne feels the familiar weight of loss settling upon her, and she looks out of the window to mask the sudden press of grief that fills her chest. Doug had been a good man, a good husband, but there were layers to him she hadn't known about till they moved to the city. On the farm, their lives were busy and their days were shaped by meaningful activity, all tied up with their rural existence. Doug was never a big talker, but in the evenings they found things to say to each other. Sometimes they played cards: five hundred, canasta, gin rummy. They were easy in each other's company. But it was different when they shifted to the suburbs.

Daphne didn't see it happening at first—she was so caught up in her own sadness over leaving the farm. At their new home, Doug seemed to live in the shed, fiddling with a mower he'd vowed to fix, the old dog lurking around his legs. Then he started to roam the streets, gone for hours, walking and not eating. Daphne noticed his silences at night, his cheeks hollowing out, the dull emptiness in his eyes. Talk contracted to short grunts and muffled answers. Daphne tried to draw him out with stories and reminiscences, but soon it was apparent that he had more time and affection for the dog, which demanded nothing of him and accepted his silences and withdrawal. Daphne was hurt.

The dog was a rusty old red heeler called Prince with a torn ear from one of his numerous fights. He was never a pretty hound, but Doug loved him in a rough manly way, and the dog was Doug's devoted shadow, following him wherever he went—from room to room (the first dog they had ever allowed in the house) and into the shed. A few weeks after they moved to Queanbeyan, Doug developed his first urban habit, which was to feed the magpies, scattering a handful of Prince's dog food on the driveway. He shouted when the old dog hauled itself to its feet hoping to chase the birds and hunt down the pieces of kibble. Instead, Doug sent the dog to its dusty pile of hessian sacks in the shed with a pointed disciplinary finger. But those were the only times Doug needed to raise his voice at Prince. They were mates, buddies with an unspoken mutual loyalty. Daphne saw it in the dog's eyes and in Doug's quiet hand, resting on the dog's head in the evenings when the TV was on.

Over time Daphne came to see the dog as a competitor for her husband's attention, but she also realised Prince was a gift. The dog kept Doug in touch with the world, even as Doug's inner hermit tightened its grip. Then disaster. A lump appeared under the dog's tail. Daphne noticed it when Prince was cleaning up his meal of dog food, tail erect and wagging as he pushed the bowl around with his tongue, trying to extract flavour from the metal. She showed the lump to Doug and wanted to take the dog to the vet, but Doug was intent on ignoring it.

The lump grew. It swelled and began to bulge and Daphne was worried about it. Eventually she persuaded Doug to visit the vet. It was a big step for him to pay money to have an animal seen to. They'd never used vets on the property—out there the cure for illness had always been a bullet. But he made an exception for the dog—his old mate—put him in the car and drove him to the local vet clinic. Prince sat like royalty on the front seat, his tongue lolling with delight.

Doug came home sullen and angry, the dog trotting miserably at his heels, uncertain of his master's mood. The vet said Prince had developed an anal tumour, seen only in male dogs that hadn't been desexed. The recommendation was to do surgery to remove the lump and Prince's testicles at the same time. The operation would cost two hundred dollars. Doug refused, outraged. Two hundred dollars to knacker a dog and cut out a lump! He'd spent twenty-five dollars of good money already just to hear this rubbish. Fancy castrating a dog at Prince's age! Doug wouldn't hear of it. He wouldn't do it to himself so he wouldn't do it to his dog. He didn't want to see Prince turn soft and fat like a backyard pet.

After that, Doug hid from the fact that the lump was growing by burying himself in full-scale denial. Daphne knew the dog needed veterinary attention, but she was afraid to raise the topic. She agreed that the cost of the surgery was exorbitant, but she knew Doug needed the dog, so she was prepared to pay to keep Prince alive. It was difficult to convince Doug, however. She tried to pick her moments, but he brushed her off, pointing out that the dog was still eating and enjoying its walks, so it must be all right. But the cancer was insidious. The lump slowly swelled until one morning Daphne saw the dog licking at its rear end. When she peered beneath its tail she saw blood and muck dripping from what had now become a grossly distended mass. She showed it to Doug, but his solution was to give the dog a rest from his morning walk so the wound could heal.

That was it for Daphne. When Doug disappeared down the street, she shoved the dog in the car and drove to the vet clinic without an appointment. In the waiting room, the receptionist berated her for not phoning first. Then she peered at the lump, crinkled her nose with distaste and went out the back to speak to the vet. They slotted Prince in between the scheduled clients, and Daphne was humbly grateful. She thanked the vet for seeing her, but was unprepared for his blunt assessment. He said Prince should have been operated on weeks ago. He could have saved the dog's life if his advice had been followed and the lump had been removed when it first appeared. Now it was too late. The lump was invasive. It was a mess. Inoperable.

With trembling hands and undisguised tears, Daphne paid the bill, unable to meet the receptionist's eyes. When she arrived home, Doug was sitting on the doorstep, hell and fury burning in his eyes—he knew where she'd been. Daphne tried to ignore him and opened the car door to let the old dog out. Poor Prince attempted to leap out like a pup, but his limbs were slow and heavy with arthritis, and he fell to the driveway with a sickening thump. Daphne heard herself whimpering as she stroked the old dog's head then turned to wipe blood from the seat and tried to wave away the rotten stench of the tumour.

An argument ensued—the worst of their marriage. Doug was furious. How dare she spend more money on the dog, and for what outcome? Another twenty-five dollars, no doubt, and they were no better off. Daphne tried to tell him what the vet had said, that Prince could have had another few good years if Doug had listened to the initial advice and paid for the surgery. But Doug wasn't having it. 'It's my dog anyway, and I'll decide what happens to it.'

His yells brought the neighbours out into the street to see what was going on. Daphne dragged the dog inside to be sure Doug would follow. Then she gave Doug a dressing down. She told him she didn't want the dog to suffer. Reminded him that Prince was a friend, not an old sick cow on the farm that could be left to die somewhere up the valley out of sight.

Something broke in Doug then, like a string snapping. He bent down to stroke the ears of the bewildered old dog where it lay on the lino between them. Then he lifted Prince in his arms and took him back out to the car.

'What are you doing?' Daphne asked, teary, following him outside. 'Where are you going?'

He walked past her back into the house and came out with a long brown vinyl bag which Daphne knew contained the gun. 'I'm going to fix things,' he said, laying the gun on the floor in the back of the car. 'Something I should have done a while ago.'

He strode to the driver's door and, as he folded himself in behind the wheel, she noticed the wateriness in his eyes, the bare grief in his expression.

'I'll come with you,' she said, rushing forward as he backed down the drive.

But he shook his head, lips firm, and then he was gone.

She sat for hours on the doorstep waiting for his return, terrified he might have shot himself along with the dog. He wouldn't do that, would he? He wouldn't leave her?

Dark came with no sign of Doug. Daphne sat through the usual TV programs oblivious to the motions on the screen. At ten o'clock she went to bed and lay there stiff with tension, listening for the sound of the car. Finally she heard the familiar rumble of the car in the street, the sound of the garage door opening and closing. Doug glided into the house, quiet on his feet. He undressed in the bathroom—she heard running water, the toilet flushing. Then he came out and slipped into bed beside her. Said nothing.

'Where have you been?' she asked.

At first there was no answer, then his voice scraped out, hard and harsh. 'Took the dog bush. Put a bullet in its head. Dug a hole and buried it.'

Daphne reached for his hand. 'It was the right thing. Best for the dog.'

For a while he left his hand in hers, then he tugged it slowly away and shuffled over on his side, his back to her. She felt the vibration of sobs shaking his body, pulled herself in close to him, wrapped an arm around him and hugged him tight.

She knew he was crying for much more than the dog.

'Why did it have to happen?' Daphne asks Abby now. 'Why did we have to leave our land?' It's a rhetorical question—she's not looking for answers. 'Nobody comes here. It's empty. Just you and me and the crows. They closed it for the public and none of them want it. What was the use of that?'

Daphne is wavering on the cliff-edge of tears. She's touched and surprised when Abby takes her hand and strokes it gently. The girl seems to understand. Daphne gathers the shreds of her self-control and pats Abby's arm. 'You have work to do, dear. You should go and do it. I'll stay here in the car. Maybe take a nap.'

She watches Abby bundle out of the car, grabbing a pack from the back of the vehicle then heading off up the valley. In the distance, kangaroos are a scatter of brown humps, resting and grazing. Abby turns and waves once then she is gone, becoming smaller and less visible among the shifting tussocks and the rolling landscape.

When she is out of sight, Daphne pushes open the car door and climbs stiffly out. She takes off slowly in a different direction. There is somewhere she wants to go.

17

Daphne walks slowly up the valley. Her hips and knees protest and she's a little light-headed and a weird thumping sound is echoing in her head. But it isn't far—if she can just find the spot where the track used to turn off into the trees. There's a special place she wants to visit, a hidden clearing in the bush where parts of her soul are buried.

As she treads along the margins of the valley where the forest reaches down to merge with the grass, kangaroos reclining among the patchy scrub push up onto their feet and watch her pass. She takes the shortest route, as best she can recall it, but she doesn't want to walk too close to any of those big old bucks.

She remembers one of her father's stockmen being mauled by a kangaroo. He was on foot and too close to a big bachelor male. He had his dog with him, a skinny mongrel of an animal that always went in too hard when it was working the stock. The stupid mutt attacked the kangaroo, and there was a dreadful howling ruckus that was heard all the way down the valley. The stockman grabbed a stick and tried to break them apart, but the kangaroo sat back on its tail and slashed out at him with a hind toe. It tore a hole in his stomach, right through the skin and into his abdomen. His screams were so loud they echoed from the crags. Later Daphne watched her mother stitch the gaping wound with a needle and thread. Then her father drove the stockman in to hospital. Her mother's repair job hadn't been ideal, but it had probably saved the man's life.

Poking around at the edge of the bush, Daphne finds the boulder which she now remembers used to mark the track into the scrub. This is what she is looking for. The trail is no longer distinct—it's more like an animal-path—but Daphne knows this is the way. Shielding her face with her arms, she pushes through a snarl of undergrowth. Crimson rosellas startle from a tree, chipping and chiming as they burst into flight. Twigs catch on her skin leaving scratches and blood spots.

In a short distance the bushes give way to a cleared area of overgrown grass and a series of crumbling white headstones lined up in two short rows. These graves mark the tragedy of her family's past. Here lie the remains of her brother who was crushed by the horse. Her mother and father rest here too; her father interred with all Daphne's unanswered questions. Four stones cover stillborn babies that her mother buried. Little Gordon too.

Daphne sits on a rock and regards this sad altar to lost human life. She thinks of her mother: a melancholy, defeated woman. It was no wonder she was like that after losing four babies—Daphne doesn't even know if they were given names. When she was little, her mother often brought her here to lay small posies of bush flowers at the feet of the headstones. She remembers her mother's tears and long face, the rush of panic she felt seeing her mother so unhinged. At the homestead her mother was always sturdily in control, a stoic hard-working woman who trudged through her daily tasks without complaint. Here in the tucked-away bush cemetery, Daphne saw another side of her mother—the raw, emotional part where life had scoured deep gorges of grief.

She is suddenly heavy with her own wash of grief. She glances to Gordon's headstone. Poor little fellow. So young. His life cut too short. She closes her eyes against the pale light and she can see him running on his skinny little legs around the homestead, beating the air with a stick. He is practising riding his imaginary horse. He's six and Doug has said he can soon learn to ride. He's a thin little boy, dark-haired like Doug, and he has Doug's pointed nose and sharp face, the same gentle smile.

He's a good helper, little Gordon. Since baby Pam was born, Doug has instilled in him a sense of responsibility. When Doug is away working up the valley, Gordon is the man about the place. He must do jobs to assist his mother and be quiet so as not to disturb the baby. Gordon's promotion makes him feel big and important. It won't be long before he will be able to ride up the valley with his father. Daphne refrains from reminding him that soon he will need to begin his schooling too.

It is a warm day, the first real taste of summer for the year. Daphne has been busy all morning, boiling water in the copper and scrubbing the dirty clothes on the washboard, passing them through the hand-cranked wringer. She is hanging the washing on the line beneath the eaves; the clothes will dry quickly in this heat. Thankfully Pam is sleeping so Daphne can complete the task uninterrupted. After this she will skin the two rabbits Doug trapped last night and set them cooking on the stove. Hopefully she will be done before the baby wakes for a feed.

The valley is at its best after a good wet spring. It is green with waving grasses, and fat black cattle spread out grazing along its length. This year they should get a good price at market. Doug has bought in an Angus bull with good bloodlines and he is happy with the new progeny. The young steers from the first drop are thickset and nuggetty. They have deep chests and straight backs, and with this excellent mountain feed they will be in prime condition when they are sold. Doug has decided to keep the heifers to boost his breeding herd. They are strong types, and it means he can get rid of some older cows that are getting long in the tooth and finding the subalpine winters hard.

Spring is Daphne's favourite season in the valley. She loves autumn too, with its spare blue skies, but spring is a time for growth and abundance. Everything is productive: the birds, the cattle, the grass, the gum trees sprouting fresh red leaves from their swaying tops. Usually this is when she manages to get out riding too. Before the children were born, she used to help run the cattle up to the High Country to the summer grazing grounds. She doesn't mind hard work, can turn her hand to fencing, making yards, marking and branding cattle.

She loves being a mother too, but often she is lonely. Doug is out most days, gone till sundown with a water bottle and a packed lunch, a dog or two at his heels. Daphne's days are centred round domestics: cooking, washing, cleaning, fetching wood, feeding the baby, keeping an eye on Gordon.

In this hot weather, the bush on the steep sides of the valley is dense with cicadas and the air seems to pulse with sound. Daphne feels small and solitary, stranded at the homestead, a speck in the grand scale of the landscape. Four days a week, just after lunch, she turns on the wireless to listen to *Blue Hills*. It only runs for fifteen minutes, but it breaks up the day, and during that time she feels she is among friends. It is reassuring to know that the author of the series, Gwen Meredith, is sitting in a cottage a few valleys away, writing about the lives of mountain people just like her, characters that might be based on people she knows of. But when the program is over, loneliness descends once more. She watches the days march through, longs for Doug's return, craves his adult company instead of the shrill demands of her small boy. She knows Doug will come home when the late orange light pinks the granite tors on the ridge and the cool fragrant aroma of alpine evening hangs over the valley.

As she hangs the washing, clinching it to the wire with wooden pegs, she hears Gordon singing down at the woodheap. He has been down there most of the morning, making a fort from chunks of wood. She sent him to fetch wood for the fire, but he's been distracted by some game that has made itself up in his head. He's so imaginative, brimming with wild stories of bushrangers and bank robberies—Doug has been filling him up with raw material at night, telling bed-time tales to put him to sleep.

It's such a relief for Daphne that Doug helps in the evenings. Most men come home from a day out on the property and slump into a chair, eat and then sleep. But Doug is a sensitive and caring man, a kind lover, and as patient as the day is long. He's wonderful with Gordon. After a quick wash in the trough at the end of the day, discarding his shirt by the door, Doug usually takes the small boy on his lap and lets him snuggle into the depths of his beard and hairy chest. There is laughter, chuckling, whispers and squeals. Weary from the demands of being a mother and housewife, Daphne likes to sit in the rocking chair to watch them, a wide smile stretching her cheeks. At night when the babies are asleep, she likes to lie in bed with her husband, her chin on his shoulder, his beard soft against her cheek. She spoons herself around his taut muscular frame, waits for his touch. He is gentleness combined with buried ferocity and passion—in his chest beats a keen love of the mountains, and of her.

She pegs the last shirt and pauses a moment to watch its tails flap in the breeze. It's late morning and the wind is already rising. She should call Gordon in for some morning tea. Using her hand as a shield against the sun, she peers down towards the yards and the woodheap. Gordon is down there somewhere, hidden by the mounds of rough-chopped wood. She hears banging—he must be bashing something with a stick. Then there is silence. She calls out to him, fresh bread waiting, a cup of water on the table.

For a while she sees no movement down there and wonders if she will have to go and fetch him. Then Gordon emerges toting an armful of wood. Smiling, she watches him. But he's slow and something isn't right. She feels the smile fade from the corners of her mouth. Gordon is staggering and swaying. He can't seem to set his feet straight. His pieces of wood topple from his arms, and he bends over. At first Daphne is unsure what he's doing then she realises he is vomiting. She sees him take a few disoriented steps and then he wavers and slumps to the ground.

Heart in her mouth, she leaps from the veranda and runs to him. The white eye of the sun stares down at her. The air beats with the rhythmic thrum of cicadas.

She reaches him and rolls him over. He is pale and drooling, floppy and unaware. 'Gordon.' She hoicks him up. 'What's wrong? What happened?' His head lolls.

She scoops him into her arms and hurries back to the homestead. Her mind is buzzing with the cicadas. She props him in a chair, waves air in his face, wipes his mouth. 'Gordon,' she is saying. 'Gordon, what's wrong? Speak to me.'

The alarm in her voice wakes the baby, she hears Pam snuffling and gurgling. It has been at least four hours since the last feed and soon Pam will start asking for it. Daphne tries to think, but her heart is heaving. Gordon needs help, but it's a long way into town. Down at the woodheap he must have found a snake. It must have struck him. She doesn't know what else it could be.

She pulls his arms and legs straight, runs her hands down them looking for a mark. Nothing. If he could speak he could tell her where the snake got him, but he's flaccid and absent. If she doesn't do something, he's going to die.

The baby starts croaking, escalating quickly to a wail. Daphne looks around for the keys. She will have to put Gordon in the truck and drive him into town. She has to get him to the hospital.

Breathing fast, she gathers her little boy up again and runs to the shed. She has to put him on the ground while she opens the doors. He is so limp it terrifies her. She lays him on the back seat, pauses to watch his chest rise and fall, then she gallops back to get the baby.

In the crib, Pam is screw-faced and screaming, her tiny fists bunched with infantile rage. Daphne feels air scraping in her throat as she wrenches Pam out and races to the shed, the baby jerking in her arms.

She hurls herself in behind the wheel, wedges the baby on the seat and cranks the key in the ignition, pumps the accelerator. The engine roars noisily, echoing in the shed. Daphne grinds the truck into reverse and trundles it out of the shadows. The baby shrieks. Light slings in through the window as she swings the truck onto the track. The white eye of the sun is still watching her.

She feels her breaths coming in gasps, something pounding in her head, fear clenching in her throat. Pam's screams are a knife in her chest. She sees the baby rock and lurch on the seat as they jolt through a dip. From the back seat there is nothing. She flings a backward glance to check on Gordon, sees his pale face and grey lips. His chest is moving with slow shallow breaths. He is still and slack.

She bounces the truck along the track, stabbing through the gears, revving the engine till it seems the pistons must pop through the bonnet. The old vehicle sways as she swings it onto the road, urging it through dappled shade, the engine growling.

Pam's screams are at a peak: she is roaring now, her entire little body tight with the force of it. Daphne's mind pings and suddenly she is strangely floaty, surreally absent, fenced off from it all. She can't drive any faster. The truck won't do it, no matter how her foot grinds the accelerator to the floor. She can't stop to feed the baby, hasn't time. She can't look back again. All she can do is to keep driving. To drive through Pam's racket; to drive beyond the road and into the sky where the fierce eye of the sun looks on.

It takes over an hour to drive to the hospital. By then the baby is still, asleep from exhaustion. Gordon is still too. He is motionless.

Daphne knows he is gone. He left her sometime along the way, his tiny slip of a soul wafting out through the window and dissipating into air. She can't say exactly when it happened, but she felt him leaving her, the feather touch of something light and buoyant, the last whisper of his breath escaping.

At the hospital she trudges inside, hefting heavy feet that don't belong to her anymore. She collapses, weeping, onto the chequered linoleum floor. A nurse points her finger to two men who exit through the doors. One of them comes back with something long and narrow wrapped in a sheet, Gordon's feet bobbing just below the hem. The other brings in a dazed baby: Pam blinks at the light, just waking.

———

Sitting on the rock in the hidden cemetery, Daphne lets her tears run loose. She has cried an ocean for Gordon, and still there are more tears to cry. One lifetime is not enough to recover from such a loss.

Eventually she stands and stretches the kinks out of her reluctant legs and back. She walks to the edge of the clearing, to a wattle tree with silvery-grey leaves. Reaching, she snaps off a sprig, clutches it in her arthritic fingers and returns to one of the white gravestones, Gordon's resting place. Tears run afresh as she bends to place the wattle on the stone.

Straightening, she looks around, the grief slowly settling back inside her. This is her family's cemetery, but there's still one grave that isn't here. Her husband, Doug. She can't visit him to say goodbye. There is nowhere she can go to release the burden of her sadness for him. His death was different—a sky burial of sorts.

She turns and walks away without looking back.

18

Cameron is reclining on his bed, arms folded behind his head, the lean length of him spread casually across his doona, when he proposes a trip to Melbourne. It's late afternoon on a Sunday and they have just made love in a crazed rush, not even bothering to pull back the covers.

Abby has been feeling more confident since her discussion with Daphne; she feels so comfortable with the old lady, and the talk comes easily, just as it used to with her Gran. After a decade of swimming through life's turbulent currents without guidance, she finds Daphne's friendship reassuring. It's good to have someone to talk to, someone she feels she can trust. She trusts Cameron too, of course, but there are some discussions she can't have with him—like how to manage their relationship. She's been hoping that maybe she can find a way to be with him. If she steps back in terms of how much time they spend together, perhaps she can steady herself.

But now, with this Melbourne trip of Cameron's hanging in the air, her optimism crumbles. She tries to force a smile while fighting a drowning sensation.

'I found some cheap flights for next weekend,' he says. 'It'll be fun. We can go to dinner. Meet up with a few of my mates. Visit Mum and Dad's.'

Abby feels chains wrapping around her wrists. 'I thought you didn't like your parents.'

'I don't much. But I'd like you to meet them. We can stay with them Friday night, get it over and done with, then the rest of the weekend is ours to have fun.'

'You told me you don't usually stay with them.'

'No, but it might be easier this way. And you can get a proper feel for my childhood home.'

Abby is still unsure, but he's so bright and hopeful, how can she say no?

She spends the week in nervous disarray, wondering what it all means, whether he's trying to harness her with a rope of commitment. She can't do it. But the tickets have been booked and paid for. How can she find a suitable excuse to wangle her way out of it now? She looks to her kangaroos out in the valley for enlightenment, but they don't help at all. They are placidly unconcerned, watching her with brown-eyed indifference as she perches on a rock to study their behaviour. They barely even move from grazing.

Cameron's parents live in a large white brick house in upper-middle-class Prahran—he points it out to her as they climb from the taxi. Privilege oozes from the street, from the dark shadows of the stately house, from the walls that surround it, and the arched metal gateway. Cameron swings the gate open and leads her through a well-watered garden. The house is partly concealed behind a large deciduous tree, and on the porch, colourful flowers spill over the rims of terracotta pots. The front door is heavy, with a polished brass knocker and shiny round handle. Cameron presses the bell.

After a few moments a tall grey-haired man opens the door and frowns out at them. He is an older replica of Cameron, obviously the father. 'You're here,' he says, without a smile. 'Come in. Your mother's been waiting.'

Cameron glances at his watch. 'I said five-thirty.'

'Your mother thought you said five. But never mind. You're here now.' He beckons them in.

'Dad, this is Abby.' A twinge of impatience colours Cameron's voice. He places a hand on her shoulder and squeezes it.

His father peers at Abby over his glasses, and this does nothing to relieve her sense of unease. 'Lovely,' he says. 'Nice to meet you. This way please.' Then to Cameron: 'Your mother is in the lounge.'

They follow his square shoulders down the corridor, their feet tapping on the wooden floor. Abby notices ornate cornices and arches, a dark antique hall stand, oil paintings in golden frames. Cameron's father leads them into a lounge room full of heavy furniture. It feels soulless, and Abby wonders at how such a home could produce someone as affable as Cameron.

A woman rises from the cream-coloured couch and moves like royalty to greet them. She is long-faced with dyed brown hair and carefully applied make-up. Her cheeks droop in sombre folds like a spaniel. Abby figures she's close to sixty.

'Darling boy,' the woman says, extending her arms to hug Cameron, a languid smile on her face.

Cameron's brow furrows. He extracts himself from her embrace and reaches for Abby's hand, tugs her forward. 'Mum, this is Abby. Abby, this is my mother, Anna.'

Abby musters a gracious smile and takes the thin white hand that is extended to her. 'Pleased to meet you,' she says.

'And delighted to meet you too, dear.'

Anna Barlow peruses Abby with a sophisticated and judgemental eye. She's smartly dressed, very boutique, dripping with gold jewellery. Abby feels like a small country hick in her brown leggings and swirly colourful top with too-long sleeves. She shakes the older lady's hand, wishing she'd worn a more modest top with a higher neckline. Cameron might appreciate a bit of cleavage, but she is suddenly very certain his parents do not.

'How about a cup of tea?' Cameron suggests, glancing apologetically at Abby.

'That would be lovely,' his mother says. 'Abby, you sit here and tell me all about yourself while Cameron sorts things out in the kitchen.'

Abby sits as instructed, trying her best to look relaxed. She wishes Cameron was still here to act as a buffer to his mother's scrutiny, but perhaps she's being unnecessarily anxious—Anna Barlow has hardly spoken to her yet. 'There's really not much to tell,' she says lightly, giving Anna a bright smile. 'I'm a country girl from Mansfield—still a student. Part-way through a PhD.'

'Very creditable,' Cameron's mother says, nodding. 'It's good for girls to study. Both Henry and I are barristers, as Cameron may have told you. Retired now, I might add. Henry still takes on the odd legal case, but I'm rather preoccupied with my art these days. I paint. It's nice to express the creative side of oneself, don't you agree?'

'I'm afraid I'm not very creative,' Abby says.

'Oh, but dear, I don't agree,' his mother protests with an amused smile. 'Look at your clothes. They're very creative.'

Abby cringes internally, but manages to absorb Anna's comment without flinching. 'What sorts of things do you paint?' she asks.

'Oh, I'm very abstract and eclectic,' Anna says. 'Portraits and still life, occasionally landscapes. I have a studio. Would you like to see it?'

'Of course.'

The studio is upstairs in a surprisingly light-filled room with abundant windows framing the sky. In the centre of the room stands an easel with a canvas mounted on it. Old bed sheets spattered with paint are strewn across the floor. On one side of the room two enormously fluffy cats lie stretched on a couch.

'Meet Cassius and Antony,' Anna says. 'My glorious couch potatoes. Living their immensely tedious lives of leisure.'

'They look very comfortable,' Abby observes.

'Comfortable but devious,' Anna declares. 'Like their Shakespearean counterparts. Their sole aim in life is to do nothing and to do it well. They've made me their servant, and I adore it. Are you a cat person, Abby?'

'More of a dog person,' Abby admits, thinking of the golden retriever with its joyful smile at home in Canberra.

'That's a shame.' Anna's nose wrinkles. 'I've always preferred cats. I like their independence.' She sighs. 'I never could tolerate dogs—all that blind devotion . . . it just isn't me.' She sashays across the studio to a series of canvasses leaning up against the wall. 'These are a few still-life studies I've done this year,' she says, beckoning. 'I appreciate lots of colour, don't you?' She indicates an impressionistic painting of a bowl of fruit on a blue tablecloth in the style of Monet. Then she pulls out another canvas. 'This is a portrait of Henry—rather experimental, but I like pushing my boundaries . . . oh, and this was just for fun . . . Cassius and Antony lolling on their couch. Do you like it? I keep intending to give it to Cameron for his flat. Such a nice little apartment, don't you think?'

'Yes, it's very tasteful,' Abby says, wondering if Cameron's mother is trying to gauge how intimate this new relationship is. 'I've been spending quite a bit of time there,' she adds, a little embarrassed.

Something flickers across Anna's face—perhaps a tinge of sourness, Abby can't be certain. 'So do you think he would like this painting?' Anna asks.

'I'm not sure,' Abby says. 'He mentioned something about a preference for dogs.'

Dinner is a politely restrained affair. They are seated at the Barlows' large, polished, antique dining table in a room spacious enough for a king. The table is carefully laid out with ornate silver cutlery, diamond-cut crystal glasses, gold-coloured placemats and pressed white napkins. The centrepiece is a large crystal bowl filled with water and floating white candles. Twisted silver candlesticks cast amber light across the table.

It's all very beautiful, very tasteful and opulent: the looping paisley drapes that adorn the high windows, the glass-fronted showcases along the wall elegantly arranged with special fine-bone china treasures, the solid, imposing buffet, bearing even more candles—Anna is obviously fond of such lighting. But to Abby it seems an intimidating announcement of wealth and status. The room is impressive, but it lacks heart. There is no passion in this house. It is all too perfect and correct. Too staged.

She feels oppressed by the dark heaviness in everything. It weighs on her and reminds her that she is not of their class, never will be, and somehow it separates and degrades her. She knows Cameron wouldn't want her to feel this way. He has fought free of all this to be his own person. But she understands now the burden of expectation his background has imposed on him. *This is what you must be*—she feels it in the solid white walls, in the massive table, set royally for four when it could seat twenty. She feels it in the proper expressions etched into his parents' faces as they share their opinions with the easy confidence that comes with significant financial security. She suspects they believe they are better than others, more deserving, more elevated, even though they are too polite and well-bred to say so. It makes Abby feel deficient and uncomfortable, and she doesn't like feeling that way.

Cameron is definitely not himself around his parents. He's tense and awkward, trying to conceal his irritation at the conservative right-wing comments his mother and father pitch constantly into the meal. The discussion roves from opera and classical music to private-school education and the entitlement of the *owning class*, as Cam's parents refer to themselves. Yes, well they certainly *own* things, Abby thinks. Here it is all around her—the evidence of their ownership. They're proud of it, and Abby supposes they deserve to be.

They've worked for it like anyone else. But why do they have to bring attention to it in conversation? Abby knows she is not of the same class, and may not have had the same opportunity as these people, but she is equally deserving of existence, she thinks. She forces herself to remain quiet for long periods, smiling blandly, not trusting herself to speak civilly if she opens her mouth.

As the evening progresses, the conversation continues to centre on topics to which Abby is unable to contribute: recent high-profile legal cases in Melbourne, issues of gangland underbelly warfare in the western suburbs of the city, the Barlows' upcoming trip to Europe to visit architectural highlights and special classical music performances in Vienna. Abby has never been to an opera and, on her student wage, it's unlikely she's about to start. And, although she likes classical music, she isn't up to a detailed comparative discussion of the music of Wagner and Rachmaninov. It seems Cameron's parents are trying to write her off as uncultured, but she mustn't let it bother her. All she has to do is survive the evening then her duty is done.

Cameron looks pained whenever he glances her way. He rolls his eyes, but refrains from standing up to them, probably to avoid a confrontation. He's admirably controlled when they stray once again into current affairs and politics, listening to their remarks with a tight grin on his face. Knowing how vastly his views differ from theirs, Abby is amazed at his restraint. She watches on, astounded, as his parents continue to bounce off each other with the finesse of years of practice. It's such a polished show, she almost expects them to stand and bow at the end of an act.

The only way to cope, she decides, is by indulging in the fine wine Henry keeps pouring into her glass. The wine softens everything. It blurs the edges of her anger. But as the evening marches on, she feels her self-control slipping. The wine, instead of mellowing her, begins to make her feel fluid and confident.

Across the candlelit table, Cameron regards her with undisguised alarm. He senses her mounting annoyance, and his expression lubricates her sense of injustice. Why should the two of them endure a dinner like this, she thinks? Why should his parents get away with their pompous opinions?

Suddenly Cameron is all over the conversation, in damage control, smoothing and sanding the rough spots that start to emerge as Abby begins to assert herself. At first, she offers only offended grunts and sniffs in response to their comments, then she gains momentum and starts asking them prickly questions. *Do you really believe all Australians have the same opportunities? Even those in underprivileged families, dealing with unemployment and domestic violence?* His parents seem taken aback and disbelieving, and Abby suspects they are unaccustomed to being challenged on their views. In this country, they say, education and chances are available to anyone who wants to work. They appear unconvinced when she points out that it can be difficult to extract yourself from poverty, and that welfare can be a self-perpetuating cycle. They smile tolerantly, and Abby can see they've classified her as a young, naïve, left-wing idealist. They shift tack, directing the discussion onto country towns as if attempting to be more inclusive of Abby. But the wine has carried her far beyond her usual capacity for rational assessment, and she feels they are intent on revealing her for an ill-bred imposter. A strange eruptive pressure begins to rise in her chest.

'So your parents, Abby? Your family?' Anna says. 'You've told us nothing about them. What do they do for a living? I can't imagine there are many options in a little town like Mansfield. Where did they do their studies? No universities out that way, are there?'

'That's right,' Abby says. 'No universities. My father's an accountant, but he's also a farmer. He likes his cows. He talks to them.' She smiles and raises her eyebrows. 'And my mother hasn't been too worried about jobs or studies in recent times. She died a decade ago.' She feels a grim pleasure when Anna recoils.

'I'm sorry,' Anna murmurs, glancing nervously at Cameron. 'What was it? Cancer?'

Now it's Abby's turn to recoil. What right does this woman have to ask about her mother? 'Yes, cancer,' she says. 'But I don't want to talk about it. Death's a private thing.'

Anna mumbles another inane apology, while Henry leaps up to open another bottle of wine.

———————

Later Abby takes a shambling, drunken, pre-bed walk, and Cameron accompanies her. She wanted to go alone, but he insisted on coming, won't let her rove the streets on her own so late at night. They head into the muted darkness of the suburb and she attempts to march away from him but he keeps up with ease, striding just behind to allow space for her anger.

'Your parents hate me,' she says. 'I'm not upper-class enough for them.'

'They don't hate you. They're appalling snobs.'

'You mean I'm not good enough for them.'

'Nobody is good enough for them; I'm not good enough either. I've had a lifetime of not measuring up. I'm not the person they wanted me to be.'

'Well, there's something wrong with them if they can't see how well you've turned out.'

His laugh has a resigned edge to it. 'Sometimes you look at your parents and wonder how you emerged from their combined genetics. Philosophically and politically I'm not like either of them. Temperamentally, I suppose I'm more similar to my father.'

'Well philosophically, politically, genetically *and* financially I fall short, in their view. That's obvious.'

He catches up and grabs her hand, pity and anxiety on his face. 'I shouldn't have brought you here, should I?'

Abby walks, half-dragging him along. 'It's been a difficult evening,' she admits.

'I wanted to make a point,' Cameron says. 'To show how important you are to me. I'm sorry about my parents. And I forgot to tell them about your mum.'

Abby tugs her hand free. 'Mum's death isn't something I like to talk about.'

'I'm sorry.' He tries to reach for her hand again, but she evades him. 'Please let's go home,' he says. 'It's late.'

'No. I need to walk. I'm not ready for bed.'

He blocks her way, shoulders looming in the dark. 'Okay, walk then. But be careful. I don't want you to get hit.'

She pushes past him, colliding with the hardness of his chest and stumbling across the nature strip, off the edge of the gutter and onto the road. A pair of headlights arcs past and Cameron grabs her into his arms.

'See what I mean?' he says. 'You don't even know what you're doing.' He presses her against him, checking her resisting limbs. For a moment, she leans into him, jolting with hard dry sobs.

He strokes her hair. 'You should talk to me about your mother,' he says. 'I know it upsets you. But I care enough to want to know.'

She drags herself loose and starts walking again. 'I can't,' she says. 'I survive by forgetting.'

The weekend is saved by a day spent wandering the streets of the city. In the morning, they escape Cameron's parents' house and head for a yum cha brunch in Chinatown where they sample dishes of chicken's feet, bean curd noodles with seafood and fungus, and chilli king crab. Then they browse through a few expensive boutiques, and Cameron insists on buying a skimpy pink dress for Abby to wear that night.

Later in the afternoon, they go to the zoo, which Abby hasn't visited in years. Her favourite exhibit is the butterfly house. She and Cameron sit on a bench seat for a long dreamy period while gorgeous butterflies dip and float around them. One lands on Abby's knee, a lovely iridescent blue creature with sculpted wings. It remains with her for an impossibly long time, occasionally opening and closing its wings, until a rowdy child dashes past and dislodges it from its quiet pew.

They finish the day with a fun and depraved evening, drinking alcohol with some of Cameron's Melbourne journalist friends in a Turkish restaurant. Around a low table, they sit cross-legged on dimpled cushions, pouring wine into tumblers and downing it like water. His friends are accepting of her, and

Abby feels warm and confident with them. They include her in the conversation, and they laugh at her comments as if she is witty and discerning. Cameron has a fine glow about him when he looks at her, a lustful aura of happiness, and it's as if he can't keep his hands off her, his fingers resting too high on her thigh. The clingy short dress must have something to do with it, she surmises, but whatever the cause, she enjoys it, and feels sexy and desirable. It's such a relief to feel so free after last night's awkwardness.

Afterwards, they sway down the street, singing. Cameron has organised a room in a ritzy hotel—unable to face another sleep beneath his parents' roof. They say goodbye to his friends at a taxi rank, and he keeps his arm around her waist, rubs his hand over her hips, wanting her.

In the room, they fall on each other, stripping clothes and taking each other on the floor. Initial lust dispensed with, they take a bubble bath together and drink champagne. Then they make love again with Abby sitting on the vanity.

The bed is the last place they explore, and it is here Abby feels the remnants of the weekend's tension leaving her. This is what she will remember: frolicking with Cameron in this sumptuous suite, giving in to the tug of desire, curling up to the warmth of his body. She suppresses thoughts of that uncomfortable evening with his parents into the mist of the past. That's what works best, she thinks: moving forward without looking back. It's a recipe that has served her well since she was thirteen.

19

Abby is eating breakfast alone in her bungalow a couple of weeks later when her father calls. Since the trip to Melbourne, she's been attempting to carve out a small amount of time away from Cameron. Cameron is hurt by it, but Abby is sure a bit of distance will be good for them. They've been so consumed with each other, to the extent Abby feels she's almost forgotten who she is. Sometimes, she's not sure she can make this thing happen anyway. She and Cameron are poles apart, opposite ends of a magnet, but attracted to each other by physics and chemistry.

Her father sounds cautious as he says hello, as if he's expecting her to say something—about what, she's not quite sure. 'How are things?' he asks. 'How's your work going?'

'Everything's good,' she says. 'Same old. How are you and Brenda? Still fighting?'

'We're okay. Same old.'

Abby laughs. Some things never change.

'Just wondered if you'd heard from Matt,' her father says.

'Why? What's up?' Abby surrenders to a moment of guilt—she's neglected her brother since Cameron exploded into her life. She hasn't kept up her daily phone calls—not that Matt seemed to need them anyway, he was so abrupt when she rang him, annoyed with her for mothering him.

'He hasn't phoned you?' her father asks.

'No. I've been busy. I haven't spoken to him for a while.'

'Damn,' her father curses. 'I was hoping he would have rung you.'

Abby swallows a clutch of fear. 'Is anything wrong?'

'We think he's taken off somewhere. His house is empty and the car is gone. He's left a note saying we shouldn't look for him.'

Abby's heart trampolines in her chest. 'How long has he been missing?'

'A week or so. We thought he might show up. Thought he might have gone hiking in the mountains or something.'

Abby turns over possibilities in her head and she doesn't like any of them. 'How was he when you last saw him?' she asks.

'He was quiet. You know Matt.'

'Did he look okay? Did he say anything?'

Her father is evasive. 'We haven't seen much of him lately. Brenda's daughter's been having a crisis and we've been caught up in it.'

'Have you talked to the police?' Abby asks.

'Not yet. He left a note. Not sure he qualifies as a missing person.'

Abby tells her father about her discussion with Matt when she was last down in Mansfield, how he might be susceptible to depression. Steve is silent, and Abby knows she's just added to his worry.

'I'll come down,' she says. If Matt has gone bush she knows where he's most likely to go. She knows his favourite haunts. He might simply be enjoying time out—she can understand that—but she can't suppress a nagging concern. The mountains cover a large area; if Matt wants to disappear she hasn't a chance of finding him.

She phones Cameron to tell him she's going away, that her brother is missing. *Missing*—it sounds so lonely and uncertain, so frightening. It seems, as she talks, as if she is somewhere else, somewhere up in the sky, watching herself talking on the phone. Cameron insists on coming with her. He says he's put in some big hours at work since the Melbourne trip, and he's also filed a couple of major feature articles so he's owed some time off. He also insists on driving. There's no way he'll let her go to Mansfield in that bomb of a Laser.

Having Cameron along isn't quite what Abby intended, but she feels fragile and guilty and worried, and it's nice to let him take charge. Plus, it could also be good to have him in the mix to defuse things. Abby is sure of one thing: she won't have patience for Brenda's dramatics this time.

Home looks incredibly normal as they turn off the road to the farm the next afternoon: the short-cropped pastures, a cow rubbing its head on a fence post, a kookaburra craning from the wires, the oak trees by the house gradually discarding their brown cardboard leaves. Cameron's car finds every dip and rut on the driveway. He takes it slowly, but the WRX bottoms out more than once. Abby sees him wince, but he says nothing. No sacrifice is too great to get her here, it seems.

Brenda meets them at the door. She reserves her best welcoming smile for Cameron—immediately impressed by his city-chic appearance. She manages to gush over Abby too, almost convincingly, but Abby isn't fooled; it's all about showing off for Cameron.

Brenda is surprisingly upset about Matt's disappearance. She talks about it as she makes tea, and she's radiating concern. 'Poor Matt,' she says. 'I hope he's all right.'

Abby never thought Brenda liked Matt very much, and now she realises perhaps the disconnection is more on Matt's side. Abby knows she's guilty of her own biases.

'We haven't looked after him enough,' Brenda says, tilting the teapot to pour strong tea into Willow cups laid out on matching saucers. 'After this, we'll make sure he isn't left alone. We just want him back.' She flusters busily in the kitchen, pulling out cake tins and laying out a stunning array of home-cooked cakes and slices. 'Steve likes a good spread,' Brenda says modestly.

Cameron is suitably flattering—Abby knows she can rely on him for tact. He tries a piece of everything and comments enthusiastically. The way Brenda blushes is almost sickening, but Abby can't bring herself to enter the conversation. She's too worried, consumed by a deep fear that something terrible has happened to her brother.

Steve comes in at last from the back paddock where he's been rolling out hay for the cattle. He's a soft touch with the cows, likes to feed them up before winter, warding off the lice that seem to appear when cattle get run-down in the cold weather. Abby watches him shake hands with Cameron. He looks thinner and more tired than usual, and he's hay-spattered and rough. He sounds rough too with a broad flat country accent. She hadn't realised how small-town he is until she sees him slouching here in the kitchen beside Cameron who is so sophisticated and smart. Cameron is significantly taller than her father, and he sits down quickly after shaking hands, sensitive to Steve's status as man of the house. Abby silently thanks him. She feels a surge of warmth towards him and is suddenly glad she brought him along.

Over several cups of tea they talk about Matt, and Abby is too preoccupied with her brother's disappearance to worry about the significance of Cameron looking in through this window on her family life. Steve has been out to Matt's house several times and he's been trying to call, but he can't raise Matt anywhere. Abby too has left about a million messages on Matt's phone since her father alerted her to his absence. She imagines him lying at the base of a cliff somewhere in the mountains, spread-eagled and still on the ground, his phone ringing into the silence. Eventually the battery will go flat and the phone will be dead. She shudders at the word. It can't be possible that Matt's not coming back.

After Brenda's cakes are packed away, Abby takes Cameron out to Matt's place. There's just enough time before dinner, and even though her father says everything seems normal out there, Abby wants to see for herself. Her father might have missed something.

Matt's digs are on the other side of town, a run-down old house on a friend's property. They drive along a dirt road and then onto an uneven farm track. The WRX scrapes along, nudging through the long grass.

The house is a dilapidated white fibro with a rusty tin roof. Unkempt scraggly rosebushes grow out the front, remnants of a previous era when this was the farm-manager's residence and a wife tended the garden. Cameron pulls up and they clamber from the car.

It's unbearably quiet, like a cemetery. The dull thud of their car doors closing echoes in the empty carport. Abby remembers visiting here in happier times. Card games with Matt and his mates that stretched way into the night: five hundred and euchre. Clusters of empty beer bottles on the table. Fat steaks on the barbecue; Matt expertly testing them with his favourite pair of tongs.

Out of habit, she goes to the door and knocks. The only sound is the wind rolling under the eaves, a cow bellowing somewhere across the paddock. The house is silent. The windows smeared with dust. All she feels is emptiness.

She turns the door handle and they go inside—no locks around here. It is deathly quiet. The fridge hums and several floorboards creak beneath their feet. Cameron follows her through the rooms. It's sad and subdued. There's not much of anything here: an empty Coke can on the kitchen table, a breadboard with a few dried out crumbs, brown-stained coffee cups on the bench, a bread knife in the sink, dead flies on the window sill, feet up.

The bed is as if Matt has just stepped from it and gone outside for a pee. Abby can see the indentation in the pillow where his head last lay. It's eerie. More than a week since Matt slept here.

She reads the note on the kitchen bench. *Gone bush. Don't try to find me.* That's it. Nothing more. What can she tell from that? Gone for a holiday? Or a need to escape, feeling down, can't cope, tussling with negative feelings, going to take my life?

She has no idea what the note means, can't read between the lines. She is the one closest to him and yet she doesn't understand. If she'd been calling like she promised, she might have had some inkling, some clue of what was going on in his head.

Cameron puts his arm around her and she leans against him, feeling exhausted in the circle of his support. But there is no consolation to be had. She has to start looking for Matt. And what will she do if she finds him?

They go home via the police station. The police record Matt's absence, but they seem unconcerned. The note, they say, suggests he is coming back. Perhaps he needs some space for a while.

Abby is frustrated by their casual attitude. One of the policemen is a mate of Matt's. When she says there's a possibility Matt might have been suicidal, he laughs.

'Not Matt,' he says. 'He's a rock. He'll be fine.'

What would they know? Abby thinks, and her guilt threatens to engulf her. None of this would be necessary if she'd kept her word. She'd have known Matt was heading downhill, she'd have heard something in his voice.

The following morning, Abby takes her father's four-wheel drive ute and starts a search. She has packed food and camping gear for an overnight stay in the mountains, which will allow her to cover more territory, although she knows she can't check everywhere. Cameron sits patiently in the passenger seat and endures her silence as they head towards the High Country, spinning first across the green river flats dotted with spreading gums and cattle and patches of remnant bush, then climbing up through the foothills into the forest.

The route winds through stringy-bark country, scrubby and stony, giving way to tall wet forest laced with the fragrant tang of peppermint and musk. Here the road narrows and roughens into gravel. Eventually the forest opens into a wide grassy clearing at Sheepyard Flat, almost park-like, with white-trunked trees. It's deserted—no battered Nissan, no Matt. Abby suppresses a tug of disappointment.

She feels close to Matt here. He's always loved this part of the bush. It's not particularly remote, but the Howqua River is nearby and good for trout-fishing. Their father used to bring them here for weekends away from home when their mother was ill. Gran would stay and tend to Grace while the rest of the family escaped. Fishing and campfires were a good cure: the lines of strain would ease from their father's mouth, Matt's silly honking laugh would re-emerge, and Abby would remember how to smile. They concocted ghost stories, played charades, cooked potatoes wrapped in alfoil in the fire.

She pulls up outside Fry's Hut so Cameron can take a look inside. It's beautifully built—one of her favourites—with a lovely deep veranda, a classic tin roof and chimney, chunky horizontal slabs for walls, and small divided windows. These days, lots of people camp here, especially weekends. The place smells of moisture and soot and ashes and dust. Weekdays, it's quiet: a hangout for bush rats and marsupial mice and magpies digging up grubs.

They leave the hut and walk down to the river. The water rolls by, chattering over rocks. Abby watches the current swirling and eddying. It swells along the shore then spirals out midstream to gather around protruding stones like a translucent scarf.

'Matt likes to fish here,' she says. 'He's a fly-fisherman—not bad at it. Ties his own flies.' She thinks of Matt sitting at the kitchen table in his house, chewing his lip as he works the delicate convolutions of completing a new fly. His instruments are laid out carefully on the table, the hook clamped in the fly-tying vice. His blunt-nailed fingers are surprisingly deft at spinning the thread around the body of the fly to perfect the taper. 'You ever tried fly-fishing?' she asks Cameron.

He gazes upstream where light glimmers on the water like silver tinsel. 'I'd like to,' he says. 'But I guess I'd be bad at it like most outdoors things.'

'When Matt gets back I'll get him to take you. He's a good teacher.'

From Sheepyard Flat they head up into the mountains proper. At Matt's secret fishing haunts, Abby pulls up and checks the river. No Nissan, no Matt. They venture onto rough tracks where four-wheel drive is necessary, and the bush whips past, damp and tangy—the lemony fragrance of eucalypts, the dense smell of rotting wood. Abby almost smiles when Cameron snaps in his seatbelt and grasps the dashboard as the ute grinds over wash-outs.

'This is not easy driving,' he says. 'You're good at it.'

The track weaves higher into snow gum country. A crowd of slender trunks reaches towards the road like eager Tour de France fans waving their arms.

'It's beautiful here under snow,' Abby says nostalgically, thinking of skiing up here with Matt. 'All the trunks and leaves crusted with ice. It's nice to put on skis and stride along the track. You go into a kind of trance. Just you and the bush. It's hard to describe.'

'I like downhill skiing,' Cameron says.

'Me too, but this kind of skiing is good too. You dissolve into the landscape and feel the air. No hurry. You listen to the wind in the branches, leaves clanking with their load of snow. And the colours in the trunks—all the silvers and greys and reds and greens. There's nobody here. Just you and a few birds. Nothing else.'

Matt loves it too—surely he wouldn't leave all that behind, his love of the bush and the snow, the feeling of carving turns downhill in fresh powder.

She hopes to find Matt's Nissan in the car park at the start of the Bluff hiking trail, but the parking area is empty and the snow gums huddle silently around the clearing, holding their secrets close.

'Should we go up?' she asks Cameron. 'It's Matt's favourite place.'

'I don't mind,' he says. 'Do we have time?'

She checks her watch. 'If we climb quickly and come straight down again we could do it. We've got lots of country to cover, but it doesn't matter if we set up camp in the dark. We should take a look up there anyway, even though his car's not here. Just in case.'

'Okay,' he says. 'Let's go.'

Abby stuffs a few things in a backpack which Cameron insists on carrying, and they take to the trail. It's steep, and they puff their way uphill, blowing like draught horses.

Cameron has a long stride, but Abby is driven. She wants to get up there—to Matt's country. She knows it's insensitive, but she leaves Cameron behind.

It's hard work, thrusting up the track, but she submerges her mind into the rhythm of breathing and walking. This is how she manages with a heavy pack on multi-day walks with Matt. You breathe and stride, pushing one leg through and then the other, feeling the way through your feet, moving like a machine, not thinking. Distance reels out slowly beneath your boots, the clean air tears deep in your lungs and sweat runs down your back, no matter how cold the weather might be.

She feels Matt with her as she ascends the trail. She sees the shape of his back, burdened with his own loaded pack, the yak in him emerging as he pulls ahead of her and skates to the top with the clouds. Eventually, as she climbs, the forest breaks open to a grassy plain studded with rocks. The craggy face of the mountain juts against the sky, and in the distance, purple peaks ripple along the horizon. Abby feels the cold wind on her damp skin. A few more weeks and snow will begin to fall here. Winter is on its way; Matt's favourite season.

Soon Cameron arrives and stands behind her, panting. He coils his arms around her, pulls her against him. 'I see what you mean,' he says. 'The view is amazing. No wonder Matt likes it here.'

She feels his lips pressing into her hair and closes her eyes. The High Plains are infinite and she can't bear to look out there across the folds of the landscape, the steep topographical lines that cluster close on a map, the vast wide valleys, the stretch of trees and bush and heath. Matt could be anywhere. How will she ever find him?

They scoff a few handfuls of nuts and chocolate and gulp water before the descent. All the way down Abby is wondering if he's thrown himself from a cliff.

Back in the car, they pass the Bluff Hut, which is all new corrugated iron, rebuilt after a bushfire razed the old building. Abby doesn't like the new hut—as much as it attempts to mimic its predecessor, it isn't the same. She took shelter here in bad weather one time with Matt. In a blizzard, they hunkered down inside the old hut, stoking a fire that shed no heat, curling up in sleeping-bags dampened by moisture. She remembers waking to a fresh white world and hummocks of powdery glittering snow, the squeaky dry crystals crunching and compressing beneath their boots. They made snowballs and tossed them to splatter against each other and the walls of the hut. Then they packed their gear and skied higher, finding clean unmarked slopes to sign with the sweeping curves of their skis.

They both discovered the High Country through their father's passion. He introduced them to the landscape and wrote the names of the peaks into their hearts. After their mother's death, he stopped coming up here, and Matt and Abby began to come alone. There grew between them a strong sibling bond—nothing weird about it, no matter what some townspeople said, but a straight and solid spiritual connection. She and Matt were simply comfortable up there together. They liked to test themselves against the weather, and they felt equipped and competent to deal with most conditions. One time they were holed up in a tent for two entire days. They slept, talked, ate, sat in silence, not needing words. Sometimes they brought friends with them too: Abby tagging along with Matt and his mates. The guys would start out guffawing at a girl trying to keep up with the men, but Abby kept pace with the best of them. She was a bush girl too, at home in the mountains, and no embarrassment to her brother.

As she drives across the slowly transforming terrain beneath the shifting shapes of clouds, Abby realises Matt is all over this country. He's wherever she looks, everything coloured by memories. He's in the peaks, the convoluted trails, the huts.

All day, she and Cameron grind up and down tracks, ticking off places Matt might have gone: Mount Magdala, McAllister Springs, Mount Howitt. Abby's eyes are constantly searching for her brother's frame—the tall lean hungry look of him, the shaggy hair, the loose shirts, his battered hat. She scans the tracks for his car, checks pull-outs in case he's parked off the road. She sits by streams and watches the current, keeps hoping perhaps Matt is at some other stream, wading up a distant river in a remote part of the park.

But as the circumference of her search expands, Abby begins to wonder what she would do if they came across his car and no Matt? Would she really want to look for him? There are plenty of rugged rock faces in these mountains . . . good for jumping from if that's what you want. She could search for months and never find him. And there are so many obscure places where nobody goes. Her heart thuds a sick slow beat as she thinks of losing him, perhaps forever. If he's gone, it's partly her fault.

On the cusp of evening, she chooses a high place to set up camp, looking out across the fading horizon of jutting peaks. In the blue light of encroaching dark, Cameron helps her fetch wood for a fire. She cobbles sticks and lumps of rotting branches together to form strong flames that flow like liquid in the lick of the breeze. They eat pesto pasta and tins of peaches, and they talk as the flames subside to smouldering orange embers—the slow trickle of fire drawing patterns on their faces.

Abby speaks of Matt, her bond with him and this country. In quiet lulls, Cameron speaks of his own family: the lack of love shown by his parents, his estranged sister living in Perth, as far away as she can get from his parents. Abby has always thought her family was dislocated and strange, but despite their difficulties, they have always enjoyed love in its convoluted and twisted shape. Cameron has lived a privileged existence, but there are gaps in his upbringing where affection should reside. His family bonds are loose at best, whereas Abby's run deep.

As the evening chill tightens its grip, Cameron moves closer and wedges her against him near the fire. She leans against his chest, soaking up the warmth. A few days ago, she was pulling away from him. Now she is closer than ever, piggy-backing on his strength. She feels a tug of guilt. It will be harder than ever to make the break that has to come.

The cold deepens, the fire subsides, and they retreat to the tent. Inside they unzip the sleeping-bags and make a cloud of down to hide beneath. Bodies close, they strip off and press skin to skin. They make slow, sad, tender love then fall asleep in a tangle of arms and legs and pillows and bags.

20

'Why didn't we ever talk about Mum's death?'

Abby is in the kitchen of the Mansfield farmhouse with her father. She and Cameron returned late that afternoon from their unsuccessful mountain search, and she's been teary and down ever since—it was far easier to keep a cap on her emotions when she was doing something constructive. Now that she is back in the house her guilt hovers like rain clouds in winter. Outside, it's a wild night. Wind roars in the pines, and the dead leaves on the oaks rattle like the voice of death. Cameron has gone to bed with a book, and Brenda is in the lounge room watching TV.

Her father leans over his cup of tea and shrugs. 'I dunno,' he says. 'It was a difficult time.'

'But we *never* talked about it,' Abby says. 'Not even after, and I mean years later. Why not?'

Steve scratches his head as if mulling on a maths problem. 'I suppose I just couldn't cope,' he says slowly. 'I was a mess.

All those years of watching out for your mother and then she was gone.'

Abby remembers the emptiness of her own struggles, and for the first time she contemplates how it might have been for her father, alone with two teenagers. Grace had been a central pillar, the lynchpin around which their lives revolved. They were bound to her cycles of depression, and then suddenly the structure was gone, and the way it was taken from them was horrific.

'I guess it was too hard,' her father is saying. 'I found it tough enough just trying to find a way to survive. It didn't seem like talking would help. I thought it would just bring up all the stuff I was trying not to think about. And I felt terrible because I couldn't help you and Matt. I was so messed up with grief.' He takes a sip of tea. 'I've always felt bad about that.'

'We managed because we had to, Matt and me,' Abby says.

'The way you kids coped put me to shame.' Steve shakes his head.

Abby hadn't even known about bipolar disorder till she was at university. She'd been at a party in Melbourne when she heard someone talking about mental illness—they were talking about someone who'd been hospitalised. It had been such a dawning to discover what her mother had suffered, to categorise it. And in some bizarre way it helped to know her mother's condition had a name. Abby had hit the internet and conducted a search. The list of brilliant and artistic people who'd been afflicted with bipolar disorder was astounding. Ernest Hemingway, Vincent van Gogh, Ludwig Beethoven, Isaac Newton, Virginia Woolf, Albert Einstein, Kurt Cobain. Reading accounts of the illness had been enlightening. It was her mother exactly: impulsivity, insomnia, mood shifts, heightened energy, fast speech, distractibility, reckless behaviour, depression, inability to get out of bed—Abby was able to tick off every one.

'The doctors thought they were pretty smart when they put a label on your mother's head, because it explained everything,' Steve says. 'But they couldn't do anything much to help her, except remove her personality with drugs—and as you know she hated that, the way the drugs wiped her out.'

'Do you think medication could have saved her?' It's something Abby has always wondered.

Her father stares into his cup and fiddles with the handle. Maybe he doesn't want to answer this question, and maybe he can't, maybe no-one can. And what difference would it make if he said yes, anyway? How would it change things, except to dredge up all those useless emotions that bog you down: regret, sadness, guilt and blame? Abby thinks of Matt and her fear swells with the destructive potential of a tsunami that might rise and rise and collapse over her and claw her out to sea.

'I could have done something for Matt, you know,' she says, guilt-racked. 'For a while I was ringing him every day because I knew he might be down. But then I got caught up with Cameron and I let Matt go, I neglected him. I've been a terrible sister.' Tears are building, but she fights to hold them back.

Her father contemplates her with a furrowed brow, serious. 'You can't blame yourself,' he says. 'Matt's a grown man. He could have asked for help—he knew you were there.'

Abby is unconsoled. 'But maybe it's not like that,' she says. 'Mum didn't call for help, did she?'

Her father's face is suddenly very grey, very haggard.

'I hate to say this, Dad, but she left us.'

Her father is shaking his head. 'She wouldn't have seen it that way. She couldn't cope anymore. Weird things went on in her head—you know that. She loved you and Matt more than anything.'

Abby hears what he says, but it doesn't help. The despair is still there, the ache of loss, and the feeling that it simply isn't fair. 'I know she loved us, Dad, but she let us down. I need her in my life. Not dead in the ground.'

Tears brim in Steve's eyes. 'Don't fool yourself into thinking she made a choice,' he says.

Abby feels a pulse of anger. She can't see how things could get that bad; her mother should have known her children needed her. 'There's always a choice,' she insists.

'Not when you are as sick as she was.'

But Abby knows her mother must have planned her death—things like that don't just happen. Her mother must have thought it through, and there must have been a point at which she made a decision. But Abby's flare of anger subsides as quickly as it arose. She doesn't want to consider what hell her mother had crossed to arrive at that place.

'It was very different with your mother,' her father says. 'Matt's not like her.'

'How do you know?' Abby asks, teetering now on the slippery edge of control, tears threatening. 'He told me he gets awfully down sometimes and can't dig himself out. What if he's done something to himself?'

Her father grips her arm with a rough dry hand. 'I know you're worried,' he says. 'We all are. But you know how Matt likes to be alone, and this isn't the first time he's gone bush for a week or two. He's bound to show up. You didn't find

201

any signs of him out there in the mountains, and that has to be a good thing. You should try to see it that way. We have to stay positive.'

Abby wipes her nose on her sleeve like a child. 'I've been worried that I might have Mum's illness too,' she says. 'It's possible, isn't it? I have her genes.'

Her father's craggy face spreads into a kindly smile. 'I don't think you're bipolar.'

'How can you know that? It might surface if I have kids, like it did for her. How can I consider having a family if there's even the slightest risk?'

Her father tightens his grip on her arm. 'Abby, you haven't got it. You're normal, not like your mother. She was always different, always a bit strange. If Gran was still around she would tell you. The illness showed up when your mother was a teenager. Her father had it too. You never knew him—he died before you were born.'

Abby looks at him as her thoughts shift slowly into place like puzzle pieces sliding together on a computer screen. Suddenly she understands. 'Grandpa suicided too, didn't he? It wasn't a heart attack.'

Her father scrapes wearily to his feet and pours the dregs of his tea down the sink. Abby knows she is right, she feels it in his silence. Poor Gran: first her husband then her daughter. No wonder she was so available to help. Maybe she felt she owed it to them.

Her father turns from the bench and sits down again, his face long and sad. 'I'm sorry I wasn't a better father,' he says. 'And I hope when you have kids, you'll understand. Because you should seriously consider having a family one day Abby, you'd be a good mum. And Cameron's a good man. I like him. He's here putting up with all this, and he's supporting you. You don't want to let that go.'

Something in Abby tightens, like water turning into ice. 'I'm not interested in getting married.'

'Well, Cameron is,' her father says. 'It's written all over him. He's in for the long haul.' He stands up, stiffness clogging his limbs as he straightens.

Abby stands too. Her father comes round the table and encloses her in a bear hug. It's hard and firm and close, good. She hugs him back, feeling the lean wiriness of his back, like Matt's, all ribs and bony knobs.

'I reckon Matt will come home,' he says, releasing her and briefly running a hand over her head. 'You have to keep your hopes up.'

'I'll try,' she says.

She follows him out of the kitchen then splits off to her bedroom where Cameron, still reading his book, looks up at her with a smile.

———◆———

The trip back to Canberra begins quietly. Cameron allows Abby her silences in which she mulls over her father's observation last night that Cameron is angling for commitment. The thought sits like a stone in her guts, and she finds it difficult not to flinch when he reaches every now and then to squeeze her leg. She knows he simply wants to show his support and let her know he's there, but fear is roiling in her like a storm. It's enough to be worried about Matt, and now she has this to think about: this plummeting feeling that she has allowed things to go too far.

She's aware that her anxiety around permanence is not a rational beast. Just by wanting her in that way, Cameron is asking more than she can give. The butterflies of escape are whirling in her feet. She needs to carve off, needs to project herself elsewhere, shift herself into a future where she is safely alone. Matt would understand.

Cameron is oblivious—he must think she is stewing on her missing brother. He plays soft music to fill the spaces: Vivaldi's *Four Seasons*, Pachelbel's *Canon in D*, Tchaikovsky's *Swan Lake*. Abby submerges in the fluctuating tide of the music. She holds her emotions inside and stares out the window.

They are spinning along the internal bypass through Albury when her phone rings, flashing Matt's number.

'It's him,' she mouths to Cameron as she rams the phone to her ear. 'Matt?'

'Hey. How's things?'

Relief floods her when she hears his voice. He sounds jolly and cheerful, unforgivably relaxed. For a moment, she wishes she could hug him then sudden anger shoots through her like a charge of electricity. 'I'm crap actually,' she says. 'Where the hell have you been?'

He hesitates. 'I've been north. Central Oz. You ever seen that country? It's bloody amazing. I walked the Larapinta Trail.'

'You've been for a hike?' She can't believe it. 'Why didn't you tell someone?'

'I left a note.'

'You call that a note? *Gone bush. Don't try to find me.* What sort of note is that?'

'I didn't think anyone would mind,' he says, stung. 'What would anyone care?'

'Well, sorry, but people do care. We've all been frantic. We thought you might have killed yourself or something.'

There's silence on the phone, then, 'That's a bit rich.'

'Last time I saw you in Mansfield, you were telling me how down you were. How you were worried you might be like Mum. Did you expect me to think you'd gone off for a picnic? I've raked the High Country trying to find you. We've all been going crazy with worry.'

Matt says nothing.

'Are you all right?' she asks, trying to stifle her rage.

'I'm fine.'

'Everything's okay?'

'Yes.'

'Then what the hell were you thinking, disappearing like that?'

Silence again, then a measure of contrition. 'There was no work on, and I was sitting there on my own, and saw a doco on Central Australia, so thought I'd go and do the trail. I didn't think you lot would go off like a pack of chooks . . .'

'What were we supposed to think? No car, no you, crap useless note . . .'

'I'll leave a better note next time.'

'No, you'll ring me next time. Then I'll know you're okay.'

'Where did you go looking for me?'

'Everywhere. The Bluff, Mount Magdala. I've been on a complete bloody tour of the High Country.'

'Nice, eh?' There's a note of humour in his voice. 'I gave you a good excuse to get out there.'

Abby's not ready to joke about it yet. 'I'm glad you're not dead at the bottom of a cliff. You've no idea how many places

I've checked, terrified I'd find your dead body. Even Brenda was upset.'

Matt scoffs. 'I didn't think she had any feelings.'

'Yeah, well your days of privacy are over. Brenda's going to take you under her wing, and Dad's rotten with guilt for neglecting you. He'll be proposing fishing trips every weekend.'

'Tell them to leave me alone.'

'*You* tell them. It's your disappearing stunt that's triggered it.'

'I'll go back to central Australia.'

'Up to you, but there's not too many vineyards round there. Can't imagine what you'll do for a job.'

'Too hot for me anyway,' he grunts.

'Then it's a roast every Sunday with Brenda. Happy days. You'll enjoy that.'

'I'll tell her to piss off.'

'I don't think so, Matt. This is part of being in a family. You should have thought a bit more before you skived off. Now you'll have to make it up to them.'

'I've got nothing to make up to anybody.'

'No? Well, you can start by ringing them and telling them you're okay. And Matt?'

'Yeah?'

'Good luck with that.'

PART III

PART III

21

The four-wheel-drive trail up into the Brindabella mountains is not as rough as Daphne expected. It's been a long time since she came this way, years and fires and roadworks have rendered the route almost unrecognisable. The government has been working to improve access since major bushfires burnt ninety per cent of the park. Now it's almost a highway.

They are in a university vehicle and Abby is driving. She organised this trip especially for Daphne, but she had to tie it in with checking her kangaroos so she could justify the use of the four-wheel drive—she said there was no way her old Laser would make it up the trails. They also had to arrange this excursion for a weekday because the rangers don't like vehicles going into the park on weekends when there might be hikers around; apparently cars disrupt the ambience of the bush.

Daphne is delighted to be here, of course. Pam wasn't very happy about her coming; she thought a whole day might be

209

too much for an old lady. But Daphne wasn't missing out for anything. The weather is fine and cool and Daphne is determined she will enjoy every moment of it. It's not often you get an offer like this: a chance to visit the locked-up parts of the mountains in a car.

Abby's boyfriend is accompanying them. He had to con his boss into letting him come by saying he had a rare opportunity to access a remote part of the park. He says he's planning to do a story about one of the historic huts, and maybe even a feature on the moon walk and the role of the satellite dish that used to stand in this valley. Daphne likes this idea, and she told him she'd be happy to share her experiences with him.

He's sitting in the back seat with his knees under his chin. Daphne offered to let him sit in the front because of his long legs, but he insisted he was fine. He said he was looking forward to being a back-seat driver so he could deflate Abby's cockiness about her driving skills.

Daphne is pleased to meet Abby's boyfriend. He's a nice young man, very solid; Abby could do a lot worse. Abby, however, doesn't seem particularly attentive to him. Daphne wants to tell Abby that good men are few and far between, but she suspects that stating her opinion would be overstepping the mark. Abby needs to make her own decisions.

Abby looks comfortable behind the wheel—she's such a competent young lady. Gates, gears, four-wheel drives, it all seems so easy to her. Daphne likes to see independence in a woman. When she was younger, she too was very capable. Nowadays, young women seem very limited, their interest absorbed by hair, fingernails and phones. Daphne is astounded every time she sees one of those nail parlours in the shopping mall. To her mind such places represent society gone wrong—people with too much money and no real purpose in life.

Fortunately Abby isn't like this, which is why Daphne appreciates her. Abby has class and individual flair, natural beauty—the very best type. She's no manicured fashion queen, but she has her own style. Daphne likes the way Abby knocks up clothes from other people's cast-offs, dividing and combining segments to create interesting garments. She says she doesn't do it often because she has so little time, but it's certainly creative and a good use for discarded clothing. Abby is definitely her own person, an alluring enigma. No wonder Cameron is in love with her—Daphne sees the rich sparkle in his eyes every time he looks at Abby. He wants more, it's obvious.

They drive up through a maze of grey trunks: mountain gums with twisted bark. Daphne remembers droving the cattle up here, using dogs and stockwhips to push the beasts away from the valley. Back then, stock work was largely men's work, although female riders sometimes came along, like her. When a lead-cow hit the front it was easy. The cow would lower her head and nod purposefully along, drawing the other cattle with her. They would wend their way up the track—a line of black shuffling backs and flicking tails, riders following. As they ascended, grassy meadows would entice the beasts off the track to graze. While they were tearing mouthfuls of wiry grass, the riders would light a fire and put a billy on to boil for a strong cup of tea. It was best not to hurry or the cattle became unsettled and difficult to handle. Once they'd eaten their fill, they were more placid and would leave slowly and lumber up the trail with the dogs panting behind, the men further back on horses. Over a number of days, they would work their way up the contours to the river flats where the cows would slow to a crawl, grazing the green pick. As the flats spread wider, so would the beasts, intent on feeding. The riders would thin out too, following small mobs that had detached from the larger whole, so they could bring them back together again at dusk.

Usually they spent a few days on the flats, letting the stock grow fat and slow and lazy, the sheen rising in their coats. The grass was rich and lush, and when the cattle were sated, the riders would push them on again, around the flanks of Mount Bimberi and up to the summer pastures where snow gums grew twisted and contorted in the ferocious winds that shredded the plateau. On still days, the cattle roamed the tops, making their way across grazing heaven.

Abby drives up into the heart of the mountains and stops at Daphne's favourite hut for morning tea. At the gate Cameron takes the keys, releases the padlock and lets them in so they can park in front of the building on the grass. Daphne opens the window so she can inhale the fragrant alpine air. The grass around the hut is cropped short by kangaroos and wallabies that have weaselled their way under the fence.

The hut has brick foundations and weatherboard walls—it's been rebuilt since Daphne's day. Back then it was a tin-roofed slab structure with thick poles for corner posts, and it provided excellent shelter, good for a night's sleep out of the weather while droving, so long as you didn't mind sharing with a few bush rats. Sometimes, if it was raining, the dogs would slink in for warmth.

Cameron does a quick inspection tour, and reports gas bottles around the side and evidence of a septic system. It's a far cry from the basic facilities Daphne and the men considered luxury many years ago. She goes for a slow amble around the hut, and when she finishes her circuit, she lowers herself into a folding chair that Cameron has readied for her. Abby produces a thermos and pours tea into mugs. They sit and eat a Boston bun, the fluffy white cream sticking to their lips. Daphne hears a shrike-thrush calling in the bush. The sound of the river rises from some distance downhill.

'Not a bad spot, is it?' Daphne says. 'Civilisation in the middle of nowhere.' She's pleased to revisit this place and share it with the young people. They must find it hard to imagine the young woman she once was, looking at her now, but to Daphne it seems not so long ago that she was last in this place. She remembers stockmen milling around the hut, horses hobbled in the clearing, the distant bellows of cattle out across the flats. If she closes her eyes, the new building is gone and the old hut is back. The bush is much the same, the mountain tops unchanged.

They finish the last of the tea and Boston bun, then Abby packs things away in a box. Daphne catches Cameron ogling the young woman's hips. She supposes they are sexually active—Pam tells her all young people are these days. Abby is lovely, and Cameron is such a good-looking man, with his dark hair, olive skin and affable smile. But there's something in their dynamic that's not quite right: a simmering tension?—Daphne's not quite sure what it is.

Back in the four-wheel drive, they retrace their route along the road above the river, a pretty watercourse, bumbling over stones and rocks. Then they turn onto the mountain trail and make their way uphill, climbing gradually through forest.

The trail is rougher and windier here, and the driving slower. Daphne wearies from holding on to the armrest as they lurch and jolt over wash-outs and gutted furrows. At times the track is steep and Abby puts the vehicle in low-four and keeps her foot steady on the accelerator while they grind uphill at a walking pace. She holds the wheel firmly and stops talking, concentrating instead on choosing the best place to direct the front wheels.

Finally they emerge from the trees onto the plateau where the land rolls in tune with the clouds. Wind scatters and fossicks among the tussocks, granite festoons the mountain tops, and ranges peel away in layers, purple and brooding, receding into the distance.

Below the walking track to one of the peaks, Abby stops the car and sets up a picnic. Cameron organises the folding chairs and helps Daphne to a seat before gathering a selection of gourmet treats on a plate for her. Daphne smiles to herself. The food is strange: marinated artichokes, chilli olives, herb bread, hummus dip, sun-dried tomatoes. The tomatoes are stiff and tough, hard work for her old teeth. She politely leaves them on the side of her plate and focuses on the more palatable morsels.

They are lucky the weather is calm up high today. On a windy day, they wouldn't be able to sit here enjoying lunch. 'This is granite country,' she tells the others as she eats. 'It's always been my favourite place. Doug's too. We used to ride here together. Kings above the clouds.' She points west towards the tree line where the open country merges into bush. 'There used to be a hut down there. Some yards too, for the horses. We camped there some years on the brumby hunt. It was a good spot. High but sheltered. We built our brumby yards down the hill a-ways and tricked the brumbies into running in. Caught ourselves some good horses that way.'

She sets down her piece of herb bread and squints across the landscape. 'This is moth country too,' she says. 'Bogong moths. You can find thousands of them up here in summer. The Aborigines used to eat them—they came for miles to catch them and cook them up. It was good tucker. They used to camp in the valleys then climb the peaks for moths.'

'Hard country to live in,' Abby says. 'Did you know many Aborigines? Were there many around when you were growing up?'

Daphne feels a sliver of cold creep up her back. 'None living up here,' she says. 'The only Aborigine I knew was that stockman I told you about who came to work with us sometimes.'

'That's sad, isn't it?' Abby muses, staring out across the landscape. 'Sad that they were all gone from this place. But the moths still come, I suppose—only no-one eats them anymore.' She points to the walking track. 'We should go up there. I'd like to see the view.'

'You young people should go.' Daphne says. 'I'm happy to sit here. I can get in the car if I get cold.'

'Are you sure?' Abby looks concerned, but Cameron is keen—Daphne sees it in the eager way he glances at Abby, as if he could eat her up.

'Yes, go.' Daphne waves them away.

Abby hesitates and casts a sideways look at Cameron. But Daphne is determined the youngsters should have time up here together without her tagging along.

'Go,' she says again. 'I don't mind being on my own. And I might take a nap. You lot have worn me out.'

She watches Abby and Cameron sort themselves with water bottles and hats then start up the track. From her folding chair, she follows their progress as they work their way along the trail up into the bush, disappearing eventually among a grove of snow gums.

For a while she hears the burble of their voices carried down on the tail of the wind. Then that is gone too, and all that is left is the rustle of swirling air, and the inherent sound of the landscape, pressing its shoulders against the sky.

She nestles deeper into her chair and looks around. Now that it is quiet, an insistent thudding sound beats in her head. It comes and goes: intermittent white noise she's been trying to ignore. But she can't help worrying about the little falling episodes that pop up out of the blue. There she was the other day in the vegie garden, planting potatoes, and suddenly she found herself on the ground. She has no recollection of anything in between. One minute, she was pushing a piece of potato into the soil, the next she was lying on the grass beside the raised vegie bed looking up at the sky. She didn't tell Pam, of course, couldn't face the fussing. And she was all right within minutes anyway. No real after-effects. These things must happen to old people all the time; you can't be running to the doctor every five minutes to gripe about every little problem.

She gazes across the stretch of wild land that surrounds her, and peace settles on her soul. Here she is, back in the higher realms of her grass castle, which she thought she might never see again. It's rugged and untamed and beautiful, even better than memory, and how wonderful it is to be immersed in it after so long. Time is meaningless in all this space. Seasons pass, years wither, fire burns, snow falls. But in essence not much has changed here since Daphne was young. The mountains will endure long after people are gone—and this is a reassuring thought. Perhaps it's good after all, that this country was parcelled into a park. What would have happened to it otherwise? Landholders would have built big houses to take in the view. They would have built sheds and fences and yards, roads, farm dams, essential infrastructure. They would have ruined it.

Land ownership is a strange thing, she thinks. If people are allowed to use the land, to own it, they make their mark, they tame things. Her family changed things in a limited way, and their impacts were relatively minimal. But what if there was no national park and they had stayed? What if they'd had to sell to other landholders—people who weren't as wedded to conserving country as her family was? What then?

In the end, maybe this was really the right outcome.

She thinks of Johnny Button the stockman, and his people. This land belonged to them before white people came. His people were pushed off by her family and other settlers. They were disconnected, cut off. But Johnny didn't blame anyone: she remembers his smile, his easy ways, unmarked by anger or resentment. He accepted it and lived his bond with country as best he could, going bush, disappearing on walkabout. She never understood it when she was young. She accepted the assessment of the other stockmen, that Johnny was a little bit crazy. But now as she sits here in this country, home of the clouds, she sees how the land lives in you, how you hold it in your bones.

Her father always said the land was empty before his family came here. But Daphne knows it wasn't and she's sure he knew it too. If only she could dig up his secrets, hear the things he knew but wouldn't tell about the Aborigines—all the knowledge that was buried in his silences. But he's been dead

KAREN VIGGERS

for decades now, and the past will have to remain in the past.
And yet it never does, does it? Consequences, punishment,
guilt, regret: these things never die. The tendrils of the past
stretch their long convoluted fingers into the present, and even
further, into the future. And there's no going back.

22

Abby and Cameron leave Daphne and follow the steep overgrown trail through the silvery grasses and up towards the peak. The track meanders around bogs and over boulders, among glades of snow gums with their narrow twisted branches spreading like thin bedraggled arms. Abby takes the lead, choosing the path of least resistance.

'If this was summer,' she says, flinging conversation over her shoulder, 'we'd be walking among wild flowers—alpine buttercups and snow daisies and everlastings and trigger plants. They're the prettiest flowers you'll ever see. And they come in the most delicate yellows and pinks and mauves.'

Cameron is frowning, she notices, focused on the ground, trying to dodge the wet patches that populate the trail. 'Where's all this water coming from?' he asks. 'I thought we were in the middle of a drought.'

'There's always water up here,' she says. 'Especially in winter. It runs out of the mosses and bogs and soaks. And

219

when clouds come across, even if it doesn't rain, you get fog drip—fine drizzle that seeps out of everything and makes it all wet.'

'Next time we should come here in summer then,' he says. 'The proper dry season.'

'So you can see the flowers?'

'No, so I can keep my feet dry.'

'Then there'd be March flies,' she says. 'So you have to take your pick. Wet feet in winter or March flies in summer.'

'We could come before March,' he grumbles. 'Then it would be perfect.'

'March flies don't follow calendars,' she tells him. 'They follow the heat. And your jeans would be a beacon. They like blue. It brings them in. You'd be a perfect magnet for bites.'

When Abby was a kid, she and Matt used to sit for hours, decommissioning March flies. They would catch them as they hovered over boots and trousers then they would restrain them and carefully pull out the proboscises before releasing the flies back into the air. Some days it seemed she and Matt disarmed an entire battalion, and yet there were always more flies to take up the charge. Now she supposes it was cruel, but she and Matt derived a depraved kind of pleasure from it—revenge for all the stings they endured over the years. Now, on the cusp of winter, there are no flies of course, and the only sting is from the breath of the wind that drives up from Victoria and accelerates across the high tops before reaching the Brindabellas. Abby pauses on a ridge to inspect the grey clouds massing to the south.

'Do you think there's any rain in those clouds?' Cameron asks.

'No,' she says. 'It's all just show and pretence. Promises

without delivery. I'm sick of believing in clouds and weather. They always disappoint.'

She glances at him and catches something in his look, a furtive intensity that unsettles her. What's he thinking? she wonders nervously. Since they came back from Mansfield, her father's words about marriage and children have been rattling in her mind like loose sharp stones. She's afraid Cameron wants to rope her in, like one of the wild brumbies Daphne used to catch. Perhaps if she keeps him walking he won't be able to speak. She puts her head down and strides fast up the path.

'Have you heard from Matt?' Cameron asks, puffing behind her.

'He rang the other day,' she says. 'He's landed a temporary job setting up tows for the ski season. It doesn't pay much, but it'll keep him out of trouble till they need him back at the vineyard.'

'Do they make wine where he works? Why can't he help out in the winery if it's quiet in the vineyard?'

'Same old,' she says. 'He never did any studies after high school. I keep telling him he ought to get a certificate in viticulture or something, but he can't be bothered.'

She pushes upslope even faster, trying to make Cameron gasp for air so he'll stop talking. She feels wild and loose and reckless and jittery. And those looks he's been firing at her all day, like he'd like to undress her and marry her all in the one breath. It wasn't decent in front of Daphne, and now they are alone she wants to discourage it. Who knows what might come out of him in this spare landscape with only the currawongs as witness.

They climb to the scabby peak and sit on a granite slab looking out over country. Clusters of boulders crowd the summits, and clouds shunt across the sky, casting shadows that race over the land. Abby draws it all in while Cameron sits beside her in silence. She's pleased he doesn't break the spell. Maybe he's let go of all that intensity and is now feeling the same as she does up here: a lovely connection with the land. But when she turns to look at him, he's watching her, and there are thoughts written in his eyes that frighten her. His gaze is serious and she wills him not to speak, but before she can turn away and mask the well of fear that's rising in her, he leans close and touches his lips to hers. She closes her eyes, absorbs the smell of him, lets him kiss the breath out of her, feels tears sliding from beneath her lids.

He pulls back as a teardrop slithers onto his cheek. 'What's this?'

She can see the questions in his eyes. He reaches for her hand and she knows he's going to speak. It's flowing from him, all those feelings. She looks away. He's misinterpreted her tears, he's going to say something and it will all be wrong.

'Abby. I love you.'

She sucks in cold air, can't look at him.

His clutch on her hand increases. 'Abby. I want to grow old with you.'

Her heart is clanging. She can't speak.

He waits for a moment, then, 'I know it's early, but this is good. It's special. And there's no rush. But I want you to know that sometime in the next ten years I'd like to marry you.'

Something tightens in her throat. She tugs her hand free and stands up. His smile is radiant as he looks up at her, patient.

'I can wait,' he says. 'It's no big deal.'

But it is a big deal. Can't he see that? Why couldn't he let them stay happy without all this rubbish about commitment? She can't cope with the pressure. Now she will have to end it.

'We should head back,' she says, avoiding his eyes. 'Daphne will be waiting. I don't want her to get cold.'

She leans down and gives him a peck on the cheek then she runs over the snowgrass and back down the track, leaving him there, sitting on the rock, watching her.

———

They drop Daphne at Queanbeyan then Abby drives them back towards Canberra, a great weight of silence sitting between them in the car. She feels Cameron watching her as she hunches down behind the wheel, focused on the road. She can tell he's been waiting to speak to her since she ran away on the mountain top. All the way home the atmosphere in the car has been thick with his confusion. It's her fault, and she knows it, but she doesn't know how to deal with this. How did she let it get so messy?

It's a relief when she pulls up outside his apartment block where the wind is blowing across the lake, chopping whitecaps on the grey water.

'Why are we stopping here?' he asks, blunt and edgy. 'Don't we need to take this vehicle back?'

She sees the mix of anger and fear in his eyes—perhaps he knows what is coming. She shakes her head and looks away.

'What's going on?' he asks, tight.

She draws a steadying breath. 'I think we need to take a break for a while.'

He slaps his hand on the dash and the sound frightens her. 'No, that is not what we need.'

She glances at him, sees the black thunder in his face. She needs more words, and quickly. 'I feel crowded,' she stutters. 'I can't breathe.'

'Since when have I stifled you?' he asks, his voice hard. 'I've done nothing but offer support.'

It's true, she can't deny it. 'It's just me,' she says. 'It's the way I am. I need space.'

'You can have as much space as you want. Just don't do this.'

'I'm used to my own company. It's been a big adjustment letting you in.'

'I can wait,' he says. 'I'm patient. I don't understand how you can like me one minute then hate me the next. You can tell me. I'll listen.'

She runs a hand across her throat. 'It's not that I don't like you. You know that I do.' Yes, her body tells him so. Can't he see how difficult this is for her? 'It's just that . . .' she dodges his eyes. 'Look, I have to take the car back. I'll call you soon. I can't do this right now. I'm sorry.'

He reaches out a hand and runs a finger down her cheek, infinitely gentle, such a dramatic switch that it unhinges her and tears roll down her cheeks.

'It's a difficult time,' she says, knowing this is all ineffectual. 'I have to start writing up soon, and it's like going into a cave. Everybody says I'll be boring and horrible.' She hates the pathetic superficial patter of her words.

'I can handle boring and horrible,' he says quietly. 'That's part of being in a relationship. I can cook for you. Bring you cups of tea.'

'I'll keep that in mind,' she says. 'I'll probably need some cups of tea.'

'Can I ring you?' he asks.

'Of course,' she says.

'Dinner sometimes?'

She fences him off, defining boundaries. 'I'll see how I go.'

He leans in and kisses her, the touch of his lips on hers drawing a ragged sob. 'You're sure this is what you want?' he asks.

She bows her head in silence and refuses to look at him, closes her eyes so she can't see as he gathers his belongings and steps out of the car. When the car door slams shut, she sits for a while with her forehead against the steering wheel, giving him time to walk away. Then she starts the car and drives off without looking back.

23

The only way Abby can cope with the separation from Cameron is to bury herself in work and close her emotional mind. She strives for recovery by taking up temporary residence in the library with her laptop as her best friend. It's a poor substitute for Cameron, but safer. When she's had enough of her electronic companion she can shut the lid and walk away. Not so easy with human relationships.

She likes the library, and she appreciates the bland impersonal silence of the place. It's almost reverent, the muted hush of people tiptoeing around trying not to disturb the mysterious workings of great minds. She sits in her favourite niche: a window overlooking neatly spaced gum trees and broad pavements where students migrate in book-carrying groups between the library and the Union buildings. Light pours onto her table. It's a good space for thinking or not thinking, as the case may be.

Sometimes she works in her office in the science building, but right now the clutter of other students, the noise of their breezy interactions, their obsession with texting and YouTube and partying, bands and cafés, is all too much for her. They ask her out, trying to include her, and even though occasionally she accepts their invitations, mostly she bows out using fieldwork as an excuse. This is one time it's good to have a reputation for keeping irregular work hours. Nobody can accuse her of being antisocial—they don't even know where she goes.

The library is gentler than the office, and wonderfully anonymous. When she's sick of data entry or exhausted from the mental pressure of trying to squeeze information from numbers using cryptic statistical programs, she can go and hide among the shelves. She can go fishing for new ideas and other worlds: history, art, philosophy—there are endless other spheres of which she knows practically nothing.

Scouring the shelves for information about the High Country, she finds a book called *The Moth Hunters* and thinks of Daphne. It's a thin little paperback by Josephine Flood. She leafs through the pages. Inside are pictures of Indigenous people, long passed-away; their eyes are sad and haunting—people displaced and deeply wounded—or is she simply reading this into the photographs? She doesn't know. Maybe she's biased.

There's also a map of different language groups in the region, all with musical names: Walgalu, Ngarigo, Djilamatang, Walbanga, Ngunnawal. Daphne would like this book, she thinks. Abby decides to buy a copy and take it to her. If it's still in print maybe the university bookshop will have it—which, fortunately, they do: old stock, tucked away on a shelf in the

Anthropology section. Abby is delighted to score it. She pays up and rings Daphne from outside the shop, arranges to visit the next day. Now that her social calendar is empty, it's easy to fit Daphne in.

Abby has been so preoccupied in recent times, she still hasn't serviced her car and the neglect is beginning to show. It used to play up only once or twice on a short trip, but now it has begun to stall every time she slows for a roundabout or traffic lights. The journey to Queanbeyan is a risk, she knows it, but she wants to deliver the book to Daphne. So she heads out the following morning even though her gut tells her it's going to end badly.

She manages six roundabouts successfully and she's almost laughing at herself—what an achievement! Then at traffic lights near the airport the Laser judders to a stop. With adrenalin-fuelled desperation, Abby grinds the ignition and pumps the accelerator. The engine slowly stutters to life, hiccupping and farting till it gains speed. It trundles along roughly, Abby hoping against hope that there won't be too many more red lights before she arrives at her destination.

She's relieved when she reaches the main street of Queanbeyan. With only one more set of lights to conquer, it looks like she's going to make it. Then the lights turn red and she's forced to stop. The Laser idles unevenly, shudders and stalls. Abby waits till the lights turn green then tries to restart. The motor turns over and whines, but the engine is reluctant. Abby's heart ratchets. She tries again. Nothing.

Cars begin to toot. In the rear-view mirror she sees the driver of a lurid red Commodore behind her brandishing a fist. Zinging with stress she tries the ignition again, to no avail. She cowers behind the wheel, wondering what to do. She can't sit here all day—the traffic is building.

She gets out and shrugs at the guy behind her who is scowling through his windscreen. It looks like she'll have to push her car off the road somehow, but she can't do it alone. She strides to the window of the Commodore and yells, 'Can I have some help?'

For a moment he stares at her, hands on the wheel, his thick black brows knitting together in one long bushy caterpillar. Then he mouths a swearword and gets out. He's not much older than her, and he's tall, imposing and bulky, like he works out in a gym. He points to the kerb. 'We'll push it across.' Then he slots himself into her car while other vehicles start to wind past them.

Abby stands alongside while he releases the handbrake, takes the car out of gear and then leaps out, leaning in to grip the steering wheel. He jams his shoulder against the canopy and shoves. 'You could bloody help,' he pants.

Galvanised, she scoots behind the car and pushes as hard as she can.

'Is that the best you can do?' he scoffs.

She pushes harder. It feels as if her abdomen is about to rupture.

The man's muscles bunch beneath his shirt and the car begins to slide slowly forward. Then it is butting up against the gutter and he swings the steering wheel and jumps in to yank the handbrake on. 'There,' he says, hauling himself out in one sinuous movement. 'At least you're out of the way.'

'What should I do now?' she asks.

'I don't know. Ring the bloody NRMA. You've got a mobile, haven't you?'

'My roadside membership's expired.' She's been so busy she forgot to pay up—that was months ago. 'Would you mind dropping me somewhere? It's not far.'

'You expect me to drive you?' He laughs, disbelieving.

'That would be kind,' she says. 'I'll deal with this later.' She's not in the habit of riding with unknown men, but she doesn't want to be late to Daphne's. It would take too long to walk. She convinces herself she can jump out at an intersection if this guy seems dodgy.

He shakes his head and waves her to his car. 'Get in.'

She grabs her daypack from the Laser then slides into the passenger seat of the Commodore while the man slams in behind the wheel.

'I can't believe I'm doing this,' he mutters, '. . . picking up chicks in the main street.' His car starts with a purr and he moves it forward to the lights, waving to an appreciative driver who honks his horn in thanks. 'Everyone's relieved I've removed you,' he says, grinning.

Now that he has a smile on his face and the crunched-down brow has lifted, he's not so intimidating. He's brown-skinned, brown-eyed and dark-haired. His shirt is neatly ironed and a masculine aroma hovers in the car despite the strong scent of aftershave.

'Where are we going?' he asks, glancing at her.

Abby gives the address.

'Massage parlour up there?' he asks, punching the details into a GPS on the dash.

'No,' Abby says. 'A nice old lady. I can direct you there. You don't need the GPS.'

'I like my toys.' He chuckles to himself. 'An old lady, eh? Meals on bloody Wheels.'

'Not quite,' Abby says. 'She's a friend.'

He swings the car round a few corners, glancing down at the GPS from time to time, then pulls up near Daphne's house.

'Thanks,' Abby says, relieved. 'I appreciate your help.'

He sniffs. 'I have my moments.'

Tentatively, she offers her hand. 'I'm Abby.'

'George.' He takes her hand and pauses as if marvelling at the tininess of it in his big brown paw. She tries to pull away but he holds on. 'How long will you be?' he asks. 'I'm not busy. I could come back and drive you home.'

She extracts her hand with a little more force and opens the door. 'I can't just leave my car there.'

'Why not? You might get lucky. Someone might tow it away.'

'That's no good to me. I'd have to pay a fine.'

'No money?'

'Student.'

That grin again—big white teeth, red lips. 'Got nothing going for you, eh?' He opens the glove box and hands her a card. 'Ring me when you're done. If I'm around, I'll help you out.'

Abby exits the car and closes the door firmly. She won't ring him. She'd prefer to walk.

24

Daphne is in the front garden deadheading roses. She works slowly and methodically, carefully positioning the secateurs then compressing the handles with two hands. It's an effort. Pam said she didn't have to do it, but Daphne likes to contribute around the place. Apart from the vegie garden, she does very little to help. It makes her feel useless just sitting in a chair.

She hears a car pull up in the street and sees Abby get out of a red Commodore. It's not a car Daphne has seen before, and she peers through the dead roses to see whose it is. There's a dark-haired man behind the wheel, wearing a wide white grin. Who is he, she wonders? Not Cameron, that's for sure. And Abby has a quizzical look on her face. Daphne wonders what the man has said in farewell.

When Abby comes through the gate and notices Daphne among the roses, her face lights up. 'Hi,' Abby says, smiling. 'How are you?'

Daphne holds up the secateurs. 'I'm having a bit of trouble with these,' she admits. 'My hands aren't what they used to be.'

'Here, I'll do it for you.'

Abby takes the cutters and snips off the rose heads in rapid succession while Daphne watches them fall to the ground. The girl makes it look so easy. Daphne has forgotten what it's like to have fingers that move willingly when you ask them to. 'Who was that?' she asks, nodding towards the road. 'The man in the car?'

'My car broke down and he gave me a lift,' Abby says.

Daphne is concerned. 'Do you often take lifts with strange men?'

'He helped me push my car off the road. I thought he seemed okay.'

Abby seems unfazed and Daphne frowns. 'That's how young girls get abducted,' she points out as she reaches for the secateurs. 'Let's go in for a cuppa, shall we?'

In the kitchen, a tray has been laid out on the bench with cups and saucers, and a plate on which there are arranged several pieces of sponge cake. Daphne feels a warm tug of gratitude. Lovely Pam must have sorted this while she was out doing the roses. Now Pam must be down in the spare room with Ben—she had it on her agenda to feed Sandy's joey at eleven. That's what she must be doing now. Daphne can hear Ben's high voice piping down the corridor.

She checks the kettle, which is already filled. Then she removes a small jug of milk from the fridge. Pam always keeps a special jug on the top shelf so Daphne doesn't have to wrestle the two-litre container; she knows Daphne's fingers won't fit into the handle anymore.

Daphne sets the milk on the tray then turns to Abby. 'How's young Cameron?' she asks. This is a question Daphne is very interested in. Judging from the atmosphere in the four-wheel drive on the way home from the mountains, she suspects trouble afoot. Something happened up there on that mountain top which neither Abby nor Cameron was willing to share. When they joined up with her after their walk, it was as if the very air had grown bristles. Daphne had been required to fill all the conversation space. She had puttied up the quiet gaps for them throughout the journey home.

Now Abby shifts edgily, a shadow passing across her face. 'We're having a bit of a break,' she says, failing to meet Daphne's eyes.

'Is he getting too serious for you?' Daphne asks knowingly. She recognises Abby's evasiveness as fear. The girl is running hard. She is scarpering into her personal hills and escaping as fast as she can.

'He's a little intense,' Abby admits.

Daphne won't allow her to dodge so easily this time. The girl needs to have it said. 'He's a good man,' Daphne says. 'I like him. He's respectful and thoughtful. Hard qualities to find these days.'

'He's a lot older than me,' Abby says. 'And I think he's looking for different things. I'm not ready for what he's offering.'

'You want to have fun.' That's how young things are these days, Daphne thinks, at least that's what Pam tells her. They're not interested in marriage anymore, all they want is sex. Daphne finds this hard to believe. When she looks at Abby, she sees a girl who badly needs marriage and children to settle her down. Family anchors you—not in a bad way—and

Abby definitely needs anchoring. She's a kite in the wind, skipping across the sky.

'I want to keep things light,' Abby says, her eyes flickering like the light outside, reflecting off Pam's wind chimes. 'Better that I step back and let him find someone else. I don't want to break his heart.'

'Perhaps you already have.'

Abby shrugs. 'I hope not.'

'He's a good person, Abby,' Daphne points out. 'That's important.'

The girl tightens and looks away. She's such a pretty thing, Daphne thinks—all that curly red-brown hair and pale skin. Daphne can see why Cameron is taken with her. There's fragility beneath that veneer of toughness and independence.

The kettle boils and Daphne smiles to herself as Abby dives to turn it off. The girl is taking the opportunity to break the conversation by becoming task-oriented. She watches as Abby pours water in the teapot and carries the tray to the coffee table. Then she goes across to her chair and sits down.

'How have you been anyway?' Abby asks.

Daphne compresses her lips—now it's her turn to dodge. 'I'm fine.' She won't mention the thumping sound that lives in her head most of the time now, like a rabbit beating its feet on the ground. Or the echoing and swishing as if she is hearing things from underwater. She supposes it is tinnitus—she's read about it somewhere: unusual stuff going on behind the ears. Perhaps she needs a hearing aid.

'I have a book for you,' Abby says, sitting on the couch. 'I stumbled over it in the library and bought you a copy. I thought you'd find it interesting.' She opens her backpack and pulls out a small thin book and hands it to Daphne.

'*The Moth Hunters.*' Daphne holds the book at arm's length so she can see the cover more clearly. It has a photo of a lean muscular Aboriginal man sitting on a rock. 'He has an impressive beard, doesn't he?' she says. 'You don't see many beards like that today. He's a fine-looking man. And lovely dark skin—they get such a healthy sheen. Quite a glow.'

The Aborigine reminds Daphne of Johnny Button, except Johnny was always smiling. This man is serious and focused, his right hand wrapped around a big stick, his other hand resting on his left knee. It looks as if he has been instructed to look like a hunter capable of violence. He wears a dried animal skin strapped around his waist to hide his manhood. Johnny wore ordinary clothes, like other stockmen. It was only the colour of his skin and his bush sense that set him apart.

Abby is watching her expectantly so Daphne obliges and opens the book. It forks out at the centrefold of glossy coloured photographs. Daphne's eyes are drawn to a picture of worked stones just like the one that is in the cardboard box in her bedroom with all her other special things. She found it at a rock shelter on the family property years ago. She points. 'Where are these stones from? I can't read the print.'

Abby reads out the location for her, and Daphne listens thoughtfully. It seems that other people—anthropologists— have visited her rock shelter. They have dug and found these stones. They have dug deeper than Daphne could when she was just a girl of eleven. She turns the page. There is a picture of the rock shelter: a large arched granite boulder with an undercut face. Beneath is a photo of rock paintings, and, seeing them, Daphne remembers. These paintings haven't changed since she was a girl. She wonders if someone has touched them up or if they have simply been preserved in the shade of the overhang.

She flicks forward two pages to the last of the colour prints. There are several plates: a Bogong moth, a rock coated with hundreds of the creatures, and three round white stones. Daphne has seen stones like these too. She reaches to pat Abby's hand. 'Wait here,' she says. 'I have something to show you.'

She goes to her room and opens one of the boxes, reaches in and scrabbles around underneath the hank of horse hair and Gordon's jumper. There it is—the dark piece of sharp-edged rock. She lifts it out, feels the chiselled margins bite her skin. Carefully she carries it back to the living room and shows it to Abby.

The girl examines the stone carefully, scraping her thumb gently across the chipped surface. 'Where did you find this?' Abby asks.

'In a rock shelter on one of our runs,' Daphne says. 'This is the only one I have, but there were two stones. A smooth white one, and this one with the sharp edges. I found them under the overhang where those paintings are.'

'That's amazing,' Abby says. 'This is a special artefact. Who knows how old it is.'

'Probably ancient,' Daphne says. Gently she retrieves the stone from Abby's hand and turns it over in her fingers again, feeling the weight of it. 'The Aborigines were there long before we came. My father insisted the land was empty, but we drove them out, I'm sure of it. I don't know if my family shot any of them, but I'm rather afraid we might have. My father wouldn't speak of it. Fact is we stole their land. Then the land was taken from us. I know how they felt. I can't forgive my family for what we did.'

Abby places her hand over Daphne's, enclosing the stone between their palms. 'Maybe you've already paid the price,' she says quietly. 'As you said, the land was taken from you too.'

Daphne hears, but she's not convinced. She looks up into Abby's clear kind eyes. 'Sometimes it would be good if we could see right back into the past,' she says, 'so we could know exactly what happened. Then I'd like to pick up a pen and rewrite history. Change things. But I can't, so I have to live with what's already been written. It seems unfair to me. But it's a fact. Not much I can do about it.'

Abby smiles and releases Daphne's hand and pours more tea. 'You're being hard on yourself,' she says, adding a dribble of milk to her cup.

And you too, dear, Daphne thinks. It's a shame you won't let yourself live.

25

That night Daphne dreams of the mountains. She's been dreaming often lately, and remembering her dreams, which is most unusual. She wonders if it's because the dreams have been coming to her like lightning flashes in the night, followed by loud thunder-like claps that jolt her from sleep. She wakes with images and reverberating sound pulsing in her head, everything clear and startling, as if it has just happened.

She dreams of dark-skinned people walking indistinct paths, following lines of connection, rocky crags jutting from the fog, wind-torn clouds seething over the high tops. In an alpine meadow a cluster of people is sitting round a fire. An old woman with long flat breasts, a wide nose and crooked eyes sings as she places a handful of moths, wing-plucked, on a rock and mashes them with a round white stone. Others of her tribe scatter more moth bodies on a hot granite slab, heated over the fire. They watch the steam rise, and they chatter over the sweet smell of roasting fat as the moths hiss and pop. When they are ready a man sweeps them from the slab with a fern frond. Hands reach to snatch up the nutty morsels and pop them into mouths. There is laughter, the calm that comes with full bellies. Nearby, tattered moth wings twirl in the breeze. They land in the fire and disappear in small crackles of flame.

Then time shifts and transforms into a mass of grey cloud swirling around granite buttresses, wind heaving over grass, whipping trees. Years and centuries tangle into knots. Flashes of light and sound jolt through the semi-conscious sky of Daphne's mind.

Now cattle are spread across the valley, grazing among the stark skeletons of ringbarked trees which poke their dead arms at the sky like stiff scarecrows. There are no more black people in the valley, none among the crags. Instead a slab homestead huddles like a beetle in the cleared grasslands, and the sun beats on the backs of several horses standing in the yards.

The rush of landscape and colour fades, and Daphne wakes to pale moonlight which falls in streaks through the curtains. Her heart is clanging in her ears and she feels dizzy, so she sits up and switches on her lamp, shuffles her pillow and leans back against it.

The stone is right there on her bedside table. She leans to pick it up, scuffs her thumb over its sharp edges. It gleams silvery-grey in the muted light, and its smooth flat sides remind her.

She is eleven years old, riding up the valley in the summer heat. She has completed her chores and she's been given the rest of the day off. She has milked the cows, checked the rabbit traps and chopped the wood. Her mother has packed her a picnic lunch of bread and cheese, and she has escaped, meandering along the trail on the old black mare.

Despite the heat, it is a beautiful morning. After good spring rains, the valley is thick with waving grasses, the soaks are still damp and full of racketing frogs, and there is green feed for the stock. Daphne checks more traps along the way, stopping among warrens to pull half-dead rabbits from the snapped-shut metal jaws of the traps. She breaks their necks by cracking their heads against a rock or a tree before hanging them from the back of her saddle.

In the open country her horse nods along, hooves picking out a rhythm on the track. The rabbits sway against her leg, flies humming around their bloodied fur. Daphne is at peace. She loves the way the horse moves beneath her, the way her body swings with the old mare's gait. Alpine grasshoppers snap into the air, catapulting around her horse's nose. The birds are quiet, subdued to lethargy by the mounting warmth. The horizon undulates with the familiar shapes of mountains.

The mare walks steadily, ears pricked, tail flicking flies from her flanks. Daphne sings songs she has learned from the stockmen: 'Click Go the Shears', 'The Wild Colonial Boy', 'The Drover's Dream'. After an hour or so she begins to look for shade to rest and have lunch. She turns the mare towards the woodland on the southern aspect of the valley where the trees thicken into taller forest reaching up-slope. Crimson rosellas rush from concealed branches as the mare treads into the dappled shadows. The old horse finds a track, maybe a wallaby trail, and picks her way along, threading among scrappy eucalypts and grassy clearings. Daphne lets the reins hang loose so the mare can choose her path. Even in the shade, the heat penetrates, and Daphne longs for a stream, somewhere to splash and cool off.

They round a patch of snow gums, and suddenly, out of the bush, the silhouettes of several large boulders loom: granite massifs like grey elephants hiding from the sun. Daphne guides the mare towards them, stopping when the rocks begin to rise more steeply. There she dismounts, lifts the reins over the mare's head and drops them, knowing the mare won't stray—her father has taught all his horses to ground-tie.

She unhooks the saddlebag and carries it round the first boulder, climbing a narrow cleft to access the rocks behind. The largest of them is underhung with a concave wall created by centuries of weathering. Daphne smells moisture and damp soil. Scrambling over a rock to reach the shade, she notices shapes painted on the rock face: outlines of animals, primitively drawn. In the cool darkness cast by the boulder, she crouches to study them, trying to work out what they are—mostly representations, rather two-dimensional, of native bush animals.

She recognises a poorly proportioned kangaroo painted in white pigment. It has stick-like front legs, ears almost as large as its legs. There is a tortoise and another kangaroo, smaller, maybe a wallaby or a joey. She sees lizards, possibly goannas or blue-tongues with their legs drawn too large. Other shapes are harder to identify. Some are long and thin, wraith-like figures as elusive as smoke. These might be humans, she thinks, but the arms and legs are too extended and they loop together in weird impossible ways. One of the shapes is unmistakably an emu, long-legged with three big toes. Often small groups of those eccentric yellow-eyed birds strut their way past the homestead, grazing with the cattle.

Daphne wonders who painted these pictures. They are childlike, very basic. She reaches a finger and touches the kangaroo, scratches at the pigment with a jagged fingernail. Nothing comes away. The paintings have about them a sense of timelessness, as if they have been there for centuries.

She ponders her father's stories of arriving in an empty land. Perhaps there were people in this place before his family came; she's heard talk of lanky-legged, black-skinned, dark-eyed people who roamed the bush like shadows. They were gone before she was born—except for Johnny Button, and he doesn't count. He's just a farmhand, and mostly he behaves like white people, despite his dark skin.

She sits beneath the rock and pulls out her lunch. Chewing on bread, she leans back, convinced that the paintings are the work of Johnny's ancestors. They must have lived here. This rock overhang would have been a good place for shelter from rain and storms and heat. They would have painted the animals they hunted. It made sense.

After lunch she scrapes around in the shade and finds an area of soil that is stained black—perhaps from campfires long ago. She sifts dirt with her bare hands, digging her fingers in. Then she grasps something, a sharp piece of dark stone that she hooks out and nearly flings into the bush until she sees its fluted edges. The rock has been chipped to create a pointed blade. She turns it over, wondering what it is; a spearhead, perhaps?

She pokes around some more and finds another stone. This one is different, smooth and round and white, like an egg. She lies back on the ground, a stone in each hand, and holds them up, squinting against the light, feeling their shapes. They are tools, she thinks: one sharp, one smooth.

Who was here? Who made them? Maybe her father can tell her. Perhaps he knows.

Excited, she emerges from the shade and clambers back over the boulders. Her horse is standing beneath the snow gums, patiently mouthing the bit. Daphne wraps the stones in pieces of old cloth she carries for wiping away dirt or mud or water or rain, and stores them in her saddlebag, then she takes a drink before beginning the ride home to share her findings.

The homestead is quiet when she reaches it. The air and the cattle and even the smoke from the chimney seem lethargic in the dreamy afternoon heat. Across the valley the bush shrills with cicadas, sound pulsing into the white sky. Daphne hitches her horse to the rail and steps onto the veranda, swinging open the door to find her father snoozing in his chair, her mother at the bench, skinning a rabbit for dinner.

Her mother turns, perspiration shining on her cheeks in the dim light cast through the small windows. 'What is it, dear?' her mother asks. 'You look flustered. Is it the heat, or is something wrong?'

Daphne hesitates—somehow her mother always seems to know what is taking place beneath her skin. It is different with her father, however. He is quick to anger, has little time for foolishness. She watches him unfold reluctantly from his nap, the smell of sweat rising from his clothes. 'I think someone must have lived here before us,' she announces.

Her father stretches his long, booted legs and frowns, tugs absently at his beard. 'What are you talking about?' he says. 'This land has always belonged to us.'

Daphne's heart knocks anxiously. 'But what about before that? Before our family came? Before it was ours?'

The frown settles deeper into the lines on her father's face, like ploughed furrows. 'It's always been ours,' he says. 'The land was empty.'

Fumbling with one of the pieces of cloth, Daphne takes the sharp grey stone from her pocket and passes it to her father, waiting while he examines it. He glances at it briefly, then sniffs disdainfully and tosses it to the floor. He is casually unimpressed.

'Just a weathering chip off a boulder,' he says, dismissive. 'There are bits of stone like this everywhere.' He scoffs. 'What did you think it was? A spearhead or something?' He shakes his head. 'What an imagination.'

Daphne squats to retrieve the stone from the floor and tucks it back in her pocket. 'Who made the paintings then?' she asks.

Her father raises a sceptical eyebrow. 'What paintings?'

'I saw them on a rock up in the bush. Pictures of kangaroos and emus and people. Somebody painted them.'

Her father laughs and she feels the harsh rub of humiliation. 'There are no paintings round here,' he says. 'You've been looking at water stains, not paintings at all.'

'I'll take you there,' Daphne offers.

He stands up and brushes her off, impatient, declaring he has enough to do without indulging her ridiculous fancies.

'Who lived here?' she persists. 'Did you see them? Where did they go?'

He turns on her, rage simmering in his eyes, and his look silences her. She feels a small white light flare in her chest, a jolt of recognition. Her father knows something, she's sure of it. He has stories he's not willing to share, information about the Aborigines, Johnny's people. And he is angry, furious.

There is a deeper reason why he hates Johnny. Is he guilty about something? Has he hurt somebody?

Questions whirl in her head, but she knows not to push further. Her father is glaring at her, thunder in his brow. She lowers her eyes and goes to unsaddle her horse. Down at the yards she pulls the sharp grey stone from her pocket and the round white stone from her saddle-bag and holds them in her cupped hands, hard and smooth, lying side by side. Then she wraps them up again and contemplates where she can hide them.

Perhaps she can ask Johnny about it. Maybe he knows what happened to his people.

———

Daphne places the stone back on her bedside table, switches off the lamp and tries to go to sleep. But her thoughts won't settle; they jiggle in her legs, making her restless and twitchy, so she turns on the light again, gets up and pulls on her dressing gown, pads quietly into the kitchen. Blearily, she makes a cup of tea. She's tired, but there's no rest to be had till all the memories work themselves through.

Johnny Button lingers with the story of the stone. When she tries to remember the first time she met him, it seems he was there from the beginning, coming and going, materialising from the bush then disappearing again. He was always kind, always finding something new to show her. Because of him she'd learned about bush tucker. And he is the one who showed her the moths.

He became her friend during her childhood. It was a quiet friendship, a concealed friendship. Daphne knew her father was uncomfortable with Johnny. There was that incident down at the yards when the horse broke its leg and Daphne's father had to shoot it—that was the first time Daphne had sensed her father's desire to lay into Johnny with his whip. But there was more. When Johnny was around, her father glowered with a particular tension. It seemed he would never reconcile this conflict: he required the Aborigine's assistance with the stock, but couldn't bear his presence.

Each year, however, Johnny showed up at the property. He arrived alone, turning up at the yards on horseback, a wide grin on his face. Sometimes he arrived bare-chested, as if he'd just returned fresh from walkabout and had been roving naked through the bush. One time he stole the shirt from the scarecrow at the vegie patch and wore it like a king, parading in front the other men. It was a bold and brash performance, destined to stir the boss's ire. No-one else would dare steal from Daphne's father, even if it was only in fun.

Johnny was clever enough to display humility and respect around Daphne's father, but when the boss was absent, his cheeky nature would emerge. Whenever he saw Daphne, his eyes would dance and he would tip his hat like a gentleman. He was a consummate prankster, unrivalled in his ability to sneak up and surprise people. Daphne was eternally being caught out by him. Once he appeared in the chicken coop and gave her a fright and she dropped all the eggs, the thick orange yolks and sticky whites spreading as fast as her dismay. That was a trick Johnny never repeated. Daphne had received a hiding for it; she could have let Johnny take the blame, but she didn't, knowing her father sought any excuse to dislike the black man.

Johnny wasn't always funny. Often he was serious, especially when he was focused on shooting a kangaroo or climbing a tree to drag a possum from a hollow to roast over his campfire. Daphne had tried many different bush meats that he'd killed: possum, bandicoot, wallaby, lyrebird. They all had varied flavours and textures—some tender, some tough. Daphne liked lyrebird best; it was like chicken, but with a stronger taste, enhanced by Johnny's smoky fire. He always roasted meat in its skin which he would later peel back like baking paper so he could bite into the hot flesh.

When Daphne was old enough to accompany the men on the brumby hunt, she rode with Johnny whenever she could. He didn't come every year—sometimes he was off back-country when the ride was on. His life seemed devoid of dates and concrete commitments. While the white men measured days and weeks by ticking off numbers on a calendar, Johnny wafted to a different rhythm, absorbed in wanderings triggered by weird ethereal things, like the flowering of the gums or the migration of the honeyeaters, indicating some great event of nature taking place elsewhere.

By the time Daphne rode into the mountains with the men, she was sixteen, and a capable young woman. She had graduated from Bessie onto a livelier horse: a brown brumby mare captured on a previous hunt, a willing but nervous horse that took quite some skill to handle. Daphne was proud to ride with the men. The invitation to join them was a rite of passage she had awaited for many summers. She was careful to be quiet and unobtrusive—some of the men were not entirely pleased to have her along. A woman had to earn her place. She had to be better than a man. For this reason, Daphne kept mostly to herself.

Those years that Johnny came along, she liked to ride near him for company, and also because his steady horse somehow calmed her own skittish mount. Often she rode to one side, or slightly behind him, and occasionally they chatted. But their conversations were rare beneath the eagle stare of her father. He didn't like her to talk with Johnny, and she learned to keep her distance, to snatch whatever opportunities arose, and to move away strategically when her father appeared on the track.

Trailing the main group of riders one day, she fell in alongside Johnny and asked if he could show her the moths up in the High Country. He answered with a nod and a grin. 'Maybe you try moths for tucker. I cook him up on the fire. Good and juicy.'

A few days later, on the slopes below a scabby mountain top, when the riders took a break for tea, Daphne saw Johnny up-slope on foot, gesturing to her. She tied her mare, grabbed something from her saddle-bag and crammed it in her pocket, then excused herself from the group and followed Johnny up the hill, remaining some twenty metres behind him. They made their way among twisted snow gums and beyond the tree line to a pile of granite slabs and boulders, jutting against the sky like needles.

Like a monkey, Johnny scaled a large flat rock then slid between the grainy faces of two boulders. Daphne followed him into a dark recess of cool shade. At first, her sun-glazed eyes couldn't locate him, but then she adjusted and found his dark shape silhouetted against the speckled silver rock. He directed her to a narrow crack and slipped his hand in. 'In here,' he said. 'You can feel 'em.'

Moving close, she reached into the crevice and her hand connected with a carpet of fur, her fingers gliding over the backs of a thousand moths, their wings like soft scales adhered

249

to the rock. Her heart thrilled at the marvel of it, at her proximity to Johnny, the raw salty, bushy smell of him, the black shadow of his arm, so near to her own, stroking the moths inside the rock crack.

Withdrawing, she flattened her hand on her chest, inexplicably breathless. Johnny pulled out too. In the dark space between the boulders, she could make out the shape of his outstretched hand, and there, on his palm, sat a brown moth slowly fanning its wings. Daphne felt her breath fluttering too. She backed away and stood where she could see the bright flash of Johnny's eager smile in the shadows. From her pocket she pulled the round white stone she'd found at the rock shelter years before, and placed it in his hand beside the quivering moth. It was with some reluctance that she relinquished the stone. She loved the unblemished texture of it, the way it fitted perfectly in her hand, worn smooth by the grasp of generations of women before her. But this summer she'd decided to give it to Johnny, and she wanted to surrender it somewhere special—here among the mountain tops where she felt close to the sky. The moths provided the final trigger: this was the time. 'It's from your people,' she said. 'I found it in a place where they left paintings.'

Johnny looked at the stone with a blissful kind of awe. He picked it up with his other hand and ran his fingers over the surface before slipping it carefully in the rear pocket of his trousers. Then he moved near, holding out the moth, his eyes never leaving her face, his skin shimmering like polished wood in the dull light.

In that moment, something took hold of her and she reached and grasped him, surrendering to a sudden urge to taste his lips. For a moment he was wooden, rigid with shock, then he flicked the moth away and curled his long sinewy arms around her, tugging her close, kissing her, his deep brown lips awakening in her an age-old desire that knew nothing of the colour of a person's skin.

With her hand she explored the bony angles of his back. His hair had the consistency of steel wool, but softer. Carried on a tide of primitive need, she unbuttoned her shirt and lifted her vest.

This is the image she always remembers: the breathtaking shock of his black roughened hand on the sacred milky white of her breast, the unspeakable electricity of his fingers connecting with her skin.

Then her father's voice barked at the edge of darkness. Everything stopped, locked into the horror of discovery: what had begun with such innocence ending with the taint of sin.

Cowering, Daphne emerged from the cleft between the rocks, Johnny following. Her father's whip tore the air around them. He slashed Daphne across the cheek, braying his anger. Then he shouted at her to go, and laid into Johnny with the lash, his eyes snapping with rage.

Daphne retreated, fearful. Just below the outcrop she waited while the whip cracked like gunshot. She wanted to scream at Johnny to get out of there—he was faster than her father—but she couldn't speak. Her voice was knotted somewhere in her throat.

Then there was silence. Her father appeared on the rocks, thunderous. He strode towards her, grabbed her arm in a mean pinch and dragged her down-slope. Peering back, she saw a shadow slipping across the landscape like a cloud—Johnny escaping.

With the red welt of her guilt prominent on her face, she packed and saddled her horse under the enraged supervision of her father. Then she rode home in disgrace, banished from the hunt. Johnny rejoined the ride the next day, but after that he was an outcast. He was shunned from local properties. Shortly afterwards, he left the district and was never seen again.

Daphne has never forgotten her humiliation that day, the judgemental looks on the faces of the men. Doug was among them, her future husband, watching as she rode off alone. Years later she married him, and he never mentioned it, but Daphne knew he hadn't forgotten. She wishes she had explained to him the innocence of what had taken place between her and Johnny that day, but she never found the courage to speak of it. Doug's silence was his forgiveness.

And yet, all these years later, she still hasn't forgiven herself for what happened to Johnny. As a result of her actions, he lost his status and the life he had known. She could have given him the stone at the farm, could have spared him the degradation of being exiled by the only workmates he knew. She could have saved him from her impetuous naïvety, her uncontrolled spontaneous surrender to her body's desires. She could have displayed some grace and respect. But it's too late for that now. She flung herself at him and ruined his life. Walking the same path as her family, she had destroyed him.

Wearily, she sets her unfinished cup of tea on the bench, switches off the kitchen lights and takes herself back to bed.

26

Abby makes a habit of morning tea with Daphne once a week. Daphne is similar to Gran, and it takes Abby back to her childhood, makes her feel secure. It's also a welcome diversion from writing and analysis, and Daphne seems to enjoy having her around. Abby likes the homeliness of visiting with Daphne. When she is with the old lady, she feels something settling inside her.

They have a comfortable friendship. Even so, in quiet moments at home, Abby has to admit she's lonely. Life without Cameron is rather empty, a bleak plain she must navigate alone. But it's better this way. On her own she can't hurt anyone, and she doesn't need to worry about promises she can't keep. If Cameron was thinking marriage, she's done the right thing unleashing him.

Morning tea with Daphne is good for her. They chat, and sometimes they just sit together watching Ben play on the floor. He is a creative child, Abby thinks, so absorbed in his Lego.

First he follows the instructions and makes the design on the front of the box then he pulls it apart and concocts his own constructions: space-age machines, towers, vehicles with all sorts of useful modifications, like guns and levers and canons sprouting fire. It seems he never tires of putting blocks together in innovative ways—except when his legs start to tingle and he explodes with the need to run. That's when Pam takes him down to the park and lets him loose on the equipment, so he can come home a more manageable little person.

Leaving the Queanbeyan house one morning after her weekly visit with Daphne, Abby sees a red Commodore parked in the street. Sitting on the bonnet, arms folded, is George, the guy who saved her when her car broke down a few weeks ago. He looks like he's been waiting for some time. Abby's heart kicks. She is not pleased to see him, hasn't given him a thought since their first meeting. His sudden appearance here at Daphne's house has a whiff of stalking about it. 'What are you doing here?' she asks, irritated.

He tightens defensively. 'You didn't call me back.'

'I didn't need to. I had my car serviced and it's going like a dream.'

He is patently disappointed. 'I thought you might ring. I've been driving past here a couple of times a week, just in case.'

Abby feels herself bristling, and she hopes he senses it too. 'You shouldn't just show up like this.'

'Why not? You didn't mind my help the other day. A bit of gratitude wouldn't go astray.'

'I thanked you,' Abby says, implying that ought to be enough. But he doesn't seem to get it.

'How about you buy me a cappuccino?' he suggests. 'You owe me for rescuing you.'

Abby is certain she doesn't owe him anything, but she can see he's unlikely to accept no for an answer and she doesn't want him following her home. She supposes a cup of coffee can't hurt, if it's on her terms.

'Follow me into town,' George says. 'I know a good café.'

She trails his Commodore through the suburb and parks behind him in the main street of Queanbeyan. He is out and opening the car door for her before she even has time to retrieve her wallet from the glove box.

'Anything for the lady,' he says with a slimy smile.

'Thank you, but I can open doors for myself.' She slips out onto the pavement and moves beyond his reach.

He makes a laboured point of holding the café door open too, and she passes inside stiff-backed without giving him the satisfaction of a response. His chivalry seems fake and overdone. He shrugs and raises his hands as if she's wounded him. Best he gets used to rejection now, she thinks. He won't be getting anything else from her.

'They do good coffee here,' he says, selecting a table and slumping into a seat.

Abby is pleased he didn't try to pull out a chair for her; maybe he's getting the message.

They order, then George leans back and inspects her across the table. She takes the opportunity to inspect him too. He's swarthy and unshaven, and his hair is wavy and dark and in need of a wash. He smiles with thick red lips and raises his bushy mono-brow as he sits legs apart, loose and casual. Abby can't help comparing him to Cameron's stylish poise.

'I'm not happy about you showing up at my friend's place today,' she says. 'I don't want it to happen again.'

He shrugs, offhand. 'How else was I supposed to find you?'

'If a girl doesn't ring, it means she's busy.'

'Yeah, well I wanted to hear it from you.'

'I have a boyfriend,' she lies.

George frowns. 'Why didn't you ring him the other day when you were stuck?'

'He was at work. When you break down in the middle of the road, you don't make a phone call and wait for rescue. You have to deal with it straightaway. You helped, I appreciated it, and that's it. End of story.'

'So you're not available then?'

'No. Taken.'

'No harm trying.' He grins. 'And here we are, having coffee. That's more than I expected.'

'The coffee is to sort this out. I don't want to be stalked.'

He smirks, unfazed. 'Sure, but since we're here we might as well talk a bit.'

Abby shifts uncomfortably. She wants out of here.

George leans forward, muscular forearms on the table, shirt-sleeves folded back to the elbows. He's tanned for this time of year—it looks like he's been hanging out in a solarium. He runs a hand through his wavy mop. 'Okay, this is me,' he says. 'I'm Greek. Grew up here in Queanbeyan. Own a courier business with my brother.'

'You're a courier?' Abby says. 'What's with the Commodore? That's your delivery van?'

''Course not,' he says. 'But I don't want to drive round in the van all the time. That's why I have the Commodore. It's my day off. A man's gotta have some fun.'

'And being a courier is good business?' Abby asks with disinterest.

'Sure is.' George sniffs and rubs his nose. 'Super-busy. I work six days a week. Delivering parcels, books, boxes of wine, all sorts of gear, including stuff you probably wouldn't want to know about.' A slippery smile slashes his face.

Abby senses he's trying to pique her interest, but she refuses to satisfy him. 'Don't tell me then, if I wouldn't want to know.'

'What about you?' he asks. 'What do you do for a living?'

'I study kangaroos.'

He chuckles, obviously amused. 'How much do you need to know about shooting? A gun licence is cheap.' He leans back, sighs and stretches. 'I admire people who study. Wish I'd done more of it myself. Wish I'd done medicine or dentistry. I can just see myself sitting in a chair with my arms folded giving out bedside manner then writing the bill.'

'So it's all about income,' Abby observes caustically.

He grins. 'Of course. Why else do you work?'

Their cappuccinos arrive and George stirs in three spoonfuls of sugar.

'I like going bush too,' he says. 'I go shooting with a mate of mine. We hunt pigs and deer up near Tumut. Sometimes 'roos and wombats, except they're too easy. Only shoot them if there's nothing else around.'

'I hope you don't go into the national park,' Abby says, projecting disapproval.

George laughs. 'That's where the best pigs are.'

Abby plasters a weak smile on her face. She can just imagine George dressed in his camouflage gear with a gun and a string of ammunition draped over his shoulder, shooting the shit out of some poor animal. Not that she minds him shooting ferals, but she knows the shooters stock the bush with piglets

KAREN VIGGERS

to keep their hobby alive. It's a joke when they say they are contributing to feral animal control.

'Shot a beautiful deer just the other week,' George continues. 'Took its head off with an axe so I could keep it for my collection. There's all sorts of stuff out there, like you wouldn't believe. I've got the best set of skulls in Australia. I've got a horse skull, cow skulls, sheep, kangaroos, a wombat, even a Tassie devil skull.'

'Skulls don't impress me,' Abby says. 'I see plenty of them out where I work.'

'I've got other things too,' George says. 'A seal skull, one from a wedgetail eagle, even a crocodile skull. Ever seen one of those? They're amazing—all this thick, hard bone with holes in it.'

'Where did you get it?' Abby asks.

'A mate found it on a fishing trip in the Kimberley. It was sitting in the mud. Bit of a risk to get it, I suppose. Must have been other crocs about. But it's one of my trophies. I was stoked when he gave it to me.' He leans forward and lowers his voice. 'I've got a human skull too.'

Abby regards him with distaste. 'That's not something to show off about. What is it, a model or something? From the medical school.'

'No, it's real,' he says.

Abby is unsure whether to believe him or not. She tries to imagine his house with shelves of skulls, and a strange smell, stale and slightly rank from lack of fresh air and the musty stench of bone. She pictures a different skull on one of the shelves. A human skull. 'You're not serious, are you? Where did it come from?'

'My mate found it in the bush. I gave him five slabs of beer so I could keep it.' He sits back, smug.

258

Abby's skin crawls. 'You mean you haven't handed it in? That's probably illegal. It could be someone's father or brother or something.'

'Nah, it's just a skull.'

'How do you know?'

George ignores this and takes a sip of his coffee. He seems very self-satisfied. 'You should come to my place and see it,' he says. 'I live just round the corner.'

Abby doesn't buy his sleazy line. Nor does she want to see his damn collection, especially not the human skull. She downs her cappuccino and checks the time. 'I have to go. Got work to do.'

He looks downcast. 'When can I see you again?'

'You can't,' she says. 'I'm busy.'

'That's a shame. I thought we could be friends.'

'Look, I'll pay for your coffee—you seem to think I owe that to you. Then we're even.' She takes some money out of her wallet and stands up.

'Well, make sure you call if you're ever in trouble again.' He reaches into his pocket 'Here's my card.'

'You already gave me one.'

'Have another,' he says with a grin. 'So you won't forget me.'

She pays the bill and heads quickly out the door. Once she's in the car and gone, she will delete him from her life like a file from her computer, and that's a good feeling. She doesn't want to see him again.

———◆———

A few days later in the office at uni, one of the other students, Nathan, calls out to her: 'Hey Abby, there's been a guy called George ringing to catch up with you.'

Abby shuffles her papers and tries to suppress a sudden tightness in her throat. How did George track her down? Perhaps on the university website. It's absolutely too creepy, and she wishes she'd never had that cup of coffee with him. She glances at Nathan. 'I don't want to speak to him.'

Nathan seems surprised. 'He sounds keen. He's rung here, I don't know, about ten times. That's pretty bloody enthusiastic if you ask me. Everyone in this room has spoken to him, and he chats away like he's mates with us all.'

'Don't be deceived,' Abby says. 'He's an idiot.'

Nathan shrugs as if to indicate that Abby is the weird one here. And for the first time, Abby sees that perhaps she should have made more effort to befriend her fellow students. They have all occupied this space for two years and she has failed to fit in.

Nathan places a slip of message-paper on her desk, along with a pile of other similar notes. 'Here's his number in case you change your mind.'

'Thanks.' Abby slides her hand over the notes and collects them in her hand.

'Give the guy a chance,' Nathan says. 'He didn't sound that bad.'

When Nathan leaves the office, Abby shreds the messages into little fragments and drops them in the bin like a handful of confetti.

PART IV

PART IV

27

Abby is en route to her study site when she hears an announcement on the radio about a kangaroo cull, and she turns up the volume to listen. Apparently there is a nature reserve near the city where the number of kangaroos has been increasing for some time. What's new, she thinks—wherever there's a suggestion of feed, kangaroos will breed, even in a drought. That's what they're designed to do.

She has been to the reserve in question. It's a haunting, bare, windy place with no grass and too many kangaroos with nowhere to go. The country surrounding it is heavily grazed treeless farmland supporting cattle and sheep. The farmers dislike having kangaroos intrude onto their land from the reserve. They see kangaroos as competitors for feed, especially in this drought. Abby's kangaroos in the mountains are equally numerous, but there's no farmland nearby, and hardly anyone goes there, so it's largely unnoticed. Because it's a national park—a natural system—the kangaroos are left to do their thing. Animals die, but it isn't close to the city, so it's overlooked. Down on the plains, it's a different matter. Farmers want to get rid of kangaroos, but there's more to the issue than that. The grasslands in the reserve also provide habitat for endangered species which the government is obligated to protect.

The radio presenter is interviewing an animal rights activist called Martin Tennant. They keep referring to an article in the morning paper by the science and environment journalist—presumably Cameron. From the content of the interview it seems Cameron has taken the side of the activist, which doesn't seem right to Abby. Cameron usually explores both sides of an argument. It would be out of character for him to align with a particular point of view, especially when he knows she supports culling to save habitat for other species—she told him that the first time they met . . . unless, of course, he's angry with her and he's trying to make an obscure attempt at pay back. But he doesn't seem the vengeful type, and from his regular phone messages, it's obvious he's still hopeful they might get back together.

Abby has been avoiding telephones as much as possible, both her mobile and the office phone. She doesn't want to speak to the ever-persistent George, who keeps trying to catch her at uni. And she also doesn't want to hear the sorrowful twinge in Cameron's voice when he asks her out and she turns him down. No to coffee. No to dinners. It's the easiest and safest way. Sure she misses him, misses the intimacy. And he seems like a knight in shining armour compared to George. But she can't help remembering the ownership tendrils Cameron kept looping around her wrists. Now she's had some time away from him she feels more herself again, just getting back to normal . . . if she can ever feel normal with George lurking in the background. Still, she's keen to make sure Cameron doesn't snowball this kangaroo issue into some media behemoth, so she decides to give him a call. It's the first time she's initiated contact since they broke up—but there's no answer. The phone switches to mailbox and the sound of his voice sets her heart knocking. She had thought she might be immune to him—not as yet, it seems. She leaves a message to let him know she's trying to get in touch. Then she's out of range; the walls of the valley block the signals out.

It's a beautiful clear day in the mountains, early winter, with cerulean cloudless skies. Abby walks up the valley uplifted by the aura of peace. Out here, it's easy to forget all the things that are troubling her. She notices there's more grass than in the reserves near the city. If any rain has fallen at all, she supposes it has fallen in high alpine places like this where the clouds graze the ridges and shed their moisture involuntarily. Even so, it's hardly grazing nirvana. There's a subtle suggestion of green, but mostly the landscape is transitioning from brown to grey. The bite of frost has nipped away all colour.

She remembers walking here with Cameron when they first met, her anxiety about that silly interview. It was the beginning of all things between them—she hadn't envisaged that at the time. Back then, she hadn't even met Daphne, and now she and Daphne are friends. She supposes she has come a long way since then, but in other ways she hasn't changed at all. This is the shape of her life, she thinks, and it's not entirely unpleasant. She'd be better off if she could permanently discourage George, but on the whole she feels okay. Since she's stopped seeing Cameron she's been ringing

Matt more often, and it's been good to hear his news. Matt is doing better. He's talking more, occasionally cracking jokes. Abby enjoys his attempts at casual banter; it has its roots in the casual comfort that comes with knowing someone all your life, growing up together. There's no awkwardness in silences between them, and there's a soothing sense of mutual support. If nothing else, their mother's illness and death has bonded them in some strange, incomprehensible way. She and Matt are similar: both navigating their solitary paths, and prone to fleeting relationships which end as soon as a suggestion of commitment rears its ugly head. This is all they can manage, the two of them burdened with the past. Abby can progress quite merrily like this, and without too much pain—which is what survival is about, after all.

She works a full day collecting data: measuring pasture, locating her collared animals, following their movements around the valley. At dusk she packs up and drives home. She is nearing the parks office when her phone beeps and, expecting to hear from Cameron, she pulls over in the fading light to check her messages. There are three from him. Yes, he would like to meet her. Sure, he'd like to discuss his article with her. Please, could she ring back to make a time.

She sits for a while wondering what she should do, whether she should simply let this kangaroo thing pass. The day in the valley has been cleansing, and she realises now that it may not be healthy for her to see him; she regrets her impulse this morning to ring him immediately after the radio interview. Perhaps she should have waited till her blood had stopped stirring, then things would have been clearer, as they are now.

Somewhere off in the scrub, she hears a kookaburra calling into the darkening sky. It's the laughter that does it—as if the bird is mocking her. She calls Cameron's number and this time she gets through. He sounds pleased to hear from her, but busy. They arrange to meet at a pub that evening—eight o'clock so Abby has time to go home for a shower and something to eat. He's thoughtful, she concedes, not caught up in his own needs like most men she's met. George comes to mind, with his sleazy manners and insensitive pushiness.

Near home she stops at the supermarket to pick up a frozen meal for dinner and a newspaper so she can see Cameron's article. In her bungalow, while the meal is whizzing round in the microwave, she sits on the couch among a scatter of scientific papers she's been reading, and unfolds the newspaper.

There it is on the front page.

A government report released last night recommends a cull on public grasslands where kangaroos are apparently on the rise. Scientists who have been monitoring the site claim there has been a decline in legless lizards and earless dragons due to overgrazing by kangaroos. These reptiles, which are listed as endangered, are dwindling across the region, and government intervention is required to safeguard against their extinction. For this reason, the cull is likely to go ahead despite community opposition. The report suggests that up to four hundred kangaroos are likely to be removed.

Animal rights activist Martin Tennant says government reports are exaggerated and politically motivated. He says kangaroos are not out of control, and culling is inhumane and unnecessary. 'Our advanced society does not need to shoot animals,' he says. 'There are many options before resorting to murder.'

Mr Tennant has been involved in many previous campaigns against kangaroo culling and he says government rhetoric is easy to recognise. "'Drought" and "starvation" are bureaucratic terms to soften the public prior to a slaughter,' he says. 'By definition, "cull" means shooting, and shooting is not humane. Animals suffer and joeys are clubbed to death. We must not accept this treatment of our national emblem.'

Efforts were made to contact the relevant government agency, but no-one was available to comment. 'This is typical bureaucratic behaviour,' Mr Tennant said. 'They plant the seed then run and hide. But we'll dig them out and force them to examine this issue properly.'

Abby sets the paper on the coffee table and goes to fetch her meal. Then she sits down with a fork and hoes in. It's not particularly inspiring—the taste of plastic permeates the meat, and the vegetables look limp and wilted. But she needs to eat, so she forces it down while reading Cameron's article for a second time.

He has definitely sided with the activist, it seems, but government ceded the right of reply, so it's hard to confirm his bias. She wonders where he's planning to take this. It's an emotive issue—she's sure he's aware of that—and it would be so easy for him to stir the pot, especially with activists like Martin Tennant waiting in the wings. But Cameron needs to be careful he isn't used as a mouthpiece. Then again, he likes controversy, doesn't he? And strategic pot-stirring may be just what the newspaper wants, to swell the issue and inflate readership.

After a shower she cycles into the city and D-locks her bike to a signpost outside the pub where smokers sit in tight clusters around gas heaters, pretending they are warm. She pushes through the filmy haze of smoke and through the swing-doors into the pub. Several sets of eyes lift to examine her with vague curiosity as she enters—humans are not so different from kangaroos.

The pub is busy. It's public-service payday and everyone is out. Restaurants will be hectic too—it's part of the culture of this town. Abby looks around but can't see Cameron, so she goes to the bar and orders a drink. She watches the barman draw the beer, his practised hand pulling the tap then letting it go with a thud. He plonks the foaming beer-mug on the bar and she pays then goes in search of a table.

She finds two vacant bar stools at the bench along the side wall and settles herself in, claiming the second seat with her helmet. It's fascinating to people-watch when you're sitting in a pub, drinking alone. Patrons passing between the bar and other tables eye her warily, as if being solo defines her as a social leper. Most people don't even notice her—they huddle in their insular groups, shouting and laughing and showing their teeth like hyenas.

Cameron is late. When he arrives Abby spots him through a sea of faces, standing at the door, scanning the room. When he finds her, his face lifts, and he makes his way across the room, parting groups of chatting people as he comes.

'Hey, g'day.' He grins down at her, eyes dancing with pleasure. She senses he would like to sidle close and kiss her, but she doesn't encourage him, so he stands back with a degree of tension, hands in pockets. After a while, he shrugs off his coat and slings it over the bar stool she has reserved for him. He notices her beer is almost empty and goes to fetch more, returning with two brimming mugs. Then he sits down and smiles at her. 'It's good to see you,' he says.

'Yes, it's been a while.' She crinkles her eyes at him in a half-smile. She can't deny she has missed him—her body tightens in his presence. Even in these few weeks, she has forgotten how tall he is, the way she is drawn to him.

'I've been worried about you,' he says. 'You haven't answered my calls.'

'Preoccupation with work,' she explains, off-hand, knowing this is an inadequate excuse.

'How's it going?' He swigs his beer and sets it on the bench, his eyes resting on her face.

'I'm doing okay. I've almost finished my fieldwork. Then the final analysis and writing begins. That won't be much fun.'

'Remember, I'm good at delivering cups of tea. And I can cook too. When you're working hard, you have to eat properly.'

She flushes. He has homed straight in on her inadequacies: her frozen meal this evening was about as nutritious and appetising as the cardboard it was packaged in, but convenient.

'How's Daphne?' he asks.

'She's good. I've been seeing her quite a bit. She likes to talk. She has lots of stories to tell.'

'And your brother?'

'Matt's fine. He's back working at the vineyard. That always helps. Keeps him busy. No more disappearing stunts. How are your folks?' she asks.

'They're still alive. You know how it is.'

'I saw your article,' she says, cutting to the chase.

He looks at her expectantly, eyebrows raised.

'I wondered what you were trying to do with it.'

His eyes darken a little. 'What do you mean?'

'Whether you were taking sides. Perhaps favouring the animal rights groups.' She knows it's a bit harsh of her to go for the jugular like this, but she wants to hear what his angle is going to be. If he's heading on the wrong trajectory, maybe she can gently redirect him.

'I wasn't siding with anyone,' he says quietly. 'It was just a preliminary report. I thought it was good to present a controversial perspective. It was hard to explore the government line when they wouldn't even speak to me.'

Abby has to agree with this. If the government hides from the media, it's difficult to paint their point of view. 'Don't forget the science,' she reminds him.

He shrugs. 'Government will trot out the science. We don't need to go through all that in the paper.'

'Of course you have to,' Abby insists. 'You need to interview a few kangaroo experts, like my supervisor Quentin. He's the guru of macropod management.'

Cameron grins with the pleasure of someone who finds themselves ahead of the game. 'I've already rung him and he's going to do an opinion piece.'

'That's a start,' Abby concedes. She's a little embarrassed. Perhaps she's making this into something bigger than it is.

He chuckles as if enjoying some private joke. 'This isn't really about kangaroo management, is it?' he says cryptically.

'What do you mean?' she asks, confused. What else could it be about?

'Think about it.' He smiles encouragingly. 'Is there really a right or wrong in this? Some people think it's wrong to degrade the environment and others think it's wrong to kill kangaroos. It's an argument about values, not management. The bottom line is that my editor's excited. He's expecting a rush of letters over the next few weeks, a good debate.'

'Just make sure it isn't one-sided,' Abby says, projecting her concern. 'These things are always complicated. Culling is a hard enough decision for governments in the first place. They don't need journalists inflaming the issue and making it even more difficult.'

He looks at her seriously. 'What do *you* think? Should they shoot these kangaroos?'

'Yes, they have to be shot,' she says. The scientist in her, the rationalist, knows this is true: the kangaroos must be shot to preserve habitat; there's no question about that. But she detests guns, and she hates the whole concept of shooting, the idea of blowing away the brains of living things. It's quick—at least it's supposed to be, and she fiercely hopes this is right. But what if it's not? Out of nowhere old visions begin to rise from the past like smoke from a smouldering fire. She tries to blank them out, to tuck away the feeling of nausea that swells suddenly in her stomach. She knows she must distract herself. It's important to keep talking. 'There's no other real option,' she says, almost choking on the words.

'Some people say the kangaroos can be shifted,' Cameron says, oblivious to her discomfort.

Abby contemplates him for a moment, slightly dazed. It's the talk about guns and shooting—she doesn't want to think about that. Her eyes are swimming, tiny black patches blotting the light. She has to bring herself back. What did Cameron say—something about moving kangaroos? She clings tenuously to the thread of conversation. 'Where would you move them to?' she asks, grasping a fragment of structured thought. 'There's no feed anywhere.'

'Apparently there might be some vacant farms around.'

'If farms are vacant, it's because they've been destocked in the drought,' she says.

'So you think shooting's the only solution?'

Back to shooting again—she feels a deep heaviness. 'They use experienced marksmen,' she says.

'But if we don't look at other options, there's no pressure to move forward, is there? Shooting becomes the answer by default.'

'Nobody likes shooting kangaroos, Cameron.'

He hesitates. 'Farmers do.'

Abby's nausea swells again, but she manages to hold it down. 'If kangaroos are grazing on your paddocks every day, and you're forever pulling carcasses off the road, then you're not too bothered if the government says they're going to shoot a few,' she says. 'Country people have a practical view when it comes to animals.'

'You mean they don't care?'

'What I'm saying is that farmers see animals in the context of running a farm,' she continues. 'When kangaroos compete with stock, it boils down to dollars and cents. Farmers shoot kangaroos and there isn't a murmur about it. But if the government wants to shoot kangaroos, there's uproar.'

Cameron is shaking his head. 'Kangaroos have to be safe somewhere.'

'And so do other species,' Abby protests. 'Reserves have to be managed as ecosystems, not as safe havens for kangaroos. It's about balance.'

He grins. 'I'm fond of balance.'

She sees he is enjoying the intellectual tussle, but she can't maintain the offensive. The room is tipping. She grasps the bench and breathes slowly.

'Are you okay?' Cameron leans forward and closes his hand over hers. 'You look pale.'

She doesn't speak as she tries to repress the bilious surge in her stomach. 'I feel a bit off,' she manages eventually. 'Maybe something I ate.'

'Let me take you home.' He stands quickly and pulls on his coat.

'What about our drinks?' she asks blearily.

'Leave the drinks.'

He hooks an arm around her and helps her up then leads her outside, pushing through the crowd. In the street they move clear of the smokers and stand on the footpath while she sucks in cold air.

'Maybe it was too hot in there,' she says. 'I feel better out here.'

He rubs his hand up and down her back. 'Shall we walk?' he suggests. 'Movement might help.'

They wander along the street, past the glowing windows of other bars and restaurants. Abby sees couples leaning towards each other across tables, bottles of wine in coolers, groups at dinner laughing and talking. Cameron's arm is steady around her—the warmth and smell of him envelop her.

'Here,' he says, slipping off his coat and putting it round her shoulders. 'Wear this. You're shivering.' He looks at her closely and shakes his head. 'That does it. I'm taking you home.'

'My bike is at the pub.'

'Too bad,' he says. 'You can pick it up tomorrow.'

He walks her to his car and slots her in. She is still wearing his coat and is thankful for its warmth. They don't speak as he drives through the night-lit streets.

By the time they pull up at her place she is feeling significantly better, but he insists on taking her through to her bungalow. She walks ahead through the darkened garden, startling a possum which scoffs and scuttles up a tree.

Inside, she flicks on the lights and the blow-air heater to take the chill off the room. Cameron enters behind her and closes the door. He moves close to inspect her face, lifting a hand to push her hair from her cheek. 'You look better,' he says.

'I don't know what it was. Maybe the smell of the beer. Maybe dinner.' She points at the empty meal packet on the kitchen bench beside them.

He picks it up and checks the ingredients. 'Who knows what they put in this stuff.' He tosses the packet in the sink then turns back to her with a smile, touches her hair again. 'You look good in my coat.'

She begins to tug it off. 'It's warm, but you'll need it for the drive home.'

He reaches and helps her, something slow and deliberate in his actions, a considered gentleness that stalls her. When she looks at him, his eyes are hopeful. He wants to take this somewhere, he wants to kiss her.

For a moment she considers weakening. It would be so easy to give in. She thinks of his big warm hands grasping her shoulders, kneading them. She imagines him bending to kiss her. Then she rallies. 'I think you should go,' she says, gathering strength from some remote place deep within. 'I need to rest.'

He hangs his coat over his arm and moves slowly to the door, his disappointment tangible. Then he turns back. 'Can we catch up soon?'

'I'm sure we'll see each other,' she says distantly. 'It's inevitable with all this kangaroo stuff going down.' She knows this isn't what he wanted to hear, but she has to hold him off. It's hard to do, but necessary.

'Take care of yourself,' he says from the doorway, a sad smile on his face. 'And no more frozen meals. It's no wonder you felt sick.'

She nods absently. As she watches his back receding into darkness, tears slip slowly down her cheeks.

28

Abby is preoccupied with the kangaroo debate being tossed around on TV, the airwaves and in the newspaper. She has almost forgotten George until she hears Nathan answer the phone in the communal office a week or so later. 'You're looking for Abby? Yeah, she's here today. I'll just get her.'

He holds the phone out to her and his brow furrows quizzically, as if he's preparing to be entertained by how she might handle this situation.

'I don't want to speak to him,' she mouths quietly. 'Tell him I've just popped out.'

But Nathan shakes his head and continues to present the phone to her. She'll have to take the call.

'Hello, this is Abby,' she says, trying to sound business-like.

'Hey gorgeous. It's me. George. Why haven't you called?'

Abby feels Nathan's eyes on her and she turns away, dragging the phone to the end of its cord so she can stand by the window looking out on the spiky native garden that shields the building from the street. 'I told you I was busy,' she says, sending out bored vibes and hoping George is clever enough to pick up on them. But he's not, of course.

'I left tons of messages. I thought we were friends.'

Abby draws breath. She's not generally blunt with people she doesn't know well. But George seems thick-skinned, as perceptive as a brick, so she'll have to muster the courage to be frank. 'George, you helped me when my car broke down, I bought a cappuccino to thank you, and then we said goodbye. That's it.'

'But I've been thinking about you. I just can't stop.'

'Well, I'm sorry,' Abby says. 'But that's not my problem. I'm just not interested.' There, she's said it. Callous and insensitive she may be, but it seems a sledgehammer approach is the only effective strategy with this guy. Ignoring his phone calls obviously didn't work.

'I want to take you out. Maybe dinner or some drinks. I know some good bars and restaurants. What do you think?'

Does this guy speak English, she wonders? What doesn't he get about *no*? 'I'm sorry George, but I really can't.' She glances at Nathan who is now sitting at his desk focused on a book and pretending not to listen, even though she knows he is. She wishes someone would come into the room and give him something else to think about.

'I can find you, you know,' George says, a smug tone entering his voice. 'I can look up your building and drop in.'

Abby's chest contracts with fear. 'But you won't,' she says, attempting to discourage him. 'It's a waste of your time. Because I won't go out with you. Not ever.'

She locks eyes with Nathan and his eyebrows rise cynically. She tries to think back—did she fob him off one night at a party? Is that why he's tuned in so attentively, still nursing a bruised ego?

The sound of George's breathing rustles down the line. She has silenced him, at least for a moment. Her mind skitters, probing for other ideas to deflect him. 'Do you still have that skull?' she asks. 'You should hand that thing in.'

'Bullshit. That's the best one in my collection.' He sounds stung—at least she has managed to get under his skin.

'You could get into serious trouble if you get caught with something like that.' She presses her slender advantage, hoping to ram home another psychological punch.

'Yeah, right,' he says slowly, and she thinks perhaps she can hear the synapse as his brain clicks in, rumbling like distant thunder. 'I'll ring you in a few days,' he adds. 'See if you've changed your mind.'

She hangs up the phone and chances a look at Nathan. He's goggling at her, apparently gob-smacked by her performance.

One thing's for sure, she thinks, as she grabs her papers and ducks out the door: Nathan won't ask her out after eavesdropping on that exchange with George.

George is tenacious, like a burr on her sock that won't be brushed off. The pile of his messages on her desk keeps snowballing every time she drops in, and she avoids the office even more than usual, terrified of being there when he calls again. It seems all the other PhD students have spoken to him: Jackson, Emily, Thomas, Beck, Felicity, and Nathan, of course. When she slinks into the office to collect documents or messages from her supervisor, they all look up at her, and a weighty silence falls across the room, as if they expect her to say something. Nervously, she grabs her mail and papers and textbooks, and departs as quickly as she can, dodging their eyes.

Everywhere she goes, she's tussling with a persistent niggling sense of anxiety. George could be outside the building waiting for her, watching her. He could follow her home. He could sit in the street outside her landlords' house and sneak up to the bungalow during the night. She begins to lock her door when she's sleeping, pulls the curtains when she's alone inside. She jumps and jitters at every unexpected sound. Possums in the garden at night become George shuffling around at her door. Wind moving in the trees becomes his breath at her window. The thumping of a loose fence paling becomes his footsteps on the path. Her rest fragments. She is twitchy, edgy, uneasy in her own company.

She thinks constantly of Cameron, how safe she felt with him, his body warm against hers at night. She can't go back to that, yet her present situation is fraught with worry. She detests the unhappiness of it, this dread and apprehension George has thrust upon her. Even talking to Matt fails to appease her. He offers to come up and smash George's head in, but Abby knows that isn't a solution. Plus, she's sure George's pig-hunting mates wouldn't stand by and watch it happen. Violence would only escalate things. And perhaps the whole scenario is an illusion anyway. George hasn't actually done anything, has he? It's just her fear that he might.

She decides she must intercept his next phone call—it's the only way to end this feeling of being a hostage. She has to get rid of him permanently, threaten him if necessary. It's the only way. She could ring him herself, of course, but he might misinterpret that as enthusiasm, no matter what words issue from her mouth.

She deposits herself in the office one day, determined to wait. Other members of the PhD group traipse in and out, and she smiles and chats with them, working hard to conceal the tension that simmers beneath her skin. They linger and drink coffee and do emails and chat on their phones, and Abby is fearful George might ring while the others are there.

But luck is on her side for once. Just before lunch, everyone disappears to a seminar which Abby ought to be attending too. She waits back, willing the phone to ring, staring out the window, unable to concentrate on her work. In the garden outside, a delicate eastern spinebill is dipping its beak into the narrow red inflorescences of a winter-flowering grevillea. It is a beautiful bird, a lovely russet brown colour with a bib of pure white and a little smudge of brown like a thumb print in the centre of it. Through the window she can hear its piping call when it pauses from sipping nectar to announce its presence to other birds. Then it cocks its head sideways and flutters off into another bush.

She is trying to find it again among the foliage when the phone rings, and her heart jolts to an instant gallop. This might not be George, she reminds herself. It could be anyone. But she recognises his voice immediately when she answers the phone, and somehow he knows it is her, even though she has only uttered a strangled *hello*.

'Hey, beautiful. I've caught you for once.'

Caught her in his slimy trap perhaps, she thinks, and it's just as well he doesn't know the truth of it, how much agitation and distress his attention has caused her. She suspects he might like the power of it, the ego trip of knowing he

KAREN VIGGERS

has wedged himself into her mind. He wouldn't care that she dislikes him; he's confident enough to assume he can change her perception of him. Last night she resolved she must go in hard from the beginning, ensure there is no chance of him misunderstanding her. 'I don't want you phoning me anymore,' she says firmly.

'Why not? Eventually you'll give in and come out with me. We've already had coffee. That was a good start.'

'I will not go out with you *ever*, George. You have to hear me. Not for coffee, not for dinner, not for anything. I'm not interested.'

'Of course you are. All girls play hard to get. It's your way of keeping me keen.'

Abby almost sobs with exasperation. 'George, if you keep hassling me I'll have to call the police. I don't want your phone calls. I don't want to speak to you again.'

He grunts, and it seems he might be listening at last.

'And if I have an excuse to call the police about you,' she says, saving her strongest ammunition till last, 'then I'll tell them about the skull. And you wouldn't want that, would you?'

He comes over defensive; she can hear it in his tone. 'You don't even know where I live.'

'I have your card, George. Two copies. You gave them to me.'

He's silent for a moment. 'All right, then,' he grumbles. 'Hint taken.'

'Leave me alone, George. Now just piss off!' She slams the phone down.

She realises she's shaking, threats not being part of her usual repertoire. But George didn't give her an option. Tears of distress slide down her cheeks and she scuffs them away with a tissue.

282

She sits at her desk for a while, eventually noticing the spinebill calling outside the window again. Exhaustion settles over her like a blanket. She picks up her notebook and hurries to the seminar.

She sat at her desk for a while, mentally noting the spindle-legged man outside the window again. He continued to pace over the like a father. She picked up her notebook and hurried to the seminar.

29

The people outside the doors to the auditorium are dressed in kangaroo suits. There are at least ten of them in furry grey costumes with uneven floppy ears, and they look ridiculous. Abby smiles as she arrives at the venue with her supervisor Quentin. If children were around they'd run away screaming. But her amusement fades when the kangaroos turn en masse and stare as she and Quentin walk across the lawns from the car park.

She wasn't going to come to the public meeting, but Quentin insisted it would be good for her, that she should come along to witness the conflict around the kangaroo issue. No need for that, she'd thought at the time. She only needed to read the papers to get the lowdown on public opinion. Now she hesitates as she hears one of the costumed characters shout, 'There's that ecologist. Let's get him. Murderous bastard.' These are serious demonstrators, and she and Quentin are in the line of fire.

She turns to leave as the kangaroos stride jerkily towards
them bearing placards and clenched fists, but Quentin marches
forward to meet them and she's forced to keep up. The pack
of angry bodies closes around them, shouting and jeering.
Abby cowers, her heart hammering hard, a quick frightened
staccato rhythm. She feels heat as they press close, smells
sweat and sour breath, mothballs and muskiness, senses the
animal strength of their rage. She's terrified—who wouldn't
be? Quentin is rattled too. He fends off the placards with one
arm, grips Abby round the waist with the other, and elbows
his way to the door, breathing fast. The kangaroos hustle
around them, firing abuse: *Murderers, Butchers.* The yells
mash together into a cacophony of insults. Abby ducks her
head, tries to shut the noise out, cold sweat icing her skin.

When they are safe in the foyer, Quentin gives her a
lopsided smile and passes a hand through his thin cropped
hair. He's as stressed as she is, that's obvious—neither of them
expected a reception like this. 'You okay?' he asks, breathing
out slowly through flared nostrils.

'A bit shaken,' she admits. It's the understatement of the year.

'Me too,' he says. 'That was really something.'

Something she would rather have avoided, Abby thinks.
The quiet of the library or even her office suddenly seems
delightfully appealing. 'Maybe I'm not cut out for this,' she says.

'Rubbish.' Quentin frowns. 'You can't be put off by loonies.
We have important work to do.'

He goes to fetch name tags from the registration table,
leaving Abby by the door. She looks around. Thirty or forty
people are gathered in groups, talking quietly. Over in the
corner a chocolate-skinned man with curly black hair and a
broad nose is playing didgeridoo. He has a photo of a kangaroo

set up on an easel beside him, and a sign that reads: *Help save my brother.* Obviously the local Indigenous people have been recruited to the cause.

Abby has been hearing plenty about the kangaroo cull these past few weeks. It's been a continuing prime topic in the media; a *hot issue*, Cameron would call it. Daily, his articles have appeared in the paper, often sensationalist and emotive, not based on science. She hears him being interviewed on the radio—journalists interviewing journalists, as they always do when there's no-one else to talk to. He's making good mileage for his newspaper, she supposes, and she has to admit some of his articles exhibit a vague attempt to remain balanced. But he still errs on the side of the activists and this bothers her. She thought he would try to be more even-handed, especially after she expressed her concern regarding his bias.

His voice evokes other sensations too. Each time she hears him on the airwaves sharp nails pierce the tight skin of her loneliness. The only way she can manage is to keep busy. Once her PhD is done, she can move on; distance and a new job might be the best cure. But even at work there has been no escape. Quentin has been calling her in to his office to discuss the cull, to voice his dismay at the ideas being aired by the public. He was chuffed when Cameron interviewed him and published a feature article on ecological perspectives. Abby wasn't so excited; as far as she can see this has been Cameron's sole attempt to give credence to the science.

Quentin returns with the name tags and Abby pins hers on, thinking perhaps she has dressed more casually than she ought to have today—crimson jeans and one of her long-sleeved patchwork tops cobbled together from St Vinnies cast-offs. It's a funky look, but probably not sufficiently conservative for a scientist. Quentin has made rather more of an effort. He's wearing an ironed shirt, a yellow tie and nicely tailored trousers. It's a far cry from his usual garb of shorts and Hawaiian tops which he wears to offend the staid old-boy network at the university, boring old men who support only the classical sciences like physics and chemistry and maths. Quentin hates being treated like a second-class citizen. The fact he's broken from habit today shows just how seriously he's taking this meeting. He wants to be respected, not seen as some misfit maladjusted geek.

They go into the lecture theatre to find seats before the growing crowd swarms in from the foyer. The auditorium is large and airy, rising from a wooden stage through multiple rows of seating to the lighting technician's box up the back. Quentin chooses a position at the front so he can gain easy access when he's called to give his talk. They sit quietly. Quentin flicks through a scientific paper he wants to refer to, frowning with concentration. Abby admires the fact he is never off duty. Whenever she sees him, at work or occasionally at his home when he invites a handful of students around to dinner, he has some scientific paper or textbook on the go, or something that he's editing: a chapter for a book, a student's thesis, a paper being reworked for submission to a journal.

While Quentin reads, people begin to file in, and Abby examines the mix. None of the faces look particularly friendly, and she wonders if everyone on earth is against culling except her and Quentin. If so, it doesn't bode well for this meeting.

Among the entering throng, she sees Cameron slip through the doors. He flushes as he catches her eye and nods at her before ascending the stairs. Abby's heart bangs uncomfortably. He looks confident and professional, laptop in one hand, phone in the other. The distance between them feels strange. It's easy to ignore when she doesn't see him, but now a pull of regret tugs deep inside her. His life has continued, of course, and she's not in it—that was her choice. She wonders what he's been doing, who he's been seeing, and her thoughts twist tight into a knot. Maybe he's found someone else while she's been preoccupied with George. It's none of her business anymore, but somehow this possibility hurts. She sees him sit by himself midway up the rows of seats, and she wishes she could sit with him, maybe hold his hand. To distract herself, she pulls a textbook from her bag and pretends to read.

She doesn't have to work on deception for long. Soon a tall man in a blue suit claims the podium and introduces himself as the facilitator for the meeting. He defers to prominent members of the audience, including the Minister for the Environment who is here to open the meeting. The minister sweeps quickly through a written speech pledging government support for the humane and ecologically sustainable management of wildlife. He stares out at the audience over his glasses, business-smart in his pinstripe suit, and all that Abby hears is soulless rhetoric—there's no heart in the words his mouth forms. This shouldn't be surprising, but she is strangely disappointed. If the minister doesn't believe in what he's saying, who can?

Next the facilitator invites to the stage a small hunched woman, an elder of the Ngunnawal tribe which is known to have lived in the region since time immemorial. Favouring her right hip, the old lady labours up the stairs to the microphone. She has short soft hair, a shapeless body, full cheeks, brown lips and gentle eyes. Her voice is quiet, and she looks frail and aged and subdued, a little afraid of the microphone. She speaks with humility of her people and their bond with the land, their respect for nature and other beings, how important it is to live in harmony with all creatures and take only what is needed. Then she finishes by delivering the traditional welcome to country and shuffles back down the stairs.

Abby is moved by her presence. It seems such a weak symbolic gesture that the government trots out—this welcome to country—and yet it is so significant. Abby can't help seeing the irony in it. The fact that this woman should thank the organisers for inviting her to speak on her people's land is weirdly unsettling. But Abby supposes it is at least an acknowledgement of sorts that Indigenous people exist. It's not so long ago they were considered non-people, not even securing the right to vote until 1967. That was before Abby was born, but it constitutes less than a lifetime.

The meeting turns out to be a talk-fest, only marginally under control. Whenever a scientist speaks, hecklers in the audience shout and interrupt. The facilitator tries to suppress them, but the mood of the gathering is unpleasant. Abby has never been to such a hostile meeting. She's affronted by the lack of respect exhibited by the crowd. She understands people are emotional about the concept of culling, but why don't they give the speakers a chance to explain themselves?

The government scientist begins by outlining the legislation governing biodiversity conservation, a boring address, peppered by endless bureau-speak. Abby is amazed that even this dry speech attracts heckling and protest. Then Quentin gets up and explains kangaroo biology in detail, focusing on the ability of kangaroos to breed continuously until they are so numerous they begin to starve. He describes the situation at the reserve where the cull is to occur. Overgrazing and habitat degradation are advanced there, he says. Other species are declining and there's no food for kangaroos. It's cruel to wait until they start to die.

Throughout the presentations, interjections and unrest are led by the animal rights activist called Martin Tennant, the one Abby heard on the radio when the cull was first announced. Abby watches him closely, astounded by his ability to galvanise support. He has the poise and voice of an actor, and he manages to twist everything the scientists say to make them look stupid. Abby wonders how he does it. She has never encountered anyone so powerfully persuasive. He's portly and arrogant, not particularly impressive to look at, and yet there's something compelling about him. He uses words like weapons. Even Quentin is humiliated by him.

At afternoon tea, she follows the crowd out into the foyer and drinks coffee with Quentin, discussing the progress of the meeting. Cameron is nowhere to be seen, but eventually she spies him in the far corner of the foyer talking to Martin Tennant. She manages to catch his eye, and for a moment she detects a flash of sadness and hurt. Then he covers his feelings with a journalistic glaze and goes back to his work. Abby feels the gulf between them, and a surge of loss rises in her.

She makes another coffee and takes it to an outside bench overlooking the long stretch of manicured lawn that surrounds the venue—obviously there's still water for showpiece public places, even though the rest of the city is under restrictions. Settling herself on the bench she leans back and draws in fresh air, letting the tension of the meeting ease from her. Cameron is right. When they discussed this topic at the pub he said it was about values, not kangaroos, and now she can see the truth of it: activist versus ecologist, city versus country, kangaroos versus plants and reptiles.

She wonders how such divided attitudes have evolved in society. Australians define themselves as outdoorsy, sporty, easygoing and friendly. But perhaps there is no real national psyche. As they've become increasingly urbanised, people have adopted city philosophies—they have lost connection with the land.

Closing her eyes and stretching her arms along the back of the bench seat, she feels the faint tingle of winter sun on her skin. It's soft red on her eyelids, gentle on her cheeks, soothing. A sigh sifts through her. It's so good to be out of that auditorium and away from the conflicting tangle of emotions and opinions. She decides to stay outside for the rest of the afternoon and avoid the remainder of the proceedings. She can meet Quentin afterwards and get a lift home.

Then a voice disturbs her reverie. 'Can I sit with you?'

She opens her eyes to see the kind, sagging features of the Ngunnawal elder who gave the welcome to country. She is standing nearby, waiting patiently.

'Sure.' Abby shifts along the bench to make space. 'There's plenty of room.'

The old woman limps to the seat and bends slowly to sit down. 'Interesting afternoon,' she says quietly, gazing across the lawn. 'What do you make of it?'

'I don't know,' Abby says. 'It doesn't seem any sort of agreement will be possible, does it?'

'No.' The woman grunts then laughs softly. 'People can't agree on anything these days. Everyone's too busy talking. Got their own views on things. What do *you* think?'

Abby hesitates then decides she must state where her learning lies. 'I think there are too many kangaroos.'

'Same as the government, eh?'

'I'm a scientist, and that's what the landscape is telling me.' Even to Abby this sounds pompous, but the old woman smiles.

'You talking to country too now, eh? You hear the land speaking?'

Abby flushes. 'Not the same way it speaks to you.'

The old woman folds her arms across her belly and regards Abby thoughtfully. 'Some white people can hear the land, but not too many of 'em.' She shakes her head. 'There sure are more kangaroos than there used to be. But it's bad news to kill 'em all. Should only kill what's needed for food. Not to throw in a pit to rot. It's a waste.'

'They say they need to get rid of four or five hundred,' Abby says. 'That's a lot of dead kangaroos.'

'Sure is. But you kill 'em and they come back again in a few years. Breed up, more babies. What do you do then? Keep fixing it whitefella way?' She lifts her fingers in the shape of a gun and points out across the lawn. 'Boom, boom.' Then she looks back to Abby.

'I don't like shooting either,' Abby says. 'But I can't see any other way.'

'No,' the woman says. 'Whitefellas never can.'

They sit for a while, breathing the afternoon air, sunlight bright on the grass, the shadows starting to lean towards the east.

'I know someone who'd like to meet you,' Abby says. 'She used to live on a property up in the mountains before that country became part of a park. She grew up there. She wants to know what happened to the people who lived there before her family came. Your people, I guess.'

'I'm Ngunnawal,' the old lady says. 'People south of the Murrumbidgee were Walgalu and Ngarigo. I can only tell her 'bout people who lived in Hollywood Mission up by Yass. Maybe that's not what she wants to hear.'

'I think she'd be interested,' Abby says. 'Would you talk to her sometime? I could pick you up, or bring her to meet you, whatever you like.'

'I'll think about it.' The old woman glances towards the building. 'See what happens here first, eh? Plenty of business to go down yet today, I reckon.'

30

After the break, Abby follows the old woman inside. She hadn't intended to go back in, but when the old woman clambered slowly to her feet, Abby felt obliged to accompany her. Now they walk together through the foyer, some sort of gentle respect settling between them. Abby helps her to her seat then returns to sit beside Quentin down the front.

The meeting dives immediately into dangerous controversial territory with a presentation on options for kangaroo population control, and Abby can't see how the audience will agree on anything. The government scientist outlines several possibilities, including supplementary feeding, surgical sterilisation, fertility control by immuno-contraception, and translocation. Then he rejects all these as impractical.

Supplementary feeding could avert starvation, he says, but it would promote breeding and lead to a further increase in numbers. Surgical sterilisation is possible, but animals would have to be captured and subjected to a painful procedure. With so many animals, the cost would be too high, and there would also be significant risk of injury. Plus there would still be too many mouths eating too little grass. Immuno-contraception might be an option for the future, but a suitable fertility control vaccine for wild animals isn't yet available. He ticks these things off the list then moves on to translocation. This option is superficially attractive because it could reduce grazing pressure, he says, but it is only approved for threatened species, which these kangaroos are not.

Martin Tennant loudly protests that these kangaroos are indeed threatened, even if the government doesn't see it that way. Shooting, he says, is without doubt a threat to life.

The government official counters that there is no logic in moving an abundant species from one place to another where they might be subject to later culling anyway. This leaves shooting as the only viable option. The government doesn't want to kill kangaroos, but there is no realistic alternative.

Protest ripples through the crowd, and Abby senses the meeting is about to get ugly. Martin Tennant is on his feet pointing a finger as if to cut the air. 'It's a public disgrace that we, as caring and concerned members of the community, have been subjected to today's agenda of lies and manipulation,' he shouts. 'There is a sensible and humane approach to dealing with this problem. With the assistance of a number of well-recognised scientists, we've drafted a plan for moving these kangaroos. But no-one is listening. Instead we have a gun-happy government that would rather kill animals than fork out money to shift them.'

Restlessness surges through the gathering, and Abby is wondering what will happen next. Then the lanky government veterinarian mounts the podium. His name is Alex Franklin, and he's the one who helped Abby put radio-transmitters on her animals out at the valley. He's a gentle and reasonable man, patient, considerate, non-confrontational, and widely respected. He stands awkwardly at the microphone, hands in pockets, tentatively leaning forward to speak. Nobody heckles.

'We've looked at translocation and there are a whole lot of issues with it,' he says quietly. 'Animals would have to be corralled, which isn't easy. Then they have to be darted from close range. It's frightening for them, so you get some pretty reckless behaviour. They fling themselves at fences and sometimes break their legs. Also their muscles can cramp up or they can die of heart attack. It's not very nice. Darted animals don't go down straight away either. They fight and thrash and scare the others. It's not pleasant and it's stressful for the animals. After that you have to find a way of getting them to a new site and holding them there till they get used to it. Once you let them go there's no guarantee they'll stay. If they wander onto other properties someone else could shoot them.'

Martin Tennant is unconvinced. 'Here's an opportunity to conduct an important scientific experiment,' he says, 'and you're all running from it. We could find out how animals respond to translocations like this *and* solve the problem in one simple act, but nobody will consider it. What's wrong with you people?'

'A crisis is not the time to undertake something like this,' Quentin says, rising from the front row. 'It would have to be carefully planned and replicated to have any worth as an experiment, and it would have to be justified. We're talking about a common species here, not an endangered one. This is also an animal welfare issue. We can't be trying these things out and have animals panicking in new locations and hurting themselves.'

'Too right it's an animal welfare issue.' Martin's face is purple with fury. 'And the only solution you lot can come up with is shooting, which is a serious welfare issue in its own right.'

He goes on to attack the vet, the government and the RSPCA. It's out of hand, and Abby wishes it was over. The arguments are circular and repetitive and no traction is being made in any positive or constructive direction. The facilitator obviously agrees; soon afterwards he closes the meeting. The issue is far from resolved, but Abby supposes they have at least gone through the motions of public consultation, which was probably all the meeting was meant to achieve. That would have been the government directive, she assumes. This is a rather tragic perspective, but she can't suppress her cynicism.

She files out of the auditorium with the rest of the crowd, listening to their hostile murmurings. Nobody is happy—this was always going to be the case. In the foyer she sees Cameron talking to Martin Tennant again, overhears him offering the activist a ride to the airport. For a moment their eyes lock and Cameron nods at her apologetically. Then he looks away and not long after he is gone, striding out through the doors with Martin.

Abby hovers among the dispersing crowd, waiting for Quentin. She feels lost after seeing Cameron, but she knows this is a situation of her own creation. It could have been very different. If she had reconciled with Cameron she could have been sitting with him today. He could have held her hand and discussed the proceedings with her.

Directionless and unsure what to do with herself, she asks Quentin to drop her in the city. It's on the cusp of evening and the walkways have thinned out, everybody has gone home to dinner. She visits the bottle-shop then wanders into a Thai restaurant and sits at a table with her bottle of wine. It's cheap rubbish, but it's all she can afford and tonight she doesn't give a damn—she has bought it for effect, not for quality . . . the meeting has left a bad taste in her mouth. She waves the waiter over to open the bottle and take her order.

'How many glasses?' he asks tactfully.

'Just the one, thank you,' she says, trying to appear comfortable in her aloneness, but in fact feeling small and isolated and sad.

He delivers a glass and she fills it, starts swigging; what else can she do? It's a stupid strategy but she sits at her solitary table by a small flickering tea-light candle and works her way through half a bottle.

When her food arrives—spring rolls and curry puffs and a bowl of white rice—she is unable to eat. She feels herself crumpling, a well of ridiculous self-pitying tears rising. Seeing Cameron today has unhinged her again, it has reminded her of her loneliness. She had good reason to end their relationship, an important inescapable personal cause. But it was good when she was with him. He was supportive and accepting, and she liked the feel of his body in bed, the smell of him, his deferential attention. Fact is, she wants him but she can't have him, and her rational self knows why. He was digging too close, cleaving to the needy parts of her soul, so she pushed him away. But it's too confronting, too raw to see him moving on with his life. He's managing without her—of course he is. She simply has to get over it.

She empties her glass of wine and leaves the rest behind, goes to the counter and pays her meagre solo bill. Involuntary tears well again and she bats them away. She's had enough of herself for one day. She has to go home.

Dazed and only marginally sober, she leaves the restaurant. Outside, the world ticks on—the city has come to life again after dinner. Couples drift by, arm-hooked, raucous groups of young men guffaw at their own pathetic humour, and late-night shoppers waltz along, strung with bags.

Abby moves uncertainly among them, seeking the nearest taxi rank. On auto-pilot she finds herself at the roadside near a café. Cars flash their white eyes at her as they plough past, and jaywalkers flit through traffic. Across the road, in glass-fronted restaurants, people chat and laugh over dinner. Watching them, Abby feels a stab of regret. That could have been her with Cameron tonight, wining and dining together, if she'd played her cards differently.

She chokes on the sour taste of disappointment, and when she sees an empty taxi her hand shoots out. It slides to the kerb and she gets in. The driver swivels to look at her, his eyes gleaming in the muted light. He is tall and dark, and for a moment he reminds her of someone. The tangle of the day roils in her like a brewing storm. She gives the address, leans back and closes her eyes.

They are there in less than ten minutes. It is shadowy and quiet among the towering apartment blocks, the light subdued. She hesitates then pays the driver, gets out and watches him pull away. Her feet are leaden as she walks to the door and presses the buzzer. No response.

She swings away, semi-relieved, walks twenty metres up the street, turns back reflexively and presses the buzzer again. There is a click then Cameron's voice: 'Who is it?'

'It's Abby.'

Silence then another click. 'Come on up.'

Tight with misgivings, she takes the lift and walks the hushed carpet to his door. In the dim light of the corridor she pauses and considers, almost turns and leaves, then lifts a tentative hand and knocks. Emptiness spreads around her. There is nothing behind the door. She wavers, gathering the internal momentum to walk away, then the door swings open and he is there, arm crooked against the architrave, his face dark and unreadable.

'I just wanted to talk,' she says.

He leans his head against his arm, sagging slightly, and emits a slow sigh, his eyes swinging away from her then sliding back. She smells muskiness on his breath, the tang of alcohol.

'I'm sorry,' she says. 'I can go away.'

'No.' He stretches like a waking cat and steps back. 'Come in if you like.'

Up close to him like this, she realises she has once again forgotten how big he is, how tiny she feels beside him. His gaze is brooding, deeper and heavier than she has seen it before. She slips by him into the apartment, unsure whether she should be here, aware of his eyes on her skin. The door closes behind her. Swallowing her anxiety, she stands tall and walks through to the lounge where the dim lights glow yellow on the artwork. The carpet absorbs all sound and when she turns he is standing closer to her than she realised. Something in her stomach contracts.

He lifts a tumbler from the chunky wooden coffee table and takes a deep swig of drink. The ice rattles and his hand curls around the glass. 'Do you want one?' he asks, raising his glass and his eyebrows at her.

'What are you drinking?'

'Bourbon. You can have it with or without Coke.'

'With, please.'

He strolls into the kitchen, something unreadable about him, and clunks his glass on the white stone bench, pulls another tumbler from an overhead cupboard. He crackles ice into both glasses from the dispenser in the stainless steel fridge. Then he sloshes in generous portions of spirit, topping hers with Coke before thrusting the glass at her. Task completed, he glides by her and slumps on the couch. 'Sit down,' he says.

She deliberately chooses an armchair diagonally across from him and sinks into the soft leather, but she's unable to relax. His vibes are less friendly than she'd expected, and there is something raw and restrained about him, as if he is curbing buried anger. 'You're not very happy to see me, are you?' she says.

'You've interrupted my private binge.'

'Why are you drinking?' she asks, even though she already knows.

'Stress relief,' he says.

The words *seeing you* hang unspoken in the air. Dodging his eyes, Abby sips her bourbon.

The apartment is quiet. In the past when she's been here, the TV has usually been on or there has been music playing. Not tonight. She hears the slow huff of his breathing and the sound of ice clinking in his glass as he takes another swig. Her heart rate ratchets up.

'Why are you here?' he asks.

She's disarmed by his directness and her courage evaporates—she shouldn't have come. 'I wanted to talk.'

He exhales as he leans forward to set down his glass. Then he sits back, his arms spread along the top of the lounge. His eyes darken as he looks at her. 'You didn't just come here to talk, did you?'

Her voice catches in her throat and there are no words she can glue together. She's suddenly shy and fluttery. Why *is* she here? Something about that taxi driver.

'Come here.' He pats the couch beside him.

She shakes her head, a small attempt to assert herself, and he gives a semi-exasperated sigh and stands up. He holds out a hand, and she accepts his warm grasp and lets him draw her up out of the chair. He takes both her hands and holds them in his upturned palms while he studies her. Then his hands slide up her arms and he moves close, touching his lips to her neck.

Yes, he is right. She isn't just here for a chat. She is here for losing and forgetting, surrender and release. When he holds her and kisses her and slides his tongue on her skin, her blood hums and her body sings and she gives herself over to the crush of desire.

It's wild and desperate love-making, hungry, as if this is the last time and the world is about to end. The intensity and emotional brutality of it breaks them both open. Abby can feel herself tearing inside—it is wonderful and terrible all at once. She wonders if it is the same for Cameron. In his eyes, she sees both ecstasy and pain.

Afterwards she presses her face against the broad hairiness of his chest and weeps. He crushes her close. She feels the power of his feelings in the hard thud of his heart beneath her ear. He knows she won't stay—she can feel it in him: a heavy sadness of premature loss.

He holds her a long time and they breathe into each other, chests rising and falling, skin against skin, their limbs enmeshed. Her fingers trace the shape of his back—the nub of his shoulder blade, the curve of his shoulder. He smells rich and humid like a damp evening after a hot day.

He tries to stay awake—she senses the effort in him—but sleep slowly takes him. He twitches with it, his limbs gaining slack stillness, his breaths deepening, beginning to rasp softly.

She disengages herself with infinite stealth, expecting to waken him, but he sleeps on.

In the lounge room she tugs on her clothes where she left them on the floor. Then she tiptoes on fairy feet to the door, escaping like a thief. In the lift her heart sinks in synchrony with her descent.

31

Daphne is standing semi-naked in the bedroom. She has fumbled undone the buttons of her cardigan and blouse and trousers and let them drop to the floor. All that is left is her bra and underpants and several folds of sagging old skin. She's no oil painting anymore, that's certain. She hasn't put on any weight since she was younger, but all the tone and elasticity have gone. When she looks at herself, she's reminded of the dog in the toilet-roll ad, all sad and droopy. There's not much she can do about that.

She dips her hands into the cardboard box on her bed and lifts out the shimmering pink dress, admiring its sheen in the soft afternoon light. She likes the smooth feel of the fabric between her fingers. It's not very fancy compared with ballgowns these days, but to her it is still the dream-filled sumptuous garment it once was.

She concertinas the dress and, with effort, lifts it up over her head. It's a struggle to insert herself inside, not because the dress is tight, but because her shoulders are weak and she hasn't the strength to keep her arms elevated for long. For a moment she thinks it is all going to end badly—she is encased in fabric and can't find a way through . . . an image of Mr Bean with his head stuck inside a Christmas turkey comes to mind and she almost laughs. But it won't be funny if she can't sort out this tangle. She will end up on the floor in a heap, and it would be far too embarrassing to be discovered by Ray, who is working in his office as usual.

Gasping a little, she lowers herself to lie sideways on the bed and rests for a moment, her arms still extended above her head, the box pressing into her back. Sound thumps in her head like a hammer—it's always worse when she's stressed. She forces herself to breathe slowly then pushes upright again and wriggles her way into the dress.

There she is in the dressing-table mirror, her face flushed and her mouth gaping. It's not a pretty sight. Her body has crumbled these past decades: her lips are thin and lined, her face has deep valleys, and her shoulders are stooped. But the dress is still gorgeous and it hangs from her in an almost flattering way. She smiles at the broad mauve-grey ribbon that is stitched around the hem, the band of matching lace around the waist, the dropped-V back, once so risqué and revealing. If only she could wind back the clock.

She reaches behind her back in an attempt to grasp the zip, but it's beyond her. She will have to leave it for later—perhaps Abby can help. That's why Daphne has pulled the dress out after all, so she can show it to Abby. She had planned to give the girl a peek into the box, but then an irrepressible urge had come over her to try the gown on again.

She slides her hands down over the fabric, enjoying its silken touch. Then she goes to the bathroom to put on some make-up. Standing in front of the vanity she smiles wryly. This could be interesting . . . she hasn't attempted eye shadow in years.

———◆———

At two-thirty, she has the kettle boiled and several pieces of Pam's lemon slice laid out on a plate. Pam has gone super-market shopping with Ben prior to collecting Jamie and Ellen from school. They'll all be home after half past three—noise and madness arriving as they surge through the door. Daphne hopes she will be done by then so she can save Abby from the onslaught of her great-grandchildren.

There's a knock at the door, and Daphne smooths her hands over the dress again, her heart bunting with excitement. Abby must be here. Daphne wonders what she will think of the dress. She arranges a smile on her lips then goes to the door and swings it wide.

Abby is looking down the street as if she might be expecting to see someone, maybe that young man in the red Commodore—Daphne hasn't heard anything more about him. But no, she thinks, as she watches the girl, something else is distracting Abby, something internal, a suggestion of melancholy and deep sadness. Daphne had intended to focus on the story of the dress today; but now she determines to alter her agenda. In the girl's dejected posture she sees there is more important work to be done. The gown is a mistake. Daphne wishes she wasn't wearing it.

At that moment, Abby swings and meets Daphne's eyes. Her reaction, her transformation, is almost comical; the melancholy slips away and her eyes widen. She hesitates then steps back as if for a better view. 'Wow. What an amazing dress.'

Daphne musters a coy smile. She will have to play the part, even though the plan has changed. 'Do you like it?' She shuffles backwards and orchestrates a slow turn, stretching her arms out for effect. When she completes her uncertain spin, she notices tears in Abby's eyes.

'You look beautiful,' Abby says.

This is a generous lie, but Daphne doesn't mind. 'I think I made a mess of the make-up,' she says.

Abby laughs. 'The lipstick's a bit wobbly, but you'll do.'

'I couldn't do the zip,' Daphne says.

'Here, I'll fix it for you.'

Abby finishes off the zip and the hook and eye while Daphne tries not to think about the girl inspecting her knobby, white-skinned back. She's beginning to think there is more humiliation than joy in parading the dress for Abby. She asks the girl to re-boil the kettle and goes to her bedroom for a cardigan to cover some of her blotchy exposed flesh. Perhaps it would be even better to take the dress off, but it is beyond her arthritic shoulders, and she can't bring herself to ask Abby for assistance in this task too.

In the kitchen, the girl is staring out the window at the yard. Or perhaps it is more like *mooching*: a dreary semi-absence as if she is here more out of duty than desire. This is not a feeling Daphne has ever had in Abby's presence before, and she knows things are not right with the girl. 'You're not yourself today, are you?' she says, gently drawing the girl's attention back into the room. Abby sets a too-bright smile on her face, but it droops at its corners, and Daphne knows she has hit a raw spot.

'It's not about me today,' Abby says. 'It's about you and your dress.'

Daphne shakes her head resolutely. 'There is a story behind the dress, but it can wait. You're feeling blue and I need to know why.'

Abby sighs and leans her hip against the bench, focuses back out the window, her hair falling about her shoulders in a disheveled and unkempt way—it appears she hasn't brushed it this morning. 'Have you been reading the papers?' she says. 'All this kangaroo stuff is getting me down.'

'You mean the cull they've been talking about?' Daphne asks.

'Yes, that.'

Daphne knows all about the cull because it has triggered even more craziness around here lately. Her granddaughter Sandy's wildlife group has been caught up trying to stop it, and, as usual, everyone has had to bend around Sandy's needs. With all Sandy's emergency meetings, the children have been practically living here. Four-year-old Ben comes nearly every day, and then Jamie and Ellen have to be cared for after school. Pam has been up late at night cooking stews and casseroles, and when Sandy comes to pick up the children each evening, they stay on to dinner. Pam and Sandy bath the children then plonk them in front of the TV, after which Sandy starts sewing pouches for the joeys that will be orphaned when the cull goes ahead. Pam has been roped into sewing pouches too; Daphne can't believe it. She watches them both—her daughter and her granddaughter—heads bowed, needle and thread in hand, tacking old jumpers and windcheaters into cosy new homes for joeys. But Daphne can't help thinking it's all a bit futile. While the others sew, she sits in her chair and reads and does crossword puzzles, keeping her mouth

tight-shut, thankful her arthritis and poor eyesight exempt
her from helping. She wouldn't be seen making pouches for
orphaned joeys that ought to be killed with their mothers.

During the sewing bees, there have been numerous discussions about Sandy's wildlife group and their plans. Apparently
the joeys will be shared among the experienced carers in the
group, which means more joeys for Sandy. Pam doesn't think
Sandy can cope, but when she says as much, it falls on deaf
ears. Sandy wants to save as many joeys as possible or the
poor things will be knocked on the head and thrown into
a pit. She bursts into tears, and Pam rushes to console her,
promising to do whatever she can to assist. It isn't a good
resolution, Daphne thinks. In fact, it's no resolution at all.
But whenever she tries to weigh in and add some perspective, Sandy becomes hostile, arguing that she doesn't expect
Daphne to understand. *Gran, you're from a time when the
rights of animals didn't matter. You fed kangaroos to the dogs.
But things are different now. Society is more evolved. We can't
just keep shooting things.* It always ends with Pam reaffirming
her support for Sandy while sending Daphne an eagle glare
that says, *Shut up, we don't need your input on this.* Daphne
generally takes the hint and goes to bed.

Now Daphne wonders if perhaps Abby's opinions are similar
to Sandy's. She'd thought Abby would be more practical, being
from the country and all. But maybe the girl has some weird
attachment to kangaroos—she does spend her days following
the creatures around the valley. 'You don't like the idea of
shooting kangaroos?' Daphne asks carefully.

Abby sighs again, as if this subject is too heavy for consideration. 'I don't like the idea of shooting *anything*,' she says.

'But I'm an ecologist, and it makes sense to shoot them. I just don't feel good about it.'

'Of course they have to be shot, dear,' Daphne says. Obviously the girl needs some reassurance. 'There are just too many; you've said it yourself. And you've seen how the countryside is suffering. What else can be done in this drought?'

Abby's face twists and she glances away. 'I know all that,' she says. 'It's just my past coming back to bite me.'

Daphne sees the opening and she determines to take it. 'Is that something you might want to talk about?' she asks quietly. She sees Abby sag slightly and knows she has found the right place to dig, but she holds back. Whatever is simmering inside the girl needs to come forth willingly, not be dragged out like a loose tooth yanked from a reluctant child.

Abby's eyes flicker briefly to Daphne's face. 'Not really, not today.'

That's it then, Daphne supposes. Conversation over. She moves around the bench to retrieve the kettle, the tulle lining of her dress rustling as she walks. It takes some effort to grasp the handle with her clumsy hands, and, as she pours hot water into the teapot, she accidentally spills some onto the plate of lemon slice, and curses. Luckily she manages not to splash the dress.

'Let me do it.' Abby dives in quickly to help. 'We can save those pieces. We'll get a fresh plate, shake the water off, and once we eat a few, Pam will never know.'

Daphne relinquishes the kettle thankfully and sits down in the living room. Easing back into her chair, she's surprised how tired she is—too much excitement for one day. A deep nagging pain tugs at her shoulders, perhaps from the effort of shimmying into the dress, and the thumping is back in her head. She is a little light-headed. She slumps among the clouds of pink material, feeling rather more like a wilted daisy than a rosebud.

Abby brings the tray into the living room. She removes the crossword book from the coffee table and sets down the tray, pours the tea. 'I bet you broke a few hearts in your day,' she says.

Daphne presses her lips together, remembering. 'Only one or two.'

'Surely more than that?' Abby is smiling.

'Sometimes you have to be careful which hearts you break,' Daphne says, and she notices the girl's smile fade. 'I never wore this dress for my husband,' she adds. 'But perhaps I should have. He would have appreciated it.'

Abby is disbelieving. 'Your husband never saw it?'

'Oh yes, he saw it, but only in the box. I never wore it to any balls—such a waste really.'

'I don't understand,' Abby says. 'A dress like that must have cost a fortune.'

'It did; all my savings. It was for a special dance. Ridiculous to put such store by a ballgown—but we didn't have many luxuries in those days, and it was my one indulgence.'

'Your parents didn't help pay for it?'

'Oh no. Definitely not. I was planning to wear it for the wrong person, you see. Not Doug, but another young man, called Stewart White. The dress was never for Doug, but in a way it led me to him.' She spreads her fingers over the fabric. 'I suppose that's why I've never been able to throw it out. It reminds me of the way life tosses up surprises. You think everything is going wrong, but somehow you end up in the right place.'

Abby looks confused. 'So that's the story, is it?'

Daphne smiles. 'That's just the beginning.' She orders the saga in her mind and begins to tell it to the girl.

———

She met Stewart White at the picnic races the year she turned twenty-three. He was a working stockman recently arrived in the region, and he was the talk of the district, quite a horseman, very flashy, and capable of racing fast horses to convincing victories at local meets. Not only was he persuasive with horses, Daphne had heard, but he was also very charming. Apparently he was clean-shaven too, which was rather a novelty for men who weren't gentry. At that stage, Daphne hadn't yet encountered him, but she knew he was riding for one of the rich landowners at that year's races.

Although her family wasn't one of the wealthiest in the region, Daphne's father had managed to accumulate a good swathe of land, and it was common knowledge that his daughter was single and available. Daphne hated the price tag she seemed to be wearing on her forehead, and she disliked the direct and enquiring looks she attracted from many of the unattached local bushmen—including Doug Norrington, who her parents considered to be high up in the eligible-bachelor stakes. Doug was the son of their neighbour, and her parents kept referring to the wisdom of a *strategic match* which would bring their two landholdings together and secure the family's status in the area. Daphne wasn't interested. To her mind, Doug Norrington was stiff-backed and serious, brooding behind that beard, and he seemed eternally entrenched in staid silence. Daphne had so much more living to do.

The local races were the domain of the big-name upper-class families who used the occasion to parade their wealth. They set the dress standards, and the bushmen and their families turned out in their best too, so as not to be completely outdone. The men wore thick woollen suits and starched white shirts, carefully secured at the neck with Windsor-knotted ties over which their bushy beards bristled. The women came in neatly pressed bright frocks and carried flowers and wore hats crafted by their own hands.

Daphne's dress that day was none too fancy, but it was clean and fresh and white and flattering. And somehow, perhaps by sheer youthful exuberance and glowing health, she must have stood out among the crowd, because she was the one who drew Stewart's gaze—not any of the other girls who were vying for his attention.

Her father had entered a horse in the main race—a half-tamed chestnut brumby mare with more than a touch of wildness in her. He was the only one who could ride her, and she had been a disaster on the farm since they'd brought her down from the mountains, wrecking fences and cutting herself, kicking and injuring other horses, biting the workmen. Nobody liked her and no-one went near her.

The mare was a handful at the starting line, and Daphne was afraid her father would be thrown. When the start gun was fired, the mare reared up, threatening to keel over before regaining balance and plunging into a mad gallop. By then the other horses had leapt away and she was some distance behind, but she ran with huge frantic strides, and Daphne knew she would soon catch the field.

Daphne was standing with the crowd near the finish line, watching the horses bolt up-slope and across the hill around the set course. She could hear the sound of hooves drumming on the ground like a miniature earthquake. Around her, people

313

were discussing their bets and chances. They'd already written off her father's mare, and everyone was focused on young Stewart White who was pushing an expensive bay stallion into the lead. Daphne was the only one who watched her father as he crouched over the chestnut mare's wither. She saw he was struggling with the mare. Madness had taken the horse's mind and she was hell-bent on her own course, swinging wide on all the corners, adding distance to the race and giving Daphne's father a hard time as he dragged on the reins to turn her. Even so, she made quick work of catching the other horses, but refused to shoulder in among them, running her own race instead, against some invisible demon.

The field threaded its way uphill and around a patch of trees before taking up the final charge for the finish line. Daphne's father lost ground in the turn, fighting for dominance until the mare settled again and started to run. By this time, Stewart, on the bay stallion, had pounded out in front and was stretching for the finish. Daphne felt the crowd rise with adrenalin, the encouraging yells intensifying. She elbowed her way through so she could see, hooking Doug Norrington in the ribs as she pushed past. She remembers him looking down at her, a dark serious light in his eyes and a small flash of white as he showed his teeth in a grin beneath his beard.

Then she was at the front, and her father's chestnut mare had caught up with Stewart on the bay, and the horses were straining stride-for-stride. The mare nosed into the lead and Daphne could see her father like a dark burr over the mare's back, the white gleam in the mare's eyes as she tore for the finish. Then some primitive part of the mare's wild brain must have registered the mass of people milling ahead of her, and she threw up her head and careered crazily sideways, lurching onto another trajectory which did not lead to the finish.

Daphne watched, dismayed, as the mare bolted away while Stewart rode over the line an easy first. The rest of the pack thundered past, riders standing in the stirrups to haul up their steeds. Daphne was caught among the throng of people jostling to see Stewart as he trotted back on the champion bay, and she heard him say *I thought I was beat.*

Of course he was beat. The mad mare was undoubtedly faster, but she was an undisciplined child, incapable of being persuaded to a different set of rules.

Daphne watched the crowd surround Stewart on the bay stallion, then she moved aside to wait for her father. Halfway up the hill, he had managed to reef the mare under control and was now jogging slowly back. When he pulled up beside her, his eyes were alight with anger. Daphne grabbed the reins while he hurled himself off and strode to the drinking tent to drown his embarrassment. Daphne felt for her father. She wished she could console him, and she knew it wasn't losing that mattered, so much as the manner in which the mare had defeated him. She could imagine the humiliation that was grating beneath his skin.

The mare was jumpy and hot, sweaty and blowing. Daphne lifted the reins over the horse's head, ignoring the spattering of sweat and foam that flicked onto her dress. She led the mare across the paddock and unsaddled her behind the old truck, leaving the saddle, pommel-down, on the bonnet.

She had taken the mare to the trough for a mouthful of water when Stewart appeared. The mare fidgeted sideways, dancing on nervous hooves.

'That's some horse,' Stewart said, as Daphne tugged on the reins to check the silly mare. 'She should have won,' he added. 'Had me cooked.'

'Tell that to the old man,' Daphne said, nodding towards the drinking tent. 'He's in there drowning his sorrows.'

'Nobody could control that horse,' Stewart said. He had his thumbs hooked in his trouser pockets and a lazy smile on his face as he inspected Daphne and the mare. 'Looks like you know how to handle her though.'

He came closer and reached a hand to touch the mare's shoulder, but the horse lunged at him and bit him hard on the leg, and he leapt back, cursing. Mortified, Daphne jerked at the mare's head, tugging her back.

Stewart managed a grin before he turned away. 'When you get rid of that horse, come and find me. I'll buy you a drink.'

Daphne watched him stride off towards the crowd, a strange hot storm of embarrassment and excitement brewing in her chest. She released the mare in a vacant wooden corral and went to find her father, who was already a drink or two down, sitting at a table with a few other bushmen. They were in full cry, unpicking the mare's wild race, so Daphne avoided them and wandered off in search of her mother.

Stewart intercepted her behind the betting tent. He emerged smiling from a fist of people and stood examining her like a horse at a saleyard. For a moment Daphne bristled then Stewart's swagger softened and he offered his arm as an invitation. 'A drink, young lady?'

'I'd prefer to walk,' she said.

His grin was wide and confident. 'Walk then it is,' he said.

She slipped her arm through his and they walked around the paddock.

He must have been sweaty after his race, she later supposed. But what she recalled was his buoyant attentiveness, the way his eager eyes rested on her face as she talked, the way his fingers drizzled slowly along her arm, arousing all sorts of scintillating sensations. They must have made several laps of the field together, talked about the race and the crazy mare and a number of other matters which she no longer recollects.

The other thing she remembers is running into Doug Norrington as they strolled along. He appeared from nowhere, his eyes glowering and his mouth invisible within his beard. Daphne felt disapproval and disappointment emanating from him in waves. 'The mare needs some attention,' he said gruffly. 'Your father's had one too many and the weather's cooling down. The mare needs walking. You should see to it.'

Daphne went to check the mare, who was standing peace-fully in the yard, head lowered, exhausted after the day's escapade. Daphne knew then that Doug's intervention had more to do with jealousy than his interest in the horse, but she hadn't the motivation to seek him out and reprimand him. No matter what Doug Norrington hoped for, the seeds of her attraction to Stewart had already been planted, and Doug's impact was less than that of a nuisance fly.

Stewart began to visit regularly at the family farm after that, arriving with flowers and compliments and cheeky propositions and kisses behind the shearing shed, and Daphne was consumed by the romance of it. Stewart was physical and insistent. When he kissed her, he pressed his tongue into her mouth and his groin against her stomach. He wanted to put his hands beneath her clothes, expected it, cajoled her into lifting her blouse so he could touch her skin.

Daphne was torn. She wanted to please him—there was status to be had with the local girls through the simple fact of holding his attention. But there was something not quite right about the way he pushed himself upon her. Even so, she was shyly overwhelmed by his affections, by the romantic things he said: how much he loved her, how much he desired her, how beautiful she was, how wildly he wanted to press her to the ground and cover her with his kisses. During the day she would imagine herself with him and become quite carried away by her thoughts. At night she would wake all hot and shaky, with new emotions and raw sensations rippling beneath her skin, urges that arose from her imaginings, thoughts of his hands on her naked body.

But it was never the same when she was with him. He was hurried, rough. He kept asking her to take off her clothes, kept saying that O God he couldn't wait for her much longer, he was so desperate to join with her.

It was all so intense, and she felt it in her bones at night that she needed this union too, that it would be beautiful. And yet something held her back. Was she afraid? Was she capable of delivering what he was asking? Or was she a mummy's girl, too polite to give in to her emotions? The thought alarmed her, that she might be as staid and correct as boring Doug Norrington. Then she realised she needed *atmosphere*, a suitable occasion to give herself to Stewart. The local dance was coming up, and that would be the night. She would use her savings to buy a dress that exceeded all dresses. She would entrance Stewart and dance for him, and then she would give in to him somewhere out in the paddock that night up in the darkness of the hill. They would be locked together, discovering each other. Then they would get married—that was the natural way of things—and they would have children.

She found the fabric on a visit to Queanbeyan and she guiltlessly handed over all her savings to buy it and have the gown made. It was a shocking indulgence, she knew it. But when she brought the dress home a week before the dance, and tried it on, and twirled around the house feeling beautiful, she was convinced the sacrifice was justified.

Her parents were disappointed she wasn't going to the ball with Doug. They didn't like Stewart and they were, at best, stiffly polite with him whenever he visited the farm, eternally suspicious of his effusive compliments. But Daphne needed a chaperone to accompany her to the dance, and she was thankful that her father agreed to take her, despite his obvious disapproval.

On the day of the dance, however, he was out shifting stock. It was a moody afternoon with clouds piled ominously on the ridge. In the homestead, Daphne bathed and dressed. In front of the mirror she carefully applied a smear of pink lipstick and a flourish of pale blue eye shadow. Then she fussed endlessly with her hair, deciding in the end to pull it up in a loose high bun, with soft strands falling beside her pretty flushed cheeks.

She was still preoccupied with herself at the mirror when the storm came in: lightning jags flashing from the steely clouds, thunder growling, rain sheeting over the mountains. She moved to the window to watch the weather, worried her father might be unable to make his way back in time. He could get caught up in the storm, trying to move cattle turned restless and stubborn in the rain. She imagined him shouting at them, wheeling and kicking his horse among them so he could angrily and impatiently ply their wet backs with his whip. He would make them do his bidding and he would be here—she was sure of it. He was a sturdily reliable man. On a chair, his suit was laid out ready, his shirt ironed, shoes shined.

The minutes went by and he didn't appear. She hovered anxiously at the window, trying to will the shape of man-on-horse from the furious lash of rain. But he didn't show and gradually her anger began to stir. Perhaps he had meant to be late or not to come back at all. Maybe this was his punishment because she had chosen the wrong man. Her father could deliberately spoil her evening. He could use the stock as an excuse, or the dogs, the weather, his horse, *anything* to avoid taking her to the ball.

Eventually the rain thinned and then stopped, and the sky brightened with patches of blue. Daphne stood stiffly by the window, fury tumbling in her heart and quickening her breath. It was so late and still her father had not come. He had let her down, and she would never forgive him.

Then she saw the neighbour's truck coming slowly along the drive, splashing through puddles left by the storm. It lumbered past the yards to the front of the homestead, and Doug Norrington stepped out and peered cautiously towards the door. He had about him the look of a haunted man, and Daphne's heart suddenly skipped to a different beat. Something was wrong. She hurried to the bed, yanked off the dress, tugged on some old clothes and yelled for her mother.

Doug met them on the veranda, his battered old hat in his hand. He had come to tell them Daphne's father was dead. He had found him in the creek near the bridge with his head under the water. Doug had seen the cattle wandering along the road, Daphne's father's horse grazing on the verge. Then he'd seen her father in the creek. There were gouges on the bridge where the horse must have slipped. Daphne's father must have hit his head on the deck then slid into the creek. Doug reckoned it had been fast.

He grasped Daphne's mother's arm to support her as she sank into the grip of shock. Then he helped her into the house. Daphne stayed on the veranda, staring numbly at Doug's truck, knowing her father's body was in there, perhaps lying on the straw in the tray-back, the life gone out of him. Her emotions began to boil: a mash of anger and guilt and dismay and disappointment, all of it rolling over her and balling into harsh jerky sobs.

Doug came out, touched her shoulder gently and asked if she was all right. Of course she wasn't, but he was so kind she couldn't shout at him, couldn't hit him with the great wall of grief that was congealing inside her. He stood nearby until her sobs had stilled then he said quietly, 'You take yourself inside and look after your mother. I'll bring your father in.'

Daphne went into the house, saw her mother crumpled in a chair weeping, but was unable to console her. An automaton, she moved to the cupboard and pulled out a sheet, laid it out on the lounge ready for her father's body. Then she opened the door to show Doug in.

He placed her father gently, respectfully, on the sheet, mindfully arranged the slack legs and arms, brushed a hand over her father's lids in an attempt to close his eyes. 'The lids are stubborn,' he said softly to Daphne with the kindest, most empathetic smile she had ever seen. 'Best I leave you with him now. But if you've any questions, anything I can do, just let me know. I'll drop in again soon.'

She followed him to the door and stretched out her hand. 'Thank you,' she said, feeling his warm grip for the first time.

The dance went ahead without her, of course. She heard that Stewart got drunk and seduced another woman who, most inconveniently for Stewart, fell pregnant. He had to marry her, and they left the district because Stewart was penniless. Daphne realised she had been lucky to escape—although it was a while before she could see it that way. After her father's death, there weren't many options. Her mother couldn't run the farm, and Daphne knew she couldn't manage on her own. She was a good horsewoman and unafraid of hard work, but it was still the era of men; without a male to run the farm, she and her mother were vulnerable. They would have to sell the land and move away.

Daphne couldn't face it. The land was in her blood, and it had been her father's reason for living. She did the only thing she could do; time elapsed then she married Doug. He was a good man, well respected, and she knew the union would have pleased her father. It was the right decision. Doug found his way into her heart and she learned to love him. He took good care of her, he was a good father, and they understood each other: they both loved the land. What more could she have wanted?

32

Daphne is exhausted; Abby sees it in the old lady's face, which is paler and more drawn than usual. Tiredness sits under her eyes. Abby knows she is supposed to glean a message from Daphne's story, that good endings are possible even in difficult circumstances. She knows the old lady wants her to resolve things with Cameron and live happily ever after. But Abby's tale is different. What was right for Daphne decades ago bears no relation to her own journey. The best Abby can do is show appreciation of the old lady's tale, smile and be kind. She tops up Daphne's teacup and offers her another piece of soggy lemon slice. Perhaps a bit of sugar will perk the old lady up.

'How's young Cameron?' Daphne asks.

It's the question that had to come, Abby supposes, beginning to feel weary herself. 'I saw him recently,' she says. 'But I think it's over. He's moved on.'

Daphne raises an eyebrow and Abby knows the old lady

doesn't believe her. It is then that the doorbell rings, and they both look reflexively to the door.

'I'll get it, if you like,' Abby offers.

But Daphne heaves herself out of the chair and wavers through the foyer, oblivious to the fact she's still wearing the dress. Abby sees the dark silhouettes of two people through the frosted glass. She stands as Daphne swings the door open to reveal two policemen standing on the doorstep. One is tall and overweight with a bunch of grey bristles on his lip which is supposed to pass for a moustache, the other is thin and clean-shaven and serious. They look grim, as if they have just come from a funeral.

Daphne tucks her cardigan close around her chest and straightens. 'Can I help you?' she asks. Then she flickers a glance of alarm at Abby before turning back to the police. 'Is everything all right?' she adds. 'My daughter? The grand-children? There hasn't been an accident, has there?'

The taller policeman smiles reassuringly. 'Nothing like that,' he says. 'Nothing to worry about. We're looking for Daphne Norrington.'

'That's me.' Daphne is holding onto the door handle. She looks down as if suddenly registering the ball gown, and the pink flush that mounts her cheeks spells embarrassment. Abby feels her discomfort. The dress was a private story, not to be shared in a public setting.

The tall policeman is fortunately professional. 'Do you mind if we come in?' he says, overlooking the dress. 'We need to speak to you. We've come across some new evidence on your husband's case.'

Daphne remains in the doorway. 'Doug died years ago,' she says. 'His case has been closed.'

'Ma'am, a skull has been found,' the thin policeman says, clearing a gravelly throat. 'We've been through our records and checked the coroner's file from your husband's disappearance in the mountains. It's early days and there are several tests to be done, but we think it might be him. Can we come in and go through some paperwork with you?'

Abby hears the word *skull* and feels a small shock of connection: George and his collection, the human skull of unknown origin. Is it possible that he has taken her threat seriously and handed the thing in? Could that be where this skull has come from? It seems too timely to be pure coincidence. She sees Daphne step back, shaking her head as she leads the policemen across the foyer with its cream-coloured tiles. Abby is not surprised the old lady is finding this hard to believe. She is struggling with the shock of it too.

Then, without warning, Daphne crumples to the floor in a cloud of pink material. Abby launches forward to protect Daphne's head, which has already thumped on the tiles with a sickening crack. She lays Daphne gently in the recovery position. It is like last time out in the valley . . . at least she hopes it is, and that the old lady has simply collapsed again. Tentatively she tucks her fingers into Daphne's neck to check her pulse, feels the solid beat and sits back on her heels, floppy with relief. She barks at the policemen to grab a cushion from the couch, which she places beneath Daphne's head.

'Christ!' she hears the tall policemen say to the other. 'You're supposed to sit them down before you give them news like that.'

'Ray,' Abby yells down the corridor. 'Some help please.'

'I'll call an ambulance,' the thin policeman says.

Abby doesn't look up. She strokes Daphne's thin white hair back from her face, feels a twist of deep affection as she tucks a wisp behind Daphne's ear. She sees the old lady awakening, quickly, like a deaf dog startled from slumber. Daphne's pale eyes stare across the floor then twitch up to Abby. 'It's okay,' Abby says. 'You tumbled.'

Ray appears from his office and pauses, bewildered, when he sees the policemen. Then he registers Abby on the floor crouching over Daphne.

'She collapsed,' Abby says as he squats beside her.

He gathers the old lady in his arms like a child and carries her to the couch. The policemen continue to wait near the front door. One of them informs them that an ambulance is on the way.

'I don't need an ambulance,' Daphne insists, batting Ray away. 'I'm fine.'

But Ray shakes his head, taking control. 'You are not fine. People don't just fall over. Has it happened before?' He follows Daphne's guilty glance to Abby, and Abby nods. 'Right,' Ray says. 'How many times?'

Daphne looks away, mumbles almost inaudibly.

'Four or five times?' Ray's lips compress. 'If that's the case we need to check it out. Let the ambulance come.'

Daphne folds her arms over the cardigan and hunches into herself, looking suddenly frail and old, ridiculous in the dress. Abby wonders if perhaps they should take her to the bedroom and remove the gown before the ambulance arrives. But there isn't time. Outside, a car pulls up and Abby hears voices: Ben's high-pitched shout. 'Look, there's a police car here.'

Then the cavalcade arrives: three children pour into the room with rapid running feet and school bags and a plethora of questions. Pam follows, eyebrows lifting into a question mark under her prim straight fringe, her mouth set in a line of worry.

And then the ambulance is there, barrelling with a shriek into the street, the two paramedics pushing less than politely past the policemen and the gaggle of children to find their patient. They bend over Daphne and examine her, take her heart rate, blood pressure, shine a torch in her eyes, look in her mouth, ask questions, start attaching leads to her arms and legs.

Pam and Ray hover, watching anxiously.

Abby, the policemen and the children are superfluous. Abby ushers the kids outside and the policemen follow, muttering something about getting back in touch when the crisis is over. The children run to the gate, yelling and squealing, awed by the emergency vehicles parked in the street. A police car *and* an ambulance—Abby supposes that doesn't happen every day. She wonders how she will keep the kids entertained while everyone else is inside worrying over Daphne. Then the idea comes to her. She puts on her most persuasive smile for the policemen. Cameron would say she was cheating, using her femininity, but hey, if it works . . .

'Can we have a look inside your car?' she asks. 'The kids would love it.'

The tall policeman's serious face splits into an affable smile. 'Sure. Part of community service, I suppose. And we're not in a rush, are we?' he says to his colleague.

Good, Abby thinks. She has a few questions she wants to ask the policemen about that skull.

33

Hospital hasn't changed much since the last time Daphne was here, and she can't quite remember when that was—maybe when Sandy had her babies. Then again, hospitals have always been the same: horrible shiny impersonal spaces full of white beds and fluorescent lights and echoing voices and machines that go ping.

Pam fusses while Daphne lies on a nasty hard bed in emergency asking repeatedly why she can't just go home. 'I'm old,' she says. 'Everyone has to die of something.'

Pam is obviously affronted. 'I'm not letting you die just yet. This might be something entirely treatable, which means you can live happily for quite a bit longer. If you weren't here, who would I complain to about Sandy's kids? Ray is too busy to listen.'

When Pam puts it like that, Daphne can see her point. And it's good to know her company is valued. Pity it takes a crisis for people to announce their feelings.

The hospital is busy. When they arrived, the waiting room was full of weary-looking people sagging in plastic chairs, watching TV with jaded faces. When Pam told the triage nurse that the paramedics had recommended Daphne come immediately to hospital for further assessment, the nurse took them straight through and found a bed for Daphne, then she drew the curtains and told them to wait. What else do you do in hospitals? Daphne thought.

They have been here at least an hour now, filling time behind the curtains, listening to the ebb and flow of voices and footsteps and beeping machines. Mostly they sit in silence. Daphne is weary. All this fuss has been too much for her, and the bright lights are uncomfortable for her eyes. She lies back and lets her eyelids droop, trying to find some peace and rest.

The doctor—when she finally arrives and yanks back the blue curtains—is a slim young woman with a dark-brown ponytail and cool hands, and a stethoscope strung round her neck like a necklace. She looks too young to be qualified, but her white coat adds a degree of authority, along with the concerned pucker of her brow as she asks Daphne to elaborate on what happened. Under direct questioning, Daphne has no choice other than to articulate what has been going on these past months. She mentions the falls and the funny thumping sound that has lodged itself in her head.

As she talks, she sees Pam's face tighten. 'Why didn't you tell me any of this?' Pam hisses while the doctor checks the records made by the nurse.

'I thought it was just old age,' Daphne says quietly. Guilt is settling on her like a blanket. Perhaps she should have told someone about those funny little symptoms. Maybe she should have acted on that referral instead of tossing it in the bin.

The doctor examines Daphne carefully, taking her pulse and listening to her chest with the chilly stethoscope which draws goose bumps on Daphne's skin. She gently probes Daphne's neck. 'Is the thumping on any particular side, or does it radiate over your whole head?'

'I don't know,' Daphne says. 'Maybe it's more on the right than the left.'

'Any numbness? In your arms or fingers or anywhere else?'

Daphne remembers waking at night unable to feel her arm. She recalls a period of three or four days when the numbness persisted. That was weeks ago but she reports it anyway, and thinks perhaps the doctor's face changes slightly as she speaks, as if suppressing a reaction.

'It's lucky you had that fall and came in here today,' the doctor says, 'or something serious could have happened. If we hadn't seen you, you may have had a stroke.' She scribbles on a form and hands it to Pam. 'I need you to take her across to imaging for an ultrasound of her neck. Then I'll see you again.'

'There's nothing wrong with my neck,' Daphne grumbles as Pam wheels her along the empty hospital corridors in a wheelchair provided by the emergency department. They are searching for the imaging rooms, which are supposed to be somewhere in this wing of the hospital. 'We'll probably be waiting for hours,' she adds. 'Nothing happens fast in these places unless you're actually dying.'

Pam swings the wheelchair round a corner. 'Sounds like you're extremely lucky,' she says. 'Sounds like you've dodged a bullet.'

Think about that, hangs unspoken in the air. Daphne supposes perhaps she *should* think about it—maybe she *is* lucky to be here. It's a steadying thought, makes her feel less like whinging and complaining. Every minute is precious.

They locate the imaging rooms and settle themselves in the waiting room. It must be a quiet afternoon because soon a smiling nurse in a green uniform emerges and scans the form Pam hands to her. Then she looks down at Daphne. 'This won't take long,' she says. 'And it's not at all invasive. It won't hurt a bit.'

She wheels Daphne into a room and helps her clamber from the wheelchair onto another hard white bed while Pam seats herself on a plastic chair in the corner. The nurse tells Daphne to lie down, and drapes a cotton blanket over her. She says she is a sonographer and that she is going to lubricate a probe with warmed gel and run it over Daphne's neck. Pictures will appear on the TV screen up on the wall, showing the blood vessels in Daphne's neck and the flow of blood through those vessels.

It all sounds very scientific and Daphne is only minimally interested. The probe is hard and uncomfortable where it presses near her throat, and the pictures on the screen are like those on an old TV set when reception was bad—mostly black and white and fuzzy and meaningless. Patches of red and blue appear from time to time, but there's no shape to anything. Daphne keeps her head still on the pillow as instructed and closes her eyes.

Pam, however, is full of questions which the sonographer says she can't answer. Her job is to take the pictures and pass them on to the doctors, who will do the interpretation. Daphne supposes this is why doctors are paid so much—they are the ones who make the decisions and deliver the bad news. She keeps her eyes closed and wishes it was over.

After the ultrasound they go back to emergency to wait for the results. All the beds are full, so they sit in reception. The faces of the waiting people haven't changed . . . or perhaps they have, but there is a sameness to boredom that makes people

331

look identical. Daphne and Pam wait for what feels like forever before the young ponytailed doctor calls them through again. Pam wheels Daphne into a small room where the doctor puts black films like X-rays up onto a white screen. She talks and points, tossing around technical words like *carotid artery* and *sclerosis* and *surgery* and *cerebrovascular episode*, which apparently simplifies to *stroke*.

The short version is that Daphne has a blocked artery in her neck and could have a major stroke at any time. She's a time bomb waiting to go off unless she has surgery to clear the blood vessel. All these strange symptoms she's been having are to do with the impeded blood supply to her brain; the thumping she's been hearing is her heart trying to push the blood through the blockage. The falls she's been having are due to small clots lodging in her brain. If a major clot breaks off she could have a stroke. The solution is to visit a vascular surgeon, which Daphne's regular doctor can arrange for her. The hospital will pass on all the information so an appointment can be made as soon as possible.

Pam seems happy to have some answers, but Daphne sinks in the wheelchair, knowing her doctor will not be happy. How long is it now since the GP recommended having those tests done? No doubt he will ask about the referral that ended up in the bin.

The ponytailed doctor is asking if Daphne has private health insurance. If she does, it's likely the surgeon will operate soon, otherwise she'll probably have to go on the list. For years, Pam has insisted on paying those ludicrously expensive insurance bills. Daphne has always thought it was a waste of Ray's hard-earned money. But now perhaps it's just as well.

34

Daphne likes the vascular surgeon—she finds she has a reluctant admiration for him. His rooms are modern and flash and expensive-looking (which will probably be reflected in his bills), but he is surprisingly human. He is smartly dressed, fit-looking and affable with a distinct twinkle in his eye which sets Daphne's concerns temporarily at ease. He talks her through the details of the operation, showing her several ghastly pictures of the anatomy of the human neck with railway tracks of coloured veins and arteries running through it.

'This is your carotid artery,' he says, pointing with his pen. 'Yours is more than ninety per cent blocked. We need to clear it out and then your risk of stroke reduces dramatically.'

As he leans forward across his desk, explaining it all to her, Daphne catches the scent of aftershave. It's tangy and masculine, not too strong. Having lived with a man with a beard all her life, aftershave is a simple pleasure Daphne has never experienced. But then women who've never made love with a bearded man have missed one of life's great intimacies, she thinks. She flushes. Here they are talking about an operation and she is thinking about sex. The good thing is no-one would suspect her of it. All they see is an old woman and they think she is past imaginings like that.

Memories of Doug have been coming to her frequently this week, more than usual. She sees him in the night, strong visions of his face, the lovely texture of his beard, the gentle intensity in his eyes when he looks at her, love written into them. Sometimes she imagines his smell—the bushy, earthy aroma of his skin. One night she finds herself reaching across the bed for him, which she hasn't done in years, decades. That was one of the hardest things to accept after he died: the loss of his comforting presence in bed, the solidity of him beside her, the reassurance that came with closing her hand over his and feeling him grasp hers any time of night, always there for her.

The surgeon is asking Daphne if she has any worries, and all the anxieties of the past week resurface: the arguments she's had with Pam, the visit from the policemen. Daphne doesn't know what to think about anything anymore, other than the fact that she doesn't want to have this surgery done. Despite her newfound enthusiasm for life, she's not sure she should allow anyone to cut into her with a knife. It might be a death sentence to dodge the operation, but the anaesthetic is a risk too. And she's lasted months without any issues, hasn't she? Who knows, she could go a few more years without any problems. If she has a stroke and goes out quickly, that's fine. She's had a good life. Why tempt fate with operations?

The surgeon places some sheets of paper on his desk in front of Daphne and offers a pen and points to where she should sign.

'I'm too old for surgery,' she says.

The surgeon nods slowly, as if taking her concerns seriously, which is more than Daphne expected of him. She thought he would strong-arm her into seeing things his way. 'I understand why you might be worried,' he says. 'But actually you are quite healthy for your age. I wouldn't recommend surgery unless I thought it was the best solution for you.'

Daphne shakes her head firmly. She sets her feet on the ground and prepares for battle.

The surgeon smiles persuasively. 'All your blood tests are good. Your heart is in good shape and your blood pressure is excellent—not in your carotid artery, obviously, but overall it's fine. There's no reason why you shouldn't have the operation. There's some risk of course, as there is with any surgery, but we work to minimise that. I have a fantastic anaesthetist who'll look after you. And you can relax knowing I've done lots of these operations before.'

Relax! Daphne almost laughs. Only a surgeon could say something like that. Relax while I cut open your neck. Relax while I slash into your blood vessel.

They talk through risks and percentages again; the chances of a stroke if she doesn't have the operation, the risk if she does. It feels to Daphne that she is caught between a rock and a hard place. Risk both ways.

Then Pam intervenes. 'Mum, the doctor is telling you that if you don't have this operation there's a very real possibility you'll have a major stroke that will leave you incapacitated.

You don't want to be left half-paralysed and unable to speak or do things for yourself, do you?'

Daphne meets the surgeon's eyes. 'Is that what you're telling me?' she asks. She refuses to have Pam putting words in his mouth.

He nods.

Daphne leans back in her chair and considers this. The concept of being brain-damaged and dependent is horrifying—she definitely doesn't want that. But Pam is being manipulative to get the result she wants. After the visit to the hospital with the ponytailed doctor, she and Pam had argued on the way home. *Why didn't you tell me about all those collapsing episodes?* Pam had asked indignantly.

You knew, Daphne had defended. *You were there when the first one happened. It was out at the valley that day Abby helped me.*

You said it was nothing, Pam had protested.

It was *nothing*, Daphne had insisted. *I recovered.*

Each one of those collapsing episodes was probably a small stroke, Pam had said. *But we didn't know because you didn't tell me.*

The argument was circular, as arguments so often are, and Daphne had found herself staring out the car window, switching off to her daughter's rave.

Now she feels resentment bubbling in her chest. 'I'd rather be dead than paralysed,' she says, turning to Pam angrily. 'I don't want to be kept alive on machines.'

The surgeon clears his throat and smiles gently. 'It's not always that simple—not unless the stroke is so major it wipes your brain out. For lesser strokes we can't always tell how a patient will recover. It takes time. We have to wait and see.'

Daphne tastes sourness in her mouth. *Wipes your brain out* is a bit blunt, she thinks, especially coming from a doctor, but perhaps he's decided to dispense with medical terms and speak plainly. 'What would *you* do?' she asks.

The surgeon sits back, steeples his hands and regards her thoughtfully, as if he is giving this due consideration. But Daphne already knows what he's going to say. She has posed the wrong question and he knows he has won. Pam is looking distinctly smug.

'I would have the surgery,' he says, and his response is no surprise. He's a surgeon after all, and surgeons like to use their scalpels.

Daphne looks to Pam and knows she is defeated. She hasn't the energy to stand against the two of them. 'When should we do it?' she asks. And everyone around her is smiling. *Great*, she thinks, *now they're all happy except me. If I'm lucky I might just die.*

But on the way home she realises she doesn't want to die. She isn't ready yet. And with that a great lump nestles itself in her guts and refuses to budge.

35

'I'm so sorry. The skull was my fault.'

It is a few days after the appointment with the surgeon, and Abby is visiting again. She insisted on coming to see how Daphne was doing after the dramatic collapse in the presence of the policemen, and she's wearing a look of guilt and apology that reminds Daphne of a reprimanded dog. The discovery of Doug's skull is only one of the many things that has been occupying Daphne's mind. There are other issues of importance she must attend to before the operation: her will, her few possessions, what she should take to the hospital.

The policemen returned only yesterday to discuss their investigation. Years had lapsed since Doug's disappearance, and Daphne hadn't expected any further evidence to turn up. Weather, snow, wildfire, predators—she'd considered the lot and come to terms with the loss of his remains. A sky burial was how she liked to think of it.

But now the story is different. The police said a man had come across Doug's skeleton in the mountains some years ago and retrieved his skull. The man hadn't considered the consequences of his find, or the meaning it might have for someone else—least of all Doug's family. He'd passed the skull on to a friend who collected bones . . . this was the worst of it for Daphne: the concept of Doug's skull sitting as a showpiece in a stranger's home. After the police had departed, she'd vomited up her distress and flushed it down the toilet. Too late for being precious now, she'd told herself . . . but it was a bit rich for someone to keep Doug's skull.

'How can it be your fault?' Daphne says, dismissing Abby's concern.

'I know the guy who had it.'

Daphne finds this hard to believe but Abby's face is serious.

'That guy with the red Commodore,' Abby says. 'He told me he had a human skull in his collection and I told him he had to hand it in.' She shakes her head. 'I never imagined it could have anything to do with you. I just thought it was wrong, that he shouldn't have it, and that a proper burial was necessary.'

Daphne feels overwhelmed by all this information. 'It isn't your fault,' she repeats.

'But what if you'd died when you found out? I couldn't have lived with that. As it was you collapsed again, and I feel so guilty.'

Now Daphne sees where the girl is coming from. 'My little episode had nothing to do with Doug's skull turning up. It was just an unlucky coincidence . . . or rather, a fortunate event, according to the doctors. Now we know what is happening with my health, they can do something about it. I'm supposed to be happy about that.'

'But you're not?'

Daphne frowns. 'Nobody celebrates having surgery at my age.'

Abby grins. 'I guess not.' Then her face lines again with worry.

'I'll be fine,' Daphne says. 'They say I'm in top shape, whatever that means. And I intend to survive. I want to live.'

It's such a ridiculous epiphany she almost laughs. *She likes being alive.* And she's good at it. A lifetime of experience and she knows how to do it; such a pity to waste all that by dying. She sees now why she is here when Doug is not. It isn't because she is weak. She chose life because she is strong, because she can face things, absorb pain. Not everyone can. Doug wasn't able to.

'My husband didn't want to live,' she says to Abby. 'That's why his skull ended up in those mountains. He couldn't cope with the suburbs.'

It had been clear from the moment they moved, and she remembers it all so clearly—how a dark entity had taken residence inside Doug. He'd folded in on himself like a closing anemone, all the soft parts hiding away, the lights going off. She'd seen it each morning when he emerged, empty-eyed, from the bedroom. He was sleeping late and it seemed a great weariness was pressing him down. On the farm, he never slept in. He was up with the kookaburras in the early pre-dawn, and by the time the morning sun crept over the ridge, he'd already had breakfast and was out with a lead-rope in his hand, looking for his horse.

'Doug just wasn't cut out for urban living,' she tells Abby. 'He'd lived almost a lifetime on the land, with air and space around him. He couldn't fit his soul into a backyard. The fences hemmed him in.'

Daphne would find him lying on the bed, hands folded on his chest, eyes closed. She would stand at the door watching him breathe, the sadness simmering inside him. More than once she offered to take him to the mountains for a daytrip or a picnic but his eyes remained shut and he refused to go, said he didn't want to.

'I tried everything,' she says. 'I suggested golf, bowls, bingo, bridge, the Rotary Club. But Doug refused everything. He said golf and bowls were for old people who couldn't entertain themselves. That he'd be damned if he would sit around talking with city folk, pretending he was interested in what they had to say. Said he'd rather be dead in his grave.'

Abby laughs. 'I think I agree with him,' she says. 'Bowls is boring. But who am I to comment? I've never played it.'

None of it had sounded particularly appealing to Daphne either, but she'd known they had to find a way to prop themselves up, and it seemed the only way was to engage with the community. There were fights every time she tried to force Doug into life. *Let's find things to do together,* she'd said. Maybe it was time for them to retire anyway. Other people retired in their fifties, didn't they? Public servants with big superannuation payouts? The payout for the farm would serve as their super. They would invest it, make it last the distance, and if it ran out they would probably qualify for the pension. Maybe enforced retirement could be a good thing. They'd worked hard all their lives. Perhaps they could stop and enjoy themselves, do some recreational things, maybe buy a caravan and travel around Australia, join the Grey Nomads.

'It was a tough thing to face forced retirement in middle age,' she says. 'Doug wasn't young, but he certainly wasn't old. He was in his late fifties with plenty of work left in his bones. But it wasn't likely he could find other employment. What would he do? Work on a road gang turning stop signs? Fill shelves at the supermarket? Of course not! And he wasn't the sort to sit around and chew the fat. Not unless it was with other farmers, discussing the cattle markets, or the price of land, problems with weeds, the cost of hiring labour. By the time we left the farm, he was definitely starting to slow down but he wasn't ready to retire. He was a worker, never idle. In the suburbs, he ground to a halt like an engine without fuel. Then our old dog died, and everything went downhill from there.'

Daphne pauses for a moment then decides to tell Abby everything—the girl is an adult after all, and there's probably not much she can't handle. She settles herself, knowing this won't be easy. But she feels she needs to do it. If Abby knows the story behind Doug's disappearance, she will understand it better. Daphne draws a steadying breath then lets the story come out.

She remembers the day clearly. It was autumn, fine and cool. Doug had woken in a strangely euphoric mood. He'd emerged early from bed and listened to the radio as he ate breakfast. Over coffee, he asked Daphne about her plans for the day, said she ought to go out and buy herself a new dress, said he might go out himself, maybe visit his friend, Sel. Selwyn owned a small property out of Queanbeyan where sometimes Doug went to help out or talk about the old days. Daphne hoped Sel might be able to lift Doug out of his gloom. Doug was always good after visiting with Sel, came home with a bounce in his stride, as if he'd found the missing part of his soul.

She didn't ask what he would do after visiting Sel, preferring to leave him in his upbeat state of mind—it was such a nice change from his moping. She decided to go shopping to buy some nice thick steaks for a barbecue dinner. Doug liked a good steak, and Daphne had found a decent butcher in town who knew his cuts. Perhaps they would have a happier evening. They might talk some more, laugh together, remember good times.

Doug came to her then, and folded her in his arms, held her strong. Daphne was surprised at this uncommon show of affection—he'd been so locked into himself since they shifted to the city but she relaxed against him, and drew in the sweet smell of his neck, the familiar mustiness of his beard. When they pulled apart, Daphne saw a bright gleam in Doug's eyes, so she pushed herself against him once more, kissed him then grabbed her handbag from the table and hurried out the door. That night she would cook him a feast and they would be together as they hadn't been in months.

When she came home from the shops, the house was silent, which was no surprise as Doug had probably gone out. She put the shopping on the table and wandered through the house looking for him, just in case he was home and perhaps sleeping. But the house was deserted. She went out to the garage, and yes, Doug's work truck was gone. On the workbench, his tool boxes sat undisturbed.

She passed the day cleaning and gardening, and by the time she went to shower and prepare dinner, she was very happy with herself. She put on a fresh dress then donned an apron while she chopped vegies and marinated the steak. When everything was ready, she turned on the TV for the evening news and picked up her knitting to kill time till Doug arrived. He should be back soon; he was rarely out after dark.

But dark came and Doug did not appear. She began to worry. He was never usually out this long, and if he was likely to be late, he generally rang. Once or twice he had met up with a friend at the pub and drunk himself silly, but this had only happened a few times and Daphne couldn't blame him. If drink was an occasional salve for despondency, she could cope. Even then, he'd called from the pub to let her know he was all right. Then he'd caught a taxi home and she'd bundled him into bed.

At seven o'clock the phone rang and Daphne leapt to answer it. But it was only Sel, and Daphne suppressed her disappointment. *Just wondering when Doug's planning on bringing my truck back*, Sel said with an edge of grumpiness. *Wouldn't mind getting my horse back too. Thought Doug would have shown up by now, with it getting dark and all.*

Surprise then irritation ran down Daphne's spine. Doug must have had plans for today that he hadn't shared with her. If he'd taken a horse in a truck, he must have gone riding somewhere. Pity he hadn't invited her too. She would have enjoyed it. *What's he been up to, Sel?* she asked. *I don't know a thing about it.*

Doug had gone round to Sel's place that morning and said he wanted to go for a ride. He had taken his saddle with him, which Sel said looked like it had been cleaned up a treat, maybe oiled not so long ago. Daphne remembered Doug pulling the saddle out from the shed just the week before. It had seemed a bit strange at the time, but Daphne had figured it was part of his healing process, to retain some links with their rural life. He'd muddled around looking for saddle soap then foamed it up and cleaned off the mould that had crept over the saddle. After that he'd gone out and bought a new pot of neat's-foot oil from the produce store. She'd watched him smooth it over the saddle to make the leather dark and supple again. She hadn't suspected he'd been planning something.

Sel said Doug had gone out for a ride, but wasn't sure where, maybe on the old property if he could find a way in. But Daphne knew you couldn't get into that country anymore, because the gates were all locked.

As soon as Sel was off the phone she rang the police. She was worried there might have been an accident. Doug could have taken a fall or crashed the truck. The police were helpful, but said maybe Doug was still on his way home, and that she should call them later if he didn't show up. Daphne sat tight in the lounge room and watched the news play out, but she didn't hear a thing. On the kitchen bench, the steaks were waiting. At eight o'clock she put them back in the fridge.

Another hour dragged by, and Daphne was exploding with tension. Nine o'clock came and she couldn't wait any longer. She decided to go out to the old farm and find him herself. She rang Pam, who wanted to come too, but a great urgency had planted itself in Daphne's chest and she couldn't delay. She took a coat, hat and torch and plunged into the night.

The road to the valley was dark and quiet, not another car passed her by; she was alone with the halo of her headlights shining on the branches of the roadside trees that reached eerily overhead. She began to wish she had waited for Pam;

the night had become huge with dreadful possibilities. She kept returning to Doug's strangely elated mood that morning, and she wondered what he had been thinking. She hadn't thought to check the gun cupboard before she left. What if he had decided to remove himself the same way he finished off the sick dog? But she didn't think he was the sort to shoot himself. And yet how well did she really know this changed man who was her husband? Before they came to the city, she thought she knew him, but he had evolved into someone else. She didn't understand the new darkness that he wore inside him like a cave, and it frightened her to consider that he might have hurt himself. She wanted him home and safe.

As she neared the valley, turning off the main road, the tightness in her throat increased. She rattled the car over the cattle grid into the park, winding through the shadowy forest and dodging a wallaby that leapt onto the road, dazzled by the headlights. At the entry track to the old homestead, she found the gate open, the chain snipped by bolt-cutters. She drove through the gateway and followed the track downhill, kangaroos bouncing out of her way like crazy wind-up toys. Straining to see ahead, she could just make out the shadowy silhouette of the homestead. Then down by the yards, her car headlights illuminated another shape—a large hulking shadow. Closer, she could see the reflection of tail-lights: Sel's truck.

She pulled up and swung out of her car. It was dark, quiet, nobody around. Wind sang in the grass and, out across the valley, a kangaroo barked. She cast the beam of her torch into the night, but it penetrated no more than five metres and all she could see were two rabbits bopping among the tussocks. She figured Doug must have ridden out from here, and she peered into the blackness as if expecting that he and the horse might suddenly loom from obscurity. She cooeed and hallooed, waiting for a reply. But all that came back were echoes, faint sounds bouncing from the boulders on the ridge.

The search began the next day. Parks and SES vehicles headed up into the wilderness, and people in fluoro-orange overalls combed the valley while helicopters buzzed over peaks. Near the homestead, Daphne waited with the director of operations and Pam and Pam's new boyfriend Ray, who had kindly come along in support. It seemed many hours elapsed before Sel's horse was found up high near Mount Bimberi, the saddle still on its back, skewed but intact. A stirrup was missing. And so was Doug.

The SES troops shifted the focus of their search to higher country where they raked the high tops and alpine meadows, the crooked snow-gum forests, walking in formation across the landscape, seeking evidence, looking for something, anything. But the day passed into night, and there was still no Doug. As each hour ticked itself off, an awful clarity settled in Daphne's mind. She was certain he was dead, that he had wandered off into his country as he had always wanted to.

Three days into the search, the missing stirrup was found near a pile of granite slabs. The search crew scoured the area, but Doug was never found. After a week, the search was called off. Doug was declared missing, presumed dead. Over time, the stirrup found its way into Daphne's box of special mementos along with the stockwhip and Gordon's jumper and the stone artefact.

'Do you think it was an accident?' Abby asks.

It's a good question, Daphne thinks, but how can they ever know? The police are asking this too, and the forensic scientists who have been poring over Doug's skull, searching

KAREN VIGGERS

for clues. Did he fall from the horse, or did he attempt to ride over a cliff? Apparently the early findings show evidence of trauma, a crush fracture over the temporal region, and it doesn't look like foul play, possibly blunt contact with a rock during a fall. There are plenty of rocks up in the mountains, Daphne thinks, and whatever the final report summary comes up with, she is sure Doug went out there to die. He gave himself to his country, offered his bones to the skies.

She explains this to Abby, who nods in understanding.

'They asked me what I want to do with the skull when they've finished with it,' Daphne says, 'and I told them I want to have it cremated.'

'No more skull collections?' Abby says with a guilty smile.

'No more skull collections,' Daphne says. 'There's somewhere I'd like to spread his ashes.'

'Can I take you there after the operation?' Abby asks.

Daphne nods. 'My family has a small cemetery, hidden in the hills.'

36

A scattered flock of chickens is pecking its way along the roadside verge, oblivious to the fast-spinning traffic that whooshes past. There are about ten Rhode Island Reds, russet-feathered, with their fluffy bottoms up, fossicking for fallen seeds among the slashed dry grass. Daphne sees them on her way to hospital for her operation. The chickens have never been here before, and their presence seems like an omen—life continuing, despite the mountain that stands before her. They have given themselves over to fate too; if one of them strays onto the road it will be squashed. Perhaps she should follow their philosophy: if the chooks aren't worried about their future, neither should she be.

She wonders if the chickens may have been here previously without her noticing them. It's certainly possible; this past week she has been noticing many things she normally overlooks in the rhythm of daily life. Yesterday she sat outside for an hour and listened to birds in the garden: wattlebirds clacking, magpies warbling, rosellas chiming. She watched as the birds fed and drifted between bushes and trees—tiny little wrens hopping among shrubs, currawongs flapping across the sky. And the clouds were amazing: fine shreds of cotton skidding across a backdrop of pale blue.

It's a pity this sense of immediacy and awareness can't be preserved in pretty bottles to be sniffed in small quantities like perfume, she thinks. Her new-found alertness is probably due to the approach of her surgery. It's no secret she might die—the surgeon said as much, and she's old for this kind of thing. If all goes well, she may still have a few good years left in her, but she also has to consider that this might be it. When they administer her anaesthetic tomorrow, her life may end. It's a levelling thought. Every waking moment seems deliciously poignant.

At the hospital, Pam drops her near the entrance then goes to find a parking space, which are rare as hens' teeth at this time of day. Daphne wheels her suitcase to a bench seat and waits. People flood by her, entering and leaving the building, intent on their own business. No-one even notices her or smiles.

Eventually Pam appears, hurrying along the footpath. She grabs the handle of Daphne's suitcase and makes a charge for the door. Daphne follows more sedately. Poor Pam has been very fluttery and nervous these past days. She's put all child-minding on hold and has been so attentive Daphne almost wants to bat her away.

When they find the designated ward, a friendly nurse shows them to a private room which is like a ship's cabin: all slick linoleum and clean surfaces and a bathroom too small to swing a cat in. It's more than adequate, and Daphne is happy not to have to share. At her age, she prefers to tend to bodily functions alone and without witness.

Pam inspects the room and organises Daphne's things into drawers. She explains to Daphne how to use the TV remote control, as if Daphne has never encountered one before. It astounds Daphne how infirmity in the aged brings out the patronising streak in others, as if being old means you lose flexibility in your brain as well as in your joints. While Pam explores the bathroom, Daphne sorts the remaining items in her bag: a crossword book and pen, her glasses, a dictionary and a novel. She figures there will be time for sitting and contemplating on her own. Pam might intend to stay, but she will soon become bored, so Daphne is armed for the filling of space once Pam departs.

The afternoon is punctuated by visits from a string of nurses requiring information and signatures, or blood for tests. Pam seems to be reassured that Daphne's facts and figures are checked and cross-checked many times, but Daphne loses count of how many times someone takes her blood pressure. A new individual from a rotating shift of nurses comes every hour to check on her. They come during the night as well, and it's most disruptive, not at all restful.

Once Pam is gone, Daphne pads out time reading and watching TV, but there's nothing interesting on the box, despite the fifty-something channels. And there's no view from the window either. A private room is more like solitary confinement, she decides. The woman next door seems to live on the telephone into which she shouts as if she's trying to speak to someone in the street. She can't be very ill if she has all that energy for talking.

KAREN VIGGERS

Pam returns in the morning to sit with Daphne till she's taken away for surgery, but she's not much use as company. She pads around the room, tidying, and looking nervously out the window until Daphne tells her to sit down. Then she perches on the edge of a vinyl chair and pokes a finger at her bun. 'It's quiet at home without you,' she says.

Daphne looks pityingly at her daughter. Surely Ben wins the prize for racket.

'You'll be all right,' Pam says, leaning forward to grip Daphne's arm too tight.

Daphne pats Pam's hand. 'Yes, I'll be fine.' It's ironic that she is sitting here reassuring her daughter when she is the one going under the knife.

'Are you scared?' Pam asks.

'No,' Daphne says . . . although that is not what the nurses tell her—they say her blood pressure has climbed today. Even though she feels a degree of outer calm, inside she must be doing back-flips. But there's not much she can do about it now. She has signed all the forms and passed all the tests. The surgeon and anaesthetist both visited this morning and they will be waiting for her when the time comes. She has to put her trust in their hands.

She smiles at Pam and gently strokes her daughter's hand. 'You're so good to me,' she says, hoping this conveys everything she wants it to.

Pam squeezes her hand and Daphne sees bright tears welling in her eyes.

They sit together for a while, holding hands and saying nothing until the nurse comes in to check Daphne's blood pressure again. Not long after, they help Daphne into a wheelchair and cart her away.

Daphne is riding in the wind. She is racing up the valley, Doug close behind. The horses' hooves slash the ground. They lurch over tussocks, flounder through bogs. Daphne looks back and sees Doug's beard pressed flat by rushing air. His teeth show white through the bushy mass of hair.

The image fades and then she sees his face again, this time twisted with grief. She is held tight to his chest. They are clutching each other, weeping for Gordon. The two of them are broken—they have holes in their hearts where Gordon has been torn out. They will stitch themselves together but they will never be the same.

Doug disappears and lovely dark-skinned Johnny Button is there, beckoning. He is on the mountain tops in the swirling shifting mist. He is pointing to the rock slabs, the rough walls of granite where the moths live. A Bogong moth wafts its wings in his hand. Daphne sees her two stones from the rock shelter: one white and round, the other sharp and black.

Then fog descends. Doug is wandering on horseback through the forest. He weaves among snow gums, reins hitched in one hand, the horse moving beneath him. Higher he rides, and higher, into cloud. She sees his shape fading—man and horse merging with the fog.

Now she sees water flowing through the hills. It begins in high alpine meadows, trickling from soaks and pools and thick boggy ground, then merging with other trickles to become rivulets that gurgle downhill along the path of least resistance. Rivulets meet, becoming creeks and then streams. The water flows, clear and sweet. It gushes down gullies, diving over rocks, plunging through cracks, surging, eddying. Lower, it

KAREN VIGGERS

widens and slows, becoming a lazy river as it wends through a valley. Then it picks up again, gaining momentum, suddenly losing altitude, meshing with another watercourse.

Rain falls, seething from the sky, splashing off rocks and the silvery skin of the stream, swelling its flanks. Ahead there is a bridge. The stream gathers to charge underneath, but there is a man on a horse pushing cattle across. He is barking at the dogs and the beasts, hustling them as fast as he can. On the bridge, the horse skitters, swings its rump into the needling rain. The man swears, slaps the horse's sides with the handle of his whip. The tetchy horse rears and jerks, jagging at the bit. Its hooves bite into the wet boards of the bridge, skating, slipping. The man cries out as the horse slams down, crushing him. Then the man is still, his face slack and ashen. The horse thrusts its legs astride and lurches up, standing on the man, heaving him sideways, and the limp body tilts over the edge of the bridge, hovers for a suspended moment, then slumps into the water. The river runs on, melding smoothly around his face.

Daphne fights the sensation of drowning. She is immersed in a heavy sludge, so deep she can't move. It is dark. There is the sound of breathing, laboured and slow. Flashes of red shoot through the blackness. Voices swim in and out, contorted, unrecognisable. Sometimes she is floating instead of drowning. There is light and she is lofting near the ceiling. She sees an old woman lying on a narrow bed, vaguely familiar, but puffy and irregular, tubes sprouting from her nose and arms and hands. Everything is white.

354

Pain stabs, like lightning shattering the sky. She sees people bending over her, senses movement, wheels rolling. Faces waft in and out. Machines hover. Day and night dissolve.

She sees Gordon: his small pale face, his dark eyes. They are Doug's eyes, the same. There are Gordon's gentle little hands touching his baby sister's face. He has a quirky smile on his face. And baby Pam's cheeks screwing up. The red burst of her infantile cries.

Then galloping again, the relentless rhythm of hooves pounding dirt. It is beneath her, beside her, drumming in her veins.

When she wakes, the room seems cloudy, as if mist has stolen unseen through the doors and filled all the spaces. She hears a voice. 'Daphne, you can open your eyes now. It's over and you're all right.'

Her eyelids are heavy. She lifts them reluctantly then lets them slide shut. She is comfortable in darkness, doesn't want to listen. But the voice is insistent.

'Come on Daphne. No more sleeping. You're okay now. Everything is fine.'

She tries again, and this time her eyes skip open and light floods in. There is a face, a nurse, leaning over her.

'Oh, that's great. You're awake, Daphne. Can you hear me?'

Of course, she can hear. 'Yes.' Her voice is a dry croak that doesn't belong to her.

'That's wonderful Daphne. It's good to have you back.'

The nurse is smiling. Daphne sees a smooth round face, honey-coloured hair cut in a short bob that tucks with a kink beneath the nurse's chin. The nurse stands up. 'I'll go and phone your daughter to let her know you're awake.'

Daphne watches her walk away. She is weary, foggy. Around her, she hears the rhythmic pipping of machines. Other patients coughing. Muted conversation.

She closes her eyes and rests.

PART V

PART V

37

Abby's mind was on other things when her supervisor Quentin suggested she go to the kangaroo cull as an observer. She was thinking of Daphne, back at home and recovering from surgery. She was thinking of Daphne's husband Doug riding into the mountains and never coming back. She was thinking of her brother Matt and his trip to Central Australia—how he too might never have come back.

Sunlight was pouring into Quentin's north-facing office and gathering around his head like a halo. He was sitting at his desk, hands folded in front of him, saying how important it was for scientists to understand the ramifications of their work. One day as a kangaroo ecologist, Abby might need to propose a cull herself. If she couldn't see the job through, she shouldn't recommend it. *They need objective observers,* Quentin had said, peering at her over his rectangular bifocals. *A country girl like you would be ideal. Practical, scientific.*

Abby felt a cold knot weaving itself in her chest. She'd rather not go to this cull, would rather read about it in an official government report or even in one of Cameron's articles in the newspaper. She tried to hide her reluctance, to appear professional. *There's no-one else?* she asked.

A frown folded between Quentin's eyes. *You'd only be expected to go for one night. And I'll be there. The vet, too.*

Abby couldn't trot out the excuse of field commitments—her work was almost done and Quentin knew it. He was waiting for her response. *I suppose I can do it,* she said. *If it's just one night.*

He'd relaxed into an approving smile, and gave her the date and the time.

Now she crests the hill in her work vehicle and stops on the road to survey the reserve. It's a bleak place, bare, dry, rocky, and the adjacent farmland is flogged and grey, grassless, scraped by wind. There's nothing but sheep and a few sad farmhouses, hunching in hollows between hills. Abby can see why the farmers might want to shoot kangaroos that rove onto their properties. There is nothing to eat.

Her eyes shift to the reserve gate and she notices movement down there, a crowd of people. She sees lines of parked cars along the road, a thread of smoke coiling from a campfire near the entry, signs and flapping banners. She wonders what's happening, maybe a demonstration . . . she hadn't thought of that. She hesitates, watching people milling and scurrying near the gate like ants. There are so many of them, and the gate is shut.

Her heart rate climbs a notch and she wonders if they will let her in. She's running late—she forgot her coat and beanie and had to go back for them. Now it is past the time Quentin told her to show up; he must have gone in without her. The shooters, the drivers and the reserve staff must have passed through the gates already. If they managed to get in, she hopes she can too. Quentin would have called if there was a problem, but her phone has been silent all afternoon. Everyone is too busy for phone calls, Cameron too—she hasn't heard from him since the night of the public meeting. But she knows he'll be at the gate with all those people. This is the biggest environmental story of the year, and she's sure he wouldn't miss out. She puts the vehicle in gear and starts down the hill.

As she approaches the gate, the crowd turns and tightens like a predator examining prey. The mass of bodies spreads, separating into small groups. Abby sees them snatch up items from the ground and bunch together before they launch towards her. She hesitates and her foot slips from the clutch, and the vehicle lurches, shudders and stalls. The protesters rush forward, leaping and jeering, pumping placards. She reaches to lock the doors.

They come at her armed with sticks and rocks, their voices raised in a battle cry. Swelling like a wave, they flow around her. She sits tight behind the wheel, cowering. She doesn't know what to do. Should she re-start the vehicle and try to push through? It seems a mistake to stop, but she doesn't want to hit anyone.

They batter the car with sticks and fists, yelling, shouting, their faces pressed against the windows. She sees mouths torn open with rage, eyes blazing, hands shoving against glass, ripping at the door handles. The vehicle rocks. There is banging. Thuds and crashes. A banner is plastered across the windscreen, KILLER glaring at her in red capital letters. Her heart is thunder. She can't see the way, can't escape the shrieking, swearing, curses. She's an animal in a trap. These people might smash the car, shatter the windscreen. They might try to drag her out. Is there anyone out there who can help her? Where is Cameron?

A deep voice sounds at her window, and a square grim face stares in at her, a man in uniform. Strong blue men are pushing the people back. The banner is dragged from the windscreen, bundled into a roll. Police guards shove through, ejecting protesters, yelling threats. The man at the window signals for her to open the door but she is gripped in a vice of fright, incapable of moving. She thinks perhaps she sees Cameron out there among the blur of faces. He will help her. He will take her away from all this.

'Come on,' the guard shouts. 'Let me in. The men will escort you through.'

Several uniformed guards have circled her vehicle now. She opens the door and scrambles into the passenger seat, shaking. The man climbs in, taut and grim-faced. He settles in the driver's seat, gripping the wheel. 'You have ID?'

'Yes. I'm here as an observer for the cull.' She scrabbles for her wallet in the glove box to show her driver's licence.

The guard starts the vehicle and clunks it in gear then he eases forward. The line of uniformed men forces the protesters aside as the car inches through. At the gate they are buffeted by a renewed surge of jeering and screaming, insults pouring down. Protesters break the line and dive at the car. A rock cracks the rear window leaving a streak of lightning. Then the gates swing open and they are through. The gates close behind them, thrust by guards leaning into the desperate force of the demonstrators.

The guard drives a short distance into the reserve then he hauls on the brake and steps out. 'Nasty lot,' he says. 'You've copped a few dents, but that's getting off lightly.'

Abby's insides feel pummeled. 'Thank you,' she says. It's the understatement of the year.

He flashes a grisly smile then slams the door and strides back to the gate.

For a few moments Abby sits there, trying to subdue her battering heart, then she crawls into the driver's seat and opens the window. Beyond the gate-hysteria, the reserve is bathed in a vast, incongruous quiet. She breathes in, seeking composure. Around her everything seems hushed, connected to another world, separate to conflict. Her heart slows. On the road, a willie-wagtail flaunts its tail and chitters. In the grass, thornbills and fairy-wrens bob. There is normality here after all. She slips the car into gear and trundles along the road.

The depot car park is bristling with four-wheel drives, all crowded in neat rows. Among them are Troop Carrier tray-backs decked out with panels bearing hooks, and topped with the silver orbs of spotlights. These must be the shooters' vehicles. On the back of one, in a wire cage, a large mongrel dog fixes Abby with a restless eye and growls as she passes on her way to the depot. Her stomach clenches—after the encounter at the gate it doesn't take much to escalate her adrenalin.

Inside the depot building it is warm and quiet. Abby follows a hum of voices to a room where men sit on orange plastic chairs facing a whiteboard to which a map of the reserve has been tacked. The reserve manager is drawing lines on the map with a texta and a ruler. He stops as she enters and waves her to a seat. From the front row Quentin nods and smiles.

Abby sinks onto a chair. She is the only double X in a room pulsing XY. In jeans and a fleece, she's a stranger among this gathering of overalls and gumboots. Girl-neat, she sits among splayed legs and hairy arms, probably thirty kilograms lighter than the smallest of them.

The reserve manager is dividing the reserve into units and assigning areas for shooters. The aim is to remove as many animals as possible in one night; the shorter the time frame, the less headache for everyone. Each shooter will start in the north of his zone and work south. There is a designated buffer area between each zone to prevent accidents. Everyone has communications equipment to use if in doubt.

Female kangaroos are to be pouch-checked and any live joeys slipped into cloth bags until they can be examined by the vet; Abby sees him sitting down the back on the other side of the room. Each vehicle will have an assistant/driver to help lift carcasses onto the truck, and also an observer. Extra staff will be spread around to help pick up bodies. They are to count animals as they are shot and make a tally. When vehicles and trailers are full, a cease-fire will be called so teams can drop off carcasses at the pit.

Abby is assigned to a shooter named Kevin. When her name is called, the men turn like folding hinges to examine her. Down the front, a stocky, clean-shaven man with a square jaw and short-cropped brown hair gives her a nod, his blue eyes flashing beneath solid brows. This must be Kevin. He looks friendly, doesn't seem to be annoyed at being lumped with her.

One of the shooters asks what they should do if protesters manage to gain access to the site—he doesn't want to shoot anyone. Grunts of concern echo among the men. The manager explains there will be an immediate cease-fire if any demonstrators breach security lines. Guards posted along the boundary will alert him if any problems arise. A discussion ensues about security protocols and procedures; the men are clearly worried about possible tactics from the activists. Abby is impressed by the attention to detail. Apart from the fact that she was somehow left out of the loop, the safety of the shooters and reserve employees has been carefully protected. While the demonstrators were performing at the front gates, the shooters entered hours ago via another access point, using side-roads where nobody could see them.

After the briefing, Quentin tells her that he came in the back way too. He says he tried to call her so she would know where to go, but she didn't answer. He left messages to warn her. She checks her phone and is embarrassed to find she has forgotten to turn it on; it's no wonder Quentin couldn't contact her. Cameron might have tried to call too. But it's too late now. She decides to leave her phone off for the duration of the cull. She doesn't want Cameron ringing when she's in the thick of things.

———❦———

At dusk, they head out into the car park, dividing into teams. Abby watches Kevin pull his weapon from a locked metal compartment in the back of his truck. It's a .223 target-grade rifle, with a thick stainless-steel shaft and wooden stock. Abby has seen guns before, but nothing like this. Guns were part of her life, growing up on the farm. Sometimes her father had to shoot sick stock—the vet's call-out fee was more than the price of a sheep. Cattle were more valuable, but if hope of recovery was minimal, it was better to end the struggle sooner.

Her brother Matt used to go out shooting rabbits sometimes. He would head into the hills behind their farm, fading into the bush with his shotgun over his shoulder, the dog slinking at his heels. Afterwards, it was rabbit stew for dinner—the skinned carcass simmering in a pot with carrots and potato. Once the meat was falling from the bones, it was ready to eat, dished with gravy onto a pile of rice. Occasionally she would bite down on pellets in the flesh, grimacing at the shock of metal against teeth.

But this is different.

She watches Kevin empty a box of bullets into a leather pouch around his waist. He extracts a fistful and slots them into the magazine. In his hands, bullets are like marbles, harmless things that click against each other, rolling and jingling. He shuffles his fingers through the pouch as if he is sifting Lego, then zips it up. Next he slides the bolt into the rifle, twisting deftly till it ratchets into place. Then he inserts the magazine which locks in with a dull click. His fingers stroke the weapon with the familiarity of a lover. The gun is an extension of self, part of his daily rhythm and routine. He slips it onto a safety rack bolted to the dashboard.

Around the car park, men are sorting themselves and swinging into the vehicles, engines rumbling. Darkness is falling, the last of blue dusk fading from the sky. Kevin directs Abby into the front of his truck: a boxy old LandCruiser modified for the job. It's dirty—dust and grass seeds everywhere. On the dash there is a GPS and a heavy sandbag. There's no windscreen. 'Increases the range of angles for shooting,' Kevin explains.

Pete the driver jumps in and slams his door. He grasps a handle dangling from the roof and smacks a switch on the dash to ignite a swathe of brilliant white light. He swivels the handle, and the light shifts from the ground and flashes up in the trees, blinding any possums that might be hiding among the foliage. He switches it off. 'Still works,' he says with a grin.

Kevin wriggles in beside Abby and grunts. 'Bit cosy.'

Abby makes herself as small as possible to allow him more room.

'Sorry about the windscreen,' he says. 'Hope you've got plenty of warm clothes. She gets a bit breezy.'

Abby huddles behind the dash as they drive out from the depot, a trailer rattling behind them. She is sandwiched on top of the gearstick between Kevin and Pete. Pete is driving first while Kevin mans the gun. When Kevin tires they will switch jobs. It's safer this way. Better for the kangaroos too, improves the accuracy of the shots.

The night is cold and clear. In convoy the vehicles drive slowly along the road, headlights dimmed and engines quiet so as not to alarm the kangaroos. Kevin and Pete are silent; Pete leaning forward over the wheel, Kevin with his elbow hooked out the window. They don't seem inclined to conversation, and that's good because Abby doesn't feel like talking.

Somewhere in the darkness kangaroos are grazing, teeth nipping and cropping, soft lips seeking blades of grass. Abby wonders if heads are already raised, watching this procession of four-wheel drives trundling down the road, now turning onto the dirt track, bouncing over wash-outs, now mounting the hill to the ridgeline.

There is no moon and the landscape sleeps in shadows. The vehicles move in the yellow haloes of dimmed headlights, blocky silhouettes tracing the line of the trail, riding the hills and gullies. At the designated location, a vehicle stops and remains idling on the ridge, its headlights off, waiting. The other trucks move on, dipping and bobbing along the track.

Abby glances at Kevin. His hands are easy on his lap as he absorbs the rough jolts of the track. His body is loose, accustomed to irregular terrain. The crackle of the radio makes Abby jerk, raising a smile on his face. 'Bit jumpy?' he says.

She shakes her head, not wanting to admit her anxiety.

'Got any earplugs?' he asks.

'No.'

'Here, have some.' He fumbles in the glove box and drops a small plastic bag in her hand. 'You'll need them. Pete and I have earphones to cut the noise. Otherwise we'd be deaf.'

She tears open the small bag and fingers the cylindrical nuggets of rubber.

'You don't need them yet.' Kevin's face glows in the light cast from the dash. 'I'll let you know when to stick them in.'

They grind up a steep hill, lurching over wash-outs. Abby tries not to stare at the rifle, cradled in its rack in front of her. It's a thick and sturdy work beast with impressive telescopic sights. The barrel shimmers greenish-silver in the muted light.

'You'd think I was married to that thing,' Kevin says, nodding at the rifle. 'I clean it daily. The barrel gets dirty. Gunpowder's messy.'

Shooting's messy, Abby thinks. *Death* is messy. She knows about that.

The track mounts a knoll and they stop while the last of the vehicles lumber on. Abby is already cold. Soon her fingers and toes will be stiff.

They wait, and there is stillness in the dark as if the night is waiting too. Minutes shuffle by. The headlights from the other vehicles ascend the next hill and disappear into blackness. A breeze shivers in the mounds of tussock grass. Time grows heavy.

Then a radio message comes through: confirmation to start. At Kevin's nod, Abby stubs her earplugs in while he slips his earphones over his head and lifts the rifle from the rack. Pete lights the spotlight, puts the truck in gear and they trundle slowly forward. With a paw hooked in the handle, he swings the spot in an arc, scanning the bush. Grass shimmers yellow and trees smoulder in the light, branches reaching.

The spotlight roves steadily then hovers on a mob of kangaroos, perhaps fifty to eighty metres away. They emerge like ghosts from the undulating slope, shadow-hummocks that lift their heads to examine the light. The long arm of the spotlight stretches and Abby sees the sideways shift of mouths still chewing. The kangaroos have paused mid-mouthful to look. There is no alarm. Why don't they flee?

Pete eases his foot off the accelerator and lets the vehicle idle gently while Kevin shifts the rifle into position, resting the stock on the sandbag nestled on the dash. The bolt clicks home. The kangaroos watch, semi-erect like a readying orchestra. They are dazzled by the beam, unsure, but insufficiently alarmed to run. On bunched muscular haunches they sit, fixed on the hypnotic eye of the light, their forearms waving.

There is a pause, pregnant with anticipation. Abby's breath locks in her throat, her fingers tingle. Her entire body tenses.

Then *bang*: an explosion in the night, her ears echoing, despite the plugs.

A kangaroo slumps sideways and the others lift as a unit and bound off in erratic leaps. Relief sweeps Abby. They are going—but no, they've stopped about ten, twenty metres from where they started. They stand upright, heads raised. There's a click then another stupendous pause; time melting before another blast. At the edge of the beam, a body lapses with a thud. Two more rapid detonations and two more bodies fold with soft swishes.

A lull ensues as Kevin searches for the next best target. The muzzle of the gun follows the spotlight, seeking other quivering faces, other eyes shining red in the dark. The mob has tightened: their bodies lifting, uncertainty swelling.

More shots crack from the gun. Kevin's body jolts as it absorbs each kickback. Closer now, bodies slump. Animals are dropping like stones, skewing sideways, legs jerking. Then the mob is moving, a few startled bounds and a gradual shifting away, kangaroos fading among trees. Abby doesn't understand why they don't rush, panic-stricken, into darkness.

The truck bumps forward among the skeletal shadows of trees, the spotlight seeking. There is another large mob, eyes shining in the light. Kevin's tongue eases across his lips as he reaches and flicks the magazine out of the rifle, deftly slotting in six more bullets, each as thick as Abby's thumb. 'Okay?' he grunts.

She nods.

'Gotta keep moving,' he says, somehow sensitive to her struggle.

He cradles the rifle in his hands. The barrel slides out the window. Again, the blast. Abby is almost half ready this time.

38

Cease-fire is called to pick up bodies.

Pete pulls up beside the first carcass, and Kevin hooks the rifle onto its rack and swings out of the vehicle, hefting the kangaroo by the hind legs and dragging it. The head dangles and blood drips, making a dark trail on the pale cropped grass. Kevin heaves the dead kangaroo onto the trailer.

Abby wonders if she should scramble from her stupor to assist, but she sits tight while Kevin slings in five more animals. She is trying to shut out the awful clunk of bone on metal, trying not to see the limbs waving in the rear-view mirror as the vehicle advances across the hill.

At the next carcass, Kevin leans in and suggests Abby do the pouch-checking. She retrieves the head torch from her backpack, slips it on over her beanie and jumps out into the night.

'Just do a hand-swipe,' Kevin says. 'Shove your hand in and have a feel around. You'll find any passengers pretty quick. If you can't pull the joey off, just cut the teat. Got a pocket-knife?'

Abby nods, sickened.

'Here's a bag.' He tosses her a soft black pouch.

She turns her torch on and starts wandering among the battlefield of slumped bodies. Kevin has dropped ten from this mob. She bends over the nearest dead animal and lifts a hind leg. This one has testicles; a young adult male. Abby ought to have known by the muscular forearms and the strong hooky claws. She lets the leg fall and brushes the dense grey coat with her hand, afraid to look at the head in case it has been blown away. The kangaroo is warm and its fur is damp with beginning dew. The rusty smell of blood is everywhere, laced with the sour smell of death. She waves to Kevin to let him know it's okay to pick up the carcass then she moves on to the next skewed hump, a female collapsed in a twist. This time there is no avoiding a full view of the head and the dark meaty hole ripped in the cranium. Abby's head throbs and long-buried visions press up from somewhere deep within. Suppressing a choking sensation, she steels herself to check the pouch.

The opening is soft and slack, reminding her of the roadside kangaroo she killed for Cameron months ago. This pouch sags open, gaping at the top and she kneels to insert her hand. It's damp inside with the musky brownish lubricant that coats the young to keep its fragile skin moist. She feels a warm mound squirm against her hand, a gawky limb pushing her away. Cupping her hand around it, she eases the pouch open further. A small pinky writhes against her fingers: a bundle of gangly legs and a little wizened head. Dark flaps for ears. Eyelids purplish—glued shut. A prickle of whiskers pierces the skin around the muzzle.

Gently she wraps her hand around the soft abdomen, trying to draw the joey out, but it's so young that it holds firm, its mouth almost fused to the nipple. She grips the long, strap-like teat between her fingers and attempts to drag the joey out, but it suctions tightly. For a moment she considers calling for help, then she realises she will have to do this alone. She'll have to cut the nipple. Groping her pocket-knife from inside her jeans, she withdraws both hands to open the blade then carefully reaches back inside the pouch. She feels for the swollen bulge of mammary tissue, locates the nipple and severs it. The joey falls into her hand and she draws it out, slides it into the cloth pouch.

Over by the vehicle the men are watching. She can see Pete behind the wheel, Kevin standing by, hands on hips, sucking on a cigarette. 'I found a pouch-young,' she calls, yelling the bleeding obvious, her voice echoing into nothing. 'I had to cut the nipple.'

Pete waves and Kevin chucks his stub on the ground, grinding it with his toe. They are not interested. Of course they're not. They do this for a job. Kevin climbs into the truck and Pete drives across to fetch the carcass.

'What should we do with it?' Abby asks as they draw alongside.

Kevin shrugs, his blue eyes meeting hers then dodging away. 'Stick it in your jacket to keep it warm. Would have been better to kill them as we go, but this is what they want so we have to do it. We've got a few more bodies to pick up yet.'

Abby loosens her coat and slides the pouch under her jumper. She can feel the small angular body writhing. The joey settles, snuggling into warmth. Abby strides across the slope to the next body, trying to look competent and unrattled, but she is shaken. Will this joey be large enough to hand-raise? Or will it receive the injection and be thrown into the pit—a tiny soft rag-doll among the hummocks of fur?

She mustn't think about it, mustn't think at all. There is nothing yet that hasn't been humane. Kevin is distant and emotionally uninvolved—of course he is: this is how he makes his living. It's tough and unpleasant, but no worse than a job in a knackery. While humans want to eat meat, animals must die. So why should it seem worse with kangaroos? Does it matter if death arrives by shooting? There are no yards, no transport, no milling among other hungry, thirsty, frightened animals at an abattoir. Maybe this is more humane than it is for domestic livestock. One moment a kangaroo is hopping free, the next moment it is dead, life over without knowledge or pain.

But how does she know there is no pain? Wouldn't there be a flashing moment of infinite, spectacular agony as the bullet strikes? Or is the impact so horrifically intense that pain is over before it begins? God knows, the bullet inflicts enough damage. Surely it is better than dying slowly.

She bends at the next humped body and pauses before she grasps the hind leg and lifts it. It's a male again, thank goodness. Not that she wishes death on males—it's just that she doesn't want to find more young, doesn't want to cut more nipples.

The next animal, slumped beneath the silver arms of a dead tree, is a female. There's a young in the pouch, a tiny wet nugget of matchstick arms and a soft domed head. It can't be long born—perhaps a week or two—and it's too small to hand-raise. She can't put it in with the larger joey or it might be torn by a jerking toe. While Kevin and Pete fling the carcass onto the trailer, she finds another bag on the front seat and slips the tiny joey inside. Then she tucks it inside her bra, closer to her warmth and her beating heart.

The next animal is female too, but its pouch is empty with no mammary development. 'Fewer pouch-young in the drought,'

Kevin says, cigarette dangling from his lip as he and Pete toss the body onto the trailer. 'That's what we've been seeing on our regular shoots. Sometimes the odd late young or the odd kidney bean. But lots of empty pouches. Usually all the females have young. But it's a cruel drought. Too many hungry mouths. Makes my job easier. Doesn't feel so bad, knowing they're starving.'

So he has a conscience after all, Abby thinks.

'I like kangaroos,' he says, finishing his cigarette and lighting another. 'I love watching them jump. Bloody impossible, the way they move.'

'Why do you do it then?' she asks.

'Pays good money. And I'm okay with not much sleep. My wife works during the day while I mind the kids. Works out fine.'

The men have started to relax with her. As they work their way across the slope, pouch-checking and picking up bodies, they talk about their home lives: how many kids they have, what sports the kids play, what TV shows they are missing tonight. Despite the low grinding feeling in her guts, Abby finds herself laughing once or twice. She hadn't thought she would relate to the shooters, but they are ordinary country folk, like her.

After several episodes of shooting and picking up carcasses they head for the pit, the trailer laden with the angular shapes of deceased kangaroos. They are dead, Abby tells herself, so it doesn't matter how they are transported. She's trying to make herself feel better, but it isn't working. Inside her jacket, the larger young still wriggles occasionally and her count of tiny fleshy babies has risen to six.

As the truck lurches across the hill, the weight of the trailer slows them down. It no longer rattles, burdened as it is with the awkward tangle of bodies. Pete and Kevin are quiet, apparently sensing her distaste. She has nothing to say. The killing has been executed with dutiful care, delivering instant death. There have been no bad shots by Kevin, though at some stage he must miss. Given his steadiness and attention to detail, Abby knows he'll be quick to finish an inaccurate shot. He'll follow up fast with a terminator, blowing a head away if necessary to end an animal's pain. It ought to be enough.

Why then is she feeling so sick? What sort of objective scientist is she? But she knows what it is that is bothering her and she works desperately not to give in to it, wonders how long she can suppress the insistent tug of her past.

At the pit she slips out of the truck and Pete backs the trailer to the lip with uncanny accuracy—the skill of experience. Kevin swings the tailgate open and the two men start to haul the pile of bodies out. It is a large pit. Nearby, an enormous yellow excavator looms in the shadows, ready to over-fill at the end of the night.

Abby looks around for the vet so she can deliver her warm cargo of pouch-young. He is leaning, arms crossed, against the bonnet of his white station wagon, a tool box of veterinary equipment on the ground beside him. 'How many?' he asks, brow crinkling into a dozen horizontal lines as she approaches him.

'A few,' Abby says. 'Most of them are too small.'

He takes the first black bag and peers inside, shaking his head. 'We're seeing quite a few small ones but not many young overall.' He sets the pouch on the front seat of his car. 'What else have you got?'

She digs into the depths of her jacket and draws out the bag containing the larger joey. 'I think this one will be okay to rear,' she says.

He glances at her. 'Not emotionally involved, are we?'

'It's hard not to be.'

'Remember what you're here for,' he says.

'I'm holding it together so far.'

'Good. The guys are stressed enough, having observers along. They don't need more pressure. This is a grim necessity.' He opens the bag and examines the larger joey. 'This one will be fine. A bit borderline perhaps, but we have to give the wildlife carers something or they'll think we're cheating them.' He tucks the joey inside another pouch and sits it in a box with a hot-water bottle. 'You should have something warm to drink,' he says, observing her with clinical intensity. 'You look peaky.'

She follows him to the back of the car where he pours thick black chocolate from a thermos and hands her a mug. Then he returns to the front seat to complete the grisly task of injecting the tiny joeys.

Abby perches on the back of his station wagon and watches the unloading. Pete is standing in the trailer, hauling on whichever carcass is uppermost. Kevin is up there too, trying to reach for the matching hind leg to give extra strength to the pull. It's hard work. As a body yanks free, they drag it from the stiffening clutch of waving legs and wrench it off the trailer, finally letting the body go on the lip of the pit where gravity takes over.

Abby wants to look away, but the work is transfixing in its awkwardness. She remembers that night on the road when she first met Cameron and dragged his road-kill into the bushes. She remembers the clumsiness of manhandling that rump-heavy body, all hind legs; those thin front feet, useless for holding, the narrow cone of the chest. It is no easier for these men, grunting and panting at the cumbersome task of shifting their load into the pit.

The worst of it is the loose slump of each body as it rolls from the tray. The clunk of bone on the edge of the trailer. The dull wallop of the body thudding into the pit, piling on top of the others. By the end of it, the men are blood-spattered. They stand aside as other loads arrive. Kevin lights a cigarette and wanders away, returning after a while to flick his glowing stub into the pit.

After the bodies are off-loaded, the men stand in a cluster by the pit, drinking coffee, the flare of their cigarettes making patterns in the darkness like fireflies. They talk in low voices, occasional jokes punctuated by muted laughter. It seems incongruous that they can manage humour with death so close. Maybe that's how they separate themselves from the mound of bodies that lies in the pit beside them.

Abby is unable to join them. A chill has entered her, a deep shivering that doesn't match the temperature of the night and all the thermal layers she is wearing. She feels nauseated and she wishes Quentin's crew would appear.

She empties her mug and walks to the edge of the pit, forcing herself to face her fear. In there, the jumble of dead kangaroos lies skewed and shadowy. There is no movement, no sound. A slim mist hovers, vapour from the mass of bodies not yet gone cold. It makes her tremble. It will be better, she decides, when the excavator has done its job and scattered a layer of dirt and clay so the burial is complete.

She peers down into the tangle of corpses, sees a blown-open head, the grey mash of brains, blood-smeared. She knows she shouldn't have looked. A tight ball is growing in her stomach. She drags herself away, stumbles back to the vet's car. He tries to make conversation, but she can't talk. The night seems to constrict around her, bands cinching her chest. She knows she is breathing too fast, too shallowly, but she can't help it.

'Are you all right?' the vet asks.

She waves a hand and blunders away from him, away from the pit and the cars and into the welcoming anonymity of darkness. The knot in her stomach is tightening. The staring eyes, that awful glassy absence. She fights with the nausea, snatching at nothing with her hands, clawing desperately to catch it all and squash it down.

And now the visions are rising, suppressed memories unfurling, her mother's death. She tries to lock it away, but the past is welling up, her head is filling with it.

The air around her contracts and expands, sound contorting. And then she is staggering back towards the cars, ejecting vomit, gagging into clumps of yellow grass, her insides emptying, her head imploding, a great purging of everything that she is and where she has come from.

When she can vomit no more, she slumps in the grass alongside the sour stench of her own gut contents. Someone places a coat over her. She hears a voice, hollow and distant. 'Quentin will take her home. I think it's all been too much for her.'

The grass prickles her cheek. She closes her eyes and gives in to silence.

39

In Quentin's car Abby huddles in the passenger seat, feeling sick and cold and small. Her supervisor is a dark sympathetic shadow beside her. He doesn't speak, doesn't ask her anything, and she is grateful. She is teetering on the lip of a personal abyss; to talk might tip her over the edge.

They drive out of the reserve via a back gate. This is probably the way the shooters and other staff came in this afternoon. Quentin has a key. He doesn't ask her to get out and unlock the gate. Instead he leaves her nestled in the car with the heater pumping while he steps out into the night and unhitches the chain. He slings back in, glances at her briefly, eyes sharp and concerned, then drives through the gateway and parks again to lock the gate.

She wonders what he is thinking—probably judgemental thoughts. She recalls his comments when he asked her to attend the cull. *If you can't see the job through, you shouldn't recommend it.* She hasn't seen the job through, and perhaps she doesn't have what it takes to be a kangaroo ecologist. Perhaps she doesn't have what it takes to be anything. All she wants to do is bundle herself into a cocoon and dissolve.

They rumble along the gravel road in the darkness, and Abby stares blankly ahead, struggling against the deep chill in her bones. Her insides are shaking and her mouth still carries the rank taste of vomit. Back at the pit, the vet had helped her to her feet and given her a bottle of water to flush her mouth. But nothing could wash the sourness away. As he walked her to Quentin's car, Abby was only vaguely aware of the shooters staring at her from their chummy cluster near the pit. She was too wasted to care, but now she wonders if that was disdain she read in their eyes, as well as disbelief. A question has been asked of her and she has failed. Now she must work through the consequences. Self-disappointment will come later, much later. The immediate fallout will be far worse; she can feel it churning in her guts. The vomiting episode was just the beginning; there is more to come.

Quentin's phone rings and he answers it quietly. He murmurs brief answers to the caller then glances at Abby. 'It's for you,' he says. 'It's that journalist, Cameron Barlow. Do you want to speak to him? He sounds worried. It might help if you put him at ease.'

He holds the phone out to her while he navigates a curve in the road, and she takes it reluctantly, shrinks even lower as she presses it to her ear and says a small hello.

'Abby. Are you okay? I've been so worried.' The force of Cameron's concern radiates from the phone.

'I'm all right,' she says softly, and her words feel empty.

KAREN VIGGERS

'I've been trying to get onto you all night. Your message bank will be full of my messages. Why didn't you have your phone on?'

To avoid speaking to you. She can't say it, even though it's the truth. 'I forgot to turn it on this afternoon. Then it was better to leave it off . . .'

'But the gate! The way those lunatics attacked your car!'

So he was there. She had known he would be.

'I couldn't do anything,' he says. 'They turned into animals. Martin Tennant stirred them up. You wouldn't believe the power of that man. He had them in a rage. Then you appeared, and they were madness let loose.'

Abby gazes numbly out the window where pale fence posts, illuminated by the side-wash of the headlights, flash past, and dust swirls in a ghostly cloud behind the car.

'So Quentin is taking you home?'

'Yes.'

'I'll come and look after you. Don't worry, I'll sleep on the couch. I just don't want you to be alone.'

'No, don't come.' She doesn't want him there. She needs to be alone, needs to crawl into her private cave.

His answer is pained silence.

'I'll talk to you tomorrow,' she says. 'I promise.'

'Okay.' Hurt jangles in his voice. 'But call me if you need me. Anytime.'

At home, Abby is teary and distraught. Alone, she has no reason, no motivation to hold herself together, and the nausea comes sweeping back, emotions welling spontaneously and pouring out. She casts about her tiny house, pacing

382

compulsively, looking for something that can't be found—a way to escape from herself.

She tries the guitar, snatches it from the corner and perches on the arm of the couch, picks out a few notes. But the musical sounds jar and clang inside her, and her mother's face rises suddenly, vivid and clear: her smile, the jingle of her eyes, the dimple high on her cheek—Abby had forgotten it. Her heart lurches sickly. Beneath the skin of these memories lies everything she's trying to suppress. One image will lead eventually to another and then to the last, the final show. She lays the guitar aside, claws at her throat, leaps up from the couch, tries to find some other distraction.

Outside in the cold night, she stares into the starry sky, watching the vapour puffs of her breath hanging in the frosty air. If only she could fly. It would be so good to scoop the night beneath her wings and race across the universe, fleeing her mind. She is so engorged with fearful energy. What can she do to calm down?

She makes a hot chocolate, watches the mug spin around in the microwave, the milk frothing and rising and spilling over the rim and spreading on the turntable. She doesn't attempt to stop it, opens the door onto the milky mess when the timer dings, wipes the bottom of the mug and sits on the doorstep.

Possums cuss and scuffle in the garden. They sound angry. Perhaps that's the best way to deal with grief: to yell and hit and scream until it has gone. But she tried that when she was young and it didn't work. This is what she is left with—this bruised shell, still full of mourning.

When finally she goes to bed she turns on her mobile out of habit, deletes Cameron's messages and then switches off the light. Sleep eludes her. She lies rigid, embedded in a kaleidoscope of images she hasn't revisited in years. She's afraid to close her eyes, terrified of slipping into unconsciousness. Death is waiting for her there. A decade ago, she lost her mother, and since then all the silly superficial bandaids she's applied to heal herself have done nothing to mend the wounds. She's still damaged, a frightened little girl hiding in a woman's body.

She coils beneath the doona, shivering, her entire body gripped by cramps of angst. She is cold, so cold. There is iciness in her chest. Something frozen in there. It holds her in its grip.

Shaking convulsively, she pushes back the doona and clambers from the bed like a stiff old woman. She makes her way to the bathroom, snaps on the light and spins the taps in the shower. With one hand gripping the towel rail, she fumbles her clothes off, waits while the water warms up. Then she steps beneath the steaming flow. She can't bear the heat. Pain contracts her extremities, forces a cry from her tight cold lips.

She twirls the cold tap till she can tolerate the temperature, then gradually eases it again as her body adjusts to the warmth. But thawing out doesn't help. The heat melts something that was holding her strong. And now suddenly, tears come gushing. Visceral sobs that rack her slender frame. She hunches beneath the blast of water, weeping.

Something makes her look up at her agonised reflection in the mirror. Water streaming over her face, her hair a wet clod draped over her shoulders, her mouth an ugly gash of grief. She glances away, can't bear to witness her disintegration.

On the floor of the shower she sees one of Cameron's disposable razors. Usually he uses an electric razor, but one time he stayed over without his toiletries, needed to shave before work the next morning, bought a packet of razors and some shaving cream at the local supermarket. She focuses on the razor, a clear, horrible steadiness taking hold of her mind. She bends and reaches for the razor, contemplates the sharp silver blade.

In the mirror she sees herself again—the grim intent in her eyes. The shaking has stopped, but there is a new destructive clench in her stomach. She needs to punish herself. To hurt herself in some lasting way that will remind her of her weakness, and distract herself from the turmoil of the past that she simply cannot evict from her brain.

She grabs the bottle of shampoo from the rack hanging off the cold tap, squirts out a handful, and lathers it through her hair till she is foaming and white. Then she lifts the razor and starts hacking, scraping her hair off at the roots in great curly hanks. She flicks the sodden lumps on the tiles, the shaggy mane of red-brown locks piling around her feet.

In the mirror, she sees her new ugly self emerge and she weeps at the awfulness of it. Bare, bald, scraped away, exposed. She has nowhere to hide from herself now. This is who she is.

When the job is done, she wipes the loose strands of hair from her body, turns off the taps and steps out of the shower, dries herself with her scratchy old towel. Then she fingers the tears from her cheeks, and the weeping stops.

Wafting like a ghost, she goes to her room, finds her pyjamas, tugs them on. She scuffs a hand through her drawer till she finds a beanie and snugs it on over her ears. Then she returns to the bathroom, swipes up the thick handfuls of hair from the floor of the shower and carries it all, dripping, to the kitchen, slops it into the bin.

She is drained now, empty. Something important has been shed with the hair. A part of herself she can't bring back. Numb, she trails to her bedroom, inserts herself under the doona, collapses into sleep.

———

Morning, and her mobile phone is ringing. It is on her bedside table, but she stays curled beneath the doona and ignores it. She hears the beep of message bank and soon after, the phone rings again. She doesn't move. She's warm and safe beneath her layer of feathers, the beanie pulled down hard over her ears.

The phone rings four times, and each time there is a message. She will not answer it, cannot answer it. Then a thought arrives. If she doesn't take the call, Cameron may come over. He may arrive uninvited on her doorstep and expect to talk. He may decide to *take care* of her.

When the phone rings again, she reaches an arm from her downy cave and pulls the phone under the covers. 'Hello?'

It's Cameron, just as she thought. 'Where are you?' he asks. 'You sound like you're under water.'

'I'm in bed.'

'Are you all right?'

'I was asleep.'

'Sorry.'

She says nothing. She is empty, doesn't want to encourage him, cannot face the concept of kindness or sympathy.

'Can I come and make you some breakfast?'

He is trying to sound chirpy, but she can't stomach it. 'I'm not hungry.'

'How about I just come and sit with you, in case you need me.'

'Please don't. I need to be alone.' She's weary, can't fathom how she would cope with his presence.

'Last night must have been awful.'

She doesn't want to have this conversation, but it seems that she must. 'No, it was very professional. It was just me not coping.'

'No-one would have coped with that.' His sympathy washes down the line.

'I thought I'd do better.'

'I'm sure you did the best you could. Let me come around. You shouldn't be alone.'

She sighs, immensely tired. 'No. Please, don't. I just need to sleep.'

Silence again. Maybe he is getting the message. 'How about I take you out to your valley,' he suggests. 'See some healthy kangaroos. It'll be good for you.'

She closes her eyes, feels tears rising and chokes them down. 'That's a kind thought. But if I go to the valley, I'll go alone. It's better that way.'

Another silence follows. Then, 'Promise you'll ring if you need me.'

'I will.'

She hangs up, flicks the phone onto the bedside table, lies back listlessly, still hiding in the soothing dark beneath the doona. But Cameron has planted a seed. She pushes the covers aside and sits on the edge of the bed, dizzy, washed out. Her head is itchy beneath the beanie. She tugs it off, runs a tentative hand over the unfamiliar terrain of her scalp. It's bristly, prickly, surreal. She weeps. What has she done to herself?

She grasps the phone again, rings Daphne's number. Pam answers.

'Pam. It's Abby.'

'Abby. You sound strange.'

She feels a crazy laugh bubbling up and stifles it. 'No. Just tired. Can I speak to Daphne?'

'Just a minute.'

Abby waits. In her mind, she sees Daphne sitting in her armchair, nodding sleepily over a crossword. She has only been home from hospital for a week, and she's weary. Abby has a proposition to make, but it may be too soon. Better she suggest it to Daphne than Pam, otherwise it would be a flat no.

She hears Daphne clear her throat as she takes the phone. 'Abby, dear.'

At the sound of Daphne's voice, Abby crumbles and is unable to speak. Tears blur her vision and knots jam her throat.

'Abby? Are you there?'

'Yes, I'm here.'

'Are you all right, dear?'

'Not really.'

'What is it?'

'I need to go out to the valley. Do you think Pam would let you come with me? Are you up to it?'

'Yes, of course.'

'You're not really up to it, are you?'

'No, but I'm coming.'

'I need some company.'

'I know how it is, dear. I'll be waiting.'

40

They drive out to the valley in silence. It is grey winter, cold, the mountains sing with the tumble of the wind. Abby unlocks the gate and drives down to the old homestead. It's a weekday. Nobody about. She parks the car in front of the building, facing up-valley.

They stay in the car and listen to the air butting against the windows, whistling through the grasses, moaning around the eaves of the homestead. Abby is so desperately tired. She is burdened, has been for a decade, is done with toting the load. She looks to Daphne who is fixed somewhere in the distance, riding on a memory.

Now Abby feels the sadness rising again. She feels the inevitability of her own story surfacing, unleashed by the cull, her mother's face looking back at her from all those mangled kangaroos.

She turns to look at Daphne, glances away again, words organising themselves in her head, images rearranging, everything preparing itself to come forth. Now is the time to talk, and Daphne is the one she must share it with. Daphne is here for her. Daphne counts. Daphne, like her Gran, will know how to hold her up when her knees fold and she breaks.

———————

The girl had walked home from school that afternoon. She was walking home because she had missed the bus—too busy talking with a friend after the home-time bell. It was hot and humid and she was sweaty, her clothes sticking to her skin like glue. Over the purple mountains, clouds were clustering in dense fluffy thunderheads, promising a cool change that seemed it would never come. Heat lay like a blanket over the paddocks, hazy warmth beating from the earth like an engorged pulse.

She plodded along the footpath, feet cooking in her shoes. At the bridge she stopped to watch a handful of kids leaping from the railing into the water. Their yells and hoots rang between the pylons: eerie echoes beneath the road. Her hot, tacky body wanted to join them, to feel the cool water drawing her in. But she didn't have her bathers, so she trudged across the bridge, the boards clacking and rattling as a car passed by. Then she took the turn onto the side road, headed for the farm.

It was a long walk, but she didn't mind. She liked the feel of the heat shimmering up from the tarmac, the mirages that painted themselves ahead in the distance, stories and landscapes forming and dissolving as she walked. Her school bag was heavy with uneaten lunch; her appetite was never good when it was hot. She stopped to haul out her sandwiches and throw them over the fence for some lucky cow or a hungry raven that happened upon them among the tall green grass which grew thick along the roadside.

She came to the driveway and wandered its length, ambling beneath the cool shade of the pines, their scent tangy in the turgid air. She was sluggishly tired and had walked more than halfway before she realised she'd forgotten to check the mailbox—an old milk urn painted silver and hammered onto a post at the gate. But she didn't turn back—hopefully her father would stop on his way home tonight.

The house nestled beneath the old oak trees which spread their branches over the roof like protective arms. Passing the sheds, she crossed the last open space of baking sunlight before reaching the door where she kicked off her shoes, not bothering to pair them on the rack. The shade of the veranda enveloped her, tracing shadows on her skin. She opened the door and slid thankfully inside.

It was quiet in the house, which was normal when her mother was navigating a slump. She tiptoed down the hall to her mother's bedroom. Usually she would creep in and plant a small kiss on her mother's marble cheek, pausing to watch the slow rise and fall of her chest as she lay inert on the bed. Today the room was empty.

She moved through the house, peering into each room, drawing consecutive blanks. Her mother was not in the kitchen—the table was still cluttered with this morning's used breakfast bowls, flies crawling in the congealed clots of Weet-bix. The lounge room was empty too; sometimes her mother would sit in a chair by the window, watching the oak trees wave their arms. But she was not in the lounge room, not in the bathroom, not in Matt's bedroom, and she was not in the laundry, where dirty clothes lay in limp neglected piles.

When she had determined her mother was not in the house, she drifted outside, stopping to watch the cows sheltering beneath the gum trees along the house-paddock fence. They were dozy and listless, their tails switching flies from their backs. She crossed the driveway to the shed, wincing as her soft sweaty feet contacted the sharp gravel. Beneath the tin roof, heat swelled and simmered. She smelled the rich oiliness of the tractor, the aroma of hot hay. Swallows scattered under the beams, circling and chattering in the dim light. Her mother was not in the shed.

She wandered down to the stables, empty now that her mother had stopped riding and the horses had been turned out for summer, until her mother called them in again, offering pieces of cut apple in the palm of her hand. Down in the horse paddock, the horses were standing in the shade, and her mother was not with them, which was no surprise.

The only remaining place was the chook shed, which was not somewhere her mother visited often. Earlier in the year a fox had invaded and slaughtered the chickens. It was murder, not even for hunger—the fox had left torn and decapitated carcasses, not even bothering to eat any of the meat. The girl and her father had buried the mangled birds down below the compost heap. Then her father had purchased from a neighbour new pullets, which had grown into fine white Leghorns. Since then her mother had refused to go down there, leaving the chooks to someone else to tend.

Now she reached the shed. The door was ajar and it was then that she noticed the chickens were out, grasping the opportunity to scratch in the garden at the back of the house, and scattering the mulch. She grabbed the handle and swung the door wide.

That was when her heart emptied and her mind stopped, her future finished.

She remembers the shaft of light cast through the open door, the drone of flies circling the shed, the rusty metallic smell of blood. On the floor, lay her mother, half-sitting, eyes starring glassily, a round black hole burnt smooth in her white forehead. Across her lap, the rifle lay fallen from her hands, and she wore an expression of surprise mingled with absence.

The girl stood there, unmoving, watching the flies crawling their way in and out of her mother's eyes and nose, the hole in her head. She heard the startled clucking of a chicken somewhere outside. Then her mind closed like a door slammed shut and silence descended—utter mental silence, as unseeing and unhearing as her mother, lying slumped and lifeless on the straw.

When the telling is done, Abby hovers in an empty space somewhere between the present and the past. She is surprised to find she doesn't need anything from Daphne. The old lady's presence is enough, the bearing of witness. She feels an odd opening in her chest, a parting, like a clearing of clouds after a storm. There is no beam of sunlight, but there is a sense of loosening, a change in the air, a lessening of the load.

The images haven't altered and the story is the same—still horrible, still shocking. But now the words are out and the facts are known. They have been announced, relinquished from the vault. The kangaroos triggered it, and because of them, the terrible thing is no longer a secret. Abby hopes that now the worst is revealed, perhaps she can start to let it go.

She meets her old friend's gaze and sees tears shimmering in Daphne's eyes, feels moisture on her own cheeks. Then she reaches for Daphne and they grip each other's hands and hold tight. All the words have been said, and there is nothing more to say.

She leaves Daphne in the car and wanders, pensive and alone, up the valley. After last night's traumas and this morning's release, she needs to recuperate now, to take pause in the soothing presence of the mountains and the trees.

The wind has dropped and the valley is quiet and still. Up ahead, her kangaroos are grazing, their jaws grinding rhythmically. She's neglected them these past weeks and they watch her with a new untrusting vigilance. Already they've partly forgotten her. That is their wildness. You can gain an edge of familiarity, but instinct is undeniable.

She sits in the dry grass and absorbs the fragrant air, the hollow echo of a currawong calling among the rocks. Despite her fatigue, she feels more settled than she has in months. She lies down in the grass and stares at the clouds, emptying herself out, trying to come to terms with the enormity of what has just passed: the handing on of her story to Daphne. It is something she's never done before, opening herself up like this, and the feeling of exposure is unfamiliar, but at the same time it is liberating. Unraveled, she stretches out, arms behind her head, adjusting to the sensation of metamorphosis.

Eventually the breeze strengthens and cold starts to set in. She climbs to her feet and turns back towards the car where, hopefully, Daphne is napping.

It is then that she sees him, standing by a snow gum along the track. She falters, sudden weakness in her knees. He shouldn't be here. She asked him not to come. Slowly she closes the distance to meet him, and he waits, awkward, his hands in his pockets, and she thinks of the first day she met him in the car park for an interview, and how much has happened since then.

'I'm sorry,' he calls before she is upon him. 'But I couldn't stay away.' He flings his arms wide, and swings his gaze over the valley, the rocky tops, the hills of rustling forest. 'Look at this, will you? How can it all be so normal after yesterday?'

She stops and contemplates him, unmoved.

'I'm sorry for what you had to go through,' he says. 'Both inside and outside the gate. I was so frightened for you.'

She stays where she is, keeping her distance, staring off down the valley, unsure what to do with him.

He walks up, stands near, close, warm. 'What's with the beanie?' he asks, smiling.

She looks at him, raises her hand and pulls the beanie from her head, waiting for his reaction.

His face crumples and tears spring in his eyes. With warm hands, he reaches for her, crushes her to his chest, strokes his hand over her scalp, softly and gently murmuring, his lips against her head. Then he pulls back slightly, his hands lightly gripping her shoulders. There is a smile in his eyes, kind, patient. 'Don't worry,' he says. 'Hair grows. And I know a good hairdresser who can fix you up. Maybe not glue the hair back on, but at least make you smooth and silky. A Sinead O'Connor. Very brave, very sexy.'

She leans her forehead against his chest, and his fingers glide over her ravaged scalp again, unafraid of the bristly texture, somehow still loving her.

Then she is crying. For herself. For her mother. For everything.

KAREN VIGGERS

He holds her till the tide of tears passes, then he bends to catch her eyes again, serious now. 'Let's walk down the valley,' he says. 'Like the first time we met.'

She moves to say something, but he shushes her gently. 'You don't have to talk,' he says. 'We can walk as long as you like. For ten minutes or forever. It doesn't matter. I'm happy to go as far as you want.'

She takes his hand and they walk through the shuffling grass with the wind chuckling in the trees like a river. Then she begins to tell him about her mother.

The valley sighs around them, and above, a flock of galahs shrieks at the sky.

EPILOGUE

The first time the two old women meet, Daphne weeps.

It is in a city café. Daphne waits at a table with Abby, while out in the street the winter wind rattles long-shed autumn leaves up and down the gutter.

Daphne's heart taps a fast rhythm. She is anxious and excited and a little afraid. This is a beginning, a small chance to make her peace. The offering she wants to make may mean nothing in the scheme of all the wrongs that have been done. But it is something she wants to do.

She doesn't know what to expect of this woman, Betty, who should soon be here. Abby has described her as damaged but wise, strong but gentle. It's a bundle of contradictions and Daphne doesn't know what to read into it. She envisages Betty might be angry. She could be indignant and self-righteous. Daphne figures she has every right to be. But whatever Betty says to her, Daphne knows she can carry the burden.

We all have matters of grief, she said to Abby in the valley that day after the cull when Abby told her story. *It's how we bear that grief which makes us who we are, and marks the strong from the weak.* Now she knows that both strength and weakness reside in everyone, along with the courage to renew. This is the journey she has undertaken: her life's journey. Today is another step on that path.

When the woman enters the café, Daphne knows immediately who she is. It's not the colour of her skin that sets her apart, although she is distinctly darker than Daphne. Nor is it anything about her features, even though she has a broadish nose and black eyes. Rather it is something about the sad, humble aura she wears like a coat: a sense of agelessness, an earthiness, a strange pull of gravity that somehow puts her at the centre of things.

Daphne watches her close the door then glance around the café with measured deliberation. Trembling with anticipation, Daphne rises slowly to her feet and extends her hands. The woman steps forward, a smile spreading her lips. They reach and clutch each other, fingers entwined.

For a whisper of a moment, Daphne remembers Johnny Button, his dark fingers against her skin. Then she is back in the present, holding Betty's hands.

The two women grip each other without speaking, eyes locked, nodding. Daphne sees that Betty already knows what she wants to say. She sees that she is forgiven. She knows this as surely as the wind lives in the mountains.

Their exchange takes place without words. Then Daphne ushers Betty to a chair, the old leading the infirm. Daphne needs words to create reality. Words unspoken have coloured her life. Today there must be no doubt.

They sit, and Daphne's eyes are already clouded by tears. She feels in Betty a wealth of kindness and compassion. She wasn't prepared for this—she'd expected rejection, hostility at least. But Betty's eyes are deep, full of life's punishment, and softened by a glow of acceptance, infused with a sliver of hope.

'Thank you,' Daphne says, and Betty chuckles: a warm bubbling sound that rises from within and rolls in her chest.

'I done nothing yet that warrants thanking.'

'You came.' Daphne says. 'That's important to me. You could have said no.'

The two women look at each other, and Daphne's tears spill onto her cheeks. She feels the trickles running warm down the creases that line her mouth. She tastes salt as the tears spread on her lips.

'Don't you cry,' Betty says, rubbing Daphne's hand in hers. 'Been too many tears over the years, and they don't fix nothing. I ought to know. I shed a few.'

Daphne's tears keep coming. The infinite well that never runs dry. For Gordon. For Doug. For her father. For her country. 'My family had a property on your land,' she says after a while. 'It was in the mountains. They lived there for many years. It was good land. Beautiful land.'

'That's good country.' Betty says. 'But I'm Ngunnawal. From further north.'

'I understand,' Daphne says. 'But it was Aboriginal land that my family took and somehow I feel that links me to you.'

'My country, my heart.' Betty touches a hand to her chest.

'I buried my son there,' Daphne says. 'Lost my husband to that country too. Part of me is with them up there.'

'Riding the wind.' Betty smiles knowingly. 'Like them old crows.'

Daphne pauses, feels the land beneath her skin, hears the cark of the ravens calling among the rocks, the wind gushing in the trees, sees the little cemetery of sad bleached stones carrying the stories of the lost. She's certain Betty has many such stories too—written into the convoluted map of life. 'Maybe this sounds strange,' she says slowly, 'but I think I understand the way your people feel about that country. The way the land lives inside you. How it owns you, and you can't let go.'

Betty's face is luminous. 'Country lives in you and you live in country. All one.' She sighs as if the weight of life is resting on her shoulders.

Daphne feels the burden too. It is heavy on her heart. 'My family settled on Aboriginal land,' she says. 'It was the way of the times, but it seems so wrong. I felt it even as a child.'

Betty's nod is small but affirmative. 'Those are hard words for white people to say. Not many see it that way. Even now.'

'I was told all the Aboriginal people were gone,' Daphne says, remembering her mother's unsatisfactory explanations. 'That you'd all died out. It's no excuse, but it's what I believed for a long time. I'm sorry for that.'

Betty sighs again. 'That's what everyone was saying for so many years. That we all died out. But we bin here all along. They wanted to forget us. But we're still here.'

Betty's story is a patchwork, quilted together from all the little pieces told to her by the old folk on the mission where she grew up. She tells it to Daphne, piece by piece. After white folk landed in Australia and the sickness wiped out hundreds of her people, what was left of them were pushed onto missions. Most of her family went to Hollywood down at Yass. But there were other missions too: Brungle up by

Tumut, Nowra, Cootamundra. In Yass, her family lived with other fragmented families on the edge of town. They lived in houses made from kerosene tins beaten flat. No electricity. No water. The only jobs were working for the white people who would have them as maids or nurses. The men worked as farmhands, picking fruit, working stock. They were away a lot or home drinking, nothing in between. It wasn't much different at the other missions she visited over the years. Those were bad times. Her people lost many things: family, language, customs, dignity. But they kept things too. They stayed connected with each other: aunties, uncles, cousins. They worked whatever jobs were going. They held on. In the seventies the missions were shut down and they all moved into towns. That's when white people thought they'd died out, because they weren't so visible anymore. But they were there. Making their way as best they could.

Daphne listens, struck by the loss that equals her own and surpasses it. But as Betty speaks there is only fact, no anger, no blame. Daphne can't understand it. The injustice. The racism. How can Betty be so calm? Where is her rage?

'All bin happen long time ago,' Betty says, a weary smile on her face. 'I've had plenty of anger, but you can't wear your hurt on your sleeve forever. Gotta get on. No point being cut up with it all your life. Anger is for the young ones who got the energy to make change. I'm past it now. Never had the rage, really. What would have been the use of it? My people, they've suffered, but they've survived. I've seen changes in my time. Lots of changes. Most of them good. My people live in houses now, instead of humpies. We can go where we like. Don't need permission no more. The children can go to school. We can give birth in hospitals. Go to movies. Sit wherever we like. Use the front door. Sure, there's a long way to go. But I'm old. It's up to others to take things forward. I done my time.'

Daphne feels the burden of shame. She thinks of her father denying the existence of Betty's people, of Johnny's people, even though he was happy to employ the black man to find his cattle. There was no-one with better bush skills than Johnny, and there was a reason for this: Johnny knew the land. He *was* the land. It was in his bones. And her father and his men had driven Johnny away. Exiled him for kissing a white girl. Where was the crime in that, compared with the transgressions of her family and all the other families who'd taken the so-called empty land? That was how her father had described it: land for the taking. It was a lie and he always knew it. But she must forgive, as Betty has forgiven her. The sins of the fathers . . . she knows what that means. Feels it.

And Doug? She never spoke to him of her guilt about her family's occupation of the mountain runs. A lifetime of love, and a lifetime of silence on this issue. Perhaps she should have talked to him. Through his connection with the land, he might have understood. But land rights had been a taboo topic among farmers, especially if you supported the Aborigines. And yet she ought to have trusted him. Now she needs to forgive him too, for leaving her. Nearly twenty years she's battled life on her own. He should have been beside her till poor health took him, not the weakness of a shattered mind. He laid down his bones and soul for the land, same as the Aborigines.

She wonders where Johnny Button's bones finished up. There was no-one to hide them among the granite boulders like his ancestors. Maybe he wandered up into the hills too, like Doug.

'How did you go on?' she asks Betty.

'Because, even though we had it bad, we also had it good,' Betty says. 'Yeah, the grog and the beatings were there. But I don't want to remember that. I want to think of happier times. I got plenty of those good memories too. Fishing down by the river. Playing music, singing all together. Caring. Loving. Getting married. Babies. That's the way forward. Not always beating yourself up over the past.'

Daphne slips her hand into her handbag and pulls out a folded piece of cloth. It's her gift—her small attempt to make amends with this woman and her people. She places it in Betty's hand. 'This belongs to you,' she says.

Betty glances at her questioningly before carefully unfolding the cloth. It's the spearhead, chiseled by ancient hands, shining dull grey in the light. Betty's fingers stroke the stone.

'I found it in the mountains,' Daphne says. 'Near some rock paintings. I was just a girl. I've kept it safe.' She looks at the stone where it lies in Betty's crinkled brown palm.

Betty is silent, feeling the stone, the forgotten lives of her ancestors.

'It's all I have to give you,' Daphne says. 'And my apology, which is long overdue.'

Betty gazes at the stone. Then, without looking up, she reaches across the table and closes her fingers over Daphne's hand. Tears drip onto the tablecloth—both women overcome by the long arm of history.

Betty looks up, her face bright. 'Everything has to start somewhere,' she says.

Abby, watching, weeps quietly too, while outside in the street the leaves rustle up and down, pushed and scattered by the breath of the wind.

ACKNOWLEDGEMENTS

Every book is a journey and this novel has been no exception. For ongoing encouragement in the evolution and development of *The Grass Castle* I thank my agent Fiona Inglis at Curtis Brown. There were times when I definitely needed you, Fiona.

For pushing me to go further and to explore deeper in order to find the heart of this story, I thank my wonderful publisher at Allen & Unwin, Jane Palfreyman. No-one has greater wisdom in knowing what will and won't work than she does. Jane, I appreciate your frankness and advice. I also offer immense thanks and appreciation to all the other fantastic staff at A & U who have contributed to refining this novel and putting it all together, including Siobhán Cantrill, Lisa White, Clare James and others who I probably don't even know. Thank you, thank you. You are a great team.

I also give special thanks to poet Mark O'Connor for allowing me to use several lines of his lovely poetry in the front of this book. To me, these lines are particularly fitting

–beautifully and accurately evoking a sense of atmosphere and time in the mountains.

Above all, I acknowledge my husband David Lindenmayer for everything. Without his positivity, patience and support, I couldn't even begin to write novels. The same applies to my children, Ryan and Nina. They are tolerant with my impatience when the story takes hold. This book belongs to them as much as it belongs to me.

For providing valuable and insightful comments at a critical time in the development of this novel, and for helping my characters come to life, I thank my sister, Fiona Andersen. And for eternal background support and diligent reading of page-proofs I thank Marjorie Lindenmayer.

The reading of many books has inspired and informed elements of this story. These books include: *Moth Hunters of the Australian Capital Territory: Aboriginal traditional life in the Canberra region* by Josephine Flood (1996); *Rugged Beyond Imagination: Stories from an Australian mountain region* by Matthew Higgins (2009); *Cotter Country: a history of the early settlers, pastoral holdings and events in and around the County of Cowley* by Bruce Moore (1999); *Kangaroos: Myths and Realities* (2005), edited by Maryland Wilson and David B. Croft; *Stories of the Ngunnawal* (2007) by Carl Brown, Dorothy Dickson, Loretta Halloran, Fred Monaghan, Bertha Thorpe, Agnes Shea, Sandra and Tracey Phillips; *High Country Footprints: Aboriginal pathways and movements in the high country of southeastern Australia* by Peter Kabaila (2005); and *Mary Cunningham: an Australian life* by Jennifer Horsfield (2004). I also enjoyed listening to several episodes of *Blue Hills* by Gwen Meredith, author of the longest running radio serial of all time which is set in the Brindabella mountains where my novel takes place.

Many friends and colleagues have assisted me in discussions and conversations about kangaroo management and ecology over the years: thank you to all of you. I also thank the numerous wildlife carers who have trusted me with their native animals—through you, I have learned so much.

Finally, I thank my parents, Jim and Diana Viggers, for giving me a country upbringing and the freedom to explore the forests and hills of the Dandenong and Yarra Ranges on the back of my crazy little pony, King. I am sure this was the beginning of my love for mountains, forests, nature and solitude. And without the gift of solitude, I could not write.